CONQUEST

S.J. FROST

mlrpress

MLR Press Authors

Featuring a roll call of some of the best writers of gay erotica and mysteries today!

M. Jules Aedin	Wayne Gunn
Maura Anderson	Samantha Kane
Victor J. Banis	Kiernan Kelly
Jeanne Barrack	J.L. Langley
Laura Baumbach	Josh Lanyon
Alex Beecroft	Clare London
Sarah Black	William Maltese
Ally Blue	Gary Martine
J.P. Bowie	Z.A. Maxfield
Michael Breyette	Patric Michael
P.A. Brown	Jet Mykles
Brenda Bryce	Willa Okati
Jade Buchanan	L. Picaro
James Buchanan	Neil Plakcy
Charlie Cochrane	Jordan Castillo Price
Gary Cramer	Luisa Prieto
Kirby Crow	Rick R. Reed
Dick D.	A.M. Riley
Ethan Day	George Seaton
Jason Edding	Jardonn Smith
Angela Fiddler	Caro Soles
Dakota Flint	JoAnne Soper-Cook
S.J. Frost	Richard Stevenson
Kimberly Gardner	Clare Thompson
Storm Grant	Lex Valentine
Amber Green	Stevie Woods
LB Gregg	Kit Zheng

Check out titles, both available and forthcoming, at
www.mlrpress.com

CONQUEST

S.J. FROST

mlrpress

Copyright 2009 by S. J. Frost

Published by
MLR Press, LLC
3052 Gaines Waterport Rd.
Albion, NY 14411

Visit ManLoveRomance Press, LLC on the Internet:
www.mlrpress.com

Cover Art by Deana C. Jamroz
Editing by Kris Jacen
Printed in the United States of America.

ISBN# 978-1-60820-088-7

Issued 2009

"Jesse, sweetheart, it's mom again. I wish you would call me back. I've been worried sick about you since last night. Your father, I know he feels horrible about what happened, and I know saying this is just going to get you angrier, but you can't blame everything that happened on him. You know how his temper is, and you still provoked him by yelling at him and shoving him. If only you wouldn't push him so hard to accept that you're…you're—"

Jesse snapped his cell phone closed to silence his mother's stammering message before the roiling disgust in his stomach rose to his throat and choked him. He lifted his left hand, gingerly touching his fingertips to the light purple bruise on the left side of his jaw. His father felt horrible? Yeah, right. If there was one thing his father felt horrible about in regards to his two sons, it was that in his father's opinion, they had fallen so short of being the men he wanted them to be.

Jesse fell over backward on the twin-sized bed that barely fit in his apartment bedroom. A growing headache caused his brain to feel like it was swelling to the limits of his skull. As if it hadn't been embarrassing enough setting foot in a house he had vowed never to enter again, to do it in order to borrow money to get his piece of crap truck fixed—money his mother had sneaked away from his father—and getting caught by his father arriving home early, had been absolute humiliation. Maybe he deserved what he got for going where he knew he was forbidden to return. Maybe, for once, his father's rage had been justified. Maybe he should have accepted being told, yet again, that he was ungrateful, that he had thrown everything away in pursuit of a pointless dream, that no little faggot was any son of his father's.

With a mental fist, Jesse punched the thoughts away. No. He didn't deserve any of that, and he held no regrets about retaliating against his father, even if it had earned him a right hook to the jaw. It was better than letting his father feel victory over him. Never would he allow himself to be defeated, not by his father, not by anyone or anything; and by staying true to himself, he knew he delivered a more devastating blow to his father than any physical hit. Though it had felt really good to shove him and feel his father's body give way under the force.

From the small stereo on the nightstand beside the bed came the smooth baritone of his favorite singer, Evan Arden. Like a soothing tonic, Evan's rich voice cooled his heated temper and mended his frayed nerves. He listened to the ballad "One More Time" and softly raised his tenor to join Evan.

> *"Despite all the tears I've cried,*
> *And all the pain they've brought,*
> *I'd shed them all one more time,*
> *To see you smile again.*
> *If seeing me hurt pleases you,*
> *Then I'll cherish this pain forever…"*

Jesse sighed and let Evan take over. The song finished, and he raised his left wrist above his head to look at his watch. Seven o'clock. He needed to get ready to meet his brother. He pushed himself upright and hopped off the bed, snatching the clothes he had laid out on his way to the door.

He opened his bedroom door and paused. It seemed so dark and gloomy in his apartment, but then he thought maybe it was just his mood. He glanced at the cracked and scratched hardwood floor, the stained countertop separating the kitchen from the living room, the secondhand furniture, the single window overlooking the dingy alley below, and decided his apartment was a gloomy shit-hole no matter what his mood.

An acoustic guitar and a battered black Gibson Les Paul sat in one corner. The Les Paul had seen better days externally, but still carried a sweet, perfect pitch when the six strings were played. Two mini amps, four microphone stands with mics, and two keyboards were close to his desk where sheets of music with his scrawling handwriting were stacked in neat piles. His bass guitar and sunburst Fender Stratocaster sat on the other side of his desk.

His eyes fell on Kenny, his oldest friend, guitarist, and roommate, on the raggedy multi-colored couch. His dark blond hair fell into honey-brown eyes that were focused on the black and white Fender Stratocaster on his lap. Jesse watched the tender way Kenny rubbed a soft white cloth over the body of the instrument, polishing it to a lustrous shine.

"Hey," Jesse said. "It sucks enough when I walk in on you and Carrie messing around, and I know you love your guitar, but you're kinda freakin' me out the way you're stroking it."

Kenny rolled his eyes up to Jesse in a look of exasperation. He repositioned the guitar on his lap to play. "I want you to hear this new riff I thought up. It's really cool."

Jesse walked across the miniscule living room and sat beside him. Kenny streaked his hand down the neck of the guitar, his long, agile fingers glided through smooth chord changes. Even without the guitar plugged in, Jesse heard the riff as if it were, high and fast, strong and catchy.

"What do you think?" Kenny asked.

Jesse placed his hand on Kenny's and slid it a fret higher to slightly deepen the pitch. "Now play it."

Kenny tore out the riff again.

"Perfect," Jesse said as Kenny finished. "Play it a few more times."

Kenny put his fingers to the frets, playing the same chord combos five times, knowing that's all Jesse needed to memorize the harmony.

"I've already got some lyrics and partial music down to a new song I think that should be perfect for," Jesse said.

"Cool." Kenny leaned back against the couch, cradling the guitar to his chest. "Mike called me. He needs directions to our gig tomorrow night, but I couldn't remember the name of the bar, so I told him you'd call him back."

Jesse let out an irritated huff. "I'll write them down and you can call him. I'm too pissed at him after he ditched rehearsal last night. He thinks he's the god of thunder, but he can't keep a good rhythm to save his life."

Kenny shot Jesse a scolding glare. "He's not as good a drummer as Justin was, I'll give you that, but since your cocky ass attitude drove him away like Andy before him, now we're stuck with Mike until he gets sick of you."

Jesse flipped his hand in a dismissive gesture. "They weren't professional quality, anyway."

"Just try not to fight with Mike tomorrow night," Kenny pleaded. "We'll never get picked up by a label if we keep changing members."

Jesse squinted at him and poked him on the chest with an accusing finger. "You should know by now to never lose faith in me. It doesn't matter how many band members we go through. You and I are the heart of Conquest." His words came faster with his mounting excitement. "Maybe we play shitty bars now, but soon it'll be the hottest clubs! Then sold-out arenas!" He leaped to his feet, his indigo eyes shining like a warrior's about to enter a battle where he knew his victory was the only possible outcome. He threw a triumphant fist high into the air. "It's only a matter of time before all of Chicago is coming to hear us play! How can they not with me, the golden god of music, singing? I *will* conquer the world!"

"Here we go again," Kenny muttered to himself, then said louder to Jesse, "shouldn't you be getting ready to meet Brandon? Carrie's going to be here soon, and I don't need you putting her in a bad mood and blowing my chances at gettin' some."

Jesse cringed with a fake shiver at the mention of Kenny's girlfriend. "Don't worry, I'll be long gone. I try to make sure I'm not within a mile radius of anywhere that thing's getting naked."

Kenny frowned up at him. "You could at least attempt pretending to be nice."

Jesse turned for the bathroom. "I'll be nice when she speaks in a pitch that doesn't hurt my ears." He paused in the doorway. "Hey, did you get the mail today?"

"Yeah."

"And?"

"And don't you think if there was anything in it other than junk and rejection letters saying how our demo isn't what every record label in the world is looking for, I would've told you by now?"

"Beautiful," Jesse grumbled, shutting the bathroom door behind him.

He leaned back against the door. Despite his confident declaration, doubt twisted his heart. Week after week he faced the rejections for their demo, from agents and labels. He wondered just how many more times he could take being knocked down before his spirit became too weak to pull him back up to try again.

He drew in a quick breath and shook his head to clear it of the depressing thoughts. He got the water running in the shower and stripped while he waited for it to get up to temperature. He stepped under the flow, and as he did, the temperature faded back down to lukewarm, then cooled to a chilly stream trickling from the showerhead before a surge of hot water blasted out with skin reddening force. Jesse scowled up at the showerhead, sending a silent curse through it to the antiquated plumbing. He turned to washing and did his best to ignore the inconsistent temperature and pressure as it repeated the pattern several more times.

When he got out, he wiped the condensation off the mirror and looked at his reflection. At five foot seven, he was lithe and fit, his biceps firm with sinewy strength, his abdomen lined in muscle, his smooth chest well-defined. He ran the backs of his index and middle fingers along his slender jaw, then lathered his face and took his razor carefully over his flawless skin. His black hair toweled and styled to accentuate the sharp, jagged angles around his face, with enough length in back to fall just to the top of his neck. Long enough to get a messy look, but able to style neatly when he wanted.

Dressed in jeans faded on the thighs and a black V-neck shirt that clung to his lean frame, he slid three small silver hoop earrings into his left earlobe and a fourth up in the cartilage, then two more in his right earlobe. Around his neck, he fastened a choker of two thin black leather cords with a gold pendant of a sixteen-rayed sun that rested in the hollow of his throat.

He stepped out of the bathroom to the living room, and after putting on his shoes, he sprang up and spoke to Kenny as he walked toward the door. "I might spend the night at Brandon's, so don't worry if I don't come home."

Kenny nodded, concentrated on his guitar once again.

With the elevator broken in the rundown apartment building, Jesse jogged down three flights of stairs to the ground floor and pushed through a front door roughly the thickness of a sheet of plywood. He turned in the direction of his brother's apartment a few blocks away. His heavy thoughts invaded his mind again and pressed down so hard they were reflected in the way he walked, dragging his feet, scuffing his already tattered Nikes on the sidewalk.

A piercing wolf whistle cut through his mind.

Jesse snapped his head up and spun toward the sound. His older brother waved to him, idling a few feet away on his Suzuki motorcycle.

"Moron!" Jesse called, walking toward him.

Brandon laughed. "Who'd you think it was? Prince Charming come to whisk you away on his gallant white and blue crotch rocket?" He pulled up next to the curb and stopped. His eyes locked on the bruise on Jesse's jaw. He caught Jesse gently by the chin and turned his head to the right, peering intently at the purple blemish. "When we talked last night, I thought you said he only clipped you."

Jesse stayed still while his brother inspected the injury. "He did. I twisted away and dodged the full impact. Mom's been calling me, but she's warped back into her classic stand-by-your-man mode. What sucks most is I was so pissed after everything happened, I refused to take the money she got for me, so now I'm going to have to dip into the funds I've been saving for a new keyboard, but I guess it's better than taking anything that's attached to him."

Brandon dropped his hand from Jesse's chin. "I'll help you out as much as I can." He faced forward, squeezing the handlebars of the motorcycle with white-knuckled force. "He could've broken your jaw. I should show him the results of all my karate lessons he paid for when I was a kid."

Jesse gazed at the distant expression and barely concealed hurt on Brandon's face. If anyone understood how their father could be, it was his older brother. There wasn't a week he remembered from when they were young where Brandon and their father hadn't been at each other's throats over something. Their relationship had been a lot more volatile than what he had with their father, and he knew he should have learned from watching it, especially when Brandon decided to major in theatre and the performing arts at Chicago University and their father turned his back on Brandon. He should have seen his own expulsion from home coming a few years later, and part of him had, but part of him wanted to believe his father would change. At least when he got kicked out he had Brandon to go to, unlike Brandon who'd had no one.

Jesse laid his hand on Brandon's shoulder, wanting to save him from reliving his dark memories. "Hey, you promised to feed me before we go out, remember? If you don't, I'll be too weak from hunger to be able to bait all the hottest guys in for you."

Brandon rolled his eyes. "Like I need your help."

"I've seen some of the people you date. You need all the help you can get."

"Jerk-ass," Brandon chuckled. "Get on."

Jesse swung his leg over the back of the Katana 750. Brandon hit the throttle and zipped the bike through Jesse's neighborhood toward his own.

Jesse leaned away from his brother and patted the back of his shirt. "You're all sweaty. What the hell were you doing before you came here?"

"What do you think I was doing? Dancing my happy little ass off in rehearsal. We gotta go to my place so I can get a shower before we go out, but we can grab something to eat first." Brandon veered the Suzuki onto South Dearborn Street and found a place to park near his apartment building.

Jesse hopped off, shaking his fingers through his hair, and fell into stride beside his brother as they walked away from the weathered brown brick building in the direction of their usual burger place up the street. "I read a review of *Cabaret* in the paper the other day. They were saying it's the best production of it Chicago has ever seen. They spent two paragraphs gushing over you as the Emcee."

"Of course. I'm only the best Emcee ever."

A humorless snort rattled from Jesse's nose. "Yeah, only because I spent every night with you for three weeks teaching your lame ass how to sing."

Brandon pushed him on the shoulder, making him stumble. "Like I don't spend hours teaching you new dance moves for your silly little rock performances."

"A lot of good it's done me," Jesse mumbled.

He lifted his eyes to the Manhattan Building, one of the largest buildings in Chicago over a century ago, now dwarfed by skyscrapers and high-rise apartments. In this area with many of the structures dating back to the end of the 19th century, it was easy to feel the history of the city closing in around him. Normally he loved admiring the old architecture, each building had some sculpture or design that made it unique, but now he walked with his eyes focused on the sidewalk.

Brandon glanced at him, taking in his somber mien. "There's more bothering you than just what happened with dad, isn't there?"

"It's a lot of things," Jesse said softly.

He stopped outside a small burger joint and pulled open the door. Crossing the pale yellow linoleum floor, he slid into the red vinyl, duct tape patched seat of a booth near a window and pulled a menu out from behind the dented stainless steel napkin holder. He gazed around the greasy spoon decorated to local flavor with pictures of past and present players from the Chicago Bears. Helmets and jerseys from the Big Ten Conference teams, including the Purdue Boilermakers, hung on another wall. He always found it cool to see memorabilia from his favorite pro and college teams, and being on the South Side, it was nice to be in a restaurant that had more White Sox stuff displayed than the Cubs. He turned his attention to the grease stained print of the menu. A sugar packet flew over the top of it, hitting him on the forehead.

"Are you gonna talk or be a pouty little punk all night?" Brandon said.

Jesse lowered the menu and met eyes a shade lighter blue than his own. People always said they looked alike, and he guessed they had some resemblances, save for the fact Brandon had three inches on him and a thicker, medium build. They shared the same jet-black hair color, though Brandon wore his a bit longer than him these days.

Jesse took a breath to speak, but stopped when their waitress walked up. After mimicking Brandon's order of a Pepsi and a bacon mushroom Swiss burger with an extra side of fries, he focused on answering Brandon. "Things have just been messed up lately. It seems like no matter what I do, I can't get ahead with my music."

"You still got Tweedledee and Tweedledum playing with you, right?"

Jesse chuckled at Brandon's nicknames for his keyboardist and drummer, and leaned back as their waitress returned with their drinks. His laugh slowed, and he took a deep breath, his moment of good humor slipping away with the exhale. "Yeah, Mike's drumming hasn't gotten any better since he joined, and Ben can't work the synth and his keyboard playing blows. I'm trying to teach him 'Shattered' but it's too complex for him. What the hell am I supposed to do? Sing, perform, play keyboard, rhythm guitar, bass, and drums? If it wasn't for Kenny, I'd be going insane."

His voice rose with his frustration. "I've sacrificed everything for this and where am I? Twenty years old and I can see my future clear as freakin' day. I'll be the stock manager at the goddamn bookstore for the rest of my life. I turned down college for this, to live in a shit-hole apartment and play in shit-hole bars, losing more money than I'm making because I've got nothing but idiots dragging me down and holding me back. Third largest city in the damn country and I can't find two people who know how to play their instruments." He collapsed back in the booth, ending his rant when he saw their waitress coming with their food.

Brandon stared at him from the other side of the table. "Damn. You're a lot more pissy than usual tonight."

Jesse glared at him while Brandon drowned his burger in ketchup and squeezed a glob on the side of the plate for his fries. "That's all you've got to say?"

Brandon shrugged and took a bite of his burger. "It's too late to be piss-eyeing over college now. Some other book smart, no common sense dork has your seat in pre-law 101."

Jesse flipped the top bun off his burger. "Thanks, jackass. That was real helpful."

Brandon lowered his burger to his plate. "What do you want me to say? When you made the decision to keep going with your music, that was the only time I ever thought you might have just a smidge of common sense, but as always, you've decided to prove me wrong by acting like you are now."

Jesse shook the ketchup bottle harder than it needed and flicked it open. "And how exactly am I acting?"

"Like a spoiled little prima donna who expected to have a record deal and a Ferrari after only a year and a half of trying to get noticed. Look at how it was for me my first year trying to be an actor and for the next couple years after that. I thought I was going to be a waiter at the Hard Rock for the rest of my life because it seemed the best I could get was doing community theatre. But I kept with it. I didn't stop. Was it hard? Hell yeah it was hard, but if it wasn't then it wouldn't be a dream now would it?"

Jesse swirled a fry in ketchup, playing with it more than having any intention of eating it. "Yeah, but now look at you. You're only going to be twenty-five this July and you're the Emcee in *Cabaret.*"

Brandon's face fell serious. "Thanks to your help with my voice."

Jesse lifted his eyes to Brandon.

Brandon picked his burger up again. "You know what? Just forget it, you should quit. You gotta have stones if you're going to pursue your dreams. I used to think you had 'em with the way you can get up in front of people and sing, the stage charisma you've got. You're a different person when you've got your music backing you. But now you can just give it up. With the grades you had and being valedictorian, I bet you could even get accepted into Purdue again, then you can work your way through school and get a nice, safe job. I really think that's the way to go. It's time for little Jesse Alexander to grow up and become a good boy."

Jesse clenched his teeth, biting his anger back as much as he could. "How can you say that? My music is everything to me! Singing, playing, writing, it's all I ever wanted to do! And I never said I was giving it up." He lowered his eyes, his voice softened. "I just said things have been rough lately."

Brandon folded his arms on the table. "Look, it's normal to doubt yourself sometimes. In fact, it's abnormal that you haven't doubted yourself until now. But don't take that self-doubt so far that it makes you fear what you love."

Jesse nodded slowly. "Your delivery was actually pretty good there."

"Why do I even try with you!" Brandon threw a fry and hit him on the chest.

"Cute," Jesse said, wiping the fry's salt off his shirt.

Brandon shoved the last bite of burger into his mouth. "Seriously though, everyone doubts themselves. Look at Evan

Arden. You don't think he was Mr. Confident his whole life before being discovered, do you?"

Jesse looked up at the mention of his favorite singer. When Evan Arden had entered the music world he was a force that couldn't be stopped. His music had a rock edge, but more depth than a lot of performers. He never held back on using violins, horns, even full symphonies to give his songs a richer, deeper sound. The fast beats attracted young audiences, the depth of the music pulled in older audiences, and his voice captured everyone. He rode the charts at Number One, selling out concerts in the largest venues across the world. He learned most of what he knew about vocal control by singing along with Evan's CDs, striving to match Evan's voice note for note. He couldn't imagine a vocalist that talented ever doubting himself.

"Okay, bad example," Brandon said. "Evan can't be touched. I Googled him the other day to see if there were any updates. Nothing. Just the same old crap on the fan-sites and forums with people gossiping about what's happened to him. This one idiot posted Evan had died of a drug overdose in China, but I don't believe it. You could tell when you saw him perform and in interviews he had too much pride in himself to get messed up like that."

"But who knows what was going on in his life when he wasn't smiling for the cameras." Jesse sat silent for a moment. He shook his head slightly. "I don't even want to think about him being dead. It would hurt too much if he were. His music has meant so much to me."

"I know, but it does make you wonder. I mean, how the hell does someone so famous just vanish off the face of the earth for three and a half years?"

"Maybe making music didn't mean that much to him."

"That's pretty shitty, to be gifted like that and take it for granted." Brandon exhaled an exaggerated forlorn sigh. "But I guess I could forgive him if I ever met him."

Jesse chuckled softly. "Yeah, I'm sure you could."

He finished his food and pushed his plate to the edge of the table. Their waitress dropped off the check, and while Brandon headed to the register, Jesse went outside. He stretched his arms over his head and gazed up at the amber sun as it made its descent from the azure April sky.

Brandon tossed his arm around Jesse's shoulders and steered him back toward his apartment. "You'll feel better after we get to a club and you hit the dance floor. But if you disappear on me like you did the last time, I'm bringing Kenny when we go out from now on so he can help me keep an eye on you."

"I'm pretty sure his kicking and screaming as you dragged him through the club doors would ruin both our chances at scoring, so you should probably rethink that idea."

After Brandon, Kenny was the second person he came out to, and though Brandon said he'd known long before, Kenny had been clueless. Maybe with him and Kenny being seventeen at the time, Kenny hadn't been ready to hear him discuss his first experience with another guy, Aaron, whose body of energy and muscle made him fully acknowledge what he needed to be happy and satisfied in life. Kenny seemed to accept it better now, but to spare him, he didn't divulge the full details of what happened between him and other men when he and Brandon went out, and he would never ask Kenny to join them at the clubs.

"You really need to start desensitizing him a little more," Brandon said. "What're you going to do if one of these days you meet a guy you really like and you want to start a relationship? Oh, sorry. I forgot who I was talking to. Guy, girl, or blow-up doll, you've never spent a full night with any, so what am I talking about relationships for?"

"You're not exactly Captain Monogamous, so I don't know why you're ragging on me."

Brandon hushed his voice, concern edged his tone. "I know, but after the last time we went out and you vanished on me, I want to make sure you're always being careful. When I didn't know where you went, it freaked me out."

"I don't know why. It's not like I ever go home with anyone. If I did, I'd have to call you and put my cell on speaker because it'd be so weird not having you at my hip."

"I'm just trying to watch out for you."

Jesse stopped and faced him. "And I appreciate it, but you know I'm always careful and you also know my limit."

"For now. In the right situation with the right guy, that'll change real quick."

"And then I'll be even more careful."

A doubtful look crossed Brandon's face.

Jesse ignored Brandon's look and climbed the concrete stairs to Brandon's building. He headed inside to the elevator, closed the rickety metal gate after Brandon entered, and hit the button for the fourth floor. The elevator creaked its way up, and they stepped out to Brandon's apartment directly across the hall.

Brandon unlocked his door, and Jesse followed him into the studio apartment, his eyes falling on a large, serene sculpture of a meditating Buddha sitting in one corner. He walked across the living area to a small jolly Hotei statue atop the TV and rubbed the Japanese deity's fat belly for good luck. On either side of the TV, two towers held fifty DVDs each, both full. In front of the towers sat two milk crates containing the overflow.

Jesse grabbed the remote and plopped down on the couch. "You collect movies like I collect CDs."

Brandon's voice echoed in the bathroom over the running water. "Comes with the trade. Gotta study the art, you know?"

"Yeah? So what's up with all the anime?"

"Maybe I'll try being a voice actor someday."

"Or maybe you just like watching cartoons," Jesse teased.

"Hey! Instead of sitting on your lazy ass, why don't you fold my laundry on the bed?"

Jesse shot a glare over his shoulder toward the bathroom. "Why don't you fold your own damn laundry?"

"Why don't you pay for your own damn dinner?"

Jesse exhaled an irritated sigh. He sat on the couch for another moment before getting up and stomping across the hardwood floor to the little nook where Brandon kept his bed and dresser opposite from the bathroom. He grabbed the blue plastic laundry basket by its broken handle and dumped Brandon's clothes on the bed. He picked up a dark maroon button down shirt and a pair of black dress pants, walked to Brandon's closet to hang them and heard the water turn off in the bathroom. He moved back to the bed, flicking a pair of Brandon's boxer-briefs away with his index finger.

"You know, we haven't lived together for three months. I thought my days of having to see your nasty ass underwear were done."

A wet towel flew out of the bathroom toward him, but fell short and slid across the floor.

Brandon walked out of the bathroom in a pair of jeans, snatching the towel off the floor on his way to the bed. He reached toward Jesse and grabbed the sleeve of the shirt he wore, rubbing the material between his thumb and index finger. "This is a cool shirt. Why do you have to be built like a damn munchkin? I never could wear any of your clothes."

"Suck it!" Jesse threw the shirt he was getting ready to fold at Brandon and headed toward the bathroom. "You got anything that can cover this bruise?"

"I'm an actor. What do you think?"

"That you're a lot more gay than me," Jesse snickered.

"Asshole," Brandon laughed. "There's some foundation under the sink. But hurry your ass up, Cinderella. By the time you're done primping, the ball will be over and the Prince will be in bed with someone else."

"Somehow I doubt I'll find my prince in Boystown."

Brandon held up the shirt, trying to decide if he wanted to wear it. "You never know. The man of your dreams could pop up when you're least expecting it."

CHAPTER TWO

Evan sat forward in the backseat of the cab. His eyes traveled up the dizzying height of the ebony Sears Tower that formed a shining shadow against the night sky. He knew it now bore the name Willis Tower, but for him, and probably so many others, it'd always be the Sears Tower. He pulled his New York Yankees cap lower over his eyes and flopped back against the seat. It felt so strange to be in the States. For three and a half years he did everything he could, gone anywhere in the world, to avoid coming back, and had managed pretty well with only having briefly returned once in that time. It wasn't that he didn't like the U.S., but even with not standing in the spotlight for so long people still recognized him. Whereas trekking through rural China, boating down the Amazon, or sleeping under the stars in the French countryside, he didn't get asked for many autographs.

"Here we are, sir," the cab driver said. "The Ritz-Carlton."

Evan took a deep breath and flung open the car door. The driver popped the trunk and came around to help him with his bag. Evan waved him away. He hauled out his heavy hiking pack with his sleeping bag tied on top and slung it over his shoulder. He glanced at the doorman, who looked confused as to whether he should help him with his bag or not. A black limousine pulled up, and the doorman darted for it. Evan shoved a few bills in the cab driver's hand and headed for the door.

"Sir!" the doorman yelled.

Without a glance at him, Evan walked into the lavish lobby. Visitors and hotel staff stopped in their tasks, conversations hushed. All stared in his direction. With his battered pack decorated in dirt from countless countries, his faded black Motley Crue T-shirt, his jeans with rips and tears, his Yankees cap frayed around the rim, and two days worth of stubble on his face, he knew he looked like a dirty vagrant. It wasn't his fault he hadn't showered in over twenty-four hours. Catching flights and living on planes as he worked his way from Tokyo to L.A. to Chicago didn't allow for such a luxury.

He stepped up to the counter and dipped his shoulder, letting his pack slide off and crash on the ground. He kept his eyes down: his cap blocked his face as he dug in his front pocket. "I need a room."

The woman behind the counter looked him up and down. A man stepped to her side, ready to assist should a situation break out.

The woman cleared her throat. "You need a room?"

"Yeah. A penthouse suite if you have one available." Evan pulled out his roll of cash, thumbing quickly through the bills, going past twenties to fifties, fifties to hundreds.

The desk clerk's eyes widened before she gathered her composure. "I'll need to see an ID and major credit card, sir."

"Why? I'm paying cash."

"It's just policy, sir."

Evan huffed in agitation, reached in his back pocket to retrieve his New York driver's license and a credit card, and flicked both across the counter toward her.

She picked them up, blinked, and held them closer to her eyes. She looked up at him, down at the license, back to him. "Are you *the* Evan Arden? The singer?"

At the mention of his name, things quieted even more in the lobby.

Evan knew everyone watched the scene, waiting to see some crazy drifter get thrown out the door. He slowly lifted his head. He fixed his bright blue eyes on her and pulled off his cap. He combed his fingers through his chestnut brown hair, and from the choked squeal that slipped out of the desk clerk's throat, he figured he didn't need to affirm his identity any further.

"Listen, I've traveled a long way, for a long time. I need three things. A suite with a hot tub, a bottle of cabernet sauvignon, and a New York strip done medium-well from the best steakhouse in town. Cool?"

She nodded quickly. "Consider it done, Mr. Arden." She signaled for a young man to grab Evan's bag, then motioned to the concierge desk. "Marcus is the concierge on staff tonight. He knows everything and anything about Chicago, and would be pleased to assist you should you have any questions. It is such a pleasure to have you staying with us, Mr. Arden. Welcome to the Ritz-Carlton."

Evan glanced over his shoulder toward the concierge desk. The man behind it waved enthusiastically to him. Evan nodded in acknowledgment, then turned to follow the young man with his pack. Once in his room, he got the hot tub filling and stepped up to the window overlooking the city below. He sighed, braced his forearm against the glass, and laid his forehead on his arm.

A knock sounded on the door.

He pushed away from the window and went to retrieve the bottle of wine. With the door secured behind him, he headed for the hot tub, shedding his clothes on the way. He eased down in the churning hot water, his tense and knotted muscles already loosening, and took a long drink of wine from the bottle. He stared blankly at the water, then closed his eyes and rested his forehead against the cool, dark glass of the wine bottle.

What the hell was he doing here? All this time of wandering throughout the world wherever he pleased, he never once felt the desire to come back to the States until he found himself in Delphi.

He hadn't been to Greece since his last world tour and figured it was as good of a destination as any, but he didn't want to go to Athens since he had been there before, so he opened a map with the plan he would go to the first place his eyes fell on. His gaze locked on Delphi. After exploring the remains of the Temple of Apollo, he took a seat on a large boulder and sipped his bottled water while watching the sunset. It was then the sensation hit him that maybe it was time to come back to the States.

At the time, he pushed it aside as nothing more than sentimental homesickness. He decided to return to Japan to shake it off, but it persisted, so he booked a flight to L.A., and hopped another plane to Chicago since he knew his old friend and former producer, Greg Hansen, had moved to the Windy City with Phoenix Records when the label had relocated from New York, and really, he didn't know where else to go. He didn't want to go back to New York, so here he was, drifting without direction in a city he had breezed through a handful of times when touring.

Evan opened his eyes and looked at the clock in his room. It was too late at night to call Greg. He'd have to wait until morning, which meant what was he going to do with himself until then? He'd been through so many time zones his body's clock didn't know night from day. He shifted in the tub and took another drink of the wine. His body might be confused as to if it wanted food or sleep, but it knew one thing it wanted.

He shoved out of the hot tub, water dripped from his sleek body as he walked to the phone. His fingertips slid down his chest and abdomen to his full arousal, and he rested his hand on the hard flesh while he dialed the concierge desk.

"Hello Mr. Arden, this is Marcus. What can I do for you?"

"I was wondering if you knew who the hottest band in this city is."

"Oh, that would be Conquest, without a doubt, sir."

"Conquest? They any good?"

"They're incredible. They came on the scene a little more than a year ago, but the second they hit, everyone was running to see them. Well actually, let me be honest. It's not that *they're* that good as in a collective group because they've changed members a few times, they're constantly changing drummers and keyboardists, but it's the singer and guitar player who are to die for. The guitarist, Kenny Cooper, is exceptional. But the one who truly makes the group is Jesse Alexander, the lead singer. His voice," Marcus sighed into the phone, "it's like ambrosia for the ears."

"Is that so? Then maybe I should go see a different band. Normally I follow the creed of wherever the hottest band is then that's where the hottest people are too, but if everyone's going to be drooling over this little vocal god you're describing, then maybe I should go somewhere else."

"I wouldn't worry about that. You're definitely fair competition for him."

Evan chuckled softly. "Only fair, huh? You just hurt my ego, Marcus."

"Forgive me. I didn't mean—"

"I'm just teasing you. Do me a solid, though. Can you find out if this band is playing tonight and where? If I walk in and everyone is fainting over singer boy, then I'll go somewhere else."

"I'll ring your room in less than ten minutes and let you know. Since it's a Friday, I'm sure they're playing somewhere."

"Good. And while you're at it, can you hook me up with a car? I don't want anything flashy, just a nice SUV."

"Certainly. Anything else?"

"No. I'll talk to you in a little bit."

Evan hung up the phone and fell back on the king-sized bed, the bottle of wine resting high between his thighs.

❋ ❋ ❋

Evan paid the coverage charge to get into the bar, listening to the last jumble of notes to a fast rock song come to an unsteady halt.

"If that's the best band in Chicago, this town needs help," he muttered to himself.

The crowd quieted in anticipation. Evan looked up on stage. The lead singer had his back to the audience, waiting for the keyboardist to move. The keyboardist hopped back, and Jesse took over at the instrument facing the crowd. He announced the next song as titled "Shattered," then followed with the opening soft notes from the keyboard. He closed his eyes, his fingers drifted across the keys, his honeyed tenor rose with the first verse of the ballad,

> *"I yelled for you as you walked away,*
> *My voice a whisper…in the crowd…*
> *And I watched our memories fall with the rain,*
> *Breaking…on the ground…*
> *I want to take it all away,*
> *And believe the truths in the dark.*
> *I want to live the fantasy,*
> *The sweet delusion,*
> *And keep you in my arms.*
>
> *What can I do?*
> *Don't leave me to drown*
> *In these shattered memories.*
> *I want to scream,*
> *But I can't breathe,*
> *I'm falling away.*
>
> *Can't you see,*
> *That I'm alone,*
> *And I'm slipping away?*
> *I can't stop myself.*
> *Can't catch myself.*
> *Take my hand,*
> *Pull me out,*
> *Please save me.*
> *I'm shattering,*
> *Breaking…"*

Evan stumbled back a step and bumped into the wall behind him. He stared up at the stage, his breath lost. Jesse had his white shirt fully unbuttoned, showing his smooth chest coated in a light sheen of sweat. The stage lights surrounded him in a halo of golden light, making him shine.

"Sir? Are you okay?"

Evan blinked at the female voice close to him. He turned to see the bartender giving him a concerned look. He pulled his Yankees cap down to hide his face more.

"Yeah, I'm fine. I've just never heard a voice like that before."

Nodding in agreement, the bartender leaned on the bar, resting her chin in her hand as she gazed up at the stage. "I hear that. He sings *and* looks like an angel. He's got it all." She glanced at Evan with an apologetic smile. "Sorry. I know guys don't like hearing a girl gush over other guys. Can I get you something to drink?"

"Guinness, please."

She ducked away and returned with his beer. Evan took his beer and began working his way through the crowd. He managed to inch to the front of the stage as Jesse wrapped up the piano interlude. The guitar joined in with the drums following, a good two beats behind where they should be. The keyboardist came to take Jesse's place, and Jesse stepped toward the front of the stage with his mic in hand.

Evan caught the irritation that flashed over Jesse's face when the keyboardist obviously hit the wrong notes. He smiled to himself. The guy was a perfectionist, he could see it. And with the talent he had already shown, why shouldn't he be?

Jesse bent down at the front of the stage to a group of swooning young women. They reached out, desperate to touch his hand. He floated his fingertips from one outstretched hand to another.

Evan watched him, his fingers tingling with the desire to feel Jesse's soft touch on them. From under his black hair, a droplet of sweat rolled down Jesse's temple, past his indigo eye, and over his elegantly raised cheekbone to linger on his delicate jaw before dripping away. He stood up straight, his white shirt slipped from one shoulder. He tipped his head back as he raised his mic, singing the second verse and chorus,

"Now I'm sitting all alone in the darkness.
Listening for your voice in the silence.
All I have left are illusions and dreams.
Your phantom body lying next to me.
Another memory trickles down my cheek,
And I slip a little bit more.

What can I do?
Don't leave me to drown,
In these shattered memories.
I want to scream,
But I can't breathe,
I'm falling away.

Can't you see,
That I'm alone,
And I'm slipping away?
I can't stop myself.
Can't catch myself.
Take my hand
Pull me out,
Please save me.
I'm shattering,
Breaking…"

Jesse stepped back from the front of the stage as the song finished. He bowed to the crowd and flashed a stunning smile.

Evan started breathing again. He staggered back to the bar and dropped down on a stool.

"Need another beer?" the bartender asked.

Evan shook his head, still in a daze. "No, thanks."

"He's some singer, isn't he? I tell ya, with all the crap on the radio these days, if ever there was a band that deserved getting a record deal, it's them. I really hope they make it someday."

Evan nodded. He sat motionless for the rest of the night, not drinking, not speaking, his eyes focused on Jesse. When Conquest finished their set and Jesse and his band disappeared into a room at the back of the bar, Evan headed out to the black Cadillac Escalade Marcus had hooked up for him. He climbed in and stared at the steering wheel, Jesse's beautiful voice resounding in his head.

"Jesse Alexander," Evan whispered, caressing the name with his tongue.

The guy was incredible. His voice, the sensual way he moved on stage, his skill at instruments, playing keyboard, guitar, and bass, switching between them in different songs with graceful fluidity all while singing and never missing a note. Jesse's talent, with a little guidance, could rival his own.

Evan paused, the realization hitting him hard. Jesse just might well be his equal. A slow grin lifted his lips. A soft chuckle slipped from his throat, and he leaned his head back on the headrest. He felt giddy, like a warm, euphoric energy was rising in him.

He wanted to talk to Jesse, to meet him, to get close to him, extremely close to him.

He stopped himself before the thoughts progressed. He didn't have the right to allow himself even the slight pleasure of little dreams and fantasies, let alone the extreme pleasure of actually being with a guy like Jesse. He didn't even know if Jesse was into it, and if he was, then what? What if Jesse started to really like him? What if *he* started to really like Jesse? He didn't deserve to be happy with someone that extended beyond a night or two of physical pleasure. What he really needed to do was go back to his hotel, get his things, go to the airport, and...

A melodic laugh like a lively violin concerto touched his ears, and he jerked his head toward the sound. Jesse walked up the sidewalk with his guitarist at his side, both carrying two guitar cases. Evan tuned his ears to catch Jesse's voice.

"See? I kept my promise. I didn't fight with Mike, even though he totally sucked. But if he blows this bad next time, I swear I'm gonna throw him head first into the drum set."

Evan laughed under his breath. Yeah, he was a total perfectionist. He watched Jesse and Kenny walk past the driver's side window.

"That's real cute, Jess. Now *I* swear, if you lose us another drummer, I'm gonna chain your skinny ass to the drums and make you play 'em."

"Maybe I should rewrite the music so I could drum in a couple of the songs, but it's 'Vanish' that's the problem, and I need to play rhythm guitar in that one."

Evan listened to their voices recede. So he could play the drums, too. That pretty much clinched it. Like himself, Jesse was a musical prodigy, and here he was stuck playing in little dives struggling to get by. He couldn't let Jesse's talent be suffocated to where he might decide to give up his music altogether. Whether or not he deserved to be with someone as special as Jesse wasn't the point, the point was Jesse deserved a chance to shine on stage before thousands, millions, of eyes.

Evan fired up the Escalade and headed back toward the hotel, deciding he liked the car enough he would buy one of his own. Buying a car meant he needed a garage, especially if he was going to bring the two cars from New York he put in storage before leaving on his travels, which all meant he needed a house.

An inward chuckle rose in his chest. He had made the decision to call Chicago his new home with hardly thinking of it. But Jesse had sparked something in him that he hadn't felt in years, inspiration. And while not directed toward his own music, to feel it in regards to Jesse's was just as good.

CHAPTER THREE

One month later

Greg Hansen sat behind his dark cherry desk and frowned at the numerical figures in front of him. It wasn't good. The new studio the owner and president of Phoenix Records, George Livingstone, had ordered built when they made the jump from New York to Chicago was incredible. But it tapped pretty deep into the already tight funds, and what was worse, they didn't have any artists worth a damn to record in it.

Greg sighed and rubbed his face with both hands. He shouldn't think that. Their artists were all good, but they had more of an Indie following than the mass popularity of Top Forty acts. What he would give to have an artist who could break into the top ten on the charts again, to be able to launch a tour playing to venues capable of holding more than a couple thousand. But, maybe he needed to come to the realization that the days of Phoenix being a label of superstar performers were long gone.

Stress churned Greg's stomach. He *really* shouldn't think like that. He had to stay positive. Someday, Phoenix would be able to attract the big name musicians again. Maybe even some of the ones who had jumped ship when the label started sinking would come back once they saw it was stable again. If they could get out of the contracts they had signed with other record companies. If not, they could always attract new ones and launch someone else to the status of music elite. If they could find someone with the talent, someone worth throwing everything they had behind.

Greg looked to the wall on his right where four framed concert posters of Evan Arden hung, one for each of his tours. Around those, Gold and Platinum records covered the wall. Beneath them, a long glass case held awards from the Grammy Awards, the American Music Awards, the Billboard Awards, the

MTV Music Video Awards, and various other award shows. At least they still had Evan, wherever in the world he was.

Though, it was probably better that Evan was hiking the Himalayas, or horseback riding across Mongolia, or scuba diving in Bora-Bora, or any of the other things Evan did in the far off places he had gotten letters from. Maybe it'd mean Evan wouldn't find out they had re-released his masterpiece album, *One More Time*, with two new bonus tracks and new liner art without his approval. Doing it was a complete breach of Evan's contract. It specifically stated no unreleased masters of his were to be released without his direct consent as Evan had full ownership rights to all his songs and had that clause written into his contract when they renegotiated it before his third album, *Allegro*. In order to keep the label's head above water, he had decided to risk it, hoping when Evan found out and flew into one of his rages, he'd be able to calm him and make him understand the reasoning behind it. In truth, it was worth the risk of raising Evan's wrath. Evan's fans were the very meaning of fanatical and gobbled up the re-release after waiting so long to be fed anything by him.

Greg turned back to the ugly figures on the papers in front of him. Fortunately, he probably wouldn't have to deal with a tirade from Evan any time soon. The last letter he got from him over a month ago said he was going to Greece, so there wasn't much point in worrying about it until the time came. He dragged his calculator across his desk to make sure the accountants had gotten the figures correct and paused, his ears catching the sound of someone humming.

He sat quiet. The humming grew louder as if someone was walking up the hall toward his office, the voice a smooth, rich baritone that could never be mistaken for anyone else's, even at so subtle a pitch. The humming stopped outside his office door.

Greg stared at the open doorway, listening, waiting.

A head peeked around the corner, a glowing smile on the handsome face that looked to be around twenty-two years old, yet Greg knew would turn twenty-seven in the coming month. A pair of purple lens sunglasses shadowed his eyes, but Greg didn't need to see them to know they were eyes of radiant blue that either enchanted or intimidated depending on their owner's mood.

"Evan," Greg whispered.

Evan stepped fully into the doorway. "Hey, Greg. Did you get all the letters I sent you?"

Greg shot up from his chair so fast it flew backward and crashed into the window behind him. He dashed around his desk to Evan, threw his arms around him, and jostled him in a rough hug. "Evan! My God, what are you doing here? I can't believe it!"

Evan laughed, patting Greg on the back. "I came to visit."

Greg pulled back, keeping both hands on Evan's upper arms. "You came to visit? Just like that after three years?"

Evan lifted his sunglasses and set them atop his head. "Has it been three years? I thought it was more like two."

Greg shook his head. "It's been three. The last time I saw you was when your mother got remarried, and you weren't in the best of moods that day. You drank more than you spoke and left without saying goodbye to anyone."

"Then I guess it has been three years," Evan grumbled. He walked across Greg's office to the large windows overlooking the Chicago River.

Greg gazed at him in sympathy. He moved to his side and placed his hand on Evan's shoulder. "It's good to see you. I can't believe you're really here, but then, you always were full of surprises. How long do you plan on staying in town?"

Evan looked at him, a soft smile on his lips. "A while."

"That's wonderful. We're going out to dinner tonight and I'm not taking no for an answer. Crystal will to go through the roof when I tell her you're back."

"How is the old lady these days?"

Greg laughed and sat on the corner of his desk closest to Evan. "Good, but whatever you do, don't call her that when you see her. She's been going through an age crisis ever since Krista started college a couple years ago."

A teasing grin crossed Evan's lips at the mention of Greg's daughter. "Krista's in college now? Then she finally broke the eighteen-year mark. You think she's still got a crush on me?"

Greg's smile faded as a withering scowl took its place.

Evan laughed, holding up both hands in innocence. "You know I'm joking! Put the look of death away!" His eyes fell on the posters of himself, the records, and awards. "You still have all that crap I see."

"Someone has to keep it."

"Better you than me." Evan pointed to the mini refrigerator in the opposite corner. "You got any water in there?"

"Help yourself."

Evan went to the fridge and pulled out a bottle of water. He faced around while drinking and walked across Greg's office to the black leather couch. He lay down on his back and put his sunglasses on again to block the fluorescent lights from seeping through his eyelids. "I'm beat. I drove all night from New York to get back home today."

Greg turned on his desk, his eyebrows furrowed closer together. "Home?"

Evan yawned and nodded. "Yeah, I bought a house up by Evanston. Oh, and about dinner tonight, we can do that, but you have to go somewhere with me after."

"Wait a second, you bought a house? Here? You've been in town long enough to buy a house, but you couldn't pick up the phone to give me a call?"

A drowsy chuckle lifted from Evan's throat. "Sorry. Do you know what a pain in the ass it is finding a decent house? Then I had to buy at least a couple pieces of furniture, you know I gave damn near everything away before I left, and I had to go to New York and get the few things I do have out of storage. I've been in town about a month, but I only got possession of the house last week. I've been going nonstop. I haven't even had time to get my hair cut. Which reminds me, I was out shopping the other day and went in a media store to get a new iPod, and I saw a funny thing."

Greg winced inside. "Really? What was that?"

"Well," Evan continued in an offhanded manner, "I came face to face with a double life-sized banner of myself with a never released picture of me from a photo shoot I had done four years ago. Now, if it was just that, I would've shrugged it off, but the funny thing was what was written on the banner in big, bold letters. I believe it was something along the lines of, 'Available now! The digitally enhanced edition of Evan Arden's masterpiece album, *One More Time*, with two never before released bonus tracks and new liner art. Experience the elegance of Evan Arden, one more time!' That's pretty funny, don't you think? I mean, how in the world could something like that happen when I own all the rights to my songs and no one is to touch my material without my explicit, unambiguous, unequivocal, precise, permission."

Greg noticed how Evan's tone sharpened as the speech wore on. He held his breath, trying to think of the best way to proceed without instigating Evan's rage. "You have to admit, Evan, getting your permission was more than a challenge when no one knew where in the world you were."

Evan bolted upright on the couch and tore off his sunglasses. "Since you couldn't get it, you shouldn't have done it!" He lay back down. "And you would choose two of my lamest ballads. Honestly Greg, 'Far Away' and 'No Longer Mine'? What were you thinking?"

"They're good songs. Nothing you've ever done is lame."

Evan let out a snort expressing he thought otherwise. "I don't want to talk about it anymore. It's just going to ruin my good mood."

Greg nodded, glad to let the matter go. If that was the worst scolding Evan gave him for releasing his material without his consent, then he would count this among his luckiest of days. "So where is it you want me to go with you tonight?"

A smile rose to Evan's lips. "To see a band. They're called Conquest. As a whole they're a little rough, but the guitarist is slick as hell, and the singer, he's got a voice that will knock you on your ass. His name is Jesse Alexander, the guitarist is Kenny Cooper. I don't know much about the drummer and keyboardist, they're not worth my time, but you've got to see Jesse perform."

Greg stared at Evan. He took a breath to pull himself out of his shock. "If he's getting an endorsement like that from you, he must be good."

"He's amazing." Evan stood and walked to Greg. "I'm going to head home so I can take a nap and be fresh for tonight." Reaching around Greg, he grabbed a pen and a piece of paper off the desk. "Here's my cell and house number. I'll leave making dinner reservations up to you, just call and let me know when and where. Conquest takes the stage at ten and they're playing at a little joint down south of The Loop. I'd like to be there when they start."

"Okay. I'll call you later then."

Evan turned for the door.

"Evan," Greg called. "Welcome back."

Evan nodded his head once and disappeared out the door.

CHAPTER FOUR

Evan stood outside the bar, his arms folded across his chest, the fingers of his right hand tapping an annoyed beat on his left bicep. "That's it. I'm going in."

Greg glanced down at his wristwatch. "He's only five minutes late."

"Five minutes means we've already missed one song. I'm not going to miss the whole set because you decided to invite your assistant who clearly isn't competent enough to show up on time."

Greg sighed. "With the cutbacks Phoenix has had to do, we couldn't be picky about who was willing to stay on the smaller salaries. All the A&R reps took off, so I need to get Tim some experience dealing with bands in the field."

"That's fine, but don't do it with this band." Evan whirled around and reached for the door.

"Here he is," Greg said, waving to a heavyset man coming toward them.

Evan tipped up the rim of his Yankees cap to get a better look at Greg's assistant. Tim walked with all the speed his stubby legs could carry him, the pudginess hanging over his belt jiggled with his rapid strides, his small dark eyes darted nervously about.

Tim drew to a short stop in front of them, puffing for breath. "Sorry I'm late. When I found myself in this neighborhood, I thought I made a wrong turn, then I checked the directions and realized I was in the right place."

"It takes a while to learn a new city." Greg placed his hand on Evan's shoulder. "Tim, I'd like to introduce you to Evan Arden. Evan, this is Tim Polanski."

Tim shoved his hand toward Evan. "When Greg said we were meeting with you tonight, I almost didn't believe it, but here you are. I've been a fan of yours since your first album. I've seen you in concert five times, too."

"Wow, that's impressive. Thanks for supporting my fetishes of fast cars and gourmet chocolate with your hard earned money." Evan shook Tim's hand, immediately regretting the action when he felt Tim's palm sticky with sweat. He grimaced as he drew his hand back and wiped it on his jeans, then regretted doing that since they were his favorite pair of Dolce & Gabbana.

"There's that wonderful sense of humor you've got," Greg chided.

"Yeah, so can we go in now?" Evan gave Greg a sharp look that told him his patience was about to break.

Greg nodded and followed Evan to the door with Tim trailing behind.

Tim hesitated outside the door, looking up at the bar. Neon signs touting the bar was open and advertising different beers flickered behind the rusted steel bars covering a large picture window, adding the only glitter to the flat, plain front.

"This place is a dump," Tim said. "What band worth anything would be caught playing here?"

Evan tugged his cap lower over his eyes to hide his irritation. "These guys have only been on the scene for a little more than a year and they've been playing anywhere and everywhere they can to get exposure. That's what highly motivated musicians do, and their talent should be judged based on their music, not the atmosphere they play in."

Tim shrugged. "If you say so."

They stepped inside to find a woman standing with a money pouch around her waist and a bouncer at her side. The sound of fast offbeat drums and a keyboard not in synch with the drums or the guitar reverberated off the walls.

"Sounds great already," Tim said, his sarcasm thick. "You may be a musical genius when it comes to your own material, Mr. Arden, but I'm not sure I agree with your taste in music for listening."

Evan balled one hand in a fist and took in a slow, deep breath, holding it to keep himself from exploding.

Jesse's tenor blasted over the instruments,

> *"This euphoria,*
> *Makes me crazy.*
> *I don't need you in my bed,*
> *Just need you next to me…"*

The sound of Jesse's voice drove Evan's anger into nothingness. He closed his eyes in a long blink and exhaled his held breath in a soft sigh.

Greg's head snapped up, cocked in the direction of the music. He ripped some cash free from his money clip to pay the cover charge for all of them, and they headed in. Up on a small stage, Jesse leaned over the edge holding the mic in his right hand, reaching out to the people with his left. The crowd focused on his every move, shoving to get closer to the stage.

Jesse snapped to an upright position, raising his voice higher for the next verse of his pop/rock song, "Euphoria,"

> *"I won't let you walk away,*
> *I won't let you leave.*
> *You finally came back to me,*
> *I'll be everything you need.*
> *Just tell me all that I did wrong,*
> *I can change it all I swear.*
> *There's nothing I won't do,*
> *Nothing I can't be…"*

"Whoa," Greg said.

Tim turned to him. "That kid can sing. Look at the way he's got the crowd. They're about to riot just to get closer to him. I can't remember the last time I saw someone sing like that."

Greg aimed a pointed look at Evan. "I can."

Evan's gaze remained on Jesse.

Greg put his hand on Evan's back. "No one's sitting at the tables. Let's grab a seat and study him for a while."

They moved over to a few tables that had been pushed toward the back of the bar and sat down. A waitress walked up to take their drink orders. When she left, Tim turned to Greg. "This place is too small for his voice. Just imagine what he'd sound like in the studio or a real concert hall."

"I was already thinking that," Greg said.

The waitress returned and deposited their drinks. Evan took his bottle of Guinness and lifted it to his lips, his eyes never leaving the stage.

A tendril of concern snaked its way into Greg's chest as he watched him stare at Jesse. "You said you haven't met him or any of the band members yet, is that right, Evan?"

Evan nodded.

Tim leaned across the table and slapped Evan on the arm. "So Greg told me you just bought a house. I bet it's some amazing place with what you can afford."

Evan slowly turned his head, locking his eyes on Tim in a silent stare.

Tim shifted back in his chair as if the cold look in Evan's eyes had physically pushed him. "It's, uh, great that you're back. The charts haven't been the same without you. When do you plan on hitting the studio?"

"I didn't come back to record." Evan turned back to the stage. "And the charts are fine. It's Phoenix that looks to be in trouble."

His voice on edge, Tim said, "Where'd you hear that?"

Evan whipped his head around. "Just because I've been out country hopping for the past few years doesn't mean I'm fucking clueless."

Greg leaped to intercept Evan's rising anger. "I'm not going to lie, it's been rough. A few months after you left, George decided to sell the label, and it went downhill fast. The investment group who bought it brought in all new staff, and just like that, businessmen instead of people who love music were running Phoenix. They were out for the quick buck, and had all the A&R reps searching for the next great one hit wonders. The goal was to pump out fast albums, then let the bands go and bring in the next round. Quantity over quality. Going against everything Phoenix always stood for.

"It didn't take long before the pile of bills was higher than the checks. The label went up for sale again, and George bought it back. Part of the reason he sold it in the first place was he wanted to be closer to and spend more time with his daughter and grandkids who live here, but seeing all he had worked for on the edge of destruction hurt too much, so he decided why not bring the label here also, but it hasn't been easy. We still have our name, and most people remember our reputation from when we were contenders, but that's about the best thing we got going right now. That, and of course, still having you. The sales from your albums are about the only thing keeping us going. The damn things keep selling after all this time. It's amazing."

Evan didn't bother looking at Greg, knowing he was trying to justify again why he had re-released his album without his permission. Not willing to let business darken his mood, he kept his eyes on Jesse and watched the sensual way he drew his fingers down his chest as he sang, how he smoothly rolled his hips in time with the beat.

Evan's rapt expression caused worry to fire in Greg's chest again. "Evan, I'm already forming an opinion of this Jesse, but you're the one who brought me here to see him, so I'd like to hear your full view on him and the band."

Evan forced his attention away from Jesse and looked at Greg. "Well, this is my fourth time seeing him, and I can tell you, he puts everything he's got into every performance. And that voice, he can really belt it out. The guitarist is pretty awesome the way he always manages to pull such clear, sharp sounds out of his instrument even in a place where the acoustics are bad, like here. I've seen him play a Les Paul, but the Strat seems to be his weapon of choice. And Jesse," he tipped his beer toward Jesse, "knows how to work a crowd."

Greg nodded. "He seems like he's got the heart for it."

"He'd have a hell of a good sound with some real musicians," Evan continued. "The only thing holding the music together now is the fast electronic backline from the synth he puts in some of his songs, the guitar, and his voice. I like what he's trying to do with the sound. He's leaning toward the rock side, it's got a nice bold edge, but it's lightened with a little pop vibe, and its real upbeat. And he's got this ballad called 'Shattered' that has some clear classical influence, so I'm thinking he's been classically trained."

"And just look at him," Tim broke in. "The hair, the clothes, he's got a nice look that's fresh without being too edgy."

They all looked at the stage. Jesse wore a pair of faded jeans and a tight black shirt with a slight sheen and red flames rising from the bottom. His silver hoop earrings flashed as he turned his head, sweat dripped from the sharp angles of his black hair.

"He's a real good looking kid, too," Tim said. "He's a little on the pretty side, but either way, every teenage girl will want his poster hanging above her bed."

Evan slammed his beer down. "Are you kidding me? That's not what you would do with him, is it? Turn him into bubblegum and lollipops?"

Tim shrugged. "It sells."

"Hey now," Greg cut in. "Let's not get ahead of ourselves. We're not going to market anyone if we don't talk to them first."

"I just hope he doesn't play on the other side of the fence, if you know what I mean," Tim said.

"No, I don't," Evan growled through clenched teeth. "Explain it to me."

Tim leaned back in his chair, gazing up at Jesse with a scrutinizing eye. "Phoenix has enough problems as it is. That's all we'd need is to throw our support behind him, only to have him get busted, ass in the air, and—"

"That's enough!" Greg said. "We're all talking too much and not listening enough. None of that makes any difference. Look at him. He practically drips sex appeal. Watch the way he dances and moves his body. He almost reminds me of you, Evan, except you had a more elegant sexual charisma on stage, kind of like, I'll wine you, dine you, then screw your brains out. This kid is more like, I'm not taking you anywhere, shut up and get naked."

Evan chuckled under his breath. "I guess that's one way to describe it. You're such a closet pervert."

"No more talking!" Greg demanded.

The three men sat back as Conquest finished their set and headed off the stage at midnight. Evan, Greg, and Tim found the manager of the bar, and after a few brief words, he let them into the back, directing them to the break room. As the three men approached the door, they paused at the sound of Jesse's roaring voice coming from the other side.

"What the hell was going on out there, Mike? You had to be jerking off because you sure as shit weren't playing the drums!"

Mike dropped down on a dilapidated couch. "It's not my fault! That electronic backbeat had me all messed up! It's too fast! Nobody could keep up with that!"

Jesse stepped up to him. "You're not supposed to keep up with it! That's why it's the backbeat, to add some extra kick to the song! You're supposed to play the rhythms I've been trying to teach you!" He snatched Mike's drumsticks off the couch and pointed them down at him. "I should shove these things up your ass since that's where it sounds like you're playing from!"

Mike shoved off the couch and stormed toward the door. "I'm done taking this shit from you, Jesse! You think you're so goddamn perfect with your music, then play it all yourself! I'm outta here!"

Jesse flipped his hand at Mike as if flicking him away. "Good! Get out! I don't need your piss poor drumming in my band!"

As Mike stomped past the three in the hall, Tim whispered, "Guess we don't have

to worry about attachments to the drummer."

Greg took a deep breath. Evan leaned against the wall, struggling not to laugh.

"Jesse, you really need to chill-out, man," Ben said, rubbing his eyes.

"Ben, I wouldn't…" Kenny started.

"Oh, don't get me going on your ass," Jesse said, turning on the keyboardist. "You don't *even* want to know how pissed I am at you."

Ben looked up at him with an apologetic face. "I'm sorry, okay? But I was nervous. It was really packed out there and people were pushing and screaming. This place is way too small for people to be acting like that."

"When people are excited over music, that's a good thing! I can't believe you missed the whole intro to 'Euphoria,' and Kenny had to try and cover your ass when you were off the keys all damn night!"

"You know, Jesse, Mike's right. Music is your life and that's great, but the rest of us have lives besides this. I don't need to be talked to like this for something that's supposed to be fun." Ben stood and moved for the door.

Jesse turned his back to him. "Fine! Go! I don't need somebody that's only going at this half-assed dragging me down!"

Silence filled the break room.

Jesse ran his fingers through his hair, still wet with sweat from the evening's performance. He clasped his hands behind his head and stared down at the floor.

"That was really brilliant," Kenny said.

"Shut up, Kenny," Jesse muttered.

"Well, we're right back where we started. *Again.* Just the two of us. *Again.*"

"I know what the situation is."

"It's like you have it on a timer or something. Same shit, just a few months later."

"I—"

"You know, screaming like that is a real good way to trash your cords," a voice from the doorway interrupted.

Jesse and Kenny both looked toward it.

Jesse gasped and spun around, instantly recognizing Evan Arden. Evan leaned one shoulder against the doorframe, his arms folded across his chest, a confident smirk on lips. Jesse's breath caught in his throat as he looked into Evan's azure eyes. It was really him. Evan Arden. The man, the singer he had admired for so many years stood right in front of him.

"Jesse Alexander, right?" another man said, walking inside the break room.

Jesse's attention stayed on Evan. He didn't look any older than when he had been putting out albums. His hair was longer now, falling close to the bottom of his neck in back, and didn't have the artificial highlights of gold and copper streaking through the rich chestnut color like he used to wear when performing, but it still looked incredible with how he had it styled in a slight wave.

Two small gold hoop earrings dangled from Evan's left ear. He wore a white shirt with silver buttons running down the front and enough left undone to reveal his smooth, fit torso. He held a Yankees cap in his hand and silver rings of various designs adorned nearly all his fingers, though the ring on Evan's right index finger looked to be older, more worn, and appeared to be made of white gold featuring an eagle set on a square piece of onyx clasping a marquise-cut ruby in its talons.

Jesse drank in every detail of him, unable to pull his eyes away. Evan met his gaze, direct and unwavering.

Greg stood holding his hand out to Jesse. "I'm Greg Hansen. I'm a producer with Phoenix Records. This is my assistant, Tim Polanski, and I'm sure you recognize Evan Arden. That was some show you put on tonight. Your energy overrode the mistakes the drummer and keyboardist were making."

Realizing there were other people in the room, Jesse snapped himself out of his stupor. He brought his attention to the man speaking. He looked to be in his mid-forties, a few strands of silver peppered his brown hair near the temples. Jesse flicked his gaze to the other man, who appeared to be in his early thirties with sandy colored hair.

Jesse took Greg's hand in a firm grip. "Thank you, I appreciate it. We always try to do our best." He gestured to Kenny. "This is Kenny Cooper, lead guitar."

Jesse shook Tim's hand, then turned to Evan. He swallowed hard, meeting his eyes again, and took Evan's hand. Heat surged through him as his skin met Evan's, his heart thumped faster. Unlike Greg's solid grip or Tim's crushing one, Evan clasped his hand gently, holding it more than shaking it.

Jesse smiled at him. "At the risk of sounding like a rabid fanboy, I've admired your music for years."

Evan chuckled warmly, his hand lingered in Jesse's before he slowly drew it back. "You don't sound like a rabid fanboy. I'm flattered to have the respect of someone as talented as you are. You put on a great show tonight, but you always do."

"You've seen us before?" Jesse asked, shocked.

"Yeah. I really like the sound you're trying to go for."

Jesse paused, his mind stuck on the word *trying*.

"And you certainly have crowd appeal," Tim said. "You perform much older than you look."

"Yeah, how old are you anyway, kid, like twelve, thirteen?" Evan said, grinning as he lifted his beer to his lips.

Jesse rolled his gaze down Evan's body and back up to his face. "No, I'm legal."

Evan lowered his beer without taking a drink, his surprised eyes staring at Jesse.

Jesse faced the others. He couldn't believe what he had just said. "I'm twenty, creeping up on twenty-one this October."

"That's about what I thought," Greg said. "It looks like you're short a couple bandmates."

Jesse forced a grin. "Yeah well, conflicting personalities, you know."

Tim let out a loud snort. "From what we heard, just about anybody would conflict with that."

Jesse glared at Tim at the same time Greg did, but his irritation slipped as the scent of the most enticing cologne he had ever smelled touched his nose, like flowers and spice melded into one tantalizing fragrance; delicate, and yet it struck his senses with arousing potency. He felt a warm presence close to him and turned his head slightly. In the periphery of his vision, he saw Evan standing less than two feet away behind him and to the side.

Kenny snapped his fingers. "Wait, Phoenix Records. We sent you guys a demo last year. You rejected it."

Jesse pulled his focus back at Kenny's voice.

"I hope you didn't take it too personally," Greg said. "Unfortunately, we get so many demos, sometimes a good one falls through the cracks."

"Maybe if you sealed up those cracks, your label wouldn't be going under," Jesse retorted.

Kenny sucked in a horrified gasp. Greg's mouth dropped open.

Tim flew into an instant rage. "What the hell would you know about our label?"

Kenny recovered and put his arm around Jesse's shoulders. "Just ignore him. Sometimes he talks without thinking. It's like his brain takes a nap and leaves his mouth in charge. It's a bad situation for him and everybody around him."

"He'll know what a bad situation is when he realizes he blew his chance at—"

"That's enough, Tim," Greg said. "Do you guys have a manager or agent that's working with you?"

Jesse heard Evan laughing and ground his teeth at his own stupidity. He shook his head in answer to Greg's question. "I handle all the managing and booking for us."

"That's the way it works a lot of the time when you're getting started. Well, we just wanted to pop back here and tell you we liked your show. We should be going now." Greg paused in the doorway. "You don't by chance have a card or a number where I could reach you in case I should want to get in touch, do you?"

"Yeah," Kenny said, moving to his guitar case. He pulled out a business card with their band name and information. He walked back to Greg and handed it to him.

Greg stuck it in his pocket without looking at it. "Great. Come on, Tim. Evan, you coming with us?"

"Yeah." Evan stepped around Jesse, his arm brushed against him as he passed by. He looked back at him and waved. "Later."

Jesse lifted his hand to wave, but Evan was already gone.

Kenny punched him hard on the arm and mocked Jesse's words. "'Maybe your label wouldn't suck if you sealed up those cracks!'"

"I didn't say it sucked," Jesse said softly, rubbing his arm.

"You might as well have! And what was up with the 'I'm legal' bullshit to Evan Arden? I can't believe you said that to *him*! What were you trying to do, flirt with him? You're lucky he blew it off! He could've been really offended! He's like a mega, superstar singer!"

"I know. I don't know what I was thinking."

"Once again, you weren't. I can't decide if this was a good night or a bad one, but I'm leaning more toward bad since your mouth just blew our shot at talking to a real record producer."

A high female voice interrupted with shrill cry of, "Hey baby, I'm here!"

Jesse cringed at the screech and turned in time to see Kenny's girlfriend, Carrie, bound in and throw her arms around his friend's neck.

"I'm sorry I missed the show," she said. "I just couldn't get off work."

"That's okay. There'll be more." Kenny glowered at Jesse. "Maybe."

"Uh oh. Sounds like Jesse screwed up again."

"It's really great to see you too, Carrie!" Jesse squealed, mimicking her high, bubbly voice.

Carrie flipped him off.

Kenny put his arm around Carrie's waist and headed toward the door. "Hey man, you know what? I'm going home with Carrie. You can load all this on your own, right?"

Jesse nodded, recognizing his punishment. "Sure."

He watched them disappear around the corner, then stood in the middle of the break room looking at all the equipment; three guitars, his bass, his keyboard, his synthesizer, their own mics, backup wires, his bag of extra clothes he always brought in case he wanted to change outfits before a show or put on clean clothes after. He sighed and shook his head.

Evan Arden. He had just met Evan Arden and let him walk away. He should have offered to buy him a beer, asked him more about what he thought of the show, anything, but what did he do? He stood there like a star-struck idiot. Now it all seemed like a dream that less than five minutes ago, Evan had stood right beside him. Jesse's mind lit at the thought. It had been less than five minutes, which meant if he was lucky Evan might still be in the bar.

Jesse dashed out of the break room. He burst through the door leading to the public seating and walked a few paces toward the bar. His eyes scanned for him, disappointment filling him with each face he saw that wasn't Evan's. He should have known. A guy like Evan wouldn't hang out in a place like this any longer than he needed to. Jesse lowered his eyes. He had missed his chance.

The delicious cologne he smelled before graced his nose. Heat from a body standing behind him warmed his back. He stood motionless, feeling as though he had slipped into a dream and didn't want to disrupt it.

Evan leaned closer to him, his breath wisped past Jesse's ear as he said, "Looking for someone?"

Jesse's breath fled at Evan's husky timbre. Slowly, he turned toward him, making sure to not take so much as a fraction of a step back that would increase the space between them. He gazed at him, noticing Evan stood only about an inch taller than himself. "I was looking for you."

Evan wet his sensual smile with a slip of his tongue. "Is that so? And why would you be looking for me?"

Jesse fought down the urge to close the meager distance between them and lay his hands on Evan's chest. Instead he smiled, keeping his eyes on Evan's. "I wanted to talk to you about my performance and see if you could offer me some tips to be better."

"Your performance, huh? Well, I suppose I could help you with that. I saw your guitar player leave with a girl. Did he ditch you to get laid?"

Jesse chuckled softly. "Yeah, and he's pissed at me because he thinks I blew it with that Greg guy."

Evan took a drink of his Guinness, his eyes never leaving Jesse's. "I wouldn't worry about it. You should hear some of the stupid shit I've done and said. Greg doesn't hold stuff like that against artists, especially artists with talent."

"That's good to know."

Evan tapped his beer bottle against his thigh as he contemplated Jesse. "Do you want to get out of here?"

Jesse nodded quickly. "Yeah. I just have to load my equipment."

Evan started for the door leading to the back of the bar. "I'll help you."

Jesse walked beside Evan, trying to control his smile from growing overly large. As it was, it took all his energy to keep from sprinting down the hall and jumping for joy in the air. Maybe Kenny thought this turned out to be a bad night, but he thought it just might be the best of his life.

CHAPTER FIVE

Jesse slammed the tailgate closed on his Ford Ranger pickup and leaned back against it, smiling at Evan standing in front of him. "Thanks so much for your help."

"It was fun. I never got to do stuff like this when I was on the road. I had staff handle everything for me."

"Well since you think it's such a novelty, you're more than welcome to help us set up and break down for every gig. You can be my first roadie. It'd be ironic, don't you think? You striving to tend the needs of the next greatest singer in the world. It's a level I bet not even you dared dream to achieve."

Evan burst out laughing. "Not only are you a cocky little punk, but you're delusional too!"

Jesse listened to Evan's laugh, amazed even it sounded clear and musical. He found in his short time with Evan, the sight of his smile, the sound of his laugh, left him incapable of doing anything but the same, and he couldn't help but study every move Evan made. He wasn't used to being around another guy who he felt was more attractive than himself. Having watched Evan's videos, read articles and interviews about him, he always thought Evan was beyond beautiful. Now standing close him, able to see each of his exquisite and refined features, he saw Evan was more stunning than all the cameras and photographs allowed for.

Jesse's mind drifted back to Evan's comment. "There're no delusions about it. I will be the next greatest performer to take the stage."

"Then I guess you don't need any tips from me since you're so confident."

Jesse laid his hand on Evan's arm. "No, I do need tips from you."

Evan looked at Jesse's hand.

Jesse eased his hand back and lowered his eyes. Now that was stupid. Just because he'd give his sunburst Strat to have Evan touch him, it didn't mean Evan felt the same way. Sure, when they were loading the equipment he thought he caught some flirtatious comments or looks from Evan, but he couldn't be sure if it was real, or if his wishful mind made him see hints that weren't there.

From what he knew of Evan's personal life, which Evan had guarded fiercely from the media, a different woman decorated his arm for every award show. Models, actresses, female musicians, Evan was used to being in the company of the most gorgeous women in the world. The last thing he'd want would be a male wannabe superstar drooling all over him. He needed to make himself realize that and calm down.

Jesse lifted his eyes to Evan's. His breath stopped at the way Evan looked at him. People often admired him with the desire to have him, but Evan's gaze held a heated carnality like he'd never seen in anyone before. His eyes, so intense, spoke a silent secret that made Jesse's heart drum a beat of attraction in harmony to the pulsing rhythm in his groin. A light breeze lifted, bringing the scent of Evan's cologne to him.

Without thinking, he blurted out, "What kind of cologne do you wear?"

Evan shifted closer to him. He stretched his right arm out, bracing it on the tailgate near Jesse's head. "Platinum Egoist by Chanel. Do you like it?"

Evan's nearness enveloped Jesse in his scent. His heartbeat reached a more rapid pace, fueling the supply of blood rushing to his cock. All night he had fought against the organ, commanding it to stay calm every time Evan neared, only to have it defy him. Now he knew he had fully lost the battle.

"Yeah," Jesse said, his voice soft. He glanced to his left at Evan's hand resting so close to him. His eyes fell on the eagle ring, and he found himself captivated by the blood-red ruby. "That ring, it's really cool."

"It's dear to me. It belonged to my father."

Evan pulled his hand away from the truck and held it toward Jesse. Realizing Evan was offering to let him have a better look at the ring, Jesse gently placed his hand under Evan's so their palms rested over each other and lifted Evan's hand closer to his eyes.

Evan's gaze moved over Jesse's face. "So now that your equipment is loaded, where would you like to go?"

Jesse looked up from the ring. "Wherever you want. If you're hungry, I know a couple all night places, but it's greasy food, so you might not like it. Or we could go to a club, or—"

"How about my place?"

Jesse felt an inward start at the suggestion. "Your place?"

"Yeah. It's kind of a drive, but it's not too bad."

His eyes locked on Evan's, Jesse nodded. "Okay."

The sound of a cell phone chiming interrupted them. Jesse allowed a burst of relief to pass through him that it wasn't his since he had Evan's ballad, "One More Time," set as his ring tone. He imagined if Evan heard it, his opinion could change of him *not* being a rabid fanboy.

Evan sighed and reached in the left front pocket of his jeans. "Sorry."

"It's fine." Still softly cupping Evan's right hand, Jesse slowly dropped his hand away. Evan's hand followed, his fingertips brushed across Jesse's palm before drawing all the way back and he turned his attention to his phone.

Jesse paced away to give Evan privacy and himself a moment to gather his emotions. Being wishful had nothing to do with it. Evan wanted him. The looks, the comments, the smiles, that touch, his senses weren't so desire laden he couldn't see the obvious. A net of nervousness tightened around his heart. He was going to Evan's home. He would be completely, totally, absolutely, alone with him. Elation filled his chest to the point where it almost broke through his nervousness. Only his worry held it in place that with someone like Evan, older, undoubtedly more experienced, who had to have countless lovers, probably male and female, where would he fit in when morning came? For all he knew, Evan could be on the phone at that very moment with one of his lovers.

From the moment he met Evan's eyes, something inside of him had started to awaken, and with each moment he shared with Evan, that roused part of himself became more alert and whispered to his heart, mind, and body, one night wouldn't be enough. Neither would two, or a week, or a month. Jesse looked over his shoulder at Evan, still on his phone. His mind forced a thought how he should just be grateful for the chance to be with Evan and not be greedy about wanting it all. But the newly stirred part of himself countered, when had he ever settled for anything less than it all?

Evan snapped his cell phone closed. Greg. He claimed to be calling because he forgot to ask him to come over to his house for dinner the following week, but he knew damn well what Greg's real reason for calling was he wanted to see if he could hear Jesse's voice in the background. Part of him understood Greg's concern. Most of him wished he'd mind his own business.

He turned to look for Jesse and saw him leaning back on the driver's side door of his truck. The streetlight shone over Jesse and gave the illusion of him being surrounded by an aura of gentle golden light. During his music career and time on the road, more beautiful men than he could remember had crossed his path, many making their way into his bed, yet he could honestly say he had never seen anyone who compared to Jesse.

Truthfully, he was moving faster than he meant to. He only intended to bring Greg to see Jesse, knowing Greg would want him for the label. Then he planned on stopping by occasionally when Jesse was in the studio to build some comfort between them and see what happened from there. But being close to Jesse made him drop all ideas of waiting to be with him.

He saw the clear signals of attraction Jesse put out, but he also felt an underlying nervousness coming from Jesse that made him tread cautiously. He knew all too well the influence his celebrity had on other people, and it made him wonder, was Jesse being compliant because he truly wanted to go home with him, or was Jesse hoping to win his way into the music business through his bed? There was another thought that Jesse could be nervous because he might not be very experienced, but he disregarded it. With as gorgeous as he was, Jesse must have a different guy for every day of the month. A jolt of possessiveness shocked Evan's chest, and he moved toward him.

"Ready?" he asked.

Jesse smiled and nodded. "Yeah."

Evan pointed up the street. "My car's parked that way in a garage. You want to give me a lift to it?"

"Sure."

Jesse jumped in his truck and reached to unlock the passenger door for Evan. After Evan got in, he put the key in the ignition and turned it. The truck let out a discontented rev. Jesse stared down at the key. This couldn't be happening. He had the beautiful rock star Evan Arden in his truck, was getting ready to go to his home, and the stupid thing had decided this was the perfect time to break down again. He turned the key a second time. Same response.

He glanced at Evan, giving him a tentative smile. "It does this sometimes."

Evan propped his head on his fist with his elbow resting on the door, watching him with an amused grin.

Jesse cranked the key again, willing with his mind for the engine to turn over. The truck grumbled, then burst to life. He nearly yelled out in joy at his victory over his mechanical adversary.

Evan chuckled softly. "I think that's the first miracle I've ever witnessed."

Jesse laughed as he wrenched the shifter into gear. "I won't deny it's a piece of shit, but it's good for hauling our gear. I'd like to get a Honda S2000 someday and trick it out." Out the corner of his eye, he saw Evan smirking, and took his eyes off the road to look at him. "What's so funny?"

"Nothing. I'm sure when you get older, you'll prefer a more big boy car."

Jesse returned Evan's smirk with one of his own. "I'd expect someone your age to say something like that. I mean, how old are you anyway, like thirty-four, thirty-five?"

Evan gasped in mock offense at Jesse repeating his earlier joke. "I'm twenty-six! I'll be twenty-seven next month!" He shoved Jesse playfully on the shoulder. "You're a funny little spud, you know that?"

Jesse choked out a shocked cough. "Did you just call me *a little spud?*"

Evan grinned at him and pointed across the street. "My car's in there."

Jesse swung into the parking garage. His gaze fell on a sleek black Ferrari backed into a parking space with the garage security guard standing watch over it from his truck.

Evan nodded toward the car. "That's me. The Scaglietti 612."

Jesse pulled near the Ferrari, though not too close for fear that even the reflection of his decrepit Ranger in the glossy paint would mar its beauty. His eyes moved over the flawless lines of the vehicles. "It's beautiful." He turned to Evan with a grin. "Now I'll admit that what I'd really love to have someday is a Ferrari F430, dark blue."

"That's more like it." Evan jumped out of the truck and waved to the security guard to let him know all was good. He turned back to Jesse. "You can look at it up close, if you want."

Jesse sprang from his truck and followed Evan to the driver's side of the Ferrari. Evan disarmed the car alarm and opened the door for him. As Jesse bent forward at the waist to peer inside, Evan battled back the compulsion to slide his fingers around the perfect curve of Jesse's ass.

Jesse gazed at the interior, the bucket seats so low they seemed only inches from the ground, the black dash accented with brushed aluminum, same as the knobs and dials for the CD player, other controls, and the brake and throttle. His eyes drifted up to the black leather steering wheel with controls for the car at Evan's fingertips and the yellow Ferrari logo featuring the black prancing stallion in the center.

He straightened and turned toward Evan. "How fast does it go?"

"It tops out at around two hundred or so."

"Have you ever had it up that fast?"

"How do you think I know where it cuts off?" Evan moved around Jesse and got in. The car roared to life at his command, and he looked up at him. "I hope you'll be able to keep up. I tend to be a bit of a speed demon, but I'll try to go slow with you."

Uncertain if Evan was referring to driving or something else, Jesse's mind went blank for a response.

Jesse's sudden speechlessness brought Evan's earlier doubts to the surface once again. "That is, if you still feel like coming over."

Jesse presented him with his brightest smile. "Of course I do. It's not even close to my bedtime."

"Then follow me," Evan said, closing the car door.

Jesse walked back to his truck. He waited for Evan to pull out of the parking space, then taking a deep breath, hit the throttle to follow him.

CHAPTER SIX

His eyes on the taillights of the black 612 ahead, Jesse didn't remember much of the drive to Evanston, his mind was occupied with the single thought that he was going to Evan Arden's home. He had only been up to Evanston a couple times before, once when Brandon scored football tickets to see the Boilermakers versus the Wildcats, and another time when he took a campus tour of Northwestern, but he liked the town, and now with the warm early May weather, the trees lining the streets burst with green blossoms.

He glanced at his cell phone on the passenger seat. He should call Brandon. He always called him after a show and if he didn't, then Brandon would start ringing him like a spaz. He was surprised Brandon hadn't called already, then remembered he was going to make his move that night on a stagehand he'd been eyeballing. He could bet as soon as Brandon finished with him, his phone would be lighting up.

But what would he tell him? He couldn't lie and tell him he was home. For one thing, his and Brandon's relationship didn't involve such deceit. For another, he couldn't lie to save his life. If he admitted he had met someone and was going to his house, Brandon would demand to know who, and if he told him, he'd never believe him. That really seemed the only way to go, though. If he was lucky he could just leave a message.

Jesse grabbed his cell phone and hit the number two to speed dial Brandon's cell, muttering to himself, "Don't pick up. Please be pounding Joe Stagehand through your bed. Don't pick—"

"Hey, this is Brandon. You missed me, sorry 'bout your luck. But don't be too sad. Leave a message and I'll get back to you eventually."

Jesse breathed a sigh of relief and lit into his message. "Hey, it's me. I just wanted to let you know my gig's over. Mike and Ben quit, I'll fill you in on that later. I'm not home right now because, you're seriously not going to believe this but, Evan Arden was at my show and he invited me over to his house, so that's where I'm going. I'll call you when I get home. Later."

Jesse hung up, chuckling to himself. Brandon would be so pissed when he got that message thinking he was mocking him for being overprotective. He'd figure out some way to convince Brandon he hadn't been messing with him. Maybe he could introduce him to Evan. Then again, maybe not. Brandon adored Evan's music and looks, he'd freak out if he was within touch range. Jesse'd worry about it later. Right now, he had more important things to stress over, like what was going to happen once he and Evan were alone together.

He knew what he wanted to happen. He wanted Evan to take his body for his own, to master it, possess it. He wanted to feel Evan's weight on top of him. He wanted to taste Evan's tongue, his skin, his ecstasy. But the thought of the coming morning continued to haunt him, and for the first time in his life, his emotions began to win over his physical desire.

He wondered if he felt this way because Evan's celebrity status had always put him at the level of unattainable. Yet even if Evan were a garbage man instead of a superstar singer, he'd still feel this way. It was how Evan looked, how he moved, how he laughed, his personality, that captured him. As a man, not the famed singer, Evan was inherently sexy. Now if only he knew how many other people in Evan's life he would have to battle if he wanted to stretch this night toward the unreachable horizon.

Jesse focused his attention on the Ferrari as it glided down the empty streets to the secluded outskirts of town. It went down a quiet road that worked its way toward the lake. The right blinker flashed, and Evan turned onto a private road blocked by a set of ten-foot high steel gates. Two tall, white brick pillars rose on either side of the gates, each mounted with a security camera. Private Property and No Trespassing signs warned against unwanted visitors. When the gates opened at Evan's approach, Jesse assumed they must be on a remote control. The Ferrari rolled through, and Jesse tapped the throttle to follow. As he looked in his rearview mirror and saw the gates closing behind him, he felt like he had just left the world he knew behind.

The private road wound through a thick copse of oaks and maples, then broke free to open space. Fields stretched out on both sides, and to his right, Jesse could see Lake Michigan dark with the night as if it were a second sky. He rolled his window down. Only the chirping of crickets and the waves sloshing in the distance came to his ears. He could smell the water of the lake, feel the cool moisture of it in the air. He absorbed the peaceful atmosphere. The most nature he ever got was when he went running in Grant Park.

He brought his gaze forward, his mouth dropped open as he saw their destination. Standing tall against the night, the front illuminated in the soft glow of ground lights, was a mansion of white brick accented with light gray stone, reminiscent of an English Victorian manor. The private road ended, and Evan swung into a drive on the right where twelve-foot high steel gates connected to a ten-foot wall made of a white brick topped with upward pointing jagged stones.

The gates opened at Evan's approach. Jesse went through, noticing the wall stretched on and on, enclosing the entire estate, and security cameras were mounted atop the wall at various intervals. Like the first set of gates, these closed behind him.

He coasted up the long drive behind the Ferrari, staring at the mansion. He didn't know why he was shocked at the size of it. With the way Evan's career had been he must have ridiculous cash, but the house and property were the largest he had ever been to. The high two-story had a long front and sharp peaks rising to the roof that made it look more like a three-story. A castle-like stone tower on the far end from the attached three-car garage rounded the corner with stained glass windows.

He saw to the left, the driveway circled around in front of the double oak front doors, to the right it wove around to a separate building off to the side that looked like a Victorian coach house and stable, though judging from the six large doors on it, he assumed it was actually another garage and from the depth of the building, it could easily hold more than six cars. The doors to the attached garage opened, and he saw two empty bays. The third held a restored black '67 Mustang Fastback. He pulled in and got out of his truck.

"That Mustang is awesome. Is it a real GT500?" Jesse asked.

Evan climbed the couple steps to the access door. "Yeah. It was my dad's. You probably saw the twelve-car garage when you came in, but all it's got in it is my beater and my baby."

"What's your baby?"

"Enzo Ferrari."

"What's your beater?"

"Cadillac Escalade. My car collection is pretty lame right now, but I'm trying to build it back up. I put in an order for a new Lamborghini Murcielago a couple weeks ago, but it won't be ready for a while."

Jesse followed Evan inside and closed the door behind him. While Evan punched his code into the security system keypad by the door, Jesse stepped down a short hall to the entrance room with walls paneled from the floor to the vaulted ceilings in richly colored wooden rectangles carved in relief. An open flight of broad, dark wood stairs was directly across from the front doors, and the wood floor beneath him shone with polish. Across from him, he could see into the family room through a wood-trimmed open doorway that arched in a sharp Gothic peak.

Everything in the house looked new and immaculate, yet underneath it, Jesse could feel the weight of history. From the architecture and interior design, he guessed the latest the main structure could have been built was the 1920s. He noticed a few cardboard boxes near the doorway to the family room.

"Did you just move in?"

"Last week," Evan said, brushing against him as he moved past.

Evan led the way across the entrance room to the right of the stairs and through another open arched doorway to the kitchen.

Jesse's eyes roamed around the kitchen. It looked larger than his apartment. It had all stainless steel appliances, dark cherry cabinets, countertops of beige granite flecked with black, and tile flooring in mixed shades of browns and tans. A breakfast counter with stools tucked underneath was across from the refrigerator.

Jesse pulled out a stool and sat down. "Your house is incredible."

"Thanks. It had been on the market for a while waiting for someone with the cash the buy it, so I was able to move in pretty quick. Everything from the first set of gates to a half mile beyond where the private road dead-ends and on both sides is mine, too."

Jesse's mind staggered at one person owning so much. "Even the beach?"

"Yeah." Evan bent down to look in the fridge. "Is Guinness okay?"

"That'd be great."

Evan pulled out two beers and popped the caps. He extended one bottle toward Jesse, then paused with it just out of his reach. "You're not going to tell on me for corrupting a minor if I give you this, are you?"

Jesse stopped his mind before it galloped away with thoughts of all the ways he'd love to have Evan corrupt him, and chuckled. "No, don't worry about it. It's not like it's my first drink, anyway."

Evan handed him the beer. He lifted his own to his lips, mumbling against the bottle, "And it's not like you'll be leaving tonight."

Jesse looked up at him. "Did you say something?"

Evan answered him with a grin as he drank.

Jesse put the bottle to his lips. Having never tasted dark beer before, he took a tentative sip, then a longer drink. "That's really good," he said, lowering the bottle.

"You want to talk about good, I practically survived off premium *sake* in Japan when I was there."

A quizzical look fell on Jesse's face. "Is that where you ran away to after you quit performing?"

"I didn't run away. I was just on an extended worldwide road trip." Evan reclined back against the refrigerator. He hooked his thumb inside the top of his jeans, splaying his fingers near his crotch.

Jesse stared at where Evan's hand rested, then realized he was staring and turned his head as if looking around the kitchen. "That sounds like a good time."

A hint of a smile touched Evan's lips. "It was. And I did it the good way. I backpacked, staying in small local places most of the time so I could get a feel for the different cultures."

"But why did you leave in the first place? After your last tour, you just vanished."

Evan shoved off the refrigerator. Leaning one elbow on the counter, he reached his other hand toward Jesse and slid the tips of his index and middle fingers under the sixteen-rayed gold sun pendant dangling from the choker around Jesse's neck. "That's really cool."

Jesse studied Evan's eyes even though they were focused on his pendant. He didn't think eyes so sharp and bright a blue could actually exist in real life. He had thought Evan might wear colored contacts to make his eyes such an astonishing blue, but now he saw that wasn't the case. He took a breath, calling his voice back to work.

"Thanks. I got it at a little jewelry artistry shop in Greektown. It's the Vergina Sun. I kinda got a thing for classical culture."

"I was in Delphi at the Temple of Apollo just before I came here. I enjoyed learning about him, being the god of music and arts." Evan lifted his gaze to Jesse's. "I especially liked the stories of his exploits with his many lovers."

Jesse's breath left him in a soft exhale, taking his voice with it.

Evan kept his gaze locked on him as he drew back. "Would you like to see some more of my house?"

Jesse nodded and followed him through another door out of the kitchen into the family room with thick tan carpeting covering the floor. Against one wall was a wide, long, light brown leather couch. In front of it sat a dark mahogany coffee table with intricate carvings on the legs, and at both arms of the couch were matching end tables. Underneath the coffee table, an oriental area rug added further to the warm feel of the room. Two plush, dark brown leather recliners were at the ends of the coffee table. A massive stone fireplace was set into one wall with a dark walnut mantel above. Directly across from the couch hung the largest flat screen TV Jesse had ever seen. A cherry entertainment cabinet held the DVD player, stereo, and various gaming systems.

Jesse walked over to the cabinet. "Not only do you have all the newest consoles, but you got all the old ones, too."

Evan headed toward another open doorway leading to the back of the house. "Do you like video games?"

"I play whenever I get a chance. I love games like the Legend of Zelda." Jesse stepped into the next room and stopped short, his eyes widening at the sight that met him.

Evan strolled into the center of the room, holding his arms out at his sides. "And this is the music room."

The music room was the largest room yet. In the back of it, windows ran from the hardwood floor to the vaulted ceiling with white columns topped in Corinthian capitals spaced every few feet between. They overlooked the back of Evan's property and the lake, but what stopped Jesse was the vast collection of instruments in the room. A Steinway ebony grand piano sat in front of the windows, where Evan stood leaning back as he watched him.

Jesse walked further into the room, turning in a circle to fully take it in. Electric guitars of numerous styles and brands hung on one wall with bass guitars and acoustics. Of the electric, Jesse guessed there had to be over thirty. Against one wall, dark walnut shelves displayed several violins and violas with two cellos and a full-sized harp sitting close by. On the other side of the room, shelves and wooden tables held still more instruments, though many of these were exotic, some of which Jesse didn't even know existed until that moment. He moved across the room to them, his fingers all but twitching to touch.

Evan could see on Jesse's face how he battled for control to not finger the instruments. "Go ahead. You can touch them. From the moment it's created, an instrument's only wish is to be held by a loving and skilled hand."

Jesse gently laid his fingers on a zither near its strings and caressed the wood. "It's true, isn't it? Sometimes I think they're almost living, the way each one has a unique voice. Kenny thinks I'm nuts. He says, a Strat is a Strat. But to me, every instrument has a subtle pitch difference that makes it its own, and when it gets held in the hands of someone who respects and understands it, the sound of that instrument becomes as individual as the soul of the person playing it." He looked over his shoulder at Evan and smiled. "You probably think I'm mental, too, for thinking like that, don't you?"

"No, not at all," Evan said softly, in awe at the serene beauty that came over Jesse's face when he was surrounded by instruments.

Jesse stopped before the violins, admiring each one. "They're so beautiful. I've always wanted to learn to play, but I haven't had the chance."

Evan headed over to him. "I could teach you. I've seen all the instruments you can play. Picking up one more would be easy for you."

Jesse turned a hopeful smile on him. "You would do that?"

"I would love to."

Evan pulled down a violin case from the top shelf and set it on one of the lower ones. He opened it, revealing a violin inside with a rich brownish-gold finish. Though it lay silent, as the light in the room washed over it, Jesse swore he could hear the echoes of the countless songs the instrument had known, and all the emotions its voice had evoked from its listeners, joy, sadness, hope, seemed to have become as much a part of it as its neck, body, or stain.

Evan lifted the instrument from its case with the tenderness of a father lifting his child from its crib. He set it against his left shoulder to check the tuning, placing a soft white cloth where his chin would go since the model didn't have a chinrest, and when the final adjustments were made, he said, "It's been a while since I've played, so don't laugh at me if I screw up."

Jesse shook his head and sat down on the stool for the harp. "Never."

Evan raised the bow and closed his eyes, calling the song he wanted to play to his mind. The music flowed through his mental ear, telling him the notes he needed. He settled the bow on the strings and played the first gentle notes of Pachelbel's Canon in D major.

Jesse's lips parted, the pure, divine sound of the violin stealing his breath to add to its essence. Like a heavenly being residing in the mortal realm, Evan wove the notes together with expert fingers and created a blanket of music that wrapped around them both. Though the piece normally called for more violins, Evan's rendition and skill made it so the other instruments weren't missed. Enraptured, Jesse stared at him, at his lips that looked so soft, at his fingers of such deft skill, and in that moment, the newly awoken part of himself became fully alert, and he knew then it was his very soul that Evan had roused. It responded to Evan, called to him, and there'd be no silence within himself until Evan was his.

Evan summoned softer notes from the violin as he brought the song to its end. He lowered the bow and opened his eyes. "So, what do you think? Think you can do it?"

Jesse blinked himself out of his daze. "What?"

"Play the violin. Do you think you can do it?"

Jesse sat silent. He had been so wrapped up in his internal musings he hadn't paid attention to Evan's fingering or strokes of the bow.

Evan laughed. "Weren't you paying attention?"

Jesse lowered his eyes. "I got wrapped up in listening."

Evan cradled the violin in his arms. "That's alright. I got wrapped up in playing."

"That violin has a beautiful voice."

"He should. He's a Stradivarius."

Jesse fixed his eyes on the violin, in shock at sitting so close to such a piece of musical history. He caught how Evan spoke of the violin as a "he," not an "it," showing the level of respect Evan held for the instrument, and thought it was only proper to do so. "They're so rare, where did you get him?"

"I had been looking for a Strad ever since I could afford one. Actually, I had come across one at an auction a few years ago, then had the opportunity to view two others from private collections, but I passed on each one. For some reason, even though they were Strads, they didn't strike me. Then I saw him." Evan ran his hand lovingly over the body of the violin. "He was part of the collection at the Nippon Music Foundation. It took me several months, but I finally convinced them to sell him. I had to have him and I wasn't going to take no for an answer." He chuckled softly and lifted his eyes to Jesse. "I guess I was a bit obsessed. Sort of like when you see someone you want so badly for your lover, your mind won't let go of them. It creates images and sounds so sharp, you feel like you already know their touch from your dreams."

Jesse glanced down at the floor. Evan couldn't know how he felt, but those words made it seem like he understood perfectly. How was he supposed to respond to something like that? His emotions would betray him no matter what he said. He turned on the stool toward the harp and ran his fingertips over the strings, creating a cascade of harmonious notes.

"I can't believe you live in this big house all by yourself. Doesn't it feel empty or lonely?"

Evan startled inside at the sudden topic change. Jesse hadn't taken the opening he'd created for him. Things had been going so well and now it felt like Jesse had withdrawn. Uncertain whether to move forward or not, Evan cleared his throat. "Well, like I said, I haven't been here very long so I'm still getting used to it. But being alone doesn't bother me. I prefer privacy to an entourage. I've thought about getting a dog, if that counts. Or maybe a cat. And who else do you think I would have living here?"

"Don't you have a few dozen girlfriends?"

Evan shook his head in confusion. "Why would you think I have a lot of girlfriends?"

Jesse shrugged and plucked a few more strings on the harp. "I just remember when you were performing you always had a different woman with you at every award show or big event. So I figured you probably have a lot of," he turned his eyes to Evan in a meaningful glance, "lovers."

Evan couldn't keep his smile at bay. And there it was. The piece holding Jesse back, and of course it would. They had only just met, so obviously Jesse would know Evan the Entertainer better than Evan the Human Being, and the persona he had presented to the world was that of a very straight male, thanks to Greg. In order to keep his sexuality hidden, Greg had insisted he take dates to events where the publicity would be hot. Greg always arranged who his date would be, and the woman, so eager and excited to be on his arm, ended up irritated and disappointed from a long evening of being ignored by him. He didn't feel it was his responsibility to keep them entertained since if he had it his way he'd go to the events alone, if he showed up at all. Unfortunately, the charade of being seen with so many different women and never having a steady girlfriend branded him with the reputation of a playboy, and he always knew it would come back to haunt him someday.

"You're right, I always did go places with a lot of different women, but out of all those women, did you ever hear of one referred to as my girlfriend?"

Jesse laid his hands on the harp strings to silence them and looked sharply up at Evan. "No, but isn't that where the whole being a player comes in?"

An amused grin quirked Evan's lips. How bold Jesse was, practically demanding to know if he had other lovers, as if already staking a claim to him. He wasn't used to people acting like this with him. Other men never cared if there was someone else in his life so long as they got their turn in his bed, but Jesse was already making it clear he wouldn't tolerate anyone else. A pleased sigh passed through Evan, and he decided to answer Jesse's question.

"Stand up," he said.

"What?" Jesse asked, confused.

"You want to try and play the violin, don't you? Stand up and come here."

Surprised by Evan's commanding tone, Jesse wondered if he'd been too pushy in trying to get him to open up about his personal life and had offended him. Now Evan was probably trying to brush it off by focusing on something they could both agree on. Music. Jesse stood and walked the few paces to Evan.

"Turn around," Evan said.

Jesse stared at him, then slowly turned his back to him. Evan moved behind him and reached around him with the Stradivarius and bow. He put the neck of the violin in Jesse's left hand, the bow in his right. Jesse froze, caught between being more alarmed at holding the Stradivarius or having Evan so close to him.

"Can't we use a different violin? I'll die if I drop him."

"You won't drop him."

Evan set the violin against Jesse's shoulder. Jesse turned his head, placing his chin on the cloth like he had seen Evan do. Evan adjusted Jesse's fingers on the bow and kept his hand resting lightly over Jesse's to guide it. He brought his left hand up to the neck of the violin.

"Wrap your hand around mine so you can feel each move I make. Move when I move and we'll create a harmony together."

Jesse nodded. Evan's chest warmed his back, his arms embraced him, his deep voice purred in his ear. It was too much. He felt lightheaded. His awareness narrowed to Evan's presence and his own erection throbbing with painful hardness.

"Here we go," Evan said.

He set the bow to the strings. Moving Jesse's hand for him, he began playing Pachelbel's Canon once again.

Jesse closed his eyes, surrendering himself to the music, feeling Evan's gift flow through him. He could read it in Evan's body, in the slightest of muscle movements, where Evan's hand and fingers would move next. The music lifted his inhibitions from him, dispelling them into the air with the floating notes.

Evan brushed his cheek against Jesse's hair and grazed his lips over the edge of his ear. "Jesse," he whispered, "you should know, I never slept with any of those women."

Evan's words began pulling Jesse from his trance.

"They were missing something so very essential for my pleasure." Evan tipped his head lower and laid a soft kiss on the back of Jesse's neck. "Do you understand what I'm saying?"

Jesse's head spun with full comprehension.

"I don't have lots of lovers. I don't have even one. Though, I was hoping to change that tonight."

Evan brought his hips up against Jesse's ass to let him feel the proof of his words. He dropped his right hand from the bow, silencing the music, and drew his hand down Jesse's chest to his stomach. He slipped it under Jesse's shirt and rubbed his bare skin stretched tight across his toned abdomen.

At Evan's touch, Jesse sighed softly and lowered the violin from his shoulder. His head fell back and to the side. Evan licked up his neck and kissed back down to suck near the curve. As Evan lightly nipped him, Jesse took in a shaking breath and pushed back hard against him.

Turning in Evan's arms, Jesse wrapped his arms around Evan's neck, the Stradivarius and bow still in hand. He placed his lips to Evan's in a warm chaste kiss, savoring the softness of them. He parted his lips at the same moment as Evan, both sharing a breath before their tongues glided together.

Evan wrapped one arm around Jesse's back underneath his shirt and buried the fingers of his other hand in his hair as he sucked Jesse's tongue deep into his mouth. Jesse tucked his hips against Evan's, shifting so their erections met through their jeans. Evan strengthened his hold around Jesse's lower back and thrust his hips toward him. Jesse pushed back, the friction of their cocks seeking each other out through their clothes made him crave the feel of Evan's bare skin.

Reluctantly, Evan broke the kiss. He smiled, looking into Jesse's eyes. "Would you like to see my bedroom next?"

Jesse had to order his arms to release their hold on Evan. "More than anything."

Evan claimed the violin and bow from him, and laid them to rest in the case. He held his hand out to Jesse. "I told you that you wouldn't drop him."

Jesse took Evan's hand. "You probably would've stopped kissing me if I would have, so that was my motivation."

Evan led Jesse out of the music room and through the family room. "Now I know the secret to getting you to do what I want. All I have to do is kiss you."

Jesse chuckled softly. "Pretty much."

Evan mounted the stairs in the entrance room. Jesse fell in behind him and gazed at his back, stunned that he was going up to Evan's bedroom. They walked down a hall to the master bedroom. Jesse's eyes widened at the sight of the four-poster king-sized bed of dark mahogany cloaked in a thick comforter of royal blue. To him, it looked like a stage built for the most intimate of performances.

Evan yanked Jesse to him and covered his mouth in a passionate kiss. Jesse's arms went around him. He returned Evan's kiss with equal fervor, allowing all the desire that had built throughout the night to break free, and pushed so hard against him that Evan stumbled back a step. He eased up a fraction, but only to work the buttons on Evan's shirt. At each one he tugged loose, his anticipation grew with the thought of feeling Evan's skin.

As the last button fell open, Jesse drew back from the kiss and settled his hands on Evan's abdomen lined with muscle, his eyes studying Evan's exposed flesh. His fingertips traveled up to his defined pectorals. He cupped them in his hands and squeezed against their strength. Though their builds were similar, Evan's frame fell more toward the small end of medium and he carried more muscle, especially in his chest. Jesse rubbed his hands over Evan's shoulders and pushed his shirt off, sliding it down his arms. He raised his gaze to Evan's and returned to his lips.

Evan fell back another step when Jesse pushed hard against him a second time. He broke their heated kiss to lift Jesse's shirt over his head. He tossed it, and before it hit the ground, he engaged Jesse in another deep kiss. Walking backward toward the bed, he enticed Jesse to follow with their lips together.

He paused to slide out of his shoes, and Jesse kicked his Nikes to the side. At the bedside, he grabbed the top of Jesse's jeans, pulled the button free, and dragged the zipper down. He wiggled his hand into Jesse's boxers, the humidity inside and slickness of his swollen cock head telling him that Jesse had been battling his attraction for him all night. He drifted his fingers down Jesse's organ, getting a feel for its length and diameter, and grinned. Jesse kept himself finely groomed, having only a small patch of silky curls above the base.

Jesse moaned loud as Evan's strong hand took hold of him, his fingers playing up and down his length with the same skill they had the violin. He hugged Evan tighter and buried his face against his neck. He wanted to touch Evan too, but his body was so desperate for release, he could only cling to him and thrust into his hand.

Evan let him go. He shoved Jesse's jeans and boxers the rest of the way down. As soon as Jesse stepped free of them, he pushed him hard, knocking him backward onto the bed, and followed by straddling one of Jesse's legs and placing a knee on the bed on the outside of Jesse's thigh.

Jesse blinked up at him, shocked by the rough movement, then grinned and propped himself up on his elbows. "You like to get rough, do you?"

Evan reached down to yank Jesse's socks off. "Sometimes. You?"

"Um, well, you see, here's the thing..."

Evan paused in unzipping his jeans and looked at him. "You've done this before, right?"

"Yeah...well, I've never gone all the way with a guy, but I've messed around and stuff."

Evan stared at him in disbelief. The one thing he had disregarded turned out to be the truth, Jesse's experience was limited. He slid his knee off the bed to stand firmly on the floor. His hands moved from his zipper to his hips. "Maybe we should slow down."

Jesse grabbed Evan's wrists. "No. If you slow down, then I'll speed up." He went to his back, bringing Evan down with him. Evan remained standing at the edge of the bed and braced himself above Jesse on both hands. Jesse lifted his head and grazed his lips across Evan's. "You started this, you're not getting out of it."

"I think it was an equal endeavor." Evan leaned all his weight on his left arm and lifted his right hand, combing his fingers through Jesse's hair. "Just so you know, we don't have to do anything you don't want to. I'll stop at anytime, just let me know."

Jesse smirked up at him. "Does talking fall into that?"

Evan laughed. "Oh, it's like that is it?"

"Yeah, it is."

Jesse snatched Evan's wrist and pulled his arm out from under him. Evan's chest crashed down on his. Without giving him a second to recover, Jesse clamped him in place with his arms around Evan's neck and his legs around his waist. Evan managed to take in a surprised breath an instant before Jesse took possession of his mouth and pushed his tongue into it in rhythmic thrusts.

Evan smiled through the kiss. He didn't realize his little bit of teasing would get Jesse so worked up. All the men he had known, all the countless times he had sex that he thought had been pretty damn good, seemed to pale compared to the way Jesse reacted to his touch. How anyone so gorgeous and passionate hadn't yet been claimed by another man was beyond him, but he'd call it his good fortune that he hadn't been, and would make Jesse his. He just needed to get him under control first.

Evan reached back with one hand and caught Jesse's arm. He pulled it away and slammed it to the bed, pinning it in place by the wrist beside Jesse's head. He grabbed Jesse's other arm and did the same.

Jesse gazed up at him, realizing Evan was taking control. He could see the dominance in Evan's eyes, feel it in the firm grip on his wrists. He was used to being in control in all he did, whether as the leader of Conquest or setting the tone for his encounters with other men, but the thought of giving himself over completely to Evan sent a tremor of exhilaration through him. He wet his lips, swollen from their intense kissing, and loosened the hold his legs had around Evan, spreading them wider for him.

Evan saw in Jesse's face his surrendering to him, and seeing it drove his passion to a new height. He lowered his head and met Jesse's lips in a rough kiss. He sent his tongue deep into Jesse's mouth along with a growling groan.

Evan tugged Jesse's wrists higher above his head. Jesse broke the kiss with a gasp and jerked his hips up toward him. He pressed Jesse's wrists to the mattress with one hand and moved his other between them to work open the zipper of his jeans. As he pushed his jeans and black boxer-briefs down, his cock came free and touched Jesse's.

A high groan escaped Jesse's throat when he felt the soft skin of Evan's erection rub against his own. He pulled his arms against Evan's hold. Evan's grip tightened. Jesse whimpered softly, raising his hips as much as he could, desperate to feel more of him.

Evan lowered his hips down on him, sliding his cock along Jesse's. He caught Jesse's bottom lip in his mouth, sucking on it and raking his teeth over it before he released it and spoke in a throaty voice, "Is there anything I should know?"

It took Jesse a second before he could compute Evan's words through his desire-drunk senses. "No. I'm clean."

"So am I. But we can still wear condoms if you want to. I don't expect you to trust me."

"I trust you," Jesse said, claiming Evan's lips again.

The wetness smearing along his cock from Jesse's told Evan how close Jesse was to climaxing. He released his hold on Jesse's wrists and slid down his body, kissing from Jesse's throat to his chest, lingering to tease each nipple, loving the way Jesse writhed and panted with every flick of his tongue. He rubbed his hands down Jesse's sides as he kissed his flat stomach. He nibbled at the soft skin where Jesse's leg met his body and brushed his palm up the underside of Jesse's long shaft. He moved his mouth over Jesse's cock, letting his warm breath caress him, then slid his tongue up the length and took him into his mouth, going deep to the back of his throat, rejoicing in finally tasting him after a month of starving for him.

Jesse clutched the comforter with one hand and tangled his fingers in Evan's hair with the other. The heat of Evan's mouth spread through his body in a dizzying rush. He couldn't believe the mouth that beautiful voice came out of was wrapped around his cock. He tightened his hold on Evan's hair. Evan moaned softly. He gave Evan's hair a harder tug, and Evan's rumbling groan of approval nearly sent him over the edge. He didn't think he could get any more turned on, but the sound of Evan in pleasure took him to another level.

"I'm so close," Jesse gasped.

Evan doubled his efforts. He sucked harder and swallowed Jesse's tip down his throat.

All night he had been dying for release and now that it was upon him, Jesse fought to hold it back. He wanted to feel Evan's velvet tongue on him just a little bit longer, to be lubricated even more in his warm saliva. But Evan's skill played to his body's dire need.

"Ev…I…I'm going to…" Jesse cried out, gripping Evan's hair as the orgasm that had been seeking freedom all night erupted from him.

Jesse's taste overwhelmed Evan's senses as his cum filled his mouth. Even when Jesse's cock stopped pulsing, he refused to take his lips away, coaxing every bit out by massaging the underside of the head with his tongue. At each stroke of his tongue, he felt Jesse take in a short, trembling breath. After a few long moments, Evan eased back.

Jesse lay motionless, panting for breath. "That was so amazing."

Evan slid up Jesse's body and whispered, "You're amazing."

Jesse pulled Evan down to his lips by his hair, devouring his tongue in a passion filled kiss. He let his head fall back on the bed and took a deep breath to steady his racing heart. Evan moved his lips to Jesse's neck, kissing and sucking at the tender skin.

Jesse smiled and buried his nose in Evan's hair. "You like having your hair pulled."

Evan chuckled as he graced Jesse's collarbone with gentle kisses. "You're the first person who's ever caught on to that."

Jesse laughed softly. He watched as Evan pushed off the bed and stood up, his jeans and boxer-briefs falling away. He sat all the way up and scooted toward the edge of the bed, gazing at Evan standing naked before him. The moonlight cast a silvery glow over his sculpted body, the thick, silken tip of his cock glistened wet with eagerness. He moved his eyes down Evan's ample length, just a touch shorter than his own, but with a bit more girth.

Jesse lifted his eyes to Evan's. "Impressive."

"I was thinking the same thing about you." Standing between Jesse's legs, Evan placed his fingertips under Jesse's chin and tipped his head back to look into his eyes. "Are you still feeling okay with everything so far?"

Jesse flashed a mischievous smirk. "No, because I haven't gotten to taste you yet."

Evan drew his thumb along Jesse's bottom lip. "Well, if that's the only problem, that's easy to fix."

Jesse embraced Evan around his hips. He nuzzled Evan's skin at the base of his cock, inhaling his masculine scent touched with Platinum Egoist. He dipped his head down and slid his tongue across Evan's smoothly shaven sac.

A soft sigh left Evan. He had dreamed of moments like this since laying eyes on Jesse, but he never anticipated Jesse would surpass the fantasies that had played out in his mind.

Jesse steadied Evan's cock in his hand and placed a line of whisper soft kisses up one side. When he reached the end, he engulfed the saturated tip in his mouth and sucked it clean. A throaty groan rumbled in Evan's throat, he rocked his hips toward Jesse. Jesse drew back, sliding his tongue down the thick vein on the underside to Evan's base. He glided up again, gently teasing with his teeth, and grinned at the little tremor that shook Evan's body.

Evan groaned louder. He rubbed one hand through Jesse's hair, bringing it to rest on the back of his head. He gripped Jesse's shoulder with his other hand and brought his hips closer to him.

Jesse took a moment to enjoy Evan begging with his body. He decided he didn't have the willpower to keep tormenting him, and wrapping his hand around Evan's base, he opened his mouth and dove down his length. He moved up and down in steady motions, sucking while rubbing with his tongue. With the palm of his other hand, he massaged circles on Evan's ass cheeks, enjoying the way the muscles would clench each time he hit him just right. He curved his fingers around one cheek and dug his short fingernails into Evan's skin; the hard groan from Evan told him he liked the force. He tugged Evan to him, encouraging him to thrust into his mouth.

Evan pushed into his mouth at a faster pace than what Jesse had started. Jesse moved with him, clamping his fingers tighter onto Evan's ass. He could feel it in Evan's body, the way his muscles constricted, Evan was on the brink of climaxing. He moaned loud, hoping Evan would pick up how badly he wanted him to release in his mouth.

Evan gasped at the feel of Jesse's voice reverberating around his cock. It was all he needed to push him over, and he gave Jesse warning. "Jess, I'm coming..." He ended the sentence with a shout as his climax surged free.

Jesse savored and swallowed the salty fluid until Evan's organ gave him no more, then lingered a few moments before he released Evan and licked his lips clean while looking up at him.

Evan had yet to move. He stood with much of his weight leaning down on Jesse's shoulder, his hand still in his hair.

Jesse ran one hand up Evan's abdomen. "Good?"

Evan took a deep breath and nodded. "So good I might die."

"That's not good. Here I thought I'd get a little more out of you, but I guess your old body just can't keep up."

Evan recovered and shoved Jesse's shoulder. Jesse fell over on his back, laughing. Evan walked around the foot of the bed, pointing at Jesse as he went to the other side. "We're going to be playing for a long time, so get ready to be schooled, brat."

Still laughing softly, Jesse climbed between the white silk sheets and slid on his side close to him. Evan flipped toward him and caressed Jesse's refined cheekbone. Jesse closed his eyes to Evan's soft touch and turned his head toward his hand, laying a warm kiss in his palm.

"You're pretty fierce until you get that first one off, aren't you?" Evan said.

Jesse pushed one leg between Evan's and draped his other on top so their legs became tangled together. "Yeah, but I don't always calm down after it. Usually I want to go fast and furious until I've got nothing left, but it feels different with you. I'm enjoying being close to you too much to burn myself out quickly."

Evan squeezed Jesse tighter to him, their chests and hips pressed together. "I feel the same way."

Jesse smiled and found Evan's lips again. Their tongues mingled their tastes. Their fingers drifted over each other's body, tracing, mapping, learning the feel of the other's flesh. The soft touches gradually changed to firmer rubs, the slow kisses more urgent. Each rocked toward the other, grinding their cocks between their bodies.

His voice hushed, breathless, Evan said, "How far do you want to go?"

Jesse kept his lips on Evan's. "As far as possible."

Evan closed his eyes in a long blink. To receive such an answer from Jesse brought his best dreams about him fully to life, but now knowing his inexperience and also that Jesse was a fan, tainted his desire with doubt. "Are you sure?"

Jesse nodded once. "Positive."

"Jess," Evan said softly, "it's okay if you don't want to. I don't want you to feel pressured because of who I am."

Jesse grinned. "Like you having a couple hit songs is a big influence in this decision."

Evan smiled at his words, then laid his hand on Jesse's cheek, his face falling serious. "I just don't want you to have any regrets. It doesn't matter how many partners you may have later in life, if we do this, you'll always remember me as the first guy that was ever inside you. You'll never be able to fully forget about me."

Jesse cupped Evan's face in both hands, locking his gaze intently into his. "I want to be with you because I *don't* want to forget you. And right now, I'm not thinking of my future with other men. I'm thinking of you, and only you."

Evan gave him a warm smile. "You certainly know the right things to say to seduce a boy."

Jesse chuckled softly. "I'm trying."

Evan placed a gentle kiss on Jesse's lips. "Roll onto your other side for me."

Jesse shifted to roll to his right side. As he moved, he saw Evan stretch across the bed toward the nightstand, reach in the top drawer, and retrieve a bottle of lube. Jesse slowly lay down on his side with his back to Evan, his heart fluttering a nervous rhythm. This was it. For so long he had wondered what it would be like to let a guy inside him and now it was actually going to happen. Several months ago, he decided he was ready, but since then, the quality of prospective partners hadn't met his standards, and he'd been waiting for someone who he felt was right, knowing his instincts would flare when he met that person. Everything inside him said that person was Evan. He heard Evan opening the bottle and swallowed hard. It didn't make him feel any less nervous, though.

Evan slid up close behind him, his lips to Jesse's ear. "We'll start slow."

Jesse's heartbeat quickened more. He managed the smallest of nods.

Evan adjusted Jesse's top leg to lie forward and settled in behind him, propping himself up on his right elbow. He nuzzled into Jesse's hair, kissed his temple, and moved the slicked up fingers of his left hand to Jesse's opening.

Jesse closed his eyes at Evan's tender touch stroking and circling outside his hole. He had touched and penetrated himself with his fingers numerous times before as he explored his own body, but the sensation of someone else's fingers was entirely different. He found himself shifting in response to Evan, a yearning growing to feel his touch inside him. He stretched his top leg further to expose more of himself to Evan.

Evan eased his middle finger halfway into him.

Jesse gasped, twisting the sheets in his fingers. His internal muscles clenched around Evan's unmoving finger. Evan's lips touched his neck in soft kisses, and their gentleness alone relaxed him. After a few moments, Evan slid deeper into him and thrust in easy, careful motions. Each push of Evan's finger sparked more pleasure, and just as he adjusted to Evan's touch, it left him. When it returned, Evan pressed two freshly coated fingers inside him.

Jesse's breath shook in his throat. When he had touched himself, the sensation, though pleasant, always fell short of what he wanted. He felt like he could never get deep enough, never quite exploit the full pleasure hiding there. But Evan's touch sent pulsing heat through his body, his fingers filled him better than his own ever had, and the feel of his muscles and skin stretching around them was incredible, as if his body had been wanting for this for years.

Evan bent his fingers to seek Jesse's prostate.

Jesse jerked back toward Evan, his body tingling from the electric shock of ecstasy. "Do...do that again."

Evan grinned, kissed him behind his ear, and gave him what he wanted, tenderly massaging around his prostate.

Jesse's breath came quick and shallow. He couldn't believe the pleasure Evan's stimulation brought. It seemed like Evan could read his body, knew just how much to press and when to back off. His cock ached with the demand to release again. He couldn't stop himself. He took hold of his shaft and pumped in time with Evan's thrusting and scissoring fingers.

Evan peered over Jesse's shoulder, watching him stroke himself. He wet his lips; his cock dripped ready drops. One thing was for certain, Jesse definitely wasn't shy about his body or in openly displaying what he wanted when it came to his satisfaction. It made Evan wonder what he had done to deserve finding such a perfect partner. He withdrew his fingers and eased three inside him on his return, stopping once he reached the center knuckles.

At Evan stretching him wider yet, Jesse's hand slipped from his cock to the bed. He gripped the sheet in a fist, feeling incapacitated by Evan's touch. He knew Evan had three fingers inside him, and though his rim felt stretched to its fullest, it wasn't unpleasant and he couldn't call it painful. He felt Evan move his hand in careful, short thrusts. Each muscle in his body began to loosen, and he sighed loud in pleasure.

Sensing Jesse's body had accepted him, Evan slowly pulled his fingers away.

Jesse turned half toward him.

Evan laid his hand on Jesse's hip, guiding him to roll onto his back. He bowed his head to Jesse's lips in a light kiss. "Try to stay relaxed for me, gorgeous."

Jesse took a deep breath, willing his body to be calm.

Evan sat back and lifted each of Jesse's legs to rest upon his shoulders. He moved over him, bending Jesse's legs back with him, and braced himself on one arm. He reached down with his other hand to guide his lube-coated cock in.

At the first sensation of Evan entering him, Jesse sucked in a sharp breath and pressed his head back against the pillow. He felt the proof of Evan's skill at preparing him in there was no pain, but the thickness of his cock filling him still came as a shock to his virgin channel. He took a slow, deep breath in an attempt to steady the rapid ones he'd been panting. A spell of disbelief passed through him that another man was inside him, and not just any man, but *Evan Arden*, the man who inspired him, who had gifted him with his music long before this night. He felt stunned and joyous at the same time.

After easing halfway in, Evan stopped and braced himself above Jesse on both arms. He closed his eyes, fighting for control. The tight, wet silk confines of Jesse's body seemed made for the sole purpose of squeezing the fluid from of him. His body begged him to slam his full length into him, to ride out a month of desire long and hard, but his heart stayed him. The last thing he wanted was to hurt Jesse and ruin this for him. He needed to go slow, to mold Jesse's body perfectly to his own. He heard Jesse's breathing even out, felt his muscles slacken, and pushed in a little more, letting Jesse's body tell him how far he should go. Gently, he brought Jesse's legs off his shoulders so Jesse could lay them wherever he felt most comfortable.

Jesse hooked his ankles across Evan's lower back, his knees fell open to the sides. With his eyes closed, he concentrated on the feel of Evan inching deeper into him. He couldn't believe how gentle Evan was being, how carefully he moved. He felt Evan's fingers brush across his forehead and down his cheek.

"You doing okay?" Evan asked.

Jesse's heart lurched at the warmth in his voice. He opened his eyes to Evan's gaze. "Yeah."

Evan lowered his lips to him. His tongue was welcomed with a sensual massage by Jesse's. He pulled his hips back and forward in a testing thrust. Jesse sent an encouraging moan from his mouth to Evan's, and Evan moved his hips slowly.

Jesse relaxed with each smooth motion of Evan's hips; more and more pleasure rose from the slick feel of Evan's cock gliding in and out of him. He felt Evan's strength with each push and opened his eyes, admiring the cut lines of muscle in Evan's torso. He was stunned at being truly connected with Evan's body, that he was sharing the most physically intimate thing possible with him. He moved his hands down Evan's sides to his hips and pulled him to move deeper, wanting every fraction of Evan's hard length inside him.

At Jesse's request, Evan gave in to his body's demands and thrust into him with a forceful push. Jesse's breath fled in a fast exhale. Evan lowered himself down to his elbows and rocked Jesse's body with deep, rhythmic thrusts. He slid his hand down Jesse's arm and took hold of his hand.

Jesse paused. That one small gesture made what was happening between them seem even more intimate. He nuzzled into Evan's neck, breathing in his cologne, and squeezed Evan's hand, holding onto him with one arm around his back. He ground his cock against Evan's stomach, heightening his rapture to another building climax.

Evan felt Jesse's body tighten under him and quickened his pace. Jesse's fingers bit into his back, he clutched his hand tighter. Evan's body trembled with the effort of holding back his orgasm, trying to bring Jesse to pleasure at the same moment.

"Jess," he groaned.

Hearing Evan say his name finished him. Jesse let out a high moan, his body shuddering in sweet release. Evan met his cry, his own orgasm tearing through him. Through his euphoria, Jesse felt Evan's cock throbbing, the heat of his cum coating him inside, and the thought fluttered through his mind that feeling Evan's climax was even better than his own.

Evan thrust a few more times, then stopped and rested his forehead in the curve of Jesse's neck. Jesse held him close, still gripping his hand. He turned his head and touched his lips to Evan's sweaty neck, feeling his quick pulse beating beneath his lips.

"Thanks," he said softly.

Evan lifted his head and met Jesse's eyes. "For what?"

"For being so patient and careful."

"You don't have to thank me for that." Evan grinned at him. "And I wouldn't be talking like we're finished. I already told you we're going to be playing for a while."

Jesse smiled and tipped his lips up to Evan for another kiss.

CHAPTER SEVEN

Jesse stretched out in the huge bed, then remembered where he was and snapped fully awake. He whipped his head to the side. The bed was empty beside him. He moved to get up, stopping at the warm ache he felt where his and Evan's bodies had been joined just hours before.

He eased back down and closed his eyes. The last thing he remembered was the feel of Evan holding him as he fell asleep. His mind flooded with how they had clung to each other, melting into each other while everything around them drifted away but their two bodies pulsing together, a blur of endless ecstasy that lasted until they both reached total exhaustion. The way Evan kissed, touched, moved, was all so sensual. He felt the same pull on his heart as when Evan asked if he was doing okay. Evan's voice had been so kind, he sounded like he truly cared.

Jesse moved his hand under the silk top sheet and wrapped his fingers around his full arousal. He looked over at the alarm clock by the bed, saw it was a quarter past noon, and felt relieved it was Sunday and he didn't have to go to work. That'd be just lovely to shuffle around a mega-bookstore trying to stock shelves with a sore ass.

The time hit him again and he realized he hadn't talked to Brandon or Kenny. He forced himself to get up and swing out of bed. He found his boxers and jeans on the floor, and pulled on his boxers while he dug his cell phone out of his jeans, not the least bit surprised to see Brandon had called six times. He knew he should call him back, but also knew it would take a while to make Brandon believe who he spent the night with, and really, he didn't want to get tangled up in a big conversation with his brother before seeing Evan. He tucked his cell phone back into his jeans and tossed them onto the bed.

He turned for the bathroom. On his way, he paused at the closed heavy curtains of royal blue trimmed in gold and peeked out to the wide French doors leading to a balcony that overlooked the back of Evan's property.

Below, a white brick patio edged with gray stone held outdoor furniture of white wrought iron. A few feet away sat a hot tub paneled in redwood. Beyond the patio was a massive in-ground pool with a separate whirlpool section, and in the far left-hand corner of it, a waterfall trickled over dark gray stones. The back of the property continued to stretch on in an expanse of thick grass dotted with maples, pines, birches, and other assorted trees. A white gravel path traversed away from the patio to a verdant garden filled with roses, and in the center of the garden stood a white gazebo. The yard progressed to the brick and stone wall where an iron gate blocked off a set of concrete stairs that led down through giant boulders and rocks to the sandy beach. White gulls oscillated over the sparkling waves of Lake Michigan.

Jesse let the curtain fall shut, a moment of disbelief passing through him. He turned for the master bathroom and stopped the instant he stepped in. He had been in there the night before, but he was in such a daze from being with Evan, he staggered in and stumbled back out when finished. Now with full daylight coming through a strip of windows above the shower, he saw a bathroom like ones he saw on TV or in magazines. Tile that looked like real pieces of stone covered the floor. The enormous glass shower took up a full corner. The whirlpool bathtub was separate, raised up on a couple steps, and could easily hold two people. To his left ran a white marble counter streaked in silver with two sinks and a long mirror above.

Jesse blinked, shook his head slightly, and walked across the bathroom to the toilet, where a bidet sat to one side. He saw mouthwash sitting by the sink and rinsed his mouth, then washed his face and combed his fingers through his hair. He headed back to the bedroom and looked at the empty bed, unable to deny the disappointment he felt at waking up alone. He considered crawling back in and waiting for Evan to return to him, then wondered if Evan was downstairs waiting for him to get dressed and get out. For all he knew, he had already overstayed his welcome. The things Evan whispered to him during the night made him want to believe Evan would like to see him again, but in truth, maybe he should look at Evan's words for what they were, the charmings of a man looking to get off.

His heart constricted at the thought. He didn't want Evan's words to be hollow. He wanted to see him again, every day, every night. He wanted Evan to be his, and his alone. But how would he go about convincing a man who was used to being the object of lust for half the world that he should be only with him?

Jesse felt the combative part of himself stir at the challenge. He could do it. After all, even if half the world wanted Evan, the world hadn't gotten a look at Jesse yet, and when it did just as many people would want him too, so didn't that mean he and Evan would be perfect together? While the whole world drooled over one or the other of them, they could find sanctuary in each other's arms, understanding each other better than anyone else possibly could. He snatched his jeans off the bed, wanting to find Evan.

"Getting ready to leave so soon?"

Jesse snapped his head up at the sound of Evan's voice. Wearing only a pair of black Adidas running pants that fell off the top of his slender hips, Evan stood in the doorway holding a serving tray with two plates of scrambled eggs, toast, and two glasses of orange juice.

Jesse dropped his jeans to the floor. "I was getting dressed to look for you."

"You don't have to be dressed to do that." Evan headed to the nightstand and set the tray down. He walked around the bed, past Jesse to the curtains, and pulled them back to fill the bedroom with sunlight. He stayed at the windows, staring out at the lake.

Jesse's breath slipped as he gazed at Evan's lean body, his skin radiant in the sunlight. Looking at him, he couldn't help but picture classical Greek sculptures that strove to depict the epitome of male beauty. It was impossible to look at Evan and think of him as anything but beautiful. Though, other words like stunning, breathtaking, captivating...

"Any regrets?" Evan asked, his voice soft.

Jesse stared at Evan's back, too surprised by the question to answer.

"I knew we should have slowed down," Evan mumbled to himself.

Jesse watched Evan's shoulders rise and fall with a sigh. He walked up behind him and wrapped his arms around Evan's waist. He kissed the back of his shoulder, laid his head against Evan's, and gave him a strong hug. "No regrets," he whispered.

Evan turned in his arms and rested his forehead against Jesse's. "How do you feel?"

With Evan so close, his breath on his lips, Jesse's earlier desire surged back to the surface. He edged his hips nearer to him. "I feel incredible."

Evan felt Jesse's cock rising against his own. "Sore?"

Jesse brushed his lips across Evan's shoulder. "A little." He licked up Evan's neck to his left earlobe and sucked the two gold hoop earrings dangling there into his mouth. "But it's a good kind of sore." He moved his lips back to Evan's neck. Evan closed his eyes and tipped his head to the side to give more of it to him. Jesse kissed the soft skin near the curve. "There's a phantom feeling as if you're still inside me." He lightly nipped him. "But it's a tease too, because it makes me want the real thing again."

Evan smiled, and caressed up and down Jesse's back with his fingertips. "You're going to become addicted to it."

Jesse traced his index finger along the inside of Evan's pants. The tip brushed over the top of Evan's hard cock. "I think I already am."

Evan grazed his lips over Jesse's. "Are you hungry?"

Jesse nodded. "I'm so starving I swear my stomach is crawling up my throat looking for food."

"That's a sexy image. I hope you like your eggs scrambled because it's the only way I know how to cook 'em." Evan lightly tugged at Jesse's boxers. "Why don't you take these off and get back in bed?"

Before Evan's fingers left his boxers, Jesse dropped them around his ankles. Evan moved his eyes over him, taking a long moment to drink in Jesse's fully filled organ. He slowly raised his gaze. Jesse's eyes showed no shyness or self-consciousness, not that Jesse had anything to be self-conscious about. His sleek, wiry body could have made Michelangelo weep at its perfection. He caught Jesse's knowing grin. Jesse knew *exactly* how attractive he was, and it was clear because of that knowledge, he was as comfortable nude as he was clothed.

Seeing Jesse's confidence made Evan's cock strain to break free of his running pants. He slid one arm around Jesse's lower back and pulled him in, covering his mouth in a kiss that sent his desire to him. He rubbed one hand down Jesse's chest to his stomach, pausing when he felt it rumble under his palm. He smiled through the kiss. "You really are hungry."

Jesse leaned forward to continue the kiss. "I can wait."

Evan gave Jesse's hand a pull toward the bed. "I have a feeling you'd starve to death before passing up sex."

Jesse let out an exaggerated sigh of disappointment, but followed. He crawled under the covers and propped the pillows up against the headboard. Evan set the tray over Jesse's lap and slid next to him from the other side of the bed.

Jesse took a bite of the eggs and looked at Evan with a smirk. "Wow. The rock star can cook."

Evan chuckled under his breath. "I do okay with some things." He lowered his eyes to his plate, his mood suddenly somber. "Is that what you see when you look at me? A rock star? A celebrity?"

Jesse heard a hint of sorrow in Evan's voice. He looked at him to see it reflected in the shadow of pain on his face. It reminded him of when he asked Evan about why he had left the music world behind and how Evan skated around the question. There was more to his leaving than wanting to explore the world. Had he grown tired of people only looking at him as a performer? From what he already learned of Evan's personality, saying he was reclusive would be an understatement. Could he no longer stand having cameras shoved in his face everywhere he went, having reporters trying to dig out the dirty bits of his personal life? It couldn't have been easy for him, being gay and trying to hide it to attain the highest level of success possible. Or did something else happen to drive Evan away from music? He couldn't imagine anything being strong enough to make himself turn away from it.

Jesse brushed the backs of his fingers down Evan's cheek. "I'm not going to lie and say I don't admire the music you've done, or that I've never watched DVDs of your concerts and sat in awe of your stage performance. But just because your music has inspired me, it wouldn't have been enough for me to be here with you like we are now. When I said things felt different with you, I meant you're the first person I've ever been so attracted to beyond just the physical."

He laid his hand over Evan's and threaded their fingers together. "And last night, I felt something with you I've never felt before. Something deep inside me responded to you, and I wanted you like I've never wanted anyone. I wouldn't have given it up to you if I didn't feel that way. That's what I've been waiting for. For a guy I felt comfortable with, someone I connected with deeper than just thinking they were hot." He paused, his next words coming softer. "Someone I felt safe with."

Evan gazed at him. Jesse felt comfortable, safe, with him. He wondered if Jesse was always so honest and open with his emotions. This was the exact thing he had feared, that he would find himself unable to resist wanting to be with him, that Jesse would genuinely like him and want more from him than only a single night of pleasure. Yet despite the trepidation, the joy he felt overpowered it to the point where he could delude himself into believing he had every right to be happy with Jesse.

Jesse gave him bright smile. "And how could I be attracted to you for your celebrity status? The Evan Arden I know is just a wicked sexy guy who hangs out in questionable parts of town desperate to catch a glimpse of the greatest singer he's ever had the privilege of listening to."

"I can't argue with that," Evan laughed.

Jesse bumped him playfully on the shoulder with his shoulder, then turned back to his food. When the last bites were eaten, Evan lifted the tray and set it on the nightstand. Jesse breathed out a contented sigh and slid down on the bed, lying on his back and stretching out.

Evan reclined on his side and propped his head up on his hand, tickling circles and swirls over Jesse's chest with his fingertips. "I still think it's amazing you don't have a boyfriend."

"I still think it's amazing you're gay. All the times I've listened to your music, watched and read interviews with you, I never got the impression you were into guys." He grinned up at Evan. "I fantasized that you were, though."

"Now that puts all sorts of beautiful images in my head. I can just envision you lying in bed, stroking yourself, listening to one of my CDs with a magazine I was in open beside you."

"You don't think I'm weird for fantasizing about you?"

"No. I fantasized about you after I first saw you. I even dreamed about you and woke up to a mess all over my sheets."

"I hope I lived up to what you dreamed about."

"You surpassed it."

Evan bent his head down and kissed him. Jesse weaved his fingers in Evan's hair. He heaved his weight up against him to put Evan on his back and rolled on top of him. Evan caught him behind his head and pulled him down harder to his mouth. He thrust his tongue against Jesse's and arched his hips up to him.

Jesse's entire body warmed as desire ignited his temperature. He ground his hard cock against Evan's hidden away in his pants, and the short, high moan that passed from Evan's mouth to his amped his passion up even more. He braced himself above Evan on both arms, breaking the kiss but keeping their lips touching, and thrust against him as he would if he were inside him.

Evan took in a quick breath, whispering "Jess" as he exhaled.

Jesse grabbed the top of Evan's pants and started to pull them down.

Evan caught Jesse's wrist. "Let's…let's shower first."

Jesse fought to refocus from his physical need and met Evan's gaze. Despite Evan's attempt to hide it, he saw a flicker of nervousness in his eyes and the slight trembling in his fingers further betrayed him. With defying speed, Jesse's mind formed an analysis of the enigma under him. For all his success and fame, for all the people who admired and adored him, Evan wasn't one who trusted easily. And yet, Evan had welcomed him into his home, so did that mean Evan wanted to trust him? From deep inside, he knew the answer was yes, and he would work to prove to Evan he could trust him.

Jesse smiled and rubbed his nose against Evan's. "Yeah, I haven't showered since before my gig last night. I'm icky, aren't I?"

Evan released the breath he'd been holding with a single short laugh. "Neither have I. So I guess we're both icky."

Jesse gave him one more light kiss on the lips, then slid off him and the bed. He stood with his back to Evan, using the excuse of stretching his arms over his head to allow Evan an eyeful of the smooth skin of his back and tight curves of his ass. He glanced over his shoulder, and at the open lust he saw in Evan's eyes, he knew he had succeeded in balancing Evan's mood again.

"I just have to run out to my truck to get my bag first," Jesse said.

"I'll get it for you. You jump in the shower. I have an extra toothbrush in the cabinet under the sink you can have if you want."

Jesse moved toward the bathroom. "Thanks."

He found the unopened toothbrush and brushed his teeth, then turned the shower on. When he stepped under the hot flow, every part of him, save one, went limp at the pressure and heat massaging his body. A small groan purred in his throat at how good it felt to be in a shower where the flow was more than a trickle and the hot water didn't fade in and out every two minutes. He washed his body, then grabbed Evan's shampoo to wash his hair. While rubbing in conditioner, he heard Evan drop his duffel bag on the bathroom floor.

"Awe, this is so cute. You have all my albums in your CD wallet."

Jesse cracked open the glass shower door and peeked out, smiling. "Snoop around much?"

Evan held up the wallet as if showing him something Jesse had never seen. "It was under your bag. Look, they're even right in front before any others. That must mean they're your favorite."

"Either that, or I want to get past them quick to the real music," Jesse teased, ducking back into the shower.

"Ouch," Evan chuckled. "Let's see what else you got in here. You can learn a lot about a person from what kind of music they listen to. We have Black Eyed Peas, Pink, Queen, okay those are all good."

Jesse laughed listening to him.

"Hmm, Mozart concertos. So you are a classical buff."

"Mozart is my boy," Jesse said, rinsing conditioner from his hair. "I played classical piano from when I was old enough to sit at the keys until I was fifteen."

"That explains a lot." Evan flipped another page and deepened his voice, making it rough, "Metallica!"

Jesse laughed harder, shaking his head at him.

"What the...Dr. Dre, *The Chronic*?"

Jesse opened the door again. "It's a classic. I have the new 50 Cent in there, too. What? You don't like rap?"

"No, I love it. I just can't see your skinny white butt cruising the streets of Chicago with *The Chronic* bumping out of your busted ass pickup truck."

Jesse forced himself to look serious. "Are you about done now?"

"No, I'm not even halfway through."

Jesse gave him a playful glare from under his wet hair. "Why don't you put the CDs down, shut your pretty mouth, and get in the shower."

Evan placed the wallet on the sink counter and pushed his pants off his hips. "Yeah, I guess I do have some more schooling to do with you."

Jesse grinned as he watched Evan's pants fall to the floor. "Just be careful. I wouldn't want you to fall and break a hip or anything."

"That's it! You're going down!"

Evan jumped in the shower and grabbed Jesse, pressing his lips to his, both laughing through the kiss. He raked his fingers up the back of Jesse's hair, took a fistful, and yanked his head back to look into his eyes, a smirk lifting one corner of his lips. "If you keep up with your smart mouth, I'll just have to keep punishing you."

Jesse bumped his rigid organ against Evan's. "You have no idea how cocky I can be. And I think you're a bit of a sadist, anyway."

"Which works out since I think you're a bit of a masochist."

"With you I am." Jesse stepped behind Evan and nudged him under the flow. He combed his fingers through Evan's hair to get it saturated, then snatched the shampoo. "But that's not how I usually am. This one time at a club, I almost ripped out a guy's nipple ring for trying to get rough with me."

Evan swallowed the instant jealousy that erupted from his core at hearing of Jesse in an intimate situation with another guy. "Have things like that happened a lot?"

"No. Most guys had to practically spar against my brother just to dance with me. If there's such a thing as overly overprotective, that's Brandon. But he means well, so I don't get upset about it."

Evan nodded, then stood silent while Jesse washed his hair and massaged his scalp. He felt Jesse's aroused cock bump against his ass, but it happened so quickly and without a second brush, he knew it had been an accident. For as hard and lustful as he was, Jesse was doing his best to not be invasive on him. The care and respect Jesse showed made his heart ache for him. Even when Jesse had been flaunting like an exhibitionist, the tenderness in his eyes was no illusion, which stunned him since Jesse had every right to be upset at him.

He hadn't meant to stop him. When Jesse gave him a taste of how hungry and aggressive he would be on top, he wanted Jesse to take him, but years had passed since he let another man inside him and he panicked at giving himself over so intimately. When he was on top, he could still maintain some distance. It was more of an act of serving physical need than emotional.

Except last night, there *had* been emotion. There had been ever since he first saw Jesse.

As Jesse finished rinsing the conditioner from Evan's hair, Evan turned toward him and kissed him. Without breaking the kiss, Jesse found the soap and lathered his hands. He rubbed them over Evan's shoulders, down his back, across his chest and abdomen. With one sudsy hand he gripped Evan's shaft, with the other his delicate sac, and gently kneaded, pumped, and stroked him clean.

Evan closed his eyes, taking a moment to enjoy the slick pleasuring before claiming the soap and washing Jesse in turn. With reverence filled fingertips, they caressed and explored every curve, each muscle, of the other.

Evan traced a line down Jesse's spine past his tailbone. As Evan's touch moved to his hole, Jesse shifted his stance wider. Evan pushed his middle finger inside him. Jesse moaned long and low, and pressed against him, the heat from the shower and Evan's touch giving him a euphoric rush. He tipped his head back. Water trickled over his face, and through it he felt Evan's moist breath on his lips.

Evan gazed at him, so wanton, so ready to accept him. Jesse was like no one he ever encountered before. He had no shame in himself, his body, or his emotions. There were no ulterior motives in him. He doubted it was even possible for Jesse to hide his feelings, let alone deceitful intentions. So maybe, it might be okay to open up to him, just a little.

Evan reached around and found Jesse's hand resting on his back. He slid his hand down and pressed Jesse's fingers between his ass cheeks. He felt Jesse exhale a fast breath of surprise, but the way Jesse's cock twitched forward told him how badly he wanted him. He eased his finger out of Jesse.

"Jess," he whispered, "you should know, it's been a long time for me."

Jesse barely heard Evan's words through the desire pounding a hard rhythm in his body like a thousand bass drums. He took a deep breath to clear his head. "Do you not like it?"

"No, I do." Evan averted his gaze. "It's just, it's difficult for me, sometimes, a lot of times, to…"

Sympathy flooded Jesse as he watched Evan struggle to explain what he had already figured out, that Evan found it difficult to open up to others, physically and emotionally, and he leaped to save him from his discomfiture. "It's okay. I understand. You're like me. It's not easy for you to trust just anyone." He smiled. "Unlike my brother. You should see some of the losers he's slept with. If I had a dollar for every time I asked him, 'What the hell were you thinking?' I'd be able to buy more Ferraris than you."

Evan chuckled softly. How was it possible Jesse knew exactly what to say and do to put him at ease? His ability to do so was almost too supernatural to believe. He looked in Jesse's indigo eyes shining with affection and humor. Adoration for him consumed him, leaving him helpless as he yanked Jesse close and claimed his mouth.

Jesse greeted Evan's sudden passion with his own. He drifted his lips down Evan's throat and gently stroked the outside of Evan's opening with his middle fingertip, waiting for a sign that Evan wanted more. He felt Evan's rapid pulse in his neck, his chest rising and falling in fast breaths. Evan opened his stance and pushed back toward his fingers. Jesse eased his middle finger halfway into him.

Evan let out a soft groan that took his tension away with the expelled breath. His shoulders relaxed, each knotted muscle untangling at Jesse's touch.

Jesse thrust his finger into him and studied him, fascinated as he explored his body. Evan felt so intense inside. The gripping tightness of him, the clenching muscles, the wet heat, the silken internal flesh, it all amazed him. He added his index finger and evoked a deep moan from Evan. He concentrated on Evan, memorizing what each caress and stroke of his fingers did so he could deliver the best possible pleasure.

His fingers found Evan's gland. He watched as Evan gasped, his body flinched in a shock of ecstasy. He looked down between them at Evan's cock, the slit filled with drops of milky white. He rubbed his thumb over it, smearing the wetness across the soft skin. A throaty groan shook in Evan's throat. Evan pushed his hips forward, and at the same time, reached back, found Jesse's hand, and drove his fingers into himself as deep as they'd go. His head fell back on his shoulders as he exhaled a loud groan.

Jesse licked his lips, his own cock demanding to feel what his fingers were.

Evan tipped his head forward, his lips a fraction from Jesse's. "Let's go to the bed," he said, his voice a husky whisper.

Jesse nodded and withdrew his fingers.

Evan turned off the water and stepped out of the shower. Without bothering to dry off, he took Jesse's hand and led him to the bed. He grabbed the comforter and top sheet, and flung them toward the foot. As he opened the top drawer of the nightstand, Jesse peeked over his shoulder.

"Holy shit," Jesse said, peering into the drawer at the lube sitting on top of dildos and vibrators of various sizes and styles, cock rings, anal beads, and other assorted sex toys. "You could open an adult store." He picked up a foot-long black dildo of an unnatural diameter. "Wow. I feel a little insufficient."

"Actually, I never use that one." Evan picked up a pink flesh colored one with a slender but full width, a near clone Jesse's organ. "This is my regular."

"That makes me feel better." Jesse reached in the drawer and lifted a black silk bondage strap on his index finger. He looked at Evan with a mischievous smirk. "Just when I thought you couldn't get any more perfect, you turn out to be a kinky boy, too."

Evan grinned at him. "You know, since my relationships don't usually stretch beyond a night, I've never gotten to play with things like that for fear of freakin' somebody out by asking them if I could tie them up and tease them with a vibrator. But you'd be willing?"

Jesse hopped on the bed and lay on his back. "I'm willing to play with anything at least once. And we're going to be moving into our second night together."

Evan crawled over the bed to him and straddled Jesse's hips. "Then you'll stay with me tonight?"

"I'd love to."

The smile Evan gave him struck Jesse in awe, not only at its beauty, but at the true happiness behind it.

Evan lowered his smiling lips to Jesse, delivering a slow, sensual kiss. So engrossed in the kiss, Jesse didn't realize Evan had opened the lube until he felt his slippery fingers slathering his cock.

Evan slowly drew back from the kiss to kneel above Jesse's jutting erection. He reached back with his slick fingers, inserting two inside his hole to line himself for Jesse. He finished quickly, and taking hold of Jesse's shaft, he lowered himself, using his weight to push the cock inside him. As Jesse's cock head passed over his rim and forced him open, he choked out a stuttering breath. He eased down a little more and moved his hand away, wiping it clean on the sheets, and placed both palms on Jesse's ribcage. He paused briefly to let his body adjust, then dropped down until he sat fully on Jesse. He closed his eyes, reveling in the feel of Jesse's hard length resting deep inside him. Never in his life had he felt so perfectly filled.

All the while, Jesse watched his cock sinking deeper and deeper into Evan, feeling each contour of his body, the moist inferno of him doubling his own body temperature, the tightness of him causing his body to shudder with the threat of climaxing.

Jesse moved his gaze over Evan. His strong legs dusted with hair leading up to his slender, angular hips. His thick cock pointed up to his belly button. The lines of muscle in his abdomen smeared with the wetness of pre-cum. The smoothness of his toned chest where his perked nipples waited for attention. Jesse ran his hands down Evan's arms, feeling the cords of strength in his biceps and forearms. He laid his hands on Evan's hands, veined and strong, and looked up at his face, so exquisitely beautiful. He stared at Evan, amazed that he was inside so magnificent a man.

Evan opened his eyes, finding Jesse's on him. No one had ever looked at him the way Jesse was. People always stared at him with a wide-eyed star-struck gaze, but that wasn't the look Jesse held for him. Maybe it was his own wishful thinking, but it seemed Jesse's expression was one of complete attraction and affection for *him*, the man bared before him, not the man who sold out concerts across the world.

The thought sent a rush of emotions through him; joy that it could be true, desire to be with him beyond the weekend, fear that when Jesse learned the truth of him, he'd walk away. Evan battled the last emotion back. He didn't want to think about that moment. He wanted this moment. He wanted to make Jesse happy.

Evan twisted his hands under Jesse's and interlocked their fingers. He rocked on Jesse's hips, pressing their palms together, using Jesse's strength to brace himself. A high moan hummed in Jesse's throat. Slowly Evan raised and lowered himself on Jesse's length, going from base to tip over and over again. He lifted up until only the head was left inside him and thrust down on it in short movements.

Jesse exhaled a hushed sigh and arched his hips up, the teasing making him desperate to have his full cock engulfed in Evan's heat once again.

Evan sank all the way down fast and hard, his head fell back with a loud groan. Jesse pressed his head back on the pillows with a moan closer to a shout. Evan pulled his hands free and laid them on Jesse's chest, riding him so hard he rocked Jesse's body on the bed. Jesse clenched Evan's hips with both hands, breathing low groans with each of Evan's thrusts.

Evan sat back, changing the rhythm of his movements by grinding Jesse deep inside him. He reached back with one hand to gently fondle Jesse's balls. Jesse moaned louder. He pressed Evan down on his cock while raising his hips. Evan gasped and clutched Jesse's forearms. Jesse moved Evan's hips for him and jerked his own up hard.

Evan held onto Jesse's forearms and let him take control of his body.

Jesse let go of Evan's left hip and grabbed his cock, grinning at Evan's loud cry that hit a note he had never heard from him before. Evan's hand slapped down on Jesse's chest, his fingers hooked into his pectoral. Jesse felt all of Evan's muscles constrict. Evan slammed back, shouting as his climax shook him. At the warm wetness splattering across his stomach, Jesse snapped his hips up with his own release.

Evan opened his eyes, watching Jesse climax. He smiled. All this time he had thought Jesse was at his most beautiful when singing. Jesse relaxed under him, and he continued to gaze at him, admiring the passionate flush in his cheeks, his lips parted to take in deeper breaths, his black hair framing his face that was still concentrated on the pleasure he just received.

Jesse slowly began to smile, then his eyes opened. He gave Evan a light tug. Evan fell forward, his lips hovering above Jesse's. Jesse brushed his fingers through Evan's hair and touched his lips in a gentle kiss. "I think I'm addicted to this, too."

Evan laughed softly and laid his head beside Jesse's. "Me, too."

CHAPTER EIGHT

The vibration of Jesse's cell phone reverberated against the wood of the nightstand, making it sound ten times louder than it was. The sound stirred Jesse, but instead of agitation filling him at being awoken before ready, he lay peacefully thanks to Evan's body pressed against him from behind, holding him with one arm draped over his waist. He had never woken up in anyone's arms before and wanted to savor being cuddled against a firm body.

His phone silenced, and he shifted back into Evan. A pleased groan rumbled in Evan's throat. He nuzzled into Jesse's hair and gave him a squeeze. Jesse smiled and began to doze off when his phone started buzzing again.

"Are you going to answer it, or do you want me to chuck it in the lake?" Evan mumbled, his voice deep with sleep.

"Chuck it," Jesse grumbled. He stretched for his phone, refusing to move from his position in Evan's arms. He dragged it across the nightstand and yawned as he flipped it open. His eyes fell on the time. "Shit!"

Evan rested his chin on Jesse's shoulder. "What's wrong?"

"It's nine-thirty. I was supposed to be at work an hour and a half ago."

Evan yawned, flicking a nonchalant hand in the air. "It's just a bookstore. Forget about it."

"That's easy for you to say. Who's gonna pay my rent when I get fired?"

"I'll pay your rent."

"Yeah? Are you my sugar daddy now?"

"I'll get my money's worth." Evan yanked Jesse closer by his hip and gave his shoulder a firm bite.

"Oww, vampire!" Jesse laughed, playfully shoving him away.

Evan flopped onto his back. "In all seriousness, you should quit that job. It does nothing but take time away from your music."

"I'll call in sick today, I'm just the stock manager so they can survive without me, but *I* can't survive without a paycheck, and even though I appreciate your offer, there's only one thing I want to suck off you and it's not money." Jesse flipped toward him and lay on his side with his head on Evan's pillow as he scrolled through his missed calls. "Damn, everybody's been calling me. Kenny called three times just this morning. That's not like him to be awake before noon. I hope everything's okay."

Evan read Jesse's phone, seeing the number fifteen next to Brandon's name. "Your brother's called you fifteen times since yesterday."

"Yeah, he's a psycho. It's not my fault he didn't answer his phone when I tried to call him. I left him a message letting him know I was fine, but it appears he's decided to keep freakin' out that I'm with someone he hasn't met yet. He's a really huge fan of yours, like scary huge, so when he does meet you he'll probably warp into fanboy mode."

"So long as he doesn't maul me, we'll be cool," Evan said, climbing out of bed.

Jesse sat up, his eyes on Evan's tight butt as he walked into the bathroom. "Has that ever happened before?"

"A lot of fans get overly touchy," Evan called from the bathroom. "I do okay if it's just a few people, but when I'd get surrounded by hordes pushing and screaming through security to get a grope in, that makes me nervous. I'd say it's part of the reason why I get claustrophobic in crowds, but I've always been that way."

Jesse quit scrolling through his phone, surprised by Evan's statement. "Is that why you quit performing?"

Silence from the bathroom answered him.

Jesse sat quiet, wondering if Evan hadn't heard him and was about to ask again when Evan's subdued voice responded, "No.

The crowds didn't bother me when I was on stage. It was different."

Jesse stared toward the bathroom. Why was it every time he brought up Evan's career, Evan's whole tone and mood changed? He became quiet and distant, and either dodged the question or replied as if in an interview with a polite response that still didn't answer the question. It was as though Evan looked at music as something he did for a while, and now he had closed the book on that part of his life. He couldn't understand how someone as gifted as Evan could turn his back on it.

He sighed and called Kenny's cell. Maybe he expected too much. Even though he felt he'd known Evan forever with all that had happened between them, he shouldn't expect Evan to feel the same way.

His thoughts halted as Kenny's voice yelled through his cell phone without a hello.

"You bastard! I don't even know where to begin with all the things I'm pissed at you about! Where the hell are you and where the hell are my guitars? I'm gonna kick your ass as soon as I see you for keeping them from me for two freakin' days!"

Jesse held the phone away from his ear and Kenny's screeching. When Kenny's voice quieted asking if he was okay, Jesse put the phone back. "I'm great, awesome, and incredible!" He listened to Kenny take a deep breath, and as Kenny spoke again, he could tell it was through clenched teeth.

"Wonderful. I'm not even gonna get into it right now. We've got more important things going down. The secretary of that Greg guy from Phoenix Records called and said he wants us to come down to their offices today at two o'clock and bring a demo."

Jesse bolted upright. "Are you serious?"

"I wouldn't joke about this, man," Kenny said, no traces of irritation left in his voice. "She tried to call you, too. This is it!"

"I can't believe it! I'll be home by noon!"

"Don't be late!" Kenny yelled, and hung up.

Jesse snapped his phone closed and looked over at the bathroom.

Evan leaned against the doorframe. "Good news?"

"Phoenix wants to meet with me and Kenny today at two o'clock!"

Evan walked back across the bedroom. "That's great."

He slipped under the covers, and Jesse bounced up to kneel on the bed.

"It's more than great! Do you think they'll sign us? I couldn't imagine, I mean, I've dreamed about this for so long, but after playing in all those shitty bars I was beginning to worry it wasn't going to happen. We just weren't getting the right exposure, and the band! The people who were playing for us—"

Jesse's words silenced as Evan's mouth closed over his.

Evan pushed him onto his back and eased on top of him. "If you have this much energy, I can think of a hundred different ways to burn it."

Jesse beamed up at him, his eyes glinting with excitement. "They're your record label too, so you know all about them. You must be pretty good friends with them since you were hanging out with them when we met."

Evan rolled off of him and lay on his back.

Jesse sprang up. "You could be on our album! You could sing a duet with me!" He crawled on top of Evan and sat on his hips. "If they decide to sign us, will you do that? Guest star on one of my songs?"

Evan brushed Jesse's hair to the sides of his forehead. "Maybe."

Jesse met his gaze, but only for a second before Evan glanced away. Jesse's heart twisted at the injured look in Evan's eyes, the strained tone in his voice. He did it again, mentioned music and caused Evan's hidden pain to surface. Wanting to elevate Evan's mood again, he glided his fingertips down Evan's chest and tweaked one of his nipples. "Thanks for helping me get this meeting."

Evan brought his eyes to Jesse's. He laid one hand on the side of Jesse's face. "Listen to me, I didn't do anything to get you this meeting. All I did was lead Greg to you. He had the final say on whether or not to bring you in. I don't want you to think you're getting this chance because we spent the weekend together. Your talent earned you this opportunity. Not me."

"I know. You could've been screwing me for a month before introducing me to him instead of stalking me at my shows. You know, I've heard of fans stalking a celebrity, but never a celebrity stalking a fan. You really do have your own way of doing things, don't you?"

Evan laughed. "I wasn't stalking you!"

Jesse took his lips down Evan's throat. "But even though you say you didn't do anything, technically you're the catalyst since Greg never would have come to see me perform if it wasn't for you. So I really should thank you."

Evan closed his eyes, his fingers tangled in Jesse's hair. "I don't deserve any thanks, but if you're going to insist on giving it, I guess I'll take it."

Jesse smiled as he kissed his way down Evan's body.

CHAPTER NINE

Jesse glanced in his rearview mirror and smiled at the black Cadillac Escalade tailing him through the city streets. Even with his sunglasses on, Evan couldn't hide how hot he was. Jesse watched the fingers of Evan's right hand tap a rhythm on the top of the steering wheel; a red flash sparkled with each flick of his index finger from the ruby set in the eagle ring. During their weekend together, he noticed Evan didn't wear his multitude of rings around the house, only the one that had belonged to his father.

Evan had yet to share anything about his family life, but from the snippets he let slip, he knew Evan's father had passed away, and from what he could tell, he must have meant a lot to him since Evan always wore his ring. Jesse wondered if he would miss his father if he died. Considering he didn't miss him while he was alive, probably not. Evan hadn't said much about his mother, but now that he thought about it, he realized even though they talked a lot over the weekend, Evan had mostly asked questions about him and listened quietly as he spilled every detail about himself, while Evan answered his questions with a two sentence maximum.

Jesse shook his head, loathing his big mouth, and vowed he would work harder to draw Evan out more. It wasn't that he wanted to pry into his life, he just wanted to know the man behind the persona who stood on stage with a mic in hand, holding thousands of people captive at his every word and movement. He knew that wasn't the true Evan. It was as if he were two different men. The one who shined and smiled for all the world to admire, and the one who lived alone in a secluded mansion where the phone hadn't rung once over the weekend.

The last thought reminded him he should call Brandon. Since it was almost noon, Brandon would be at the theatre, but he might still be able to answer his phone. He opened his cell phone and almost hit the number two to speed dial Brandon out of habit, having momentarily forgotten he bumped everyone's number down one to put Evan's cell as the first. He hit three instead. The phone didn't get to finish its first ring before Brandon's voice sounded through the other end.

"Well, well, well, look who finally decided to call."

Jesse winced, knowing he was in for a scolding. "What're you talking about? I've left you two messages."

"Yeah, I got your stupid messages!" Brandon raised the pitch of his voice to mimic Jesse's. "Hey, asshole, it's me. Just wanted to let you know I'm running off with some guy to prove to you I can take care of myself!" His voice deepened back to its normal baritone. "Fine! I get it! I watch over you too damn much! You know what? Too freakin' bad, because it's not going to change!"

"I knew you'd take the messages like that, but it's not how I meant them. And I was being honest. I didn't go running off with just *some guy*."

"Oh, that's right. You went running off with Evan Arden. Real cute, Jess. You have the stupidest sense of humor."

"I'm not joking. I'm on my way home and if I look in my rearview mirror, I can see him following me."

"Fine. Then I'll meet you over there so you can introduce me to him."

"Now's not a good time. I'm only running home so I can change, then Kenny and I are going to a meeting at Phoenix Records. They might sign us! Isn't that awesome?"

"Uh huh," Brandon said, his voice flat and unbelieving. "Well, whenever you decided to quit this stupid joke, then you can give me a call. Until then, think about what you put me through the past couple days. Talk to you later."

"Brandon, wait! Don't hang up like that!" Jesse listened to the silence on the other end. "Are you still there?"

"I'm not talking until you quit being a moron."

Jesse took a deep breath, willing his voice to come out as calm as possible. "How about this? If everything goes good at

Phoenix, then all of us will go out to celebrate, and I'll introduce you to Evan, that way you can feel like a major jackass and learn to believe me when I tell you I'm not joking."

"For your sake, he better at least look a little like Evan Arden with the way you've been clinging to this dumb joke."

"Whatever. I'll see you tonight."

"Fine. Bye."

Jesse hung up his phone to the satisfying mental image of flinging it out the driver's side window and watching it crash and roll across the pavement. He swung onto his street, found a place to park where Evan could park behind him, and hopped out of his truck.

Evan met him at the tailgate and took off his sunglasses, looking up at Jesse's apartment building, the brick discolored from years of city grime. He glanced over his shoulder at the rest of the stained and weathered structures on the street. Most of the buildings seemed somewhat inhabited, though nearly every one had sheets of plywood covering a few windows. The majority of cars on the street were battle-scarred derelicts that looked like they hadn't seen a carwash since they were built.

A young woman with a black eye and cracked lip staggered across the street toward a group of young guys throwing dice, her blond hair hanging in limp strands around her skeletal face. The vinyl purple miniskirt she wore was askew on her bony hips, her white halter top barely fit her flat chest. She fell into one of the guys, offering to let him do whatever he wanted for twenty bucks. In a look of disgust, the guy shoved her away, and she slunk off with his cursing chasing her.

"I see what you meant now by saying this isn't that bad of a neighborhood." Evan grabbed Jesse's guitar and bass from the truck. "The crack whore and gang bangers really create a nice ambiance."

"There're worse neighborhoods." Jesse hefted Kenny's two guitars and led the way inside. "Sorry, I'm on the third floor and the elevator's broken."

Evan glanced at the yellow paint peeling off the walls of the stairwell.

They reached the third floor and walked down a short hall. Jesse set one of the guitars outside his apartment and turned to Evan. "Hey, I'm not sure how Kenny's going to react to knowing that it was you I spent the weekend with, so try and stay cool if he freaks, okay?"

Evan looked at him, confused. "Doesn't he know you play with guys?"

Jesse lifted one hand, teetering it back and forth. "Yeah, but we don't really talk about it, and I've never brought anyone home. Of course, I've never met anyone worth bringing home, but that's neither here nor there. What I'm trying to say is, don't take it personal if he gets a little funny."

Evan chuckled softly. "Great."

Jesse cracked the door open. Kenny flung it the rest of the way.

"I'm gonna beat your..." Kenny stopped, his eyes off Jesse and on Evan.

"Kenny, you remember Evan from the other night, don't you?" Jesse said, walking inside. "So you see, your guitars were more than safe. Navy SEALs couldn't break into Ev's house with the security he's got."

Kenny stared at Jesse, the realization of what he was saying sinking in. He stood dumbstruck, his honey-brown eyes round, his mouth agape.

Evan held out his hand to him. "I didn't get a chance to tell you this Saturday, but you're a real slick guitar player."

Kenny looked down at Evan's hand. Tentatively, he took it, muttering, "Thanks."

Evan nodded and moved to Jesse's side as he sat on the couch.

Kenny's gaze darted back and forth between them. "You mean, you two, but he's...he's..." He collapsed down in a chair next to the couch, rubbing one hand through his shaggy, dark blond hair.

Jesse leaned toward Evan. "I think his little hamster is running too fast on its wheel. He's about to have a meltdown."

Evan smirked at him. "I can't believe you two are in a band together. Sometimes you *can't* shut up and this poor guy can't even get words out."

"Hey!" Jesse reprimanded him with a light shove on the shoulder. He looked back to Kenny. "Yes, Kenny, he's Evan Arden. What's the big deal?"

Kenny shook his head and looked away from him. "Just go get ready."

Jesse gazed at him for a moment, then slowly rose from the couch. He gave Evan a look asking if he would be okay, to which Evan flicked his hand in a shooing gesture. Jesse headed toward his bedroom, glancing back at them before stepping in to change.

Evan sat quiet, feeling the tension swirling in the room like a heavy invisible fog. This was not something he was used to. Since he rarely stuck around long enough to say "good morning" to his lovers, he never had to deal with meeting their friends or family, and really, he never wanted to. It was too committal. But with Jesse, it seemed perfectly natural to meet the people in his life. He just hadn't anticipated obstacles like this.

Kenny cleared his throat. "So, do you, uh, like Chicago?"

Though he could hear how uncomfortable Kenny was by the tone of his voice, Evan smiled at his attempt at conversation. "Yeah, it's a nice town."

"Are you here long? I thought I heard once that you lived in New York."

"I live here now. I just bought a house up by Evanston."

"That's a haul from up there all the way down here."

"I don't mind it, but I'm worried Jess's truck won't make the trip too many more times."

"I'm surprised it made it once. I've been telling him to get something better, but he can't really afford anything newer."

Evan nodded.

Silence filled the room again.

Jesse's bedroom door opened. A rush of relief washed through Evan at Jesse's reappearance. He craned his head around to look at him, his body warming at the sight. Jesse had changed into a pair of black dress pants and a midnight blue button down shirt of light, airy material that flowed around his slender torso and drew out the indigo in his eyes. He'd used hair wax to accentuate the layers, and it all combined to give him a look of trendy sophistication.

"You look amazing," Evan said.

"Thanks." Jesse sat down beside him and rested his hand on Evan's thigh. He looked into Evan's eyes, recognizing an already familiar glint. He smiled and wet his lips with a slow lick of his tongue to let Evan know they were thinking the same thing.

Kenny loudly cleared his throat.

Jesse flicked him a quick glance, then turned back to Evan. "Can you give us any idea of what to expect?"

Evan took a deep breath, exhaling slowly. "Well, I was seventeen when I got signed, went on my first tour at eighteen, and even though my contract was updated before I started my third album, *Allegro*, some things have changed."

"Hmmm, right," Jesse said. "So, what you're saying is that it was so long ago you can't remember, and the stone tablet your contract was on got washed away in the Great Flood."

Evan aimed a sarcastic smirk at him. "I'm sorry, I was going to tell you about record contracts, but since you're still working your way through *Curious George Goes to the Zoo*, it'd go right over your pretty little head. However, I *will* talk to Kenny since he's a lot nicer than you."

Jesse let out a cynical snort. "He just hides it better."

Kenny punched Jesse on the arm. "Please, for five minutes, just close it! Some of us are nervous about this."

Evan put his index finger to Jesse's lips. "Shhh, be a good boy for five minutes."

Jesse caught Evan's finger in his mouth and sucked it down to the middle joint before slowly drawing back and letting it go. Out the corner of his eye, he saw Kenny's mortified expression and fought to keep from yelling at him to chill. He knew Kenny would be shocked at finding out about him and Evan, and maybe springing it on him like this wasn't the best way to go, but when Evan asked if he could come with him to see his apartment, he couldn't say no. He wanted to greedily snatch every second with Evan he could, and he figured Kenny would freak out for a moment, then shrug it off and go back to being his laidback self. That's how Kenny was, he accepted everybody, so he didn't understand why he was being intolerant now.

Evan chuckled at what Jesse did and Kenny's reaction to it. "*If* you are offered a contract today, get ready for some heavy reading. Record contracts are made with the label in mind, not the artist. They want to make sure they have their asses covered every which way they can and squeeze out every penny that's possible. There'll be points set aside that are supposed to summarize what's of interest to you, but read the whole thing. Really, you should have an entertainment lawyer with you or at least a manager, but," he gazed around their apartment, "I can see your extravagant lifestyle doesn't leave you with a lot of extra cash."

Jesse bumped his shoulder against Evan's. "Hey, you may have a kickass view of the lake, but you should try looking out our window between midnight and four and watching what goes on in the alley. It's better than TV."

"Yeah, I bet. So anyhow, with the cutbacks Phoenix has had I'm thinking you'll be dealing straight with Greg and he's pretty honest. He used to handle everything for me from managing to publicity. Granted, I might have driven him into the ground, but I don't like having a lot of people in my business. So don't worry, he'll explain everything. You'll probably still end up feeling like a two dollar hooker on a discount dollar day, but at least you'll understand why."

"Damn," Kenny muttered.

"What else?" Jesse asked.

"Watch your royalty percentage. Depending on where an album is sold, your royalty rate can fluctuate. Normally you'll get more when your CD is sold through normal retail stores, but its all about Internet downloads now, so make sure you're not getting screwed on a low percentage for album or individual song downloads, and watch that the points are coming out of retail sales not wholesale."

"What's the average percentage?" Jesse said.

"It varies, but if you get ten points out of Phoenix, then that's about average for a new band. Even though Phoenix isn't the size of the big boys, they've always been able to hold their own, even before I signed with them."

Kenny said, "I bet you could go into any record company and demand the highest percentage you wanted."

Evan shook his head. "When I renegotiated my contract before *Allegro*, Phoenix got me locked into a ten album deal, moving it up from the five I had originally signed for."

Jesse snapped his head toward Evan. "Does that mean you have to make six more albums?"

Evan let out a single humorless laugh. "Don't get your hopes up. All it means is that if I do decide to make another album, I can only do it with Phoenix unless I get out of my contract or they let me go, neither of which will likely happen. It's not unusual for record companies to do that, especially if they think the artist has some staying power. But it doesn't mean you're guaranteed to make ten or however many albums either. If your first one doesn't sell they can cut you loose and there's nothing you can do about it. Also, when they throw the advance at you, don't get excited over the large number. It includes your recording budget. You won't see any royalties until that's paid off first. On the plus side, if your album bombs you don't have to pay that cash back, so shoot for as high an advance as you can. It might be the only cash you'll see."

"Well, that's good at least," Kenny said.

"It's a plus, but you have to sell a lot of albums to make that money back. It takes selling 500,000 just to hit Gold, 1,000,000 for Platinum, and there's a hell of a lot of expenses in between to eat up your royalties before you ever see a check."

Kenny stood up. "This is a lot to remember."

Evan rose and walked toward the door with Jesse. "You'll be fine. Just don't sign anything if you have any doubts, not even a Post-it note. And don't agree to anything verbally either. You'd be amazed at what a label can turn into a binding agreement."

Kenny led the way down the stairs. Jesse lingered beside Evan, walking so close their shoulders touched. He grazed his fingers against Evan's hand, and Evan lightly hooked his fingers with his.

"That was the most I've heard you talk," Jesse said softly.

Evan gave him a sideways glance, his lips curved up in a wicked grin. "Well, that's because my mouth has been full most of the time since we met."

Jesse laughed. "And I thought I had a perverted sense of humor."

Kenny leaped down the last two stairs and darted for the door. He held it open for them, standing with his eyes focused out on the street.

Evan pulled Jesse to a halt by his hand. "I'm going to be in the city for a while doing some shopping. If you have any questions or need anything, call me. And don't take any shit off Greg or anyone else down there. Like I said, Greg is trustworthy enough, but his bottom line is always making money. Your music is a commodity to him, and you wouldn't be going to his office if he didn't think he could make money off you, so keep that in mind while you're negotiating."

Jesse nodded. "Okay. Thanks, for everything."

Evan caressed Jesse's cheek with the back of his hand, then kissed him. Jesse heard the door slam close and knew Kenny had moved away. He leaned into Evan, wrapping his arms around him. Evan held him tighter, and it was all Jesse could do to force himself to break the kiss first.

"Quit trying to make me late. I have a contract to sign, music to make, and all your record sales to break."

"That's so cute. You really think you can compete with me," Evan said, tousling Jesse's hair.

Jesse ran his fingers through his hair, trying to fix it by feel. "You're just nervous because you know it's true."

Evan opened the door for him. "I don't think I'll lose any sleep over it."

Jesse walked him to the Escalade and leaned through the open driver's side window once Evan climbed in. "I'll call you after we wrap things up."

"Alright. Good luck."

"Thanks."

Jesse backed away from the truck and watched the taillights disappear around the corner, already missing Evan's warm body beside him. He took a deep breath and spun toward Kenny's car.

CHAPTER TEN

Jesse stepped into the building containing the Phoenix Records corporate offices on Wacker Drive, a little disappointed the actual recording studio was elsewhere. He headed into the elevator with Kenny, hit the button for the tenth floor, and stood quietly beside him. A hundred times during their drive he wanted to talk to him, but hadn't because at his first attempt of, "Hey, about me and Ev," he got cut off by Kenny sharply uttering, "I don't want to talk about it now." Under different circumstances, he would have told Kenny he didn't give a rat's ass whether he wanted to talk about it or not, they were going to, but he knew Kenny was stressed enough over the meeting.

Really, he should be concentrating on it too, but Evan kept slipping into his mind without his realizing it until he caught himself thinking about his azure eyes, the smell of his cologne, his body so warm and firm, the sound of his voice in pleasure, the taste of his...

Jesse took a deep breath, trying to clear his head.

The elevator doors opened to an office assistant smiling at them from behind her large half-circle desk. Her gray eyes focused on Jesse, her olive-colored complexion pronounced with her black hair pulled up.

"Jesse Alexander and Kenny Cooper?" she asked.

"That's us," Jesse said.

"I'm Renee, personal assistant to Mr. Hansen and Mr. Polanski." Renee's gaze drifted down Jesse's body. "You're dressed more like a model than a musician."

Jesse flashed a bright smile. "Well, if there's one thing I've learned, it's a performer's looks are more important than talent. Luckily, I have both so I'm guaranteed to be loved by millions."

"And not a bit of modesty to get in the way," Renee giggled. She pointed toward a door to her left. "Mr. Polanski is waiting for you in his office."

"Thanks." Jesse turned toward the door. He couldn't fight down his agitation over meeting with Greg's assistant. Tim had irritated him when they met and he got a slimy vibe off the guy.

Tim looked up at their approach. His gaze passed over Jesse and landed on Kenny. He rose from behind his black lacquer desk, extending his hand to him. "It's great to see you again, Kenny. And right on time. That's wonderful."

Kenny shook Tim's hand. "It's great to see you again too, Mr. Polanski."

Jesse held his hand out to Tim.

Tim gave it a quick, rough shake and sat back down behind his desk. His eyes returned to Kenny. "Did you bring the demo?"

"Yeah." Kenny handed him a CD. "Sorry if the quality isn't the best. We couldn't afford to record in a studio, so we set up a recorder during one of our shows, then burned the songs onto discs using Jesse's computer."

"That's fine. I've already got a good feel for your sound after hearing you play the other night."

Tim put the disc in a player on his desk. The fast beats of the pop/rock track "Euphoria" sounded through the office, Jesse's tenor lifted over the instruments. Despite the bad drum work and shoddy keyboard, Jesse knew he and Kenny sounded great. Any person in music could tell that.

Tim leaned back in his chair, listening with his eyes closed. When "Euphoria" ended, the classically inspired ballad "Shattered" came on. The song finished, Tim ejected the CD, and tossed it on his desk. "It's not bad."

Jesse sucked in an offended breath.

"It needs work," Kenny quickly intervened. "But with the right people playing with us, we could have a really awesome sound."

Tim tapped his fingers on his desk. "Look, I'm going to be straight with you guys. The beat is awesome, I love the attempts with the keyboard, the electric backline from the synth in the first song is great, I get the sound you're going for. Kenny, your guitar work is clean and precise." He turned his eyes on Jesse. "But I honestly don't think you've got what it takes to be successful."

Tim's words struck Jesse's chest like a sledgehammer. He exhaled a hard breath to bring his voice to the surface. "Me? What's wrong with me?"

"You're volatile and unpredictable. After what I saw at the bar, I'm concerned how stable you'd be working with anybody. I could put you with some of the best musicians in the business, but they're not going to tolerate that attitude you throw around."

"What happened the other night was a freak occurrence. That's not how—"

"How many band members have you been through in one year? Four? Five? You mean to tell me the fault lies with them and their personalities? Come on."

Jesse clenched his teeth and clamped his mouth shut. He couldn't trust himself to open it. He nearly jumped when Kenny spoke up.

"Actually sir, it wasn't all Jesse's fault. He's very passionate about music, more passionate about it than I've ever seen anybody over anything. Sometimes his intensity *can* be a little hard to handle if you're not used to him, and he doesn't tolerate laziness or halfhearted playing. He wants the people who play with us to be the best they can be, not just for Conquest, but for all the people who come to hear us."

Jesse's lips twitched with wanting to break into a smile. If they weren't sitting in an office trying to get a record deal, he would have thrown his arms around Kenny for saying that.

"That's not to say that he can't be a little high-strung at times, but it keeps things interesting," Kenny added.

Jesse lost the desire to smile and changed his mind about wanting to hug him.

Tim looked away. "It doesn't matter. Greg wants you on the label." He picked up two thick packets of documents from his desk. He lightly tossed one to land in front of Kenny and flung the other at Jesse. It shot across the slick surface of the desk and fell in a crumpled heap at Jesse's feet. "So, Phoenix Records would like to sign you for a five album deal. Your royalties will be ten percent of standard U.S. retail sales and you'll get an advance of $200,000."

Jesse looked down at the contract, then slowly raised his eyes to Tim, piercing him with a sharp glare. "If you're a representative of how Phoenix is, I don't think I want to sign with a label so unprofessional."

"Jesse," Kenny pleaded in a panicked voice.

Tim snorted in disgust. "You're calling me unprofessional? I just assumed you'd be more comfortable getting on your knees to pick it up."

Jesse leaned over the edge of the desk toward Tim. "If you've got a problem with me, say it!"

Tim's eyes narrowed, his voice lowered to a hiss. "We both know how you got this deal. As much as I hate to admit it, you're pretty sharp to have figured out that the right kind of attention to the right person can get you big favors."

Jesse shook his head slightly. "I don't know what you're talking about."

"Let's cut the oblivious act, okay? I know what you are. When we went to see you guys last Saturday, a few minutes after we went back into the bar after meeting you, we saw Kenny leave with a girl, but you were nowhere to be seen. Greg and I left, but Evan claimed he needed to use the restroom and then would go home. Greg and I talked at my car for a while, then when I tried to get out of that hellhole of a neighborhood, I saw you and Evan standing by a truck, and you were holding his hand."

Jesse forced his face to be impassive. The only thing that stopped him from screaming his sleeping with Evan had nothing to do with his being there was knowing Evan had never openly admitted his sexuality, and he sure as hell wasn't about to be the one to out him. "So what? He was showing me one of his rings."

The contempt in Tim's expression deepened. "Yeah, I bet he was. The second I saw you I had my suspicions, but Evan Arden, that I just can't believe. You must be damn good to have gotten him to arrange this for you."

Jesse balled his hand in a tight fist. "He didn't have anything to do with this!"

"Keep using that. Maybe someone will eventually believe you." Tim stood up and walked around his desk. "I'm going to get some coffee. Sign the contract and be out of my office before I get back."

Jesse stared down at the floor, his right hand trembled from the force of his white-knuckled fist. Kenny picked the contract up from the floor and handed it to him without looking at him.

"It's not true, Kenny," Jesse mumbled.

Kenny nodded, his head turned away from him.

Jesse snatched Kenny's wrist, forcing him to look at him. "It's not true! I didn't sleep with Evan to get us a contract! You believe me, don't you?"

Kenny averted his eyes from him and sat quiet for a moment as if carefully choosing his words. "I believe you probably didn't do it on purpose. But you have to admit, the timing is pretty impeccable. Maybe he acted on his own, thinking it'd make you happy. Or maybe he had already set this up, thinking he could use it to get you to show your gratitude to him afterward and you moved a step quicker than he anticipated."

Jesse adamantly shook his head. "You're wrong. Ev wouldn't do that. You don't know him."

"And you do?" Kenny snapped. "You've known him two days, Jess. For all you know, this is your payment for giving him a good time."

Jesse coughed at the pain Kenny's words caused. A deep ache constricted his chest and closed his throat. He set the contract on Tim's desk, stood, and turned to leave.

Kenny jumped up, catching him by his upper arm. "Where're you going?"

"I'm leaving."

"You can't leave! We have to sign the contract!" Kenny snatched the contract Jesse had set down and shoved it against Jesse's chest. "Everything we've ever dreamed about and worked for is right here!"

"And it doesn't mean shit if you believe I whored myself out to get it!"

"Stop acting like this! What difference does it make? Let's just sign it and move forward!"

"I'm not signing it until you say you believe me!"

"Fine! I believe you!"

Jesse lowered his gaze from Kenny. All his life, he had been proud to know there were two people who would never lie to him. Now, he only had Brandon. He set his hand on the contract Kenny had pinned to his chest and eased back down in the chair. Kenny sat beside him and began reading his copy, or at least, made a good show of trying. Jesse stared blankly at the first page.

"Hey, guys. How've you been?"

Jesse and Kenny both turned to see Greg standing in the office doorway.

"Great, Mr. Hansen. How about you?" Kenny said.

Jesse ground his teeth at Kenny's cheerful, everything-was-lovely tone.

"I'd be better if you just called me Greg. I'm sorry I couldn't be here for the start of the meeting." He gazed around the office, his eyebrows furrowing closer. "Where's Tim?"

"He went to get some coffee," Kenny said.

"Did he go over the contract with you already?"

"He mentioned a few key points," Jesse grumbled, and thought he saw a flash of annoyance on Greg's face before his demeanor shifted back to friendly business oriented.

"I apologize for Tim getting a caffeine craving in the middle of your meeting. Let's move down to my office where it's more comfortable and we'll go over the contract page by page. This is where you're going to take the first steps toward success with your music, so if you have any questions, don't hesitate to ask."

Kenny bounced up to follow Greg. Jesse rose and trailed behind them down a hall leading to Greg's office. He wondered if he should tell Greg about Tim's accusations, then refused to entertain the thought. That's all he needed was to get a reputation for being difficult when he hadn't even signed the contract yet. Once he signed the contract, he'd be locked into Phoenix and there wouldn't be anything Tim could do to get rid of him, then he could retaliate.

He felt a little more ease at the thought and turned into Greg's office, twice the size of Tim's with a view overlooking the Chicago River. His eyes fell on the four framed concert posters of Evan, the Gold and Platinum records, the case filled with awards. He pointed at the wall and case. "Those are all Evan's?"

"Yes," Greg said. "He covered a lot of ground when he was performing. All of his albums went multi-Platinum, and his fourth, *One More Time*, was a masterwork."

Jesse went to the case and gazed down at the awards. "I knew he won a lot of awards, but I never knew it was this many."

Greg moved to Jesse's side, also looking down in the case. "Well, they never meant much to him. That's why I have them. It was always such a pain to get him to those award shows unless he was booked to perform. He'd go up on stage smiling for everyone, say a quick charming acceptance speech, then walk offstage, shove the award at me, and wait until he was called up again."

Jesse looked at the awards, wondering why Evan didn't want them. It was a huge accomplishment for a musician to win as many as he did. For every album he released there were awards.

Greg gave him a warm smile. "Evan was very taken with your music. That's a great compliment coming from him. He doesn't acknowledge other musicians unless he truly feels they have talent, so you can imagine that's a rarity with him since he's well aware of the enormity of his own gift."

Jesse faced Greg and met his eyes with an unwavering stare. "Is that why you called us for this deal? Because he told you to?"

Greg's smile shifted from warm to sympathetic. "You're a fan of his, aren't you? I could tell when you met him. You must have been very excited to speak with someone who carries as much weight in this business as he does, but the truth is Evan has little interest in the careers of other artists. He brought me to see you guys because he saw your talent, he gave me his input on your style, but that's it. I'm sure you admire his work and would like to see him again, and if he's still in town by the time we hit the studio, if all goes well today, I might be able to convince him to come down, but I couldn't promise anything."

Jesse stood silent. Either Greg was doing a hell of a cover job pretending to not know about him and Evan, or he really didn't know. Pure elation began to fill him. Greg didn't know. Evan really hadn't set this up. He had been honest when he said all he did was bring Greg to see him. Not that he thought Evan had lied, but with all the accusations from Tim and Kenny, his belief in Evan's words had gotten a little shaken. And that meant Tim really didn't know either, but had assumed it from what he saw and his impression of him.

Jesse shot Kenny a triumphant smirk. Kenny pointedly looked away.

Greg patted Jesse's shoulder. "I said I couldn't promise anything, so don't get your hopes up. Right now, we should concentrate on getting down to business." He walked to his desk and took a seat in the chair behind it. "I take it Tim already discussed the advance amount with you, but just so you know, that's where all your recording costs are going to come out of, so try to optimize your studio time. If you have a dream of recording in New York, L.A., or anywhere else, we can send you there, but it's going to cost more than if you use our private studios here in Chicago."

Jesse sat down beside Kenny. "Is this a warning to not blow all the cash on booze and strippers?"

"Pretty much. You could do that, but then you'd end up more in debt to the label."

"Well then, maybe our advance should get bumped up," Jesse said.

Kenny choked out a horrified gasp.

Greg leaned back in his chair, grinning at Jesse. "Are booze and strippers key elements to your creative process?"

"No, but Pizzeria Uno's and a shopping spree at Saks are."

Kenny buried his face in his hands.

"I'll see what I can do," Greg chuckled. "Let's start working out some of the other details, and we'll negotiate at the end."

Halfway through Greg's explanations of the countless clauses in the contract, Jesse sat back in the chair, rubbing his eyes. "From what I'm getting out of all this crap in the promotions section, we pretty much have to do whatever Phoenix tells us to do since you're handling all our publicity and promoting. You basically own us. We're your indentured servants."

"I prefer to think of us as all on the same team, striving for the mutual goal of your ultimate success," Greg said.

"That's some nice sugarcoating."

"Yes, I thought so. But you could seek outside representation in the form of an agent to handle your publicity if you're not comfortable with Phoenix doing it."

"So long as your people can get the job done, one evil's just as good as the other as far as I'm concerned. And just to make sure I'm completely clear on this, the songs we record become the property of Phoenix, even masters that aren't released. Then if you guys decide to let us go, we can't record those songs again with another label?"

"That's the gist of it, but it doesn't mean forever. After a certain time period we can relinquish those songs back to you. See here, it's written in case you are cut loose by us, after a period of five years from that date, you can release the songs under another label."

"I understand you guys need the copyrights so you can distribute and promote the music, but the last thing I want is to be watching TV and hear 'Shattered' as the background music for a tampon commercial because you guys got offered an endorsement deal. I want a clause written in that no songs bearing songwriting credits by myself or any other member of Conquest can be exploited or released for endorsements or other promotions without my direct written consent."

Greg's lips parted in shock. "I'm not sure I can agree to that."

"Then I'm not sure I'm capable of holding a pen."

Kenny looked at Jesse in alarm. He glanced at Greg and watched him and Jesse stare each other down.

Greg's face broke into a slow smile, and he scribbled down Jesse's demand. "The attorneys will adjust this into the final contract."

Jesse glowed at his victory as he flipped to the next page. He didn't care what Tim said. He knew he had everything it took to reach the highest levels of success in music, and he wasn't going to stop until he stood on top of the world, the conquering hero for all who had ever doubted him to look upon.

CHAPTER ELEVEN

Jesse stretched his arms high over his head and looked at his watch. "It's already past seven. That took forever."

Kenny stood beside him, rubbing his forehead. "My brain hurts."

Jesse tossed his arm around Kenny's shoulders. "But we did it! I told you never to lose faith in me!"

"We have to go out and celebrate! I can't wait to call Carrie and tell her."

Jesse rolled his eyes. "Does she have to come?"

"What do you think? She's my girlfriend. Besides, this is a perfect excuse for getting laid."

"You shouldn't have to use excuses. You should just be able to say, 'I'm horny, satisfy me,' and get results."

"And that's why your relationships never last beyond a night."

Jesse leaned toward him, speaking in a singsong voice, "Not anymore."

He felt Kenny's shoulders tense under his arm and saw the joy in his countenance wither. Anger welled up inside him. Even after hearing from Greg that Evan had nothing to do with the meeting, Kenny still believed he had slept with him to get the contract. He dropped his arm from Kenny's shoulders and dug in his front pocket for his cell phone. "I'm calling Evan."

Kenny's expression turned apprehensive. "Is he going to go out with us?"

"If he wants to."

Kenny opened his own cell phone and turned away from him.

Jesse glared at the back of Kenny's head while listening to the phone ring. On the fifth ring, Evan answered with, "Hey, gorgeous. How'd things go?"

Evan's warm greeting and the sound of his voice extinguished Jesse's irritation at Kenny. "We got signed! I even got us a higher advance and had our royalties bumped up a couple points!"

"That's wonderful. Congratulations."

"Thanks! I guess I really can quit my job now."

Evan laughed softly. "Yeah, that'd be a good idea. Listen, I hate to cut this short, but I'm kind of in the middle of something. Are you heading back to your place now?"

"Yeah."

"I'll see you there in a little bit then."

"Alright. Later." Jesse snapped his phone closed and spun toward Kenny.

Kenny closed his phone and headed up the sidewalk. "Let's get going. The sooner we get home, the sooner we can party!"

The earlier tension between them vanished on the ride back to their apartment, with excited conversations of what it'd be like to record and tour. When they arrived home, Jesse let Kenny shower first, then claimed the bathroom, showering and making sure every part of his body was perfectly washed and groomed for Evan. He stood in front of the mirror in a pair of jeans, working on his hair. As he finished, a knock sounded on the apartment door.

Jesse sprinted out of the bathroom and slid to a stop at the door. Taking a deep breath to steady his rapidly pounding heart, he flung open the door.

His lips graced in a sensual smile, Evan brought one arm from behind his back and held out a bottle of Dom Perignon. "Congratulations, gorgeous."

Jesse ignored the champagne and hurled himself at Evan, slamming into him in a rough kiss.

Evan stumbled back, trying to catch his balance and not drop the champagne. He laughed through the kiss. "Miss me?"

Jesse kept his arms clamped around Evan's neck. "You have no idea how much."

"I can't say I'm not happy to hear that." Evan held up the bottle of champagne. "Now are you going to let me in, or should I drink this stuff straight from the bottle in the hall like a bum?"

Jesse took the champagne and let Evan inside. "You'd be one high society bum to be drinking this." He closed the door and turned around as Evan took off his Yankees cap. "You got your hair cut and highlighted."

Evan shook his hair out with his fingers, now shorter in the back, falling to the middle of his neck, layered, and staggered sharper around his face to pull out his refined features. Gold and copper highlights streaked through the natural chestnut color. "That's where I was when you called. The guy doing my hair was so nervous about screwing it up, his hands were shaking. Sorry I had to cut our conversation short, but I was afraid my being on the phone would distract him even more."

"It looks wonderful. It's just like when you were performing."

"Yeah, I've always liked it like this."

Jesse set the champagne on the card table that acted as a kitchen table and walked toward him, his eyes locked into Evan's, his lips lifted with a mischievous smirk. He wrapped one arm behind Evan's back and reached up with his other, taking a fistful of Evan's hair behind his head. "I'm glad you didn't get it cut too short. I still have something to hold on to."

Evan grinned and moistened his lips with the tip of his tongue. He brushed his fingers down Jesse's bare chest, moved to kiss him, and paused when Kenny walked into the room. "Hey, Kenny. Congratulations on the contract."

Kenny glanced at them standing chest to chest, embracing each other, and sped toward the kitchen. "Thanks. Are you going out with us?"

Evan looked at Jesse. "You're going out?"

"I meant to ask when I called if you wanted to join us, but if you don't feel like it, we could do something else."

Kenny stared at Jesse in disbelief.

"I'll go," Evan said. "Where?"

"We haven't decided yet," Kenny said.

"We could stay here, or go back to your place," Jesse suggested.

Evan raised one slender eyebrow. "Are you trying to get me alone?"

Jesse lingered his lips a fraction from Evan's. "Maybe."

Evan gave him a light slap on the butt. "Go get ready to go out."

Jesse sighed in defeat and released his hold on him. He walked into his bedroom and went to his dresser to flip through his shirts. His bed creaked behind him, and glancing over his shoulder, he saw Evan lay back on it, propped up on his elbows with his legs hanging over the side.

"My closet is bigger than this," Evan said, gazing around the room.

Jesse grinned at him. "Wait until my record sales surpass yours, then we'll see who's got the bigger closet."

"My my, aren't we setting high goals for ourselves?"

A knock on the apartment door forced Jesse to turn his eyes away from him, then Carrie's squeal of, "Baby! I'm so happy for you!" broke through the apartment.

Evan snapped his head toward the door. "What the hell is that?"

"The dreaded Carrie beast, also known as Kenny's girlfriend. It's an obnoxious animal that should be destroyed for the sake of humanity's eardrums." Jesse went to his door and kicked it closed. "And I'm not ready to deal with it yet."

As he moved to walk past his bed, Evan snagged him by the belt and pulled him toward him. "You said you wanted me alone."

Jesse ran his fingers through Evan's newly cut hair. "And you told me to get ready."

"Well…" with quick movements, Evan clasped his arms around Jesse's waist, lifted, and tossed him to the bed. Jesse landed on his back, laughing. Before the bed had stopped bouncing from the impact, Evan was braced above him on both arms. "I've changed my mind."

Jesse caught Evan behind his head and pulled him to his lips, transferring the joy he felt through the kiss.

"Hey!" Kenny yelled from the other side of the door. "Are you ready?"

Jesse slowly withdrew from the kiss. Without taking his eyes from Evan's, he called out to Kenny, "No. You guys go ahead. I'll call you in a little bit and we'll catch up."

Kenny breathed a loud, frustrated sigh. "Fine."

Evan stroked Jesse's hair near his temple. "I don't know what you've done to me, but I haven't been able to stop thinking about you all day."

Jesse slid his hands under Evan's shirt and up his sides. "I haven't been able to stop thinking about you either."

"So how'd things really go? You said you negotiated for a higher advance and royalties, so Greg must've been treating you pretty fair."

"Greg did at least," Jesse mumbled, turning his head to the side.

Concern darkened the joyous glow on Evan's face. "What do you mean? What happened?"

"Just a bunch of bullshit." Jesse shifted to sit up, forcing Evan to climb off him. "Do you want some champagne? I'm dying to try it." He got up from the bed and walked out of the room.

Evan followed him, catching him in the kitchen. He gently gripped Jesse's upper arm, halting him from getting occupied with the champagne, and laid his other hand on the side of Jesse's face. "I can see it in your face and hear it in your voice that you're upset. Tell me what happened."

Jesse met Evan's eyes. Whether it was the worry he saw there or the warmth in Evan's voice, he wasn't sure, but he found himself spilling everything that had happened, from Tim's accusations to his argument with Kenny, and even Greg's comments about trying to convince Evan to come down to the studio to visit him, which looking back on he found it pretty hilarious, though if Evan did no humor entered his expression. Evan stood silent, focused on his every word while he sat on the kitchen counter delivering the events like a skilled orator.

Evan gazed down at the kitchen floor, his somber face set with a frown as Jesse finished. "Why didn't you call me when all that happened?"

Jesse let out a sarcastic huff. "Yeah, that would've looked real cool. I could've jumped up, brandished my cell phone, and yelled, you better stop picking on me or else I'll call my boyfriend, and he'll come down here and kick your ass!"

Evan looked at him from under his eyelashes, one corner of his lips turned up in a grin. "Your boyfriend, huh?"

Jesse lifted his chin and gave Evan a smirk. "That's right. I assume you don't have a problem being called that since it basically means you're mine."

Evan wrapped his arms around Jesse's waist. "None whatsoever."

Jesse cupped Evan's face in both hands and covered his mouth in a kiss he put all his happiness behind. As the kiss ended, Evan reached for his glass of champagne. He lifted it and paused, his head tilted to the side as he gave it a curious look.

"What's the matter?" Jesse said teasingly. "Not used to drinking Dom from a seventy-five cent glass bought at the dollar store?"

Evan laughed and shook his head. "It's a first." He looked at Jesse. "But I've had a lot of those the past few days." He raised his glass to him. "Here's to you, commander of Conquest. The world is your battlefield. Now all you have to do is conquer it, a feat I have total faith that you can do."

Jesse touched his glass against Evan's. Both drank at the same time and lowered their glasses to bring their lips together.

CHAPTER TWELVE

The sound of jewel cases clinking together pulled Jesse awake. He opened his eyes, waited a moment for the haze of sleep to clear, then looked toward the sound and saw Evan sitting naked on his bedroom floor, flipping through his CDs.

"That has to be some kind of sickness you have," Jesse said.

"I know, I can't help it. I see discs and I have to know what ones they are."

Jesse swung his legs over the edge of the bed and grabbed his iPod off the nightstand. "Here. You should like playing with this. It's got the stuff I listen to the most on it." He tossed it, Evan caught it. He yawned, stretching his arms over his head. "I can't believe we drank that whole bottle of Dom last night."

"Drank, licked, sucked." Evan smirked with his eyes on the iPod as he scrolled through the songs.

Jesse grinned at the memory of leaning against the kitchen counter while Evan dribbled champagne down his body and followed the rivulets with his tongue. As his cock showed appreciation for his thoughts, he got out of bed and walked over to him. Evan placed a tender kiss on the inside of Jesse's thigh.

Jesse combed his fingers through Evan's hair. "I was thinking we could do something fun today, like go down to Navy Pier, or the Field Museum, or Shedd Aquarium."

Evan lowered his eyes back to the iPod. "If I want to look at fish, I'll get sushi."

Jesse shoved him on his shoulder. "C'mon, it'll be fun! I'll even load your walker in the Escalade for you so you can outrun the two fans you have left, geezer."

Evan looked up at him with a playful grin. "Okay, let's go. It'll be a cheap date since I can get the kids' discount on you."

Jesse burst out a fake laugh and cracked open his bedroom door to find the kitchen and living room empty. He stepped out and crept over to Kenny's room. The door was open, the bed empty. He couldn't tell if it had been slept in since Kenny never made it, but he imagined he would have heard him and Carrie if they had come back. Then again, maybe he and Evan drowned them out.

Jesse sighed. After all they had been through together, when the time came their dream was in reach, they didn't even celebrate together. He hadn't meant to ditch him. It just happened, and if Kenny kept his attitude over him and Evan, they probably would have ended up bitching at each other again.

"Looks like we have the place to ourselves," he said.

"Great. I'm getting a shower, then we can get out of this shit-hole," Evan said, walking to the bathroom, his clothes tucked under his arm.

Jesse gazed at Evan's elegant form and felt a little less guilty about ditching Kenny.

"Any extra toothbrushes?" Evan called from the bathroom.

"Use mine. It's the blue one," Jesse said, heading into the kitchen.

"Gross!"

"Think about our past three days together and say that again!"

"That's different! I don't get off on your nasty ass tooth plaque!"

Jesse laughed and took a few drinks of orange juice from the container. He walked into the bathroom, stopping to admire Evan's foggy figure from the other side of the shower curtain. He looked at his toothbrush, saw it was wet, and chuckled to himself as he globbed it with toothpaste. When he finished brushing his teeth, he pulled back the shower curtain and climbed in behind Evan. He wrapped his arms around his waist and kissed the back of his shoulder. "I think I prefer your shower. It's a lot bigger."

"Everything I have is."

Jesse slid his hand down Evan's abdomen. "Mmm, we're pretty close with some things."

A booming knock on the apartment door stopped Jesse's actions. Exhaling a hard sigh, he dropped his forehead against Evan's back. "If Kenny forgot his keys again, I'm going to kick his idiot ass."

He ripped open the shower curtain, snatched a towel off the rack, and stormed out of the bathroom, trying to adjust the towel to somewhat hide his erection. As he whipped open the door, he bellowed, "Listen, moron!"

Brandon stomped into the apartment, nearly slamming into Jesse. "Don't you call me a moron, you little bastard! Thanks a lot for leaving me hangin' last night! But I guess it's my own stupid fault for believing you could be considerate!" He shoved a white paper bag against Jesse's chest as he passed by. "Here! I brought donuts!"

Jesse couldn't help but laugh at the last sentence and the anger it tried to keep, and closed the door behind him. "I'm sorry. Ev and I got wrapped up last night."

Brandon faced him, running his fingers through his windblown black hair. "*Ev?*"

Jesse fixed Brandon with an are-you-stupid look and pointed toward the bathroom where the shower was still running.

Brandon leaned toward him, his blue eyes squinting in a scrutinizing stare. "So lover boy's in the shower, is he? Maybe I should peek in and say hello."

"Don't you dare," Jesse snarled under his breath. "Actually, why don't you take off and come back in a little bit? I don't want him to feel weird coming out of the shower and having a stranger standing in his face."

"I'm not a stranger, I'm your brother!" Brandon snapped. He paced away from Jesse in an attempt to collect his patience. "What's his name?"

"I already told you."

Brandon spun toward him, ready to unleash another tirade, then stopped and forced his voice to be as calm as it could with his impatience. "Jess, stop this already. If you're not willing to tell me his name, then all that shows is you're not very proud to be with him. How far have you gone with him?"

Jesse smiled, his eyes glazed over in a dreamy look. "All the way. I know you told me how good it can be, but I don't think even you've experienced anything like what he's capable of. He's got skills you wouldn't believe!"

Brandon stared at him in stunned silence for a moment. "You're being careful, right? You're using protection?"

Jesse heard the water turn off in the bathroom and glanced toward it. He looked back to Brandon, his smile dimmed to tentative. "Here's the thing, I know I'm clean, and he said he was, so—"

"Idiot! What the hell is wrong with you?"

"I trust him."

"You trust him?" Brandon roared in disbelief. "How stupid can you be? If he had any respect for you, he would've wrapped it!"

"Can you tone it down, mouth?" Jesse said in a low voice. "He can probably hear you."

"Good! Let Johnny No Condom hear me!" Brandon snatched Jesse by his upper arm and dragged him toward his bedroom. "Get your ass dressed and kiss lover boy goodbye. I'm taking you to get checked out."

Jesse staggered behind Brandon, trying to keep his towel in place and free himself from Brandon's viselike grip. "You're not taking me anywhere, psycho! Let go!"

"This is the last time we do this at your place. Your hot water sucks," Evan said, walking out of the bathroom wearing only his jeans and a towel over his head as he dried his hair. He brought the towel down, draping it over his shoulders, and looked at Brandon.

Brandon gasped and released his hold on Jesse. "You're…you're really him! I don't believe it! You're really Evan Arden!"

"Shit," Jesse muttered, flopping down on the arm of the couch.

Evan startled back a step, peering at Brandon with a wary expression as he spoke to Jesse. "Is he okay?"

"Yeah, but remember how I told you that he's a freaky big fan of yours?"

Brandon raced toward Evan. Evan held out one hand to slow him down. Brandon snatched it with both of his. "I can't believe this! I love your music! I actually saw you in concert for the *Allegro* Tour!"

Jesse scowled at Brandon. "Settle down, jerk-ass. You're having a conniption and you're creepin' *me* out, so I can't imagine what you're doing to him."

Evan met Brandon's eyes, a smirk playing across his lips. "It's Brandon, right? Jess has talked so much about you, I've been really looking forward to meeting you. And please, just call me Evan, or Johnny No Condom. Whichever you're most comfortable with."

"Yeah, about that—"

Evan held up his hand to silence him. "It's alright. Jess told me how protective you are of him, and I think that's awesome, so you don't have to apologize."

"I wasn't going to," Brandon said, his gaze unflinching from Evan. "You should've wrapped it, especially considering what you do for a living, I'm sure you've been with a few more people than the average guy."

Jesse sprang to his feet toward Brandon. "What the hell's the matter with you, asshole!"

"No, he's right," Evan said, looking at Jesse before turning back to Brandon. "But it wasn't an issue of not respecting him. It was an issue of getting carried away in the moment. It happens to everybody, and I'm sure it's happened to you.

Regardless, I can assure you that Jess's wellbeing is in better care with me than *anyone* else. So let's move on, shall we?"

Jesse looked from Evan to Brandon. By Brandon's expression, he could tell Evan's less than subtle way of telling him to back off had slapped the last bit of star-struck daze from him. He knew this was difficult for his brother. Brandon had always been the number one person in his life, and he was the last person he wanted to have tension with Evan. It was bad enough Kenny was distant because of their relationship, he couldn't let that happen with his brother. He smacked Brandon on the arm to get his attention and break the tense moment. "I guess now you know to believe me when I tell you who I'm hangin' with."

Brandon slowly turned his sharpened gaze from Evan to Jesse. "You can't blame me for not believing you. Who would've thought that someone like him would put up with you for long enough to get your clothes off?"

"Well, I do have incredible patience," Evan said. "So you saw me for the *Allegro* Tour. I hope I put on a good show for you."

"It was an amazing performance. You were on stage for two and a half hours, then came back for two encores."

"It was all he could talk about for days," Jesse said.

Evan turned to Jesse. "Why didn't you go?"

Brandon laughed. "Our parents wouldn't let him. They said he was too young. And when you came around again for the *One More Time* Tour, the tickets sold out so fast we couldn't get any and the scalped prices were ridiculous. It's pretty hilarious when you think about it. When you were on your third concert tour, he was just starting high school."

Evan's smile shared none of Brandon's humor. "Yeah, that's pretty funny." At the sound of Jesse sniggering, he glanced at him.

"Just so you know, even back then I had a crush on you," Jesse said.

Evan smirked at Jesse. "And just so you know, I'm glad I didn't meet you back then since I have a feeling prison life would cramp my style." He looked back to Brandon. "Jess tells me you're one hell of an actor and dancer."

Producing a shy smile, Brandon lowered his eyes. "I do okay, I guess. There are far better actors out there than me. And my dancing is nothing compared to what you used to do on stage."

Jesse rolled his eyes at Brandon's feigned humility, then caught Brandon's gaze drifting down Evan's body, blatantly checking out his lean, fit torso. Obviously Brandon wasn't too upset over Evan usurping his position in Jesse's life.

"Well, that was a long time ago," Evan said. "I doubt I could pull half those moves anymore, and I'm way behind on the latest trends."

Brandon waved Evan's excuses away. "You talk like it's been decades. Dancing's like riding a bike. If you're free tonight, we should go to dinner, I know the best Italian restaurant, then we could go back to my place and I'll show you all my best moves."

Evan opened his mouth in as much shock as to protest the offer, but before he could get a word out, Jesse lunged at Brandon and shoved him back a step.

"I can't believe you! I'm right here, and you're hitting on him!"

Brandon rebounded and retaliated with a hard push to Jesse's chest. "All I did was ask him out to dinner!"

Jesse stepped up to Brandon's face. "And invite him to your apartment for '*all your best moves*'! What a lame ass line!"

"It's better than making him stay here! You should be ashamed of yourself for making him come to this dump!"

Evan looked back and forth between the two of them, barely restraining from breaking into hysterics. "Wow. I've never had two brothers fight over me before. This is hot. We can move it into the bedroom if you boys like."

Jesse sucked in a horrified gasp. Brandon started snickering. Jesse spun to walk away from him, but Brandon snatched his arm.

"Wait. Since you weren't playing around about him, then does that mean you really did meet with Phoenix Records yesterday?"

Jesse's chin raised in pride. "That's right. We're all set to make our first album. Well, we will be after our producer finds us a drummer and keyboardist, but he said he's already got a couple people who might be interested and he'd arrange for us all to meet down at the Phoenix Studios next Monday, so by this time next year the whole world will know my name."

Brandon threw his arms around him. "I knew you could do it! Didn't I always tell you that?"

"Yeah, you did," Jesse laughed as he hugged Brandon with one arm while still maintaining a grip on his towel. He stepped from Brandon's embrace and headed toward the bathroom. "I'm going to finish showering, then we'll go out to breakfast. I'm starving and those donuts you brought aren't going to cut it."

"Hurry and get ready," Brandon said, chuckling again. "I've got to show you guys this stripped out Escalade parked up the street before the owner finds it and has it towed away. The damn thing's up on blocks, the whole front clip is gone, tires, everything! It got stripped right on the street! I almost died when I saw it! What moron leaves their Escalade parked on the street in this neighborhood?"

Jesse snapped his head toward Evan.

Evan stared at Brandon. He blinked once. "Was it black?"

Brandon's laugh slowed, then stopped as he cleared his throat. "Yeah."

Evan took in a long, deep breath and exhaled slowly.

Jesse put his hand on Evan's shoulder. "I'm so sorry."

Evan lifted Jesse's hand to his lips and placed a soft kiss on his fingers. "Don't worry about it. This just gives me an excuse to get a Porsche Cayenne." He turned for Jesse's bedroom. "Let's get ready to go."

Jesse faced Brandon and saw his eyes were focused on Evan's ass as he disappeared into the bedroom. He punched him hard on the bicep. "Hey! Can you behave around him while I get a shower? You're not going to try and compromise his honor or anything, are you?"

Exasperation fell across Brandon's face. "Will you hurry and get ready?"

Jesse gave Brandon a final warning look before going back into the bathroom. When he finished his shower, he stepped out to Brandon rambling about theatre and his roles to Evan, having already forgotten about his humble routine. He ducked into his bedroom and was pulling on a shirt when Evan stepped in.

"Is he driving you nuts?" Jesse asked, sitting on the bed to put on his shoes.

Evan shook his head. "No, but he talks almost as much as you do when he's excited." He stood in front of him and placed his fingers under Jesse's chin. "Why don't you pack a few things and come stay with me for a while?"

Jesse's expression glowed with a bright smile. "Really?"

"Yeah."

Jesse stood up and pulled Evan into a kiss. As Jesse's tongue glided into his mouth, Evan tightened his hold on him, pressing Jesse's hips against his.

Jesse caressed Evan's cheek, then turned to pack his Chicago Bears duffel bag. Once finished, he left Kenny a note and they headed out of his building to where Evan had parked his Escalade.

Evan stumbled to a halt, a shocked cough slipped from his throat at the sight of it. The SUV sat stripped to the frame on the front end, mounted up on cinderblocks with the wheels and tires gone. The seats were missing and the instrument panel had been torn apart. Evan took a halting step toward it, then paced around it.

Jesse saw something on the SUV's roof and pointed to it. "What's that?"

Evan pulled it down. "My CD wallet." He flipped through it. "Oh, how nice. They took the time to look through and only steal the ones they wanted."

Jesse bit his bottom lip to keep from busting out in laughter. Brandon turned his back to Evan and rested one hand on Jesse's shoulder, squeezing it as he struggled to keep his laugh under control.

"Well, we have pretty classy thieves here on the South Side," Jesse said.

Evan glanced up at him. "I told you this was a bad neighborhood."

"You did say it was your beater, though."

A slow smile spread across Evan's lips.

Brandon faced around, chuckling with each word he spoke. "If you need to go anywhere, Evan, I'd be happy to take you. I got my motorcycle parked up the street. You can ride behind me."

Jesse jabbed his elbow into Brandon's ribs. Brandon's breath shot out of him, and he lost the last bit of control he had over keeping his laughter in check. Evan shook his head, chuckling softly as he pulled out his cell phone to call for a tow truck. Jesse took a seat on the steps to wait.

Brandon sat down beside him and leaned close to his ear. "Hey, is he really that good in bed?"

Jesse looked at him with a smirk that gave Brandon his answer.

Brandon huffed and reclined back on the steps. "Lucky little slut. It's not fair. So you were really at his house? What's it like? Is it a big ass mansion?"

"Yeah, it's awesome," Jesse said, and began filling Brandon in on details.

Evan finished his call and sat down on the step behind Jesse with his legs on either side of him.

During the hour it took for the tow truck to come, Brandon dominated the conversation by asking Evan questions, and Jesse noticed how Evan would deftly turn the topic away from himself and back to Brandon. When Brandon asked what Evan had been up to for the past three and a half years, Evan simply said traveling and talked about a few of the places he'd been. Then Brandon queried Evan as to what it was like being on tour, and Evan answered it wasn't much different from being a stage actor in a traveling troupe and swung the dialogue back to Brandon's acting career.

Listening to him, Jesse had to admit Evan's mastery of conversation was impressive, if not a little unsettling. Evan was always honest in the answers he gave, but he didn't give more than he had to, and now sitting back and paying attention made him realize all the more that Evan had been doing the same thing to him. Before, he'd been hurt by Evan's refusal to open up to him, now his determination strengthened to get Evan to trust him.

When the tow truck arrived, Jesse overheard the conversation between Evan and the driver, the driver commenting how in his experience, insurance companies didn't usually pay up unless there was a police report. Evan shrugged and told the guy to take the Escalade away.

Jesse stood as Evan returned. "Aren't you going to call the cops?"

Evan shook his head. "The paparazzi have a knack for sniffing out stuff like this. I've been doing pretty good at staying below their radar for the past few years, I don't need to send up a signal flare by reporting this. If I did, the next thing you know, there'd be articles in every tabloid about me being a burned-out has-been trolling bad neighborhoods looking to buy crack and a hooker."

"But what about the insurance?" Jesse asked.

"It's not like I need their money. Tomorrow we'll go shopping for a Cayenne. Right now, I can't even think I'm so hungry. It's closer to lunch than breakfast. Let's go get some food."

Jesse and Brandon glanced at each, both in disbelief. Jesse could hardly fathom purchasing a vehicle the cost of an Escalade, let alone shrugging off the loss like it was a pair of ten-dollar sunglasses. He took a breath, doing his best to comprehend Evan's reasoning, and focused on Evan's food comment.

"If you're that hungry, then let's go to Uno's. I guarantee you've never tasted anything so good in the world."

Evan stepped close to Jesse and nuzzled next to his ear. "But I've already tasted the greatest thing in the world."

Brandon watched Jesse glow under Evan's attention and the affectionate way Evan whispered to him. Having never seen Jesse look or act in such a way with anyone, he was more than a little surprised, but he also couldn't shake his concern about Evan. He noticed the way Evan gave virtually no information about himself, and though he played along as if oblivious, it made him uneasy that Evan was hiding something.

Brandon came out of his thoughts as Jesse walked away with Evan's arm around his shoulders. He left them at Jesse's truck and hopped onto his Suzuki motorcycle, leading the way down side streets and short cuts to get to Ohio Street and Uno's. He headed in before them, as it was easier for him to find a place to park his bike, and put his name on the waiting list.

As the hostess called his name, the door opened with Jesse bouncing in at Evan's side. They followed him to their table, and after ordering an appetizer of pizza skins and a deep-dish pizza with extra sausage and pepperoni, Jesse took a quick sip of his soda and excused himself to go to the restroom.

Brandon watched Evan smile at Jesse as he departed. Slowly, Evan brought his gaze to him. He met Evan's eyes peering out from under the pulled down rim of his Yankees cap, amazed at their radiant beauty. He had been a fan of his since Evan's first music video nine years ago and now he sat across from him in his favorite restaurant. If that wasn't enough to blow his mind, Evan being his little brother's new partner was, and that's what dampened an otherwise fantastic moment for him.

Evan leaned back in the booth and stretched one arm across the top. "Well, we're alone now, so get it off your chest."

Evan's astute perception came as no surprise to Brandon. One thing he had noticed about him was that those beautiful eyes of his were incredibly sharp, never missing the most subtle nuances around him, but at this moment, there was a coldness to them he found disquieting. Most men he knew would seek his approval and friendship if they wanted to be with Jesse, yet Evan sat with an air of detachment as if he couldn't care less whether or not he liked him. Brandon glanced behind him to check for Jesse, then looked back to Evan, deciding he needed to make it clear to him that he wasn't about to back out of Jesse's life just because Evan had stepped in.

"I'm going to start this off by saying that I don't have anything against you personally. In fact, from what I've seen of you so far you're pretty cool, but you've gotta understand, Jess is my top priority. I've been watching out for him since the day he was born. I was there for him when he needed someone to talk to about the things he was feeling toward other guys. I was there for him when he kissed his first boy and freaked out about it later. When our father kicked him out like he did to me, I took him in and took care of him. And I'm the one who made sure no lowlife losers took advantage of him because they thought he was nothing but the hottest piece of ass to walk through the club door that night.

"I know how things work. You meet someone, hook up for a weekend or a few days, then move on. If he's just a passing fling for you, then don't lead him to believe you want something more. You have to understand one thing about him, Jess is ruled by his emotions. And from what I'm seeing, he already looks like he's damn near smitten with you. So I just want to know what you want from him."

Evan's lips lifted with an amused smirk. "You mean, since you've already made it clear you think I'm a man whore, you want to know that I want more from him than just his ass, is that right?"

Evan's condescending tone broke Brandon's patience. He leaned forward on the table, his voice dropping to a growl as he glared into Evan's eyes. "You may think you're big shit sitting there with your arrogant little rock star attitude, but to me, you're just the lucky one who beat out seventy-five percent of the gay populace of Chicago that would give their right nut to get him in bed. And I don't give a rat's ass how fat your bank account is, how many Ferraris you own, what your mansion looks like, or what celebrities have sucked you off, none of it proves to me you're good enough to be with my brother."

Brandon finished and stared at Evan, waiting for his retaliation.

Evan took a sip of his soda and casually glanced around the restaurant. "If you're waiting for me to say something like, wow, Brandon, I've never been talked to like that before and now I really respect you, and then see me change from being the *arrogant little rock star* to a warm and compassionate person, then we'll keep sitting here until one of us kicks it because that's not going to happen." He brought his eyes to Brandon's, all amusement vanished from his expression and voice. "I don't respect you for having the balls to stand up to me, and I can assure you, I was arrogant long before I ever stepped foot in a recording studio."

He chuckled, his countenance shifting once again to light and nonchalant. "But I do respect the love you have for Jess and feel in your debt for acting as a barrier between him and so many men, so if there's anything I can do to pay you back, let me know."

Before Brandon could retort that Evan's dancing around every question was really starting to piss him off, Jesse slid into the booth at Evan's side, sitting so close there was no space between them.

"What're you guys talking about?"

Evan raked his fingers through the back of Jesse's hair and toyed with it. "Just how grateful I am to him for being your gallant protector."

Jesse lightly kicked Brandon under the table. "Even though you made me want to choke you sometimes, considering how things have worked out, I'm pretty grateful, too. Thanks, jerk-ass."

Brandon let out an indiscernible grunt for a response as he sipped his soda, feeling an even greater unease. Evan's fortifications against showing his true self seemed impenetrable and he fiercely guarded his emotions. He wondered if Evan's walls would be too much for even Jesse to breach.

CHAPTER THIRTEEN

Jesse waved to Brandon from the front porch as his brother coasted toward the gates. When Brandon passed through, Jesse turned inside, shut the one front door, and leaned back against it smiling at Evan, who was closing the gates from the security keypad by the door while watching the small monitor screen so as to open the second gates for Brandon.

"Thanks for letting him come over," Jesse said.

"I could tell when we finished lunch that he wanted to spend more time with you. And I don't want you to thank me. While you're staying with me, I want you to look at my house as your house. If you want Brandon to come visit, then invite him whenever you want."

"You might regret that. We're used to hanging out together whenever we can. Even though our schedules would conflict with how I had to work during the day and he had his rehearsals and theatre stuff, on top of his performance nights and my gigs, we always made time for each other, and if we couldn't get together, we called each other every day just to see what was going on."

Evan finished at the keypad and faced him. "You guys really are close."

"He's always been there for me. When I would get in trouble and our dad would go on one of his rampages, Brandon always stood up to him to get the heat off me. He's my best friend, even more so than Kenny." Jesse chuckled. "We might bicker a lot and call each other names, but it's how we show our love."

Evan lowered his gaze. It had been years since there'd been anyone in his life he could count as a best friend. The closest was his former guitarist, Jerry Jeffries, or JJ as everyone called him, and when he'd been making albums they were pretty close, but since he quit performing he had only seen JJ twice, called him a handful of times, and sent a few letters. The only person who he considered a true best friend had been his father.

"Ev?"

Evan raised his eyes to Jesse's questioning face and summoned a smile for him. "The last thing I want is to come between you two. Is he seeing anyone right now?"

Jesse's countenance deepened from questioning to concerned. "Not anyone serious. Is everything okay? Just now, you looked kinda sad."

"Sad?" Evan said in a doubtful voice with a forced chuckle. "Well, I *am* out a brand new Escalade. Wouldn't that make you sad?"

Jesse averted his gaze, his voice came soft. "But, you've gotten that look before, and it makes me feel like there are things you're thinking or feeling you don't want to talk about. I guess I can understand since we haven't known each other that long, and everyone has things they'd rather keep to themselves, but," he brought his eyes back to Evan's, "I know I feel safe telling you everything about myself and I want you to feel the same way. I'd never betray anything you confided in me. I swear it on my life and music."

Evan opened his mouth to speak, then closed it without a word. He dropped his gaze from Jesse's, blinking rapidly a few times, and shifted his stance backward, then forward again, looking as though he wanted to flee but not knowing how.

Jesse mentally chastised himself for making him uncomfortable, and yet at the same time, felt a little bit of triumph at touching something in Evan that made it difficult for him to maintain his cool front. Evan took a deep breath, and Jesse saw he had managed to gather some of his controlled demeanor back, but still seemed shaken, and there was a soft desperation in his eyes that made Evan appear almost fragile.

Evan moved close to him and braced one hand on the door beside Jesse's head. He placed his other under Jesse's chin and brushed his thumb along his slender jaw. "I know I can trust you. If I didn't believe that I could, I never would've brought you here. I would've screwed you in my hotel room the first night I saw you, then I would've been gone before you woke up. But I felt something when I saw you, and for the first time in a very long time, I wanted to be able to believe in someone. When I finally talked to you, I could sense your honesty, and you've shown me nothing but sincerity since that night. You don't know how much it means to me to find someone who is truly genuine with me. Almost everyone who has ever been in my life has been nothing but greedy fools wearing fake smiles and showing kindness to me because they wanted a piece of my success."

Evan's words spiraled through Jesse's mind. He couldn't think of a response until he muttered without thinking, "What do I need your success for when I'm more than capable of gaining my own?"

Before he could close his eyes or tip his lips up to him, Evan's mouth closed over his in an intense kiss. Evan pulled him away from the door, spun him toward the stairs, and pressed him back without taking his lips away. Jesse walked backward, his eyes closed. Something in his response had struck Evan. The thought passed through his mind that he should stop Evan's abrupt passion, he should keep him talking, but he decided against it. If this was where Evan's emotions wanted to be, then he would follow them. When Evan halted them both, he assumed they must be near the stairs, and broke the kiss to see he was right. He turned to climb them, and Evan walked behind him, his hands on Jesse's hips.

Jesse looked over his shoulder, grinning with mischief. "I'll race you to the bed. If you can catch me, I'll let you do whatever you want to me for the rest of the day and night."

Before Evan could respond, Jesse sprang up three steps in one leap. As he landed, he launched into a sprint up the rest of the flight. Evan dashed after him. Jesse reached the top of the stairs and raced toward the bedroom. With each stride, he heard Evan closing in on him. He veered into the bedroom, seeing the bed only a few strides away, then felt Evan's hands on his waist.

Evan clasped him tightly, forcing him to stop, and trapped him in his arms. "It appears I win."

Jesse laughed between quick breaths, "I guess it does. So what are you going to do with your victory?"

Evan released him and pushed him hard, knocking him forward onto the bed. Jesse flipped from his stomach to his back, sliding fully onto the bed as Evan brought his body over him. Evan pressed his mouth to his, diving his tongue deep inside, and worked his hips against him. A short, high groan sounded in Jesse's throat. The friction of their clothes between them made it feel as if they were chaffing his sensitive cock. He realized the chase brought Evan's passion to a fiercer level and stored the trick into his permanent memory.

Evan lifted himself up and grabbed the bottom of Jesse's shirt. Jesse wiggled beneath him to aid in getting it off. Evan flung the shirt away and pulled his own over his head. He came back down on Jesse, bringing the bare skin of their chests together. Jesse exhaled a soft groan, his hands moved over the smooth skin of Evan's back. Evan drifted lower on him, his lips devoting attention to every inch of Jesse's skin, causing Jesse to lose himself in the feel of his explorative tongue. Evan tugged Jesse's button and zipper loose, his hand dove into his boxers and pulled Jesse's cock free as his lips reached his chest and he covered one nipple with his mouth.

Jesse moaned and writhed, weaving his fingers in Evan's hair. The beautiful sounds Jesse made heightened Evan's pleasure. He wanted to evoke more of those noises from him. He pressed Jesse's cock to his own abdomen. Jesse gasped loud, and Evan grinned at his reaction. He pushed off the bed and dragged Jesse's jeans and boxers off his legs. He removed Jesse's socks, then shed his own clothes. Jesse held both arms up to him. Evan climbed onto the bed to lay in his embrace. Jesse's mouth opened for Evan's tongue before their lips touched.

After a few long moments, Evan withdrew from Jesse's lips and crawled half off him to reach the lube on the nightstand. He picked it up, shook it, and sighed. "I forgot we killed this the other day, but I've got more in the bathroom."

"I know. I saw your stash under the sink when I was looking for the toothbrush. You've got like a year's supply down there."

"More like a couple weeks with the way we've been going at it." Evan stepped into the bathroom to get the lube. He headed back to the bedroom, halting in the doorway at the sight before him.

Jesse lay sprawled across the bed on his back, his eyes closed, his head turned to the side, his black hair framing the fair skin of his face. He had one leg cocked up, the other spread wide to the side. His left arm was tossed behind his head, his right hand worked in slow strokes up and down his erection.

Evan found himself unable to move or speak, capable of only taking in Jesse's slender body. His heart tightened as the thought passed through his mind of how Jesse's was the kind of exquisite beauty that inspired artists to create masterpieces.

Jesse opened his indigo eyes, a sensual smile graced his lips. He propped himself up on one elbow and beckoned Evan to him with his index finger. "I'm all yours. Do whatever you want to me."

Evan didn't think it was physically possible for him to get harder, but Jesse's words made it painfully so. He marched across the bedroom and jumped onto the bed, forcing Jesse down to his back once again as he met him in a kiss, only to draw back so he could slather his fingers in lube. He lifted Jesse's right leg to rest on his shoulder, and when he found his lips again, he pushed his middle finger inside him.

Jesse's body temperature flared at Evan's touch. He draped his other leg over Evan's back. After only a few thrusts of Evan's finger, he wanted more and let out a pleading moan. Evan responded by adding his index. Jesse sighed softly, amazed at how well Evan could read him. Steady and firm, Evan pushed into him, but he craved more force and more of Evan. He reached down, grabbed Evan's wrist, and with a sharp yank and snap of his hips, he drove Evan's fingers deep and hard, gasping and arching at the sensation.

Evan tried to pull his hand back, but Jesse tightened his fingers around his wrist, and he couldn't help but chuckle. "You want more than just my fingers, don't you?"

Jesse grumbled and let go of his wrist.

Evan drew his hand away and lowered his lips to Jesse's ear. "Get on your knees."

Jesse flipped over and moved up to his hands and knees, glancing over his shoulder at Evan with a teasing smirk. "You're awfully demanding in what you want."

"Yes, it's a shame you're not more assertive," Evan said sarcastically. Kneeling behind him, he pulled one of Jesse's arms out from under him and slapped Jesse's hand down on the top of the headboard. "Remember when you asked if I liked to get rough?"

"Yeah."

Evan moved Jesse's other hand to grip the headboard. "You're going to need to hold on to that."

Jesse blinked down at the headboard, his heart drumming hard and fast. Evan's fingertips drifted down his back in a caress firmer than usual. When his fingers reached his lower back, Evan hooked them and scratched his short, manicured nails over Jesse's ass, creating streaks of pale red against the ivory skin.

Jesse fed his rapid heartbeat with shallow, quick breaths. He could tell from Evan's methodical touch, from the intensity in the air surrounding them, that Evan was studying his reactions, gauging how much force he could use, and he found himself overflowing with the same emotions he had felt their first night, the desire to surrender to Evan's dominance, to have Evan master him.

Evan's nails dug in harder. Jesse moaned high and pushed into his touch. Evan grabbed Jesse's hips and tugged his back end to him. With a hard thrust, he shoved his cock inside him. Jesse sucked in a sharp breath and flinched at the force, then exhaled hard and leaned back toward Evan for more. Evan pulled him back as he moved forward, sinking into him deeper and deeper until his body was flush with Jesse's, and still he continued to press in and tug him back.

Jesse panted in short, hard breaths. Evan's strong grip held him in place. It was the deepest he had ever been. It hurt a little, and Evan pressed against him so hard Jesse swore his ass was going to have bruises from Evan's hips, but he didn't want to stop him. As deep as Evan was, it still didn't feel like enough.

Without pulling so much as a fraction out of him, Evan jerked his hips forward in small hammering thrusts. Jesse's cock pulsed with every push. Evan drew his length out halfway, and he instantly missed the deep pressure. A choked whimper escaped him, followed by a high cry as Evan slammed into him, causing him to fall toward the headboard before he caught himself, his body throbbing from the impact.

Evan stopped and eased back, fearing it'd been too much for him, but as he did, Jesse moved with him, as though desperate to keep every inch of him inside him.

Jesse looked at him. "Again, Ev. Do it as hard as you can."

The need on Jesse's face severed the last of Evan's self-control. He rammed forward. Jesse dropped his head between his stretched out arms, expelling a loud moan. Gripping Jesse's hips, Evan pounded into him. Jesse's arms trembled with the effort of keeping his elbows locked against the strength of Evan's thrusts, each one driving gasps and high cries from him. His cock ached, but he couldn't release the headboard to give it the attention it wanted. From the warmth circulating in his sac, he didn't think he would have to in order to reach climax. At that thought, Evan's right hand released his hip, his fingers clamped around his shaft.

A high groan came from between Jesse's clenched teeth, not only at the overwhelming pleasure of finally having his organ touched, but also at the way Evan stroked him, hard and rough, tugging and pulling. Never in his life had someone taken possession of him like Evan was. It felt like his body belonged more to Evan than to himself.

Evan brought his torso over Jesse's back, thrusting faster. With his other hand, he grabbed a fistful of Jesse's hair and yanked his head back and to the side. A choked breath shook in Jesse's throat, his muscles tightened as his ecstasy built. Evan nipped down his neck, then reaching the tender curve near the shoulder, sank his teeth into his skin in a solid bite.

The pain of the bite intertwined with Jesse's pleasure. He bucked back hard against him, yelling Evan's name as his climax burst free. A rumbling groan came from Evan's throat. His teeth still gripped Jesse's skin as he pushed every inch of his length inside him, releasing deeper in him than ever before.

Evan dropped his torso down on Jesse's sweat slick back, which rose and fell under him as Jesse tried to catch his breath. Though his arms and legs felt weak, Jesse supported their combined weight.

Evan wrapped his arms around Jesse's waist, pressing their bodies tighter together. He nuzzled into Jesse's hair. "Why can't I control myself with you?" he whispered. "I have no defenses against you."

Jesse turned his head to look at him. Evan's face remained buried in his hair. There was a vulnerability in Evan's voice that made an ache rise in his chest. He didn't know what Evan was referring to, but he was positive it wasn't sex. He laid one hand over Evan's, silently telling him his defenses were no longer needed.

CHAPTER FOURTEEN

Jesse sat beside Evan on the steps of the Field Museum of Natural History. He picked at the frozen lemonade cup in his hand. Even though he had a blast spending the morning meandering around the museum, he couldn't shake his concern about Evan. He thought he made a breakthrough on Tuesday with the amazing afternoon and evening they spent together, but the next morning Evan had collected his composed character once again and took him along to purchase a Porsche Cayenne.

Granted, the last time he'd gone shopping for a vehicle, he and Kenny had cruised around in Kenny's battered old Honda Civic as they scoured every used car lot on the South Side looking for a truck. So rolling into a Porsche dealer in a Ferrari 612 was a pretty mind-blowing experience. It led to further astonishment when Evan climbed into his new metallic black, fully loaded Cayenne Turbo S and tossed him the Ferrari keys. And he had been so excited the night before when Evan let him drive it to pick up Chinese food for dinner. That was nothing compared to being able to get on the gas on the highway.

But as much fun as playing with the cars was, it served as a distraction that gave Evan an excuse to not talk about himself all day. When evening came and Evan suggested they go for a swim, they wrestled in the water, one thing led to another, and before Jesse knew it, all opportunities to learn about him had passed.

This morning in the museum, he asked Evan if he would come with him to the studio on Monday, to which Evan replied, "Look at that crazy lookin' turtle," as he strolled away to inspect the fossilized prehistoric creature. Despite feeling a twinge of discouragement at Evan's elusive ways, he was far from admitting defeat.

Evan pushed his Yankees cap up so it rested on the top of his head and leaned back on the step behind him. "This was a pretty good idea."

"I was afraid you'd be bored. You really liked it?"

"Yeah, those dinosaur bones were pretty cool. I like stuff like that."

Jesse looked at Evan through his sunglasses. "What other kind of stuff do you like?"

Evan turned to him with a smirk. "You know, since we've already slept together, you don't have to pretend to be interested in my likes and dislikes."

Jesse exhaled a frustrated sigh. "You're really difficult, you know that? Do you ever just answer a question?"

"I didn't think I had to. You grew up reading all the little music mags. I bet you already know my favorite food and color."

Jesse shook his head and chopped at the frozen lemonade with the plastic spoon.

Evan watched his frustrated movements, then smiled. "What do you want to know?"

"Tell me anything about yourself that's not music related."

"I like the Giants and the Yankees."

"I like the Bears and the White Sox, big freakin' whoop. C'mon."

"Okay. I prefer dark chocolate over milk chocolate."

"That's fine," Jesse grumbled. "I don't need to know anything about you outside of the bedroom, anyway."

Evan leaned toward him, putting his lips to Jesse's ear. "No? Then how's this? I love how noisy you are when we play. All those sexy little sounds you make get me so hot." He let out a throaty moan and flicked his tongue over the two earrings in Jesse's right earlobe. "And you're so gorgeous, I want you all the time."

"Damn it," Jesse breathed out. "I've been half up all day, now I could crack diamonds. Thanks."

"You were more than half up in the ancient Egyptian section," Evan whispered.

"I can't believe you groped me in front of the mummies."

"You did tell me you had fantasies about doing it anywhere, anytime, and I know those poor crusty guys haven't seen anything that good in two thousand years."

Jesse laughed and shoved him away. "You have the most twisted sense of humor! Now tell me anything that's not related to music *or* sex."

"You just killed eighty percent of my personality right there! You already know I like cars, and I'd say that's a good ten percent. And I'm really serious about the dark chocolate thing. Good dark chocolate is really important to me, so I'd chock that up to another two."

"Evan," Jesse growled.

Evan burst out laughing. "You must be really serious! The only time you say my full name is when I'm working you really good and you're screaming it out."

Jesse's efforts to maintain a serious countenance faded, and he chuckled.

"Alright," Evan said, still laughing softly. "Something that's not music or sex related. I'm going to have to go back pretty far to find anything that meets those requirements." He took the frozen lemonade cup out of Jesse's hand and ate a couple bites. He paused, thinking with the spoon in his mouth, then whipped it out. "I know. I was almost held back in the first grade because my teachers didn't think I was ready to move on."

"What?" Jesse said, shocked. "Why not?"

"I wasn't a very good reader."

"I can't picture you struggling at school with how intelligent you are. Why weren't you held back?"

"My dad threw a fit, so the school pushed me through. It was one of only two times that I ever saw him get really upset. My mom thought it might be good for me to be held back, but he stood up for me saying the teachers and the school were the problem, not me. The truth is, written words confused me because I was so used to reading music. While other kids were reading *The Pokey Little Puppy*, I was picking apart 'Fur Elise.'"

Jesse stared at him. That certainly helped him to understand why Evan was such a loner. Even at so young an age, Evan's talent isolated him from his peers. He caught what Evan had said about his father, and asked, "What was the other time your dad got upset?"

Evan looked out over the glassy waters of Chicago Harbor.

Jesse could see his eyes from the side of his sunglasses and could tell from their distant look that Evan was replaying the memory, probably deciding if he wanted to share it or not. He watched Evan's gaze lower behind his sunglasses, the forlorn expression he'd seen before flickered across his face. He suddenly felt selfish for pushing him to talk and was about to tell him to forget it when Evan cleared his throat.

"It was the summer I was sixteen. The guy across the street from our townhouse was washing his new Harley in the street, and I was standing inside our house watching him. I was so focused on him, I didn't notice that my dad had walked up behind me until he asked, 'Did Anthony get a new bike?' I freaked out. Here I was getting hard over the neighbor guy, and there's my dad. I was so embarrassed that I just blurted out, 'yeah,' and took off upstairs to hide in my room.

"My dad came up, whipped open my bedroom door and yelled, 'What just happened down there?' I didn't say anything. I couldn't. Now I wasn't just embarrassed to all hell, I was shocked that my dad was mad at me and I thought for sure he had figured it out, and I was right. He stormed across my room, took my face in both hands, put his face in mine, and said, 'Don't ever run and hide from me like that again.' Then he wrapped his arms around me, and said, 'Human feeling has complexities that can't be understood. The only thing you can do is try to be true to what's in your heart. Always do that and I'll always be proud of you. And there's nothing you could ever do to make me not love you.'"

Evan finished the memory and stared down at the steps. He hadn't talked about his father to anyone since he had died, and never shared what happened between them that day. Loss started to tighten his chest, then stopped as Jesse's hand fell on his. Jesse slid across the step until they were sitting so close their legs, the sides of their hips, their arms and shoulders touched.

"He sounds really cool," Jesse said, his voice soft with compassion.

"Yeah. He was from England, and he had some pretty good success singing in operas over there until he moved here."

"What was his name?"

"Ethan."

"Your middle name."

Evan smiled at him. "You remembered. I'm impressed Jesse Michael."

Jesse laughed. "Don't call me that. I'll feel like I'm in trouble."

Evan rocked affectionately against him. "So what about you? I bet the worst grade you ever got was an A minus."

"As if I'd get a lowly A minus. Haven't you figured out that I'm a genius yet?"

"I know two places you're a genius. One's behind a mic. Can you guess where the other is?"

Jesse winked and kissed the air toward him. "School came really easy for me. When I was in elementary school, I went through a bunch of tests that said I was gifted. My teachers tried telling my parents that I needed to be in accelerated schooling, but my dad wouldn't listen. He said I'd outgrow it and fall back in line with the other kids in a couple years, but I never did. You'd think a professor at a community college would be a little more into his own kid's education, but he had always pretty much ignored me unless I did something wrong.

"Brandon thinks our dad hated him worse because he'd always fight with him, but I look at it that our dad cared more about him because he at least took the time to bitch at him. I think he could tell early on that I was going to turn out to be gay and thought I wasn't worth the effort from day one, but he still had some hope for Brandon. If you asked Brandon now, he'd deny he's ever done anything to try to please our father, but that's probably why Brandon was screwed up for so long, trying to come to terms with his sexuality, and bounced between guys and girls for a few years before he realized he couldn't force himself to be straight or bi."

Evan gazed at Jesse, too stunned to speak. He couldn't imagine what it was like growing up with such a poor father when his own had been so dear to him, but what shocked him more was the carefree way Jesse talked about the situation, as if discussing last night's baseball game. It seemed Jesse accepted his father's disownment, but a person didn't get over being rejected by their parent. The scar may become easier to hide with time, but it was always there.

"So anyway," Jesse continued, "I was in advanced classes and even they were easy for me, but I've always loved to read and study history, especially ancient Greece. With my grades and high SAT scores, I got a full academic scholarship to Purdue, but I passed it up to pursue music fulltime, and that's when my dad jacked me in the cheek and threw me out. Not that it mattered. I had already been planning to move in with Brandon after I graduated high school."

Evan looked at the partially melted frozen lemonade cup he had forgotten he was holding and took a bite in an attempt to cool the fury rising in him that anyone would hit Jesse. Deciding it'd be best to change the topic, he stood up and held his hand down to him. "Let's go into the fish house. I'm starving, and I bet for the right price, they'll throw just about anything on a plate in there."

Jesse rolled his eyes and took Evan's hand. "Do you know how many endangered species the Shedd has?"

"I guess they'd be the more expensive dishes."

Jesse chuckled under his breath. "That's not even funny."

"Then why are you laughing?"

"Out of pity that you'd make so bad a joke."

Jesse tried to duck when Evan moved to rumple his hair, but was too slow. He sighed, looking up at the messed up cluster of hair hanging above his eyes, and did his best to fix it with his fingers. He dropped his hands and Evan slid his arm around his waist. Jesse matched the movement. He noticed a group of people looking at them, then quickly averting their eyes, only to peek back at them in a weak effort to be sneaky.

"People are looking at us weird," Jesse said.

"Well, we're probably giving them a mixed signal trying to figure out if we're really good friends or lovers." Evan moved his arm from Jesse's back and shoved his hand into the back pocket of Jesse's jeans furthest from him. "There. That should clear up any confusion."

With each stride, Jesse felt Evan's hand pressing against his left butt cheek, and as much as he wanted Evan to keep his hand there, he felt nervous for Evan knowing how closely he had guarded his sexuality. "Aren't you worried someone will recognize you? I mean, the hat and sunglasses are *not* that slick of a disguise."

"I'm not worried about it." They began climbing the stairs to the Shedd Aquarium, and Evan clamped his fingers onto Jesse's ass cheek. "And I thought your ass felt good when we were walking. It's so firm when you're going up stairs. I think tomorrow we'll go out shopping for a stair-stepper so I can sit in a chair behind it and watch you work out."

As they mounted the last step, Evan pulled his hand away to retrieve money for their entrance.

Jesse moved in close to him. "And if you're a good boy, I'll do it naked for you. I'll climb it until I'm panting and dripping in sweat, then you can grab me, throw me over the bench-press, and ride me as hard as you did the other day."

Evan breathed a heated sigh over Jesse's lips. "Now I'm the one that could smash a diamond to dust."

Jesse gave him a smug grin and strolled into the aquarium. He walked to a large gallery and stood looking at the brightly colored fish, the small ones darting about, the larger ones drifting through the water with lazy swishes of tails and fins. Evan stepped up behind him. His lips brushed the back of Jesse's neck in a whisper soft kiss.

They turned from the gallery of tropical fish and worked their way to the underwater viewing gallery in the Oceanarium section to see the Pacific white-sided dolphins and beluga whales.

Evan turned his head to look at Jesse, watching his eyes follow the sea creatures. No matter how much he looked at them, they were still the darkest, deepest blue he had ever seen, like twilight when night was about to take full claim of the sky from the sun. All the people he had ever met, all the places he traveled, and never had he seen eyes of such royal indigo. Then to have those stunning eyes accentuated by hair of rich ebony. How could one person be so exquisitely beautiful? He caressed his fingertips down Jesse's arm.

"Hey," he said softly. "You want to know something else about me?"

Jesse faced him and nodded.

"I've never done anything like this before, just hung out with someone I was sleeping with. If I wasn't screwing them, I didn't care to be around them. I'm almost twenty-seven years old and I've never been in a real relationship."

A smile touched Jesse's lips. He put his arm around Evan's shoulders. "Neither have I. I guess this is one more first we're experiencing together."

Evan wrapped his arm around Jesse's waist and leaned his weight against him.

CHAPTER FIFTEEN

Jesse listened to Evan's breathing next to him in bed and knew he was still awake. During their day at the museum and the aquarium, he never thought he would get so much joy from hearing someone talk about themselves as he got when Evan finally started to open up, even though there was one topic he still adamantly dodged.

Jesse brushed his hand up and down Evan's chest. "You did it again today. You didn't answer my questions about why you quit making music."

Evan kept his eyes closed. "I never quit making music."

"But you haven't put out any new albums."

"That doesn't mean I quit making music." Evan took a deep breath and sighed. He pushed himself up and got out of bed, swiping his boxer-briefs off the floor as he headed for the door. "Come on, if it's so important for you to know."

Jesse sprang out of bed and hopped into his boxers as quickly as he could to follow Evan. He reached the hall and saw Evan moving down the stairs in the dark. Silver light from the moon streamed through the windows to illuminate Evan's skin, making Jesse feel like he was chasing a specter through night. He caught up to Evan as he turned right at the bottom of the stairs, going to the opposite end of the mansion from the kitchen and family room.

Evan led him through the dining room to a closed wooden door that peaked high and sharp in Gothic style, carved in arches and lines, making it look as though it'd be at home in any seventeenth century church. When Evan had given him a tour of the house, Jesse remembered this door led to Evan's office in the tower that rounded the far corner. He'd only gotten a quick peek inside when Evan cracked open the door saying, "And this is my office. All boring, nothing interesting," and shut it again. Now he became instantly enamored with the space.

He walked into the middle of the circular room. Dark walnut bookshelves curved around the walls and towered above to a second landing. A narrow flight of spiral wooden stairs wound up to the second landing and still more bookshelves, though all the shelves on both levels were bare save for a handful of car magazines and maps of various countries.

Two large, arched stained glass windows overlooked the front lawn, one on the first level, one on the second, and under each was a wide plush seat built into the light gray stone wall. The wall to his right was paneled in dark wood squares carved in relief and climbed to the second level, where the wall continued to the ceiling in the light gray stone. Swords of various designs hung on the wall; an English long sword, a rapier with a sweeping hilt, two Chinese broadswords, three katana, and two wakizashi.

Evan stood in front of the wood paneled wall behind a massive desk of dark mahogany that had a laptop computer, a printer, pads of paper, pens, and empty sheet music all neatly organized. He pressed on the square of one wood panel. It sank in, clicked, then slid to the side, showing a safe behind.

"Are these real?" Jesse asked, admiring a katana. "Like true historical pieces?"

Evan punched a code into the safe and opened the solid steel door. "Yeah, I'm sort of a collector when I see one that strikes me."

He retrieved a fireproof box from inside the safe and set it on the desk. He opened it, revealing pages and pages of sheet music. He sat down in the black leather chair behind the desk and pushed the box toward Jesse.

Jesse sat on top of the desk and leafed through the songs. "There has to be over fifty songs here. And they're complete with lyrics, music, everything. If you have all this music, why haven't you recorded a new album?"

"I guess I haven't felt like it."

Disbelief dropped Jesse's jaw. "Haven't felt like it? How can you say that? What about your fans? Don't you think you owe it to them—"

"I don't owe anybody, anything," Evan said sharply.

Jesse stared at him in silence for a moment. "But, I don't understand. You don't want to make albums, but you keep writing music. Why?"

Evan brushed Jesse's hair back from his forehead. "What difference does it make?"

"I want to know."

Evan slid the chair between Jesse's legs and put his hand behind Jesse's neck, pulling him down for a kiss. He rubbed his other hand up Jesse's thigh. His fingers slipped in the front hole of Jesse's boxers and grazed his cock. Though it responded instantly to his touch, Jesse broke the kiss and pulled Evan's hand away.

He kept Evan's hand in his and tried to will his steadily rising organ to lay at rest, but it now listened better to Evan than to him, and despite seeing the hard line pushing against Evan's boxer-briefs, he knew Evan was trying to escape talking by arousing him.

Jesse laid his hand on the side of Evan's face and bent toward him, keeping his voice gentle, but firm. "I want to know." He sat back, holding up the sheet music and gesturing at the house. "There has to be a reason for all of this. You disappeared, running all over the world, *alone.* Then you come back and buy this house, *alone.* I know you like your privacy, but all the time I've been here I haven't even heard the phone ring, so you must not have that many friends anymore."

"I never had that many to begin with," Evan mumbled. He stared down at the desk. "Do you ever give up when you have your mind set?"

"No."

Evan thumbed at the corner of a pad of paper, his voice barely audible in the silent room. "You know, when I first started singing, I never expected it to take off the way it did.

Being a one hit wonder was fine in my book. All I wanted was to earn a lot of money really quick to help my dad. When I was sixteen, he was diagnosed with throat cancer, and by the time the doctors caught it, or I should say by the time he went to a doctor, it was already very advanced. He went through treatments and operations to have tumors removed, and finally his whole voice box had to be taken out. Even though he hid his pain, I know it broke his spirit to lose his voice, even if it was only a shadow of what it had been when he was healthy. It was my mother who convinced him to do it, and he did it because there was nothing he wouldn't do for her.

"I told you earlier today he was from England. When he lived there, he worked steadily as an opera singer in a midsize opera house in London, and he would have made it to the highest level, but he met my mother when she was in London on an exchange student program, and when it came time for her to return to the States, he came with her. Before he could even try to start his career here, my mother got pregnant with me. So he gave it up and spent his whole life working as a mechanic to support us."

Evan raised his eyes to Jesse, a sad smile on his lips. "He used to call me his little prodigy. He taught me to sing and all he knew about music, and worked twelve to fourteen hours a day to pay for lessons on whatever instrument I decided I wanted to learn next. After I played one for a while and mastered it, I'd get bored and want to switch. There were times when I'd have two instructors at once, and never did he complain that it was too much."

Evan's smile faded, and he lowered his gaze again. "When he got sick, I was willing to do anything to save him and decided the best way to do it would be to take advantage of the skills he had helped me hone. I knew that if I could get the right exposure, my voice would be able to take care of the debt from the doctors and him not being able to work, and I thought once I signed with a record label, I'd have enough money where I could send him to the best treatment centers in the country. So when I learned that a huge classic car restoration shop was doing a hot rod Christmas float for the Macy's Thanksgiving Day Parade and they needed a singer, I jumped all over it.

"I went down to their shop to audition and instantly got it. When I was on the float, I made sure to fluctuate my range and improv with the crowd so there was no question that what people heard was my real voice. After that, the car shop was flooded with labels looking to sign me, but I went with Phoenix because my dad felt he could trust Greg, and Phoenix actually cared about the product they were putting out. I didn't care either way so long as I saw a check." Evan took a deep breath as he finished.

"He must've been really proud to see you hit it big," Jesse said softly.

"He was, but all the money in the world can't keep cancer from spreading. He died right before my first tour started. I guess that's why I threw myself into music so hard. I felt like it was all I had left. I felt like I had to do it for him."

Jesse stroked Evan's hair from his eyes. "I'm sorry."

Evan looked up, forcing a smile, but Jesse could see the tears in his eyes. "Do you want to see a picture of him?"

Jesse nodded. Evan swiveled his chair toward the safe. He pulled out a photo album and turned back to the desk. He scooted back in the chair, patted it between his legs, and Jesse hopped off the desk to sit in it with him. Evan wrapped one arm around him and laid his chin on Jesse's shoulder as he opened the cover.

Jesse's eyes widened at the picture of a breathtaking man with amazingly blue eyes holding a beautiful little boy on his lap while they both played the piano. "You look just like him."

"Yeah, quite a bit."

Jesse chuckled and pointed to a picture of Evan and his father sitting on the floor playing with Matchbox cars. "Look at little baby Evan. You were so cute."

Evan laughed softly and nuzzled Jesse's hair. "Don't tease me."

"I'm not. You were adorable."

Jesse looked at a photo on the next page, showing Evan as a toddler held in the arms of a stunning woman with long, dark brunette hair. "Is that your mom?"

"Yeah," Evan grumbled.

"You don't sound real pleased about it."

Evan gazed at the picture of his mother. "Things are tense between us. They have been ever since my father became sick. She'd get so angry at him, as if it was his fault he got cancer, then I'd get pissed at her and we'd end up fighting, but I think there's a part of her that resented him for never continuing his career and when he got sick, she couldn't keep it in anymore. When they were young and first met, he had probably seemed exciting to her, being an opera singer. Then he ends up becoming a mechanic to support his family, and I think she looked down on him for that.

"After he passed away and my career was rolling, I never saw her except a Christmas here and there, then three years ago she decided to remarry and begged me to come to the wedding and meet her new man. I went, and never felt so disgusted in my life, watching her hang on him, him on her. The guy's a no-talent hack of a painter and it was so obvious he was only with her because I set her up very nicely financially, as my father asked me to do, and to top it off, the guy's daughter, my new *stepsister*, was trying in every way possible to let me know she was game for being more than siblings by law. When my mother started cooing how the jackass was her one true love, I left without saying goodbye.

"The last time I talked to her was a couple months ago and she spent the conversation trying to convince me to wire some extra cash to her account because her man had lost his ass, or that is to say, a good portion of the money I gave her, playing stocks. I hung up on her and haven't talked to her since."

Jesse laid his hand over Evan's. "I'm so sorry."

Evan shrugged. "It's not a big deal, really. We were never that close. She used to complain all the time about my father spending money on lessons and instruments for me. He always gave her everything she wanted and did whatever she asked, except when it came to me. With me, he did what he thought was best for *me*."

Jesse looked at him, a warm smile on his lips. "He was an amazing person, wasn't he?"

"He was."

Evan slowly turned the pages of the album, telling Jesse memories from some of the more humorous photos. Jesse listened and laughed at the stories, all the while feeling that with each memory Evan shared, they were growing closer, and even though Evan hadn't specifically said why he quit recording music, he felt that all Evan shared with him was a big step.

Evan flipped the last page of the photo album and closed it.

"Do you have any more?" Jesse asked, not wanting the sharing to end.

Evan embraced Jesse with both arms and laid his head against him. "A couple, but I'll show you another time. I'm feeling pretty beat right now."

Jesse laid his hands on Evan's forearms. "Thank you for telling me about your dad."

Evan nodded. He tightened his hold on Jesse. "Did you mean what you said earlier today? About wanting to have a real relationship with me?"

"Of course."

"You really... *like* being with me that much?"

Jesse looked, trying to see Evan's face, but couldn't since he had it turned away. "Well yeah. Why are you asking things like that?"

"It's nothing."

Jesse knew it wasn't "nothing," but also knew Evan didn't want to talk anymore. He patted Evan's arms. "How about we go back to bed, and I'll give you a backrub until you fall asleep?"

"That would be amazing."

Jesse hopped up from the chair. He wrapped one arm around Evan's waist, glancing at the photo album before walking out of the office.

CHAPTER SIXTEEN

The sound of a piano floated up from downstairs. Jesse bolted upright, instantly awake, and saw the bed empty beside him. He jumped out, snatched his boxers off the floor, hopping toward the door on one foot, then the other as he struggled to put them on and dashed down the stairs. The music grew louder as he neared the bottom. He sprinted across the entrance room, through the family room, and slid to a halt in the doorway of the music room.

Sitting shirtless in his black running pants, Evan's fingers glided over the keys of the ebony grand in his classically inspired ballad "One More Time" from his fourth album of the same title. The morning sun fell over him, the gold and copper streaks in his hair shone against the backdrop of darker chestnut. Though his eyes were closed, his fingers never touched a wrong note. He took a breath and began to sing,

> "*I walk alone,*
> *Still feeling the warmth*
> *Of your body close to mine.*
> *The seasons change,*
> *Night turns to day,*
> *But I remain the same.*
> *My tears chill my skin,*
> *Imitations of the ones*
> *I caused in your eyes*
> *The night I said goodbye.*
>
> *Despite all the tears I've cried,*
> *And all the pain they've brought,*

> *I'd shed them all one more time*
> *To see you smile again.*
> *If seeing me hurt pleases you,*
> *Then I'll cherish this pain forever.*
>
> *I'll never ask you to forgive me.*
> *How could I after all I've done?*
> *But before my body leaves this world*
> *I beg for the gift of your smile one more time.*
>
> *One more time,*
> *That's all I ask.*
> *One more time,*
> *That's all I need.*
> *It'll be my greatest treasure forever,*
> *To see you smile one more time.*
>
> *One more time,*
> *For all my life.*
> *One more time*
> *For all our pain.*
> *It'll bring me just enough hope,*
> *To face one more day…"*

Evan's fingers drifted over the piano in the interlude, playing high and mid-range notes, weaving them into soft, mournful harmonies. He took another breath, letting his smooth baritone flow out again,

> *"My loneliness has become the seasons,*
> *Continuing on*

It never weakens
Leaving me haunted by the memory,
Of your spirit broken in your eyes,
The night I walked away.

I know my lies
Were truths to you.
And the truths I spoke,
Were so very few.
I'll never hurt you again,
By looking in your eyes
With betrayal on my lips.
I'll go away forever,
If it would make you smile,
Just one more time.

One more time,
That's all I ask.
One more time,
That's all I need.
Can't you see my joy is gone forever?
That's why I need your smile one more time.

One more time,
For all my life.
One more time,
For all our pain.
To remind me of what I've lost,
And get me through one more day…"

Evan's voice hushed as he finished the song, his fingers caressed the final gentle notes from the piano.

Jesse stood mesmerized in the doorway. All the times he had listened to the ballad on CD or the radio seemed distorted compared to the clarity with which Evan had just sung.

"Did I sound that bad?" Evan asked with an anxious chuckle.

Jesse realized he should breathe. "You sounded beautiful."

"Well, I'm a little rusty. You don't get much practice just singing in the shower." Evan winked at him. "But you never got to hear me sing live, so now you've had your own private little performance."

"Your voice, it's amazing. I must sound like an old crone compared to you."

"Now that you mention it," Evan snickered, turning back to the piano.

Jesse laughed softly and walked to him. He wrapped his arms around Evan's shoulders from behind, watching him play. Evan played whatever his ear thought sounded right. Jesse sat beside him, caught the melody and harmonies Evan did, and laid his fingers on the keys to play along with him.

Evan looked over at him. "Aren't you going to start pestering me to answer why I quit performing?"

Jesse shook his head and stretched his long fingers over the keys. "I've come to the decision that when you want to tell me, you'll tell me. I'm just going to say this. Even though I don't know why you quit performing, whatever it was that made you leave it all behind couldn't have been worth sacrificing your gift, and you *are* gifted, Ev. What your music gives to the world is far too beautiful and precious for you to throw it away."

Evan stopped playing. "There's nothing beautiful or precious about my gift." He stood up and walked away from the piano, gazing out the tall windows at Lake Michigan, his back to Jesse. "Do you remember during my last tour when my guitarist, Brian Carney, died?"

Jesse's hands slipped off the piano to his lap. "Yeah, it was all over the place. He committed suicide. He only played with you because your regular guitarist, Jerry Jeffries, quit before the tour started since his wife was about to have a baby. But I thought Brian was just a fill-in until JJ was ready to catch up after the baby was born."

"Well, that's what we told the media. The truth is, I kicked Brian off the tour."

"Kicked him off? Why?"

Evan turned back to the piano and sat down on the bench beside Jesse. He took in as deep a breath as he could, letting out a shaky exhale. "Because I was sleeping with him and when I broke it off, he wouldn't accept it, so I got rid of him. When I first met him I knew he wanted me, but it wasn't because he was attracted to me for who I am, it was because he was attracted to the *idea* of me, the person he thought I was from seeing me on stage, in interviews, and all that bullshit. I tried to ignore the whole thing at first. He had a wife and two little girls, and I didn't want to come in between that. But, he was persistent."

Evan hunched forward with his elbows on his knees, his eyes focused on the floor. "So I decided, what the hell? If he wants it so bad, who am I to deny him? And I thought maybe after he was with me once he'd be satisfied and go back to his wife and kids. So, one night I showed up outside his hotel room door. But afterwards it didn't work out the way I thought. He wanted to keep the affair going, and I'll admit I caved a few more times. There's only so much you can do when your mouth and mind are saying no, but your body is pleading yes, and I'm sure you've seen pictures of him."

Jesse nodded slowly, not wanting to openly acknowledge how attractive the other man had been and trying to ignore the jealousy permeating every part of him at hearing Evan talk about a former lover.

"But things got out of control," Evan said softly. "He would knock on my hotel room doors at all hours of the night. I didn't get much sleep when I was on the road to begin with, so you can imagine how pissed I was getting, not to mention, I wasn't always alone when he was pounding on the door. And he was starting to mess up a lot during concerts, which didn't help my patience. Then during a show, I was doing my thing singing next to him, and he stopped playing, threw his arm around my neck, and tried to kiss me. That was it. I told him I was finished with him, that he was the worst lover I had ever had, and I fired him from the tour, then to add insult to injury, I got him cut from Phoenix so he couldn't even be a studio musician with them anymore. I ruined him. I used my influence and ruined him."

Jesse sat quiet, his stunned mind stumbling to absorb all that Evan said.

Evan cleared his throat, trying to find his voice again. "Except for Greg, no one knew the details of our relationship, but either way, I couldn't risk letting any of it get out, so Greg begged JJ to leave his new son and come on tour as a cover-up, and like a true friend, he did. Then a week after I had fired him, Greg came to me and told me Brian had killed himself with a shotgun.

"I didn't know what to do, but I couldn't stop my tour. And when it was finished, I couldn't bring myself to go back into the studio. How could I? I had destroyed a man's life. I couldn't stand the limelight and the adoration of everyone around me. It made me sick to think of all the people who admired me not knowing what kind of person I really was.

"And when I cut Brian's wife a check to make sure that she and the little girls would be taken care of, people sang my praises thinking I was so generous and kind. Not a fucking one of them knew it was nothing but guilt money. I couldn't handle it. So I left the country and went anywhere I thought people wouldn't recognize me."

As Evan finished, a protective rush surged through Jesse, and with it, a feeling that had been lingering below the surface of his consciousness waiting for him to acknowledge it. He turned his head toward Evan. All of Evan's defenses, all his walls were down. His pain, his fear, bared raw and open. In that moment, he knew without a doubt he had fallen in love with him.

But there was one thing he had to know. Jesse drew in a long breath and said on the exhale, "Were you in love with him?"

Evan's head snapped toward Jesse. "No," he said quickly, desperately. He shook his head, his voice softened. "I wasn't. I don't know if that makes it worse or better. I've tried to answer that for years. Worse because he died for nothing, having never obtained my full affection, or better because I at least came to the conclusion that..." he swallowed hard and gripped his legs near his knees to hide the sudden trembling in his fingers. He forced his eyes to stay focused on Jesse's. "That...the man I love would never receive such treatment from me." He broke their gaze as soon as he finished the last word, his eyes going to the floor again.

Jesse slowly turned his eyes away from Evan, his heart pounding.

Evan eased to his feet and moved for the doorway. "So, now that you know, I understand if you don't want to stay here or hang out with me anymore."

Jesse jumped up and grabbed him by the shoulder. He spun Evan around to face him. "All this time I've been thinking you might just be smarter than me, and then you go and say something like that."

Evan blinked at him. "How can you still want to be with me after knowing how I disregarded another person so callously?"

"Because it wasn't your fault he died, Ev. The guy clearly had some serious issues, and if you didn't trip him off, someone or something else would have. How were you supposed to know what he was going to do? You couldn't have. If you did, you would've gotten him help, I know it."

"I think you're taking this too lightly."

Jesse laid his hand on Evan's cheek, trying to tell him with his eyes what he felt in his heart. "If I am, then it's because the only thing that matters about your past is that it brought you to me now. Nothing you've ever done will make me walk away from you."

Joy, relief, pain, grief, choked Evan's throat. He wrapped his arms around Jesse and leaned against him. "Jess," he said, his voice hardly a whisper. "I don't know why I've told you everything. It's not the way I am to talk and express my feelings to someone else. But with you...you've broken me down. You make me feel so vulnerable."

Jesse strengthened his hold on him. "I'm sorry. I shouldn't have pushed you."

"No, it's okay." Evan pulled away enough to look into his eyes. "It shouldn't be, but it is, because I know my vulnerability is safe with you." He lowered his head and shook it. "I'm sorry. I'm not making sense."

Jesse combed his fingers through Evan's hair. "You are making sense, and you're right. I'll never do anything to hurt you." He kissed Evan's forehead, his cheeks, and lifted his chin to kiss him lightly on the lips. He drew back and kissed Evan on the tip of his nose. "Unless you keep dropping your head and making it hard for me to kiss you. Then I might be forced to get rough with you."

A ghost of a smile flickered on Evan's lips, and he rested his forehead against Jesse's. "Can we go back upstairs? I really need to be close to you right now."

Jesse startled at Evan asking if they could go back to bed. When Evan wanted it he took it, but he sounded so fragile, almost desperate. Jesse drew his fingertips across Evan's chest, took him by the hand, and led him out of the music room and upstairs.

Evan sat on the edge of the bed with his back to him, listening as Jesse retrieved the lube. He stared down at his hands, wondering why he felt so nervous as if it was his first time. The answer flared in the front of his mind. He pushed it away, too fearful to face it.

Jesse glanced at Evan, his heart constricting at how strained he looked, so different from the confident man he had grown used to. It made him fully understand how much the guilt over

Brian's death had weighed Evan down as he carried the pain of it alone for nearly four years. He crawled across the bed and knelt behind him.

"Maybe we should wait until later," he said softly.

Evan turned his gaze back toward him. "No. Please, Jess."

Jesse shifted to Evan's side. He placed one hand on Evan's chest, the other on his shoulder, and guided him back to lie on the bed. Evan moved at Jesse's commands, lifting his hips up to push his running pants off. Jesse took over for him, shed his own boxers, and brought his body over him.

Jesse caressed Evan's face with his fingertips, having so many things he wanted to say to him, to tell him he had fallen in love with him, that he could never picture any of his days to come without him, but feared saying the words so soon.

Evan gazed up at Jesse, seeing an emotion on his beautiful face, in his stunning indigo eyes, that he prayed was true, and at the same moment, knowing he didn't deserve it. He lifted his hand, resting it on the side of Jesse's face. Jesse closed his eyes. He turned his head toward Evan's hand, laying a warm kiss in his palm.

Evan drew his legs along Jesse's sides. Jesse leaned his weight down on his left elbow and slipped his right hand with lube-slicked fingers down Evan's body. He gently massaged and worked Evan open, wanting to make him feel as physically special as he had become to Jesse emotionally. He felt Evan's body melt under him. He slowly withdrew his fingers, took hold of his own arousal, and guided it into Evan.

Evan exhaled a ragged breath and wrapped his arms around Jesse. Jesse lowered his head, brushing his cheek against Evan's and softly kissed his throat and neck, moving his hips in gentle thrusts. He took one of Evan's hands and raised it to his lips, kissed along the back of it and locked their fingers together.

Evan buried his face against Jesse's neck, realizing that for the first time in his life he wasn't simply having sex, he was making love.

Jesse could feel Evan's turmoil of emotions and lifted his voice in a comforting whisper. "It's okay, Ev. You don't have to be alone anymore."

Evan squeezed his eyes shut, allowing two tears to escape and roll down his temples. "Stay with me," he said in a trembling voice.

Jesse nuzzled into Evan's hair. "I will. I'll always take care of you."

Evan let his head fall back on the pillow and met his eyes. "Jesse."

Evan's soft murmuring of his name told Jesse he felt the same for him, that those three words were lingering on Evan's tongue as well, and Evan held the same fear of saying it too soon. He didn't understand how it was possible to feel something so powerful for someone he had only known a few days, but he did, and he knew from the sheer intensity of his emotions it was more than a crush, more than a fling. He gazed down into Evan's azure eyes. Too soon or not, he didn't care. A time frame shouldn't be placed on when emotions should be articulated. When they were felt and known to be true, they should be expressed.

Jesse lowered his head, his lips touching Evan's in the softest of caresses. "Evan, I love you."

Evan pulled Jesse's breath into his body. "I love you too, Jess. So very much."

Jesse felt Evan's pain and fears retreat against the joy their confession brought. He put his smiling lips to Evan's and met him in a deep, slow kiss as he continued to make love to him.

CHAPTER SEVENTEEN

Jesse grinned at the sight of Kenny's silver Honda Civic swinging into the parking garage ahead of him, across the street from the Phoenix Studios. Using the pass Greg gave him that allowed him access to the private garage, he pulled into a space next to Kenny, grabbed his sheet music and a stack of apartment listings off the passenger seat, and climbed out of the black Enzo Ferrari.

"Holy shit!" Kenny said, bending down to peer inside the Ferrari. "I was looking at this thing when I pulled in. I hoped it was a chick driving so I could work a little of my magic."

"You don't want to try working your magic on me?"

Kenny stood up straight and scowled at him. "Funny."

Jesse watched Kenny walk toward the exit of the parking garage. He hadn't seen him since Evan had spent the night at their apartment, and thought by lying low it'd give Kenny time to adjust, but he acted even more pissed. During the past week, Jesse called him a few times and invited him over to practice some music, but Kenny said he wasn't feeling well. Now he realized Kenny had been avoiding him.

Jesse marched after him, snatched him by the upper arm, dragged him around and back toward the Enzo.

Kenny tugged against Jesse's hold. "What the hell are you doing?"

"Get in the car," Jesse demanded, hitting the remote to disarm the alarm.

"We're gonna be late!"

"So what if we are? They can't do shit until we walk in."

Jesse opened the passenger side door of the car. With a heavy sigh, Kenny climbed in. Jesse walked around to the driver's side, got in, and faced him.

Kenny gazed at the interior of the Ferrari. "This is so freakin' cool."

Jesse huffed out an impatient breath. "Right now, the only two members of Conquest are preparing to walk into a recording studio and they can't even be around each other without there being tension. I think getting that cleared up is a little more important than how cool this car is."

Kenny slumped down in the black leather seat, his eyes on the floor.

Jesse took in the distraught expression darkening Kenny's face. He mentally chastised himself for his impatience and spoke in a gentler voice. "Kenny, you and I have been due to sit down and talk about some things for a while now. And I'll admit, I've been avoiding it just as much as you because I haven't wanted to upset you, but we can't avoid it anymore.

"You've never cared what a person looked like, where they came from, how much money they had, you've always looked past those things to see what their personality was. You never even got mad when someone picked on you in school, well, except for that one kid who pushed you down in fifth grade and broke your Game Boy. I still don't know how I got stuck with detention and you didn't."

Kenny chuckled softly. "Because before I could get up, you had thrown him on the ground and were making him eat dirt until he apologized to me."

Jesse laid his head on the headrest, smiling from the memory. He rolled his head to the side and looked at Kenny. He didn't want to break the little bit of comfort they had gathered, but he also didn't want to have only brief moments of camaraderie with Kenny, he wanted every minute to be so. "I guess what I'm getting at is you've always accepted everybody for who they are, so I don't understand why it's so difficult for you to do that with me."

"It's not that I don't accept you," Kenny mumbled.

"But it is. You've known I'm gay since we were seventeen, but the first time I bring a guy home, you freak out on me."

Kenny spun in the car seat, anger flooding his face and voice. "And you think because of that I don't accept you? Did you ever stop to think maybe it was *the guy* you brought home who freaked me out?"

Jesse shook his head, confused. "Ev? Why would he freak you out?"

"Oh, I don't know. Maybe because he's one of the biggest recording artists in the last twenty years. Maybe because he always used to put on a show that he was into girls, then I get to witness him hanging all over you. Maybe because you never bothered sharing that half of your life with me, acting like I couldn't understand because I'm straight, and the first time you decide to let me in on it, you're shoving rock star Evan Arden in my face and telling me you spent the weekend at his mansion!" His voice quieted. "Or maybe because since you met him, you've been acting like no one else exists."

Kenny's sharp words stabbed into Jesse's chest with as much physical pain as a dagger. Jesse looked away from him. All this time he thought he was doing good by Kenny and their friendship by shielding him from his sexuality, he never thought he was actually damaging it.

"I'm sorry," Jesse said. His words sounded feeble to his own ears, he knew they sounded even weaker to Kenny's.

His voice dripping sarcasm, Kenny said, "Oh, well, that makes up for it. Thanks."

Both sat quiet. Jesse stared down at the Ferrari logo on the steering wheel, Kenny out the passenger side window. Tension hung in the car like a miasma. Jesse had heard silence could be deafening, but never really understood what it meant until that moment.

Kenny took a quick breath and held it, as if trying to decide on his words. "Will you answer one thing completely honestly for me?"

Jesse looked toward him. "I always answer you honestly."

"Did you sleep with him to get our contract?"

"No! I already told you that! You say I haven't confided in you about what I do with other guys, but here you sit accusing me of being a whore when I've laid everything out in the open for you about my relationship with Evan!"

"I'm not accusing you of being a whore! But I had to know."

"You knew when I told you last week," Jesse snarled between clenched teeth.

Silenced filled the Ferrari once again.

His gaze focused out the passenger side window, Kenny said softly, "You really like him, don't you?"

"I'm in love with him."

Kenny jerked his head toward him. "You just met him!"

"I can't help it. It's the way I feel, and he feels the same way. There's something very special between us. I don't know how to explain it, or if words even exist to begin to. I just know when I think about him, when I look at him, touch him, kiss him, hear him laugh, the feelings I get go so far down inside me that I know they have to be reaching my soul because I can't see the end of them."

Kenny stared at him for another moment, then slowly glanced away.

Jesse nudged Kenny with his elbow. "Not to mention how great the sex is. I thought I could be wild, but he's unbelievable!"

Kenny laughed under his breath and shoved Jesse on his shoulder. "Idiot."

"But hey, if you're so curious about my sex life, I'm more than willing to start bragging, and *damn*, do I have a lot to brag about. You already know about the first one, that Aaron guy on the beach, there's no point in reliving that, and I can skip over everything else and go straight to bragging about Ev, because all the stuff in between really isn't very entertaining. It's just been a lot of making out, groping, a blowjob here and there—"

"Alright! Can you at least ease me into hearing stories about my best friend doing things with guys I'm only used to seeing chicks do?"

A mischief filled smirk claimed Jesse's countenance. "But I can do things a girl can't, unless they have artificial aid, that is."

Kenny sighed in exasperation and looked down at his watch. "It's ten after nine. We better get in there."

Jesse caught Kenny's forearm to halt him from reaching for the door handle. "We're cool now, right?"

A smile warmed Kenny's face. "Yeah, we're cool."

Jesse leaned across the center console and puckered his lips. "Make up kiss?"

Kenny slammed him on the chest with the heel of his hand. "Dumbass!"

"Ow," Jesse whimpered, rubbing his chest as he climbed out of the car. He fell into stride beside Kenny and handed him the apartment listings. "Here, take those. The other day I told Ev that I was worried about you living in our apartment all alone, so he called his real estate agent and had her look up some apartments here on the North Side."

Kenny flipped through the listings as they crossed the street. "Did he bother telling her I'm not a multi-millionaire rock star like him? I can't afford any of these places. I can't even afford the shit-hole if I have to live there by myself."

"You'll be able to once our advance money comes in. I've already calculated a solid estimate of what it'll cost to record and promote the album, and how much we can safely take for ourselves to live off, including setting aside two equal amounts for our new band members. These places are well within reach, and I figured since rent is due next week on the shit-hole, I'll lend you the money to pay the first month's rent at one of these places and you can pay me back whenever."

"You were working this out the whole time you were gone," Kenny said quietly.

Jesse smiled, the look on Kenny's face and the tone in his voice telling him how happy Kenny was that while he had been with Evan he hadn't stopped thinking about him. He opened one of the double glass doors to the studio and stepped into the lobby.

They showed their driver's licenses to the security guard, and a blonde receptionist told them to wait while she informed Greg they were there. They stood in the lobby carpeted in dark maroon with small blue heraldic crests patterned on it. A large tapestry of a gold and red phoenix with flames for feathers and its beak opened wide in call hung on the wall to their left. A wooden plaque above it inscribed in Old English letters read,

Phoenix Records
Always Soaring

Jesse turned when he saw Greg walking down the hall directly across from the doors.

"Good morning, guys," Greg said. "I hope you took advantage of resting up this past week, because we'll be busting butts from here on out."

Jesse shook Greg's hand. "We're ready. I'm sorry we're late."

"Don't worry about it. Your prospective band members are here, but I'll give you a quick tour before I introduce you." Greg turned, leading the way back down the hall. He stopped and pointed to a small booth on their right. "This is the vocal booth with its own control room. This is where we can listen to you solo, Jesse, and make sure that we're optimizing your voice to its fullest potential."

Jesse looked in the room where a large microphone hung down from the ceiling.

Greg continued his march up the hall. "We have three full-sized live rooms with individual control rooms. We were pretty creative when we named them. They're Studios A, B, and C. We just passed Studio A, it was on the left. We also have a drum room deeper in the studio." He turned into a control room on the right. "And this is Studio B."

The large control room had a thick glass window above the control desk that overlooked the live room. Jesse stared at all the equipment and recorders, his head spinning at the sight of the control desk. He couldn't even begin to count all the knobs and switches for adjusting volume, pitch, bass, tempo. Huge speakers were set in the wall above the window and on the sidewalls.

"How can anyone know what all this stuff does?" he asked.

"That's where he comes in," Greg said, turning around.

A man in his early thirties with dark brown eyes and wavy black hair bound in a ponytail stood in the doorway of the control room. He had a white coffee mug in his right hand with a yellow smiley face on it, but the smiley face had one eye closed, its tongue sticking out, and a little yellow hand flipping the bird.

"This is Jeremy Kane," Greg said. "He's an amazing sound engineer and will be one of a few people who will work with you on this album to make it flawless, but for now, he's your main guy. He'll help you get just the right sound you want."

Jeremy shifted his coffee mug to his left hand and held his right out to Jesse. "I'm really looking forward to working with you, Jesse. I've listened to your demo a few times and your voice is freakin' unbelievable, dude. We're going to have a blast recording this."

"Thanks. I'm really looking forward to it, too. This is Kenny Cooper, he plays guitar."

Jeremy took Kenny's hand. "You don't need introductions. You got mad skills on a six string."

"Thanks, man," Kenny said.

Greg headed toward the door. "Well, I guess we should introduce you to your possible new bandmates. They're down in the chill-out room."

"The what?" Jesse asked.

"The chill-out room. Some studios call it the green room, we call it the chill-out room. It's an area where you can escape the music, because let's face it, there will be moments when you need to step back from it."

Jesse and Kenny followed Greg down the hall and stepped in to what seemed like a mini apartment. There were two light tan couches in the room, one against a wall opposite the door, another across from it with an oval wooden coffee table in between. Four plush red chairs sat near the arms of the couches, two at each end. To the right of the door was another sitting area with a TV, and to the left, a small kitchen.

Jesse briefly glanced around the room, but his attention was more on the people sitting on the couches. One he already knew, Tim. He didn't bother acknowledging him and looked away to the man and woman sitting on the couch by the wall. He met the deep green eyes of the woman first, who he guessed to be in her early twenties. She wore a pair of khaki Capri pants and a tight powder blue baby-doll T-shirt that hugged her curves and showed off her well toned biceps. Her dark red hair was pulled up in a long braid.

Jesse shifted his gaze to the young guy sitting on the couch beside her. He didn't figure the guy could be over twenty-four, but he also didn't look like a potential member of a rock band with how he wore his straight pale blond hair pulled back in a smooth, neat ponytail that ended at the top of his shoulders. The guy's clothes were immaculate; black dress pants perfectly pressed, a white shirt with a high button collar, and a black jacket without so much as a hint of lint. He moved his eyes from the guy's light blue ones when Greg spoke up.

"Well, introductions first. Guys, this is Trish O'Connell. She's been a studio drummer with Phoenix for nearly two years and is extremely skilled on the skins. I think you'll be very impressed when you hear her play." Greg motioned to the blond guy. "And this is Julian Forrester. He's a Julliard trained classical pianist who's guested with several orchestras, including the New York Philharmonic, but now he's looking to break into something a little more lively, and we were the fortunate ones who learned of him before anyone else snatched him up." He gestured to Jesse and Kenny. "Trish, Julian, this is Jesse

Alexander, vocalist, songwriter, and multi-instrumentalist. And this is Kenny Cooper, lead guitar and co-songwriter."

Both Trish and Julian rose and walked to greet them.

Trish smiled and extended her hand to Jesse. "I'm so happy to finally meet you. I almost died when I heard your voice on the demo. It's so beautiful."

"Thanks," Jesse said, thinking he caught a flirtatious tinge in her voice. "I'm kind of surprised to see a woman drummer. If you're so good, why aren't you in a band?"

"Jesse!" Kenny scolded. He quickly offered his hand to Trish. "Sorry about him. His mouth and brain work on separate systems."

Trish giggled. "I can see that." She turned to Jesse. "I don't have a band because, as you have so astutely noticed, I have boobs instead of balls, and that can be an issue for some boys. I'm good enough to give them the clean, solid beats they need for their albums, but when tour time comes around, my job is done. When you play live the audience accepts mistakes and sloppy sounds a lot more readily than on a studio recorded album. If this is an issue for you, it's not a big deal. I can drum on your album, and when you hit the road, you can find a boy to play with."

Jesse decided to keep the cocky comment that danced on his tongue in response to Trish's end remark to himself. "The only issue is what you expected when you got propositioned for this gig. If you're expecting to only be our studio drummer, then this isn't going to work. If you drum on our album, then you'll tour with us too, and do all the other stuff like videos and interviews. You'll be a full member of the band. I just want to let you know so you can decide what's best for you. I'm not playing games here."

Trish's full lips parted with a soft gasp. "I don't know what to say."

"Of course, this all depends on if you can really play," Jesse added, giving a nonchalant flip of his hand. "This is serious music, not Barbie Makes a Record."

Trish laughed. "Why you little jerk."

Jesse gave her a wink and a smile, then took a step toward Julian. He looked him up and down as he offered his hand, and decided to test a suspicion he had. "Julliard, huh? Impressive. Just so you know, because I want you to be comfortable in this band from the start, I'm gay."

"Son of a bitch," Kenny muttered in disbelief, turning away from Jesse.

One corner of Julian's lips lifted as he shook Jesse's hand. "And you won't be the only one if I get this gig."

"I hope I'm not your type. It could make things a bit awkward."

"I think you're probably about everyone's type with that pretty face, though I normally go for more of the tall, rugged, athletic boys. And you?"

"I only have one type, and he's the most breathtaking and talented man in the world."

"That's quite a reputation you give him to live up to, but since you're in a relationship things should be perfect. I absolutely loathe cheaters and have a personal vow to never become one." Julian's eyes moved down Jesse's body. "Your taste in clothing is superb. Versace T-shirt, Gucci belt, Armani jeans…and the most beaten pair of Nikes I've ever seen."

Jesse laughed. "Actually, the Nikes are the only things that belong to me. All the rest are my boyfriend's. I've been staying with him and he doesn't care if I raid his closet."

"He's a true gentleman of sophistication then."

Jesse nodded and glanced around the room. His smile wavered at what he saw. Kenny stared at him, his mouth agape in a mortified expression. He met Trish's eyes, but she flicked them away as if pretending they hadn't made eye contact. Tim looked at Greg with a glory filled sneer that spoke of I-told-you-so, and Greg had an expression akin to someone who had bet their lifesavings on the favorite to win the Super Bowl and had just finished watching the team get pummeled. Other than

Julian, the only one who didn't seem rattled was Jeremy, who stood leaning back against the wall sipping his coffee.

"I'm sorry if this is a shock to some of you," Jesse said. "But it had to come out sooner or later if we're all going to be working together. If it makes anyone uncomfortable, I guess the only thing I can say is to get the hell over it because it's just the way things are."

"Jesse!" Kenny yelled. "Subtlety, dude! Seriously!"

Jesse moved toward Greg, meeting his eyes with a steady stare. "Is this a problem?"

Greg looked into Jesse's eyes, then shook his head. "No, though Kenny has a point about subtlety. But we'll discuss that later. Right now, we need to put our attention to the issues of the moment and that's giving Trish and Julian an idea of your vision for the sound of this album."

Jesse decided to grant Greg his escape and turned toward the couches. He sat on the one closest to the wall with Kenny on his left, Julian taking a seat on his right, and began passing around his sheet music.

Julian grinned at him as he took his copies. "You're a bold one, aren't you?"

Jesse answered him with a smirk and handed Trish her copies. She gave him a weak smile before lowering her gaze to the papers. He had only made enough copies for Greg and two others, so he handed Jeremy his originals to look over since he and Kenny had every note and harmony memorized.

He turned a harsh eye on Tim. "There's not any left for you."

Tim shrugged. "I don't need to look at them."

"I didn't figure you did."

Greg glanced back and forth between them. His gaze came to a rest on Tim. "That's not exactly the attitude I expect you to demonstrate, Tim."

The muscles in Tim's jaw clenched. A strained smile curved his lips, and he leaned over the arm of his chair to look off Jeremy's papers.

Jesse forced down the burst of glee at Tim's reprimand and brought his attention to his music. "I guess as far as a vision for sound goes, we're definitely focused more toward the rock side, but my main thing is to not have it too heavy. I like keeping things light, fast, and fun. That's why I lay down an electronic backline from the synth in some of our songs, to bring in that extra kick and add some diversity. Between the electronic backbeat and the front rhythms of the drums, that's why we don't feel we need a bass player, plus I can play the bass myself in the songs that I feel need it. Basically, we have a lot going on in our songs. They're refined, but also carry a strong, bold edge. We get our strength from the guitar and drums, our refinement from the keyboard, and the fun, lively part from the electric beat. And obviously, my voice is of unquestionable importance since it's what everyone really wants to hear."

Julian sat forward, his thin eyebrows drawing closer in concentration. "In 'Shattered,' you go through some fairly complex movements with the piano."

Jesse nodded. "Yeah, but sadly I've always had to use the keyboard to substitute for a real piano during performances, but that won't be the case anymore since I'm assuming I could have a piano on stage during our live shows."

"Absolutely," Greg said.

After an hour of reviewing Conquest's songs, Greg stood up. "How about we go down to Studio B and have Jesse and Kenny play for us, since if you guys are feeling anything like I am, you're dying to hear these two without the background static and a hundred drunken women screaming for Jesse to take his pants off like what was on the demo."

Jesse chuckled as he got up. "Being wicked hot is as much of a curse as it is a blessing sometimes."

"That ego of yours truly is magnificent," Julian teased.

"It's not an ego when it's the truth," Jesse retorted.

Everyone followed Greg down to Studio B. They stepped into the live room paneled in golden oak and stocked with a full drum kit, bass guitars, six different types of electric guitars, two acoustics, four keyboards, and a black grand piano. Greg, Trish, and Jeremy gave Jesse, Kenny, and Julian an introductory lesson in setting up the equipment, and an hour later everything was ready to go.

Jesse sat at the piano, doing his vocal stretching exercises by matching his voice to the notes he played.

"Let's start off with 'Shattered,' Jess," Greg said through the control room P.A.

Jesse nodded and continued warming up while Kenny finished perfectly tuning a borrowed Fender Stratocaster.

Greg turned to Tim. "I forgot to tell them they could help themselves to what's in the fridge. Would you go get him a bottle of water so he can wet his throat?"

"Sure." Tim shoved his chair away from the control desk. He managed to keep his cool until he stepped out of the control room, then allowed rage to contort his face, and his hands to clench into fists at being the one who had to cater to Jesse. He stomped down to the chill-out room, rounded the corner of the doorway, and stopped in mid-stride at who he was confronted with.

Evan stood by the refrigerator taking a drink from a bottle of water. He lowered the bottle, twisted on the cap, and raised his gaze to Tim.

The lethal glare that greeted Tim forced him to stumble back half a step before he realized he had done so. He caught his reaction and straightened his posture, reminding himself of what Evan was, and almost laughed aloud at being unnerved by one of his kind, but the urge to laugh died quicker than it arose when he saw Evan advancing toward him in long, stalking strides. He stuck out his hand under the pretense of wanting to shake Evan's, but more to keep distance between them.

"This is a surprise. It's great to see you again, Mr. Arden."

Evan smacked Tim's hand aside with a loud crack and stepped forward until they were inches apart. He lowered his voice to a growl. "Don't you dare offer your hand to me as if we're friends."

Tim swayed backward as though his will battled his body to not back down. "Is there a problem?"

"Yeah, there's a problem. Did you really think he wouldn't tell me what you accused him of?"

For an instant, Tim forgot the threat standing before him and let his repulsion slip through. "I knew it. He didn't confirm it that day, but I knew it."

"You don't know shit!" Evan roared.

Tim flinched at Evan's booming voice and fell back a step.

Evan moved forward. "I'm going to make this real clear, and you should consider yourself blessed that you're getting this warning; if you so much as breathe and it offends him, you'll be shitting your own teeth for a week courtesy of my fist. You got me?"

Tim gave the smallest of nods.

"Now move the fuck out of my way."

Tim scurried from Evan's path.

Evan walked past him, not deigning to spare Tim another glance. As he approached Studio B, the sound of piano and electric guitar leaked through the open door. When he arrived at the studio, he peeked in and saw Jesse didn't have anything to drink. Knowing how he personally needed lots of water when singing, he decided to get some for Jesse. He stepped into the control room with everyone's back to him and saw who he assumed was the sound engineer bouncing behind the control desk, saying, "I'm so excited! I'm so excited! I'm so excited!"

A red haired woman smiled down at the bouncing engineer. "You're a happy little fellow, aren't you?"

"He's got a great voice. I feel like I'm getting ready to listen to Evan Arden."

"So that's why my ears were ringing. And here I thought it was one too many concerts."

All the heads in the control room turned to Evan.

"Evan," Greg said, almost too shocked to get his name out.

Trish sprang between them and pushed her hand toward Evan. "I can't tell you what an honor it is to meet you, Mr. Arden. I've always wanted to play with you."

Evan took her hand and presented her with a teasing smirk. "My my, aren't we a forward girl."

Trish's cheeks flared to crimson. "N-no, that's not what I meant."

"Evan, don't tease her," Greg intervened. "She's quite possibly the new drummer for Conquest, Trish O'Connell. And this is Julian Forrester, pianist and prospective keyboardist."

After introductions, Greg turned to Evan. "I can't believe you're here. What made you come down?"

Evan nodded toward Jesse. "Him."

"Are you guys ready—hey!" Jesse yelled from the live room, waving wildly at Evan.

Evan smiled and waved back. "He asked me to come here."

Greg's brow furrowed, his mouth set in a frown.

Evan sat down beside Julian and grabbed the P.A. mic. "Well, are you going to sing, or just sit in there like a little boy with stage fright all day?"

Jesse threw him a playful glare and turned back to the piano. He sounded the first notes of "Shattered," took a breath, and lifted his tenor in harmony with the instrument.

"I knew he had a voice from the demo," Trish said, "but it's nothing like hearing him in person. He's so clear and pitch perfect."

"He's a sound engineer's wet dream," Jeremy said.

"His style of playing is very classical, too. Very Mozartesque," Julian added.

"He's gifted," Evan said simply, resting his chin in his hand with his elbow propped up on the control desk, gazing at Jesse as if entranced.

Greg glanced at him out the corner of his eye, then turned back to Jesse. "This song is a destined top single, but I'm thinking I'll have it released as either the second or third single from the album and come out with 'Euphoria' as the first. 'Euphoria' has such a good beat and guitar, and I want to set the precedent that Conquest is a rock band who can jam hard as well as put out works like this. Though, the lyrics are weaker in 'Euphoria.'" He looked at Evan. "He's not as much of a lyricist as you are, but then, he hasn't lived as much, either."

Evan glared at him. "You're underestimating him."

Jesse coaxed the last soft note from the piano and looked up at everyone. "How was that?"

"Not bad for a rookie," Evan answered.

"Hmm, is that jealousy I hear?" Jesse quipped.

"Alright, let's break for lunch," Greg said, already walking toward the door. "When we get back, we'll get you guys out there so they can hear you play, then hopefully we'll have everyone jamming before the day is over."

Evan rose to greet Jesse when he walked into the control room, a knowing smile on his lips.

Jesse's gaze moved slowly over him. Evan wore black leather pants pulled over a pair of black snakeskin boots. His dark blue shirt clung tight to his torso, the front cut open from the collar to mid-chest to resemble a cross. Small blue mesh crosses hinting at his skin beneath patterned the shirt. Silver and thin black leather bracelets dangled from his wrists, and each finger was adorned with silver rings, some set with blue gemstones. He had changed out the two gold hoops he wore in his left ear for two large diamond studs, and in addition, up on the cartilage of his right he had a silver cuff with a cross hanging from it and a blue sapphire in the center. Resting on top of his head was a pair of silver-rimmed, blue lens sunglasses.

Jesse stepped close to him and wrapped his arms around his neck. The instant their bodies met in the embrace, heat rolled through his groin. "Did you get all rock-starred out just for me?"

"Yeah. I remember you telling me how hot you always thought I was done up and how fine my ass looked in leather pants. Do I still look good dressed like this?"

Jesse pushed his hips toward him. "Everyone's left us for a moment. Let's lock the door and I'll show you how good I think you look."

Evan grazed his lips over Jesse's. "Your first day in the studio and you already want to do naughty things here. How about we drive to lunch separate from the others and I make sure we hit all the red lights so we can play a little bit along the way?"

Jesse looked at him with a pouting expression. "I guess that will tide me over."

Evan laughed softly. "Horny little brat." He slipped his fingertips under the black leather chords of the sun choker around Jesse's neck, gently touching his throat. "You sounded incredible."

"Would you expect anything less?" Jesse snickered.

Evan tousled Jesse's hair and handed him the bottle of water, then slipped his arm around his waist and led him toward the chill-out room. They walked in to a discussion of what to have for lunch. Jesse tensed when he saw Tim, knowing his and Evan's relationship was now fully revealed, but Tim kept his back to them and his mouth shut.

Kenny left the group to stand by them and rolled his eyes. "I suggested Uno's, but apparently no one wants to listen to the Chicago native on restaurant ideas."

"Maybe tonight the three of us can go," Jesse said. "Oh, and Carrie, if you want to invite her."

Kenny shook his head. "We can go, but since I broke up with her two days ago, I doubt she'd want to come."

"That's awesome!" Jesse blurted out, then quickly softened his voice and forced some sympathy into it. "I'm sorry, man."

Kenny laughed and shoved him. "No you're not! You couldn't stand her."

"Yeah, but you seemed to like her, for some inexplicable reason. Why'd you break up with her?"

"Ever since I told her about the contract, all she could talk about was money this and money that. She kept pestering me to buy her a new outfit, asking when I was going to get a new car, and crap like that. And I thought, damn, if she's grubbing for cash this bad now, what's she gonna be like when we hit it really big? Not to mention, why the hell would I want to tie myself down to one girl when there's gonna be hundreds, *thousands*, of so much hotter ones to sleep with?"

"Very logical reasoning," Evan said. "And at least you're lucky that you don't have to compete with a hot lead singer for the ladies."

Kenny looked at Evan, his eyes slowly widening as his words sank in. "You're right. That's never even hit me. And Julian's gay too, so I wouldn't have to compete with him, either. And Trish seems like a really straight chick since she was looking pretty hot for Jess when we all met."

Evan aimed a sharp look at Jesse.

Jesse forced out a chuckle and waved his hand at Kenny's words. "She was not."

Lost in his fantasy, Kenny continued, "I'll be the only straight guy in the band, so all the women will be mine. All the models, actresses, fan girls, big boobs, little boobs, long legs, blondes, brunettes, younger, older, all races, all colors, they'll all be mine." He grabbed Jesse's shoulders, shouting his elation. "They'll all be mine!"

"Yeah, freak!" Jesse laughed. "They'll all be yours, and everyone here knows it."

Kenny glanced over his shoulder at the others, who from the entertained expressions seemed to have caught a fair bit of the conversation. He let go of Jesse and shifted his weight from one foot to the other in his embarrassment.

Evan flicked his head toward the door. "You guys decided on Lawry's, right? Let's go, I'm starving."

Kenny gave Evan a grateful smile for taking the attention off him and sped for the door. Evan kept his arm around Jesse's waist and followed Kenny's lead out of the studio.

Greg caught Evan's shoulder as he stepped outside. "Can I talk to you for a minute?"

"Yeah, sure." Evan dug in his front pocket for his car keys and handed them to Jesse. "I drove the Cayenne here. Let's take that instead of the Enzo."

Jesse started across the street. "Don't keep me waiting."

"Don't worry, gorgeous. I'll be coming soon."

Greg waited until Jesse disappeared into the parking garage, then leaned toward Evan, his voice just above a hiss. "What the hell are you doing?"

"Going to lunch," Evan said, putting on his sunglasses. "Prime rib sounds really good, don't you think?"

"Don't pull your little question dodging bullshit with me. I guess now I know the real reason you canceled coming over to have dinner at my house last week. Are you insane? Have you completely lost it? Why don't you go to the tabloids and pose with your tongue down his throat and end both your careers right now!"

"I think you're overacting. These people would have to know about our relationship if they're going to be in a band with him."

"No they wouldn't. No one who played for you ever knew about your sexuality except for JJ and Brad Delfini. Not to mention, these are people I'm not yet one hundred percent certain can be trusted with this information. It's not like you to be so reckless. But besides that, how the hell can you be sleeping with that kid?"

"He's not a kid and lighten up." Evan moved to walk away, but Greg yanked him back by his shoulder.

"I should've known better than to think you were interested in his career because of his talent. I know you don't give a damn about your own career, but don't go screwing up his just because you want to have a fling."

Evan slapped Greg's hand off him and stabbed his index finger into Greg's chest. "I care for you greatly, but if you ever say something like that to me again, I will lay you the fuck out. What I do in *my* personal life is *my* business."

"If only you could keep it your business." When the last word left his mouth, Greg thought Evan really was going to hit him. He saw Evan's arm twitch, his fingers balled into a fist, but somehow, Evan restrained himself at the last second. He had seen Evan's temper unleash at less provocation than what he just gave him, and felt a pang of guilt that Evan's words had been true about caring for him.

Greg softened his voice. "I'm only trying to protect you. Both of you. And after what I saw of Jesse today, I'm not sure I'll be able to."

Evan shook his head slightly. "What do you mean?"

"He announced being gay to a room full of strangers with such brash and basically told everyone they had no choice but to accept it."

Evan laughed under his breath. "He's a confident little thing, isn't he?"

"This isn't funny, Evan. I'm not sure he'll be able to hide it when he hits the public eye."

"Who says he has to?"

Greg frowned at him. "You know firsthand how these things work. It's not that there aren't gay or bi performers out there, but most of them only come out after they've been around for a few years, and let's face it, in this country it's safer to start out pretending to be a straight entertainer to build up your fan base. With Jesse, I could almost believe his talent would carry him past the prejudices, but add him singing to the world that he's Evan Arden's lover and it'd be a disaster. You may not have released new material in a while, but you're still one of the most loved singers in the world, and for this new singer to come out saying you're a couple, can you even begin to imagine the consequences?" He paused, and spoke his next words cautiously. "That is, if you're genuinely serious about him."

"I'm real serious about him." Evan sighed and turned to walk across the street toward the parking garage, talking more to himself than to Greg. "It'd figure I'd fall in love with someone who wanted a life in the spotlight."

Greg stopped walking when he heard Evan's words.

Evan reached the sidewalk on the other side of the street and turned around. "I know this is a surprising revelation, but you should probably get out of the road before you get run over."

Greg blinked his shock away and hurried across the street. He walked beside him into the parking garage and put his arm around Evan's shoulders. "You're going to be the death of me, I know it. The next thing you're going to tell me is you want to start recording again."

"Actually, I wanted to talk to you about that."

Greg stopped, his arm dropped off Evan's shoulders.

Evan faced him. "How long would it take you to get me a band? I've got some new material I want to lay down."

CHAPTER EIGHTEEN

Jesse stood behind Evan, waiting for him to unlock the access door to the house, unable to move his eyes away from his black leather clad ass. All afternoon he had been tortured by the sight of it, tormented by the need to grab and grope it, so much so he nearly bowed out of having dinner with Kenny to get Evan to himself. But after hearing Trish and Julian play, he and Kenny decided they needed them in the band and taking them out to dinner was the right thing to do, despite it leaving him unbearably hot for Evan a few hours longer.

Evan opened the door and stepped in. "How's your throat feeling? I know you said it was still bothering you at dinner."

Jesse leaped up the steps and kicked off his shoes by the door. "It still feels a little scratchy. I really don't think it was necessary for Greg to be so damn hard assed today. I've never sang so much in one day in my life."

Evan headed into the family room. "He was testing you to see what you're capable of, but I agree, I thought he was pushing you too hard. I almost stepped in, but I thought you might get upset."

Jesse flopped down on the couch and sprawled out. "I wouldn't have."

"I'll remember that for next time. The last thing you need is to get nodules on your cords." Evan turned toward the kitchen. "I'll make you some green tea. It'll make your throat feel better."

"Thanks." Jesse closed his eyes to recharge his body and be ready for the physical actualizations of the fantasies he'd had about Evan throughout the day. His mind drifted to Julian and Trish.

When Julian took to the piano, he sat beside him, awestruck by his ability as he watched Julian's graceful fingers work the keys in Chopin's Polonaise No. 6. Not to be upstaged, he felt it necessary to combat Julian's artful style with his own by playing the Rondo alla Turca from Mozart's Piano Sonata No. 11. When he finished in triumph, he glanced at everyone's stunned expressions, except for Evan and Kenny, who both knew his classical capabilities. Julian had laughed and flung up his hands, asking what the hell he needed him for, and he knew then that Julian would be a perfect addition to Conquest, especially after hearing him play "Shattered" without a single misstep and seeing him handle the synth and keyboard with masterful skill.

Trish was without a doubt the best drummer he had ever played with, despite a couple errors during his song "Vanish," but he didn't hold that against her considering how heavy and fast the rhythms had to be and it was only her first time playing them. It nagged at him that his first impression of her flirtatiousness was accurate since Kenny picked up on it, too. He imagined her hope of anything with him got pretty well squashed with his declaration of his sexuality and Evan's appearance.

Even with Evan's footfalls silent on the carpet, Jesse didn't need to open his eyes to know he had entered the family room. He was so tuned to Evan's presence, he no longer needed sight and sound to detect him.

Evan stopped in front of him and held out a warm mug. "Here you go."

Jesse opened his eyes and sat forward to accept it. He blew away the tendril of steam rising from the liquid and took a sip. He let it trickle down his throat, the heat of the tea comforting the scratchiness he felt. He took a longer drink, then set the mug down on the coffee table. He smiled and looked at him. "Thanks for coming to the studio today. I was really surprised when I saw you standing in the control room."

"Why? You asked me to come down there, didn't you?"

"Yeah, but it was when we were at the museum, and you didn't answer. You just walked off to go look at that funky prehistoric turtle."

Evan stroked his fingers through Jesse's hair. "Whenever you ask me to do something for you, you should know the answer will always be yes, even if I don't say it. I would never deny any request you ask of me."

Jesse's smile brightened further. He wrapped his arms around Evan's waist and laid his head against Evan's firm abdomen.

Evan continued to softly stroke his hair. "Is your throat feeling better?"

"A lot." Jesse nosed under Evan's shirt. "But I know what'll make me feel even better." Near the button of Evan's leather pants, he took the top fold in his teeth, gave it a sharp tug, and freed the button. "That little appetizer you gave me on our way to the restaurant wasn't nearly enough." He stood, sliding his body up Evan's, and with both hands, grabbed Evan's ass in a squeezing grip. "I've been dying to do that all day, and you've been such a tease strutting around in these things. It borders on cruel."

Evan laughed softly. "Sorry. I won't wear leather pants ever again."

"Don't you dare make a threat like that." Jesse dug his fingers into Evan's ass cheeks and jerked him forward.

Evan sucked in a sharp breath, his head fell back slightly.

Jesse licked a line up Evan's exposed throat and nipped lightly under his jaw. "It looks like the sadist is in a bit of a masochistic mood tonight."

Evan grinned, his head fell back further to give more of his throat to Jesse. "Maybe a little."

Jesse moved his hands under Evan's shirt. He rubbed his chest and squeezed against the strength in Evan's pectorals, then circled his nipples with his thumbs.

Evan laid his hands over Jesse's, halting his motions. "Before we get carried away, there's something I want to talk to you about."

Jesse halted his affections and took a half step back, looking at Evan in concern. "What is it? Is everything okay?"

Evan took Jesse's hand and led him to the couch, guiding him to sit beside him. "Everything's great, but I have something important I want to tell you." He sat quiet for a moment, his eyes focused on the floor rather than on Jesse. He filled his lungs with a deep breath and turned on the couch to face him. "I've been thinking a lot about all the things we've talked about and I've decided to hit the studio and record a new album."

Jesse stared at him. He blinked a couple times, then stammered out, "Are...are you serious?"

"Yeah."

Jesse flung his arms around Evan's neck. "That's awesome! You don't know how happy I am to hear that!"

Evan held him tighter. He squeezed his eyes shut, his voice came soft. "I thought you would be."

"When are you going to start?"

"Probably after my birthday. That should give Greg time to contact the people who played with me in the past to see if they want to suffer through another album with me. I think I'll call JJ myself, though, and see what he's up to." Evan relaxed his embrace. "But, I don't want you to think I'm trying to steal your thunder. I'm already planning on releasing my album a couple months after yours so yours won't get overshadowed."

Jesse arched one slender eyebrow. "Really. That's so considerate of you."

Evan caught Jesse sarcastic tone. "I didn't mean that as an insult. It's just the reality of how things will be when I release new material."

"Uh huh. Well, I want you to know I'll do everything I can to help you make a successful comeback. I'll even talk to Greg about having you be my opening act."

"Opening act!"

"Yeah. I'm a very generous guy," Jesse chuckled.

"You better be after that comment," Evan said, and silenced Jesse's snickering with his lips.

CHAPTER NINETEEN

"Brandon Alexander?"

The door to the Phoenix Records studios hadn't closed behind Brandon when he heard a female voice call his name. He looked toward the blonde receptionist sitting behind her large desk and the security guard leaning against it. "That's me."

The receptionist gave him a welcoming smile. "I thought so. Jesse told me to expect his older brother about this time and you two look a little alike. If I could ask you to show me an ID to confirm it, then you can go in."

Brandon dug in his front pocket and pulled out his money clip where he kept his credit cards and driver's license. He handed her the license.

She looked at it and handed it back while pointing to the hall. "Jesse will either be in the first studio on your right past the vocal booth, or further down the hall in the chill-out room on your left. The pizza they ordered just arrived, so my guess would be the latter."

"Thanks," Brandon said, and headed down the hall.

The last time he saw Jesse had been two weeks ago when he first met Evan. They hadn't gone so long without seeing each other since the period when Jesse still lived with their parents and he had already been kicked out. He didn't like it. Even though they talked on the phone every day, between Jesse being busy the week before with his new band members, and his being wrapped up with his latest audition, they couldn't fit a visit in. But that wasn't the way things should be. They were brothers, not someone to be squeezed in between obligations. And he almost forgot the other reason they hadn't hung out, Evan.

Brandon gritted his teeth. He wondered if Evan was there. If he was, he wouldn't let him slip by like the last time. He had thought a lot about their encounter, and the more he did, the more Evan's snide comments and air of superiority pissed him off. The only thing that confused him was how quickly Evan shifted from aggressive to congenial when Jesse walked up at Uno's. He couldn't figure out if Evan tried to hide how he actually was from Jesse, or if he covered the tension between them to not distress Jesse. He wanted to believe it was the latter. He hoped with all his heart it was for Jesse's sake.

He heard Jesse's voice coming from an open door on the left side of the hall, and chuckled to himself. Jesse babbled about how his birthday was October 7th and Kenny's August 12th, then questioned others on their birthdays. A male voice answered he would turn twenty-five in November, a female replied she had turned twenty-two that past January. Jesse called her an "old lady," and the next thing Brandon heard was Jesse yelling "Ow!" He stepped in the doorway and saw Jesse sitting on a couch rubbing his arm, and an attractive redheaded woman, who could only be Trish from Jesse's description of her, smirking at him. His eyes fell on the marvelously hot blond guy whose demeanor spoke of sophistication and knew he must be Julian.

"Damn girl, you punch like a guy," Jesse said.

"And don't you forget it," Trish retorted.

"So this is the busy life of a rock star," Brandon said.

"Brandon!" Jesse leaped up and dashed toward him. He threw his arms around him in a crushing hug. "You're late, asshole!"

"It's good to see you too, jerk-off," Brandon laughed, embracing him in return.

"It feels like it's been forever! I was talking to Ev this morning about how it sucks that we haven't gotten to see each other and he said we should set aside a specific night every week for us to have dinner so we'll always see each other. I think that's an awesome idea, don't you? I know Friday, Saturday, and Sunday are out because you always have shows those days. But hell, sometimes you're performing or rehearsing six days in a week, so I'm not sure what night would be best. What do you think?"

Trying to catch up with Jesse's light speed oratory, Brandon said, "I think you need to cool it on the caffeine, spaz boy."

Jesse huffed and frowned at him.

Brandon chuckled. "I think it's a great idea, and we can always get together before I have to be at the theatre on performance nights. Tuesdays are usually quiet. How about then?"

"Sounds fine to me, and since today is Tuesday, we can get together tonight."

"That works out perfect because we actually have something really big to celebrate." Brandon grabbed Jesse by his upper arms. "Guess who's going to be playing the Phantom in the new production of *The Phantom of the Opera*? That's right! Only the greatest stage actor to ever hit Chicago! Playing the Emcee in *Cabaret* was one thing, but this is the freakin' Phantom! It's gonna be a huge production! And it's set to run for a whole year!"

Jesse wrapped Brandon in another embrace. "That's incredible! I didn't even know you were going for that role. Why didn't you tell me?"

"It all went down so fast. I just auditioned Saturday, and then I thought it'd be a good surprise in case I got it."

"It's a great surprise! I'm so proud of you!"

"Thanks," Brandon said softly, "but I never would've gotten it if it wasn't for you."

Jesse startled at the confession. "Me? What did I do?"

"All that time you spent helping me with my voice when I was going for *Cabaret* really meant a lot. I never would have gotten the part if it wasn't for you, which means I never would have been given the chance to audition for *Phantom*. The director of *Phantom* was only seeing the big boys for the role, but he had seen me in *Cabaret* and called me to come in."

"Well, I'm glad you think I helped so much, but you need to give yourself some props, too. If you didn't have the skills, all the coaching in the world couldn't have gotten you where you are. I can't wait to tell Ev. He's going to be so happy for you."

Brandon nodded, but looked doubtful at Jesse's words. He caught Jesse's wrist and pulled him out in the hall away from listening ears. "So how are things going with you guys? Is he treating you good?"

Jesse smiled and leaned one shoulder against the wall. "He treats me like a prince."

Brandon looked him up and down. "Well, you look good. You look like you've put on a little weight, actually."

Jesse sucked in a horrified gasp. "I have *not* put on weight! If I've put on anything it's muscle, because I'm working out a lot since he's got an entire gym in the house."

Brandon let out a sarcastic snort. "Yeah, that must be it. And settle down. I didn't mean you look fat. I just meant you look healthy, like you're eating better."

Jesse winked at him. "Well fed and well fucked."

Brandon rolled his eyes. "Cute. I'm kind of surprised you haven't gotten bored with him yet."

"You wouldn't say that if you had any idea of what he's like."

"Well how am I supposed to know when your stingy ass hasn't given me hardly any details?"

Jesse squinted at him in an accusing glare. "Do you think I don't remember all the things you used to say that you'd like to do to him during your fanboy days? You're hard enough for him without me feeding it."

Jesse looked past Brandon and saw Evan walking toward them. He moved to greet him, but Brandon pushed him on the arm and stopped him.

"You're not getting out of it this time," Brandon said. "I've always shared all the details of my sexcapades with you. Be fair."

Evan stopped behind Brandon and cocked his head, smirking as he listened to him continue.

"He's got those slender hips that are built for sex and an ass so perfect it had to have been chiseled by a god. I bet he takes it as good as he gives it, doesn't he?"

"Actually," Evan said, "I'm a lot like a snake. I can do it for twenty-four hours straight and I swallow everything whole. Does that help?"

Brandon jumped and spun around.

Jesse burst out laughing. "And there you have it. Anything else you want to know?"

Brandon laughed softly and held his hand out to Evan. "Sorry about that."

Evan took Brandon's hand and laid his other over top of it. "Don't be. I'm flattered."

Brandon stared at him, shocked by the warmth in Evan's voice.

Evan let go of his hand and went to Jesse.

Jesse embraced him and placed a soft kiss on his lips. "We've got plans tonight. We're going to take Brandon out to celebrate. He's just landed the role of his life playing the Phantom in a new production of *The Phantom of the Opera*."

Evan turned toward Brandon. "That's wonderful! Congratulations!"

Brandon nodded in appreciation. "Thanks."

Evan put one arm over Jesse's shoulders, the other around Brandon's. "You pick the place, Brandon. Anywhere you want to go and don't even think about prices, because it's all on me tonight."

Brandon suffered another moment of total shock. "You don't have to do that."

"But I want to and I'm going to whether you like it or not. Then afterward, you can come over to our place, and we'll express our deepest congrats and happiness all through the night in the comfort of our king-sized bed."

Jesse exhaled an exasperated sigh. "You really need to let that demented little fantasy go. It's never going to happen. He's my brother."

Evan looked at him with a wicked smirk. "But that's what makes it so hot. It's so dirty and wrong."

Brandon patted Evan on the back. "Sorry, Evan, but he's right. However, if you'd be cool with having him stand aside and just be the cameraman, I could probably handle that."

"Alright!" Evan laughed.

Jesse shook Evan's arm off his shoulders and jabbed him on the chest with his index finger. "What makes you think I'd ever share you with anyone? And you," he whirled toward Brandon and shoved the same finger under his nose, "don't encourage his twisted sense of humor! Now c'mon! I've gotta introduce you to Jules and Trish."

He snatched them both by their wrists and dragged them into the chill-out room. He listened to them snickering behind him, then stopped by the couches to introduce Brandon.

Kenny stood and hugged him. "Dude, it's been forever."

"I know. I heard you moved up to this side of town. I'm looking at a couple places on North Dearborn, so we'll almost be neighbors again."

"That's sweet!"

Trish rose to greet Brandon, offering her hand and a flirtatious smile. "Jesse's talked so much about you. It's wonderful to meet you."

Jesse caught her attempts to entice his brother. "Forget it, Trish. After years of self-deprivation, he finally decided to let himself be fully queer."

"Damn it!" Trish dropped down on the couch. "Is that all there is in this town?"

Jesse grinned at her. "All the best ones are."

She scowled up at him. "Obviously."

Julian slid into Trish's place. "I'll take over then." He held his hand out to Brandon. "Julian Forrester. It's a pleasure."

Brandon gently took Julian's hand and presented him with his most charming smile. "Mine as well. Jess told me you attended Julliard and that you've played with orchestras all across the country. I can't believe someone with so much talent would want to go slumming with him."

"Hey!" Jesse yelled.

Julian ignored Jesse. "Well, I am a man who enjoys diversity. You'll have to forgive me for eavesdropping, but I could have sworn I overheard you saying that you were going to be playing the Phantom. Am I correct?"

"Very much so."

"Then my sincerest congratulations to you. That's always been one of my favorite plays. I actually dated an actor once who was a stand-in to Raoul in a small production of it. He was dreadful on stage, but excellent in bed."

"Well, if you don't have the talent for one, you better be good at the other," Brandon laughed.

"So true," Julian chuckled. One eyebrow raised. "And, where do your talents lie?"

Brandon leaned toward him. "I'm one of those rarities who excels at everything."

Jesse stepped in between them. "This whole thing is creepin' me out." He faced Brandon. "Jules has way too much class for you and we both know you only date losers." He turned to Julian. "And you said that you go for the tall, rugged, athletic type, and he's a theatre freak. There's nothing rugged about him."

"No, but he is rather tall and looks quite athletic," Julian said.

"Well, I did practice karate for ten years when I was younger, and I've had seven years of ballet, not to mention, tap, swing—"

"No one wants to hear your résumé, dork," Jesse said. "Sit down and have some pizza."

Brandon threw a grin at Jesse, sat beside Julian, and immediately took over the conversation with talk of theatre and the new Suzuki GSX-R1000 motorcycle he was picking up that afternoon.

Evan handed Jesse a plate with two slices of all meat pizza when he sat down beside him. "You should've let them continue," he whispered. "It was fun watching them."

"You're such a voyeur. That's all I'd need is Brandon to sleep with him, then pull one of his I'm-just-not-looking-for-a-commitment acts and get Julian so upset that he leaves the band. Brandon doesn't have the best track record with relationships, and he really does always fall for losers. You know, for as much as he always took care of and protected me, he's the one who gets taken advantage of a lot. He tends to be a little on the gullible side when it comes to the guys he's dating."

"That's so sad."

Jesse nodded and took a bite of his pizza.

After lunch, everyone made their way back down to Studio B to begin the afternoon of recording, and since he had some free time, Brandon decided to stay and watch Jesse work. He started to walk into the control room, but Evan caught his wrist and pulled him back.

"I want to talk to you."

"Okay," Brandon said, confused. He glanced back toward the control room, saw Jesse and the others tuning and getting things ready, and turned to follow Evan up the hall.

Evan stopped near Studio A, standing with his arms folded across his chest. "So listen, I know when we met I was sort of a dick and I didn't talk to you in the best way, so I just wanted to say sorry."

Brandon stared at him. For the third time that day, shock jolted through him, and this time, so strong it forced his mind blank.

"I'm not really good at this kind of thing," Evan continued. "Meeting friends and family of lovers. I've never been with anyone long enough to get involved in all that, but it's different with Jess."

Brandon's mind began to function again. He looked at how tense Evan stood, listened to the hesitation in his voice. He could easily tell Evan wasn't accustomed to apologizing and definitely wasn't used to speaking his emotions.

Evan took a deep breath and spoke again, his voice softer. "I don't have a lot of friends, Brandon. I could count the people I truly trust on one hand, and even then I wouldn't use all my fingers, but I'd like to count you among them. You're very special to Jesse, and he's very special to me, so that makes you special to me, also." He unfolded his arms and moved to walk past Brandon. "So anyway, I just thought you should know."

Brandon snagged Evan by his bicep. "I appreciate it. Nothing would make me happier than to be counted among the people you trust. The truth is, I don't have a lot of friends either. I know tons of people, but there's a big difference between that and calling someone a friend, isn't there? For me, Jess has been my best friend forever, so to be able to call the man he's fallen in love with a friend, that's something I've always hoped for."

The apprehension on Evan's face was vanquished with a bright smile. "I'm glad we've got that cleared up. Now you can take me for a ride on your new motorcycle tonight."

"Only if you take me for a ride in your Enzo," Brandon laughed.

"It's a deal." Evan walked toward Studio B. The sound of Jesse singing "Shattered" drifted out into the hall through the open door. He stopped and turned to Brandon. "You asked me that day at the restaurant what I wanted from him. Remember?"

Brandon nodded.

"I wasn't ready to answer then, because at the time, I was still afraid to admit it to myself. What I want from him is, everything he is, everything he has ever been, and everything he will ever be. I want him and only him."

Brandon smiled and laid his hand on Evan's back, guiding him into the control room and to Jesse.

CHAPTER TWENTY

Jesse hurried toward the studio doors. After the long hours in what seemed an endless week in the studio, all he wanted was to get home, tear off his clothes, and jump in the pool with Evan. He looked up. Almost to the doors, almost to escape, just a few more feet.

"Jess! Hold up!"

Jesse faced around to see Trish jogging down the hall. "Did I forget something?"

She stopped in front of him. "No. Well, Greg was looking for you, but that's not why I was chasing you down. I didn't get a chance to ask because you took off so fast, but do you feel like going out? Just me and you. We could hit a few clubs and listen to some bands."

"I'd like to, but I'm going to have to take a rain check. I really want to get home to Ev."

Trish let out an indignant snort. "You talk like you haven't seen him in days. He came down to have lunch with you today. He comes down *every day* to have lunch with you. And you live together for Christ's sake. Don't you need some time to yourself?"

"No. I like spending time with him. And he doesn't come down every day. He stays home when the housecleaners, the pool people, and the gardeners come."

Trish lifted one eyebrow in a critical expression. "Don't you think it's a little obsessive to hang on someone like that all the time?"

"I never said our relationship was normal," Jesse laughed. "We both have obsessive personalities when it comes to the other and we both know how mental it is, but it works for us." He caught her hand and swung it back and forth between them. "We'll all go out another night. Or you know what? I'll talk to

Ev, and maybe we'll host a big cook-out this weekend and have everyone over."

"Hmm," Trish grumbled. She sighed loudly and lowered her gaze. "That's fine. Don't worry about it. It's just, I moved all the way from New York with Phoenix a couple months ago and I'm still trying to get to know this town. When Greg told me he had a band for me, I was so happy because it's been hard meeting people. How was I supposed to know that my sweet and sexy singer wouldn't want to make the time to do any bandly bonding?"

"That's not fair! Don't go pulling a guilt trip on me."

Trish shrugged. "It's not like I'm meaning to."

"Yes you are. Girls always pull out the guilt trip when they want something. It's one of their favorite tricks against guys."

Trish put her hands on her hips. "And what would you know about the tricks girls play?"

Jesse looked at her as though he pitied her slow-wittedness. "I *have* dated a few girls in my day, you know."

Trish's eyes widened, her hands slid off her hips to leave her arms hanging limp at her sides. "So, you're actually bi?"

"No. That was way back when I was trying to figure out the whole sexuality thing." He laid his hand on her upper arm. "I really gotta get going. But I'll call you tomorrow morning and let you know if we're all getting together, okay?"

Trish nodded slowly. "Yeah."

"Later." Jesse spun toward escape. He would make it this time. Just a few more steps. The handle was in reach. He stretched his right hand toward it.

"Jesse! Great, I caught you!"

"Son of a…" Jesse growled under his breath and turned to Greg. "Did you need something?"

"I need to talk to you." Greg put his arm around Jesse's shoulders and steered him back toward the depths of the studio.

Jesse cast a wistful glance over his shoulder at the doors, watching them grow smaller as he walked away. He looked forward and saw Kenny, Julian, and Trish coming down the hall.

"Isn't Evan waiting for you?" Trish mocked.

Jesse shot her an unappreciative glare.

Greg guided him into the chill-out room. "Sorry for keeping you. Do you and Evan have plans?"

"Yeah." Jesse plopped on the couch and looked up at Greg expectantly.

"I'll try to make this quick then. I wanted to tell you that you've been going beyond my expectations these past couple weeks, and I'll admit my expectations were rather high. You've taken full command of working in the studio as if you were a seasoned pro. Most young musicians need time to get used to studio work, but you've already mastered the equipment and your work ethic borders on workaholic. And your skill with communicating the music to your members and Jeremy has been incredible. You truly were meant for this, Jess. I really believe that after working with you."

"Thanks. It means a lot that you think so," Jesse said, and started to rise.

"I'm not quite done yet."

Jesse sat back down with a thump.

Greg paced behind the couch opposite Jesse. "I was looking over the final documentation of everything last night and I noticed your address looked familiar. Is what you put down your official residence?"

"Well yeah."

"So you and Evan are living together now?"

"We've been living together for the past few weeks."

Greg stopped pacing. He rested his hands on the back of the couch and looked down at Jesse. "You do know that you're not going to be able to acknowledge your relationship with him publicly, don't you?"

"I don't see why not."

"You don't? Then you must be living in a country other than the one I'm in, because in the one I'm in, there's still a hell of a lot of discrimination against homosexuality. Do you believe that you can come out as an openly gay singer with one of the most popular artists in the world as your partner and everything will be fine?"

Jesse shifted on the couch. "Well, I know it would probably be a big scandal, but we'd get through it. It's better than lying to everyone."

"No, Jesse, it's not. Lies are what this business is, and if you want to make it, you better wise up and learn the game. Not to mention, what about Evan? After all this time, he's decided to make a comeback. I never thought I'd see the day when he would step foot in a recording studio again, but now he is, and you need to think about how something like this could affect not just your career, but his as well."

Jesse gazed at him for a moment, then slowly lowered his eyes. "I guess I haven't thought about how it could affect his career. As far as my own, I just never worried about it. I figured I'd be who I am, and people could either take me or leave me. But the last thing I would want would be to hurt Ev's career."

"I know that, and I also know you probably hadn't thought about it, so that's why I wanted to talk to you about it now. If this were a perfect world, then this wouldn't even be an issue. You and Evan could be out in the open, holding hands, and doing all the things straight couples do without having people sneering and passing judgments. But this isn't a perfect world. In fact, it's a pretty damn shitty world sometimes, but it's the world we live in."

"Yeah," Jesse said softly.

A heavy silence filled the room for several moments. Jesse finally broke it by drawing in an audible breath and asking, "Is that it?"

"There's something else I wanted to talk to you about." Greg walked around the couch and sat down across from Jesse. "This is about Evan personally," he said, his words hesitant.

"He'll probably be upset knowing that I talked to you about these things, but I think they're things you should know, and I don't think they're things he would tell you on his own."

"If you're going to tell me about Brian Carney, he already did. I know the whole story about their affair, and we've moved beyond it together."

"He told you about Brian?" Greg paused in stunned disbelief. "Did he also tell you about Ethan, his father?"

Jesse nodded. "He told me he passed away from cancer right before his first tour started."

"Did he tell you that all throughout Ethan's illness, he had been the one who cared for him?"

"No," Jesse said, surprised at the new information.

"Well, he probably didn't want to evoke pity from you. It's not an easy thing, caring for and watching the person you love most in the world slowly fade away, and that's what Evan did. His loyalty and love for his father was so deep, it broke my heart watching him. But if there was any man in the world worth admiration, it was Ethan Arden. I first met him when I went to their house to discuss bringing Evan under Phoenix. You see, after his performance at the Macy's Thanksgiving Day Parade, a lot of labels were after him, but he refused to meet with representatives anywhere other than his home because Ethan was too ill to travel around the city and go to meetings, so right from the start, Evan set the precedent that if someone wanted to deal with him, they did it on his terms."

Greg leaned against the back of the couch. "I arrived at his family's home early and an A&R rep from another label was still meeting with Evan and Ethan, but Evan's mother, Sophia, let me in and put me in the den. I was sitting there when all of a sudden there was a huge crash and yelling. I jumped up and ran to see what was going on, and there was seventeen-year-old Evan dragging a man three times his age and twice his size through the house and out the door. He literally threw the man in the street, then faced me with those eyes of his and said, 'I guess we'll take your appointment now.'"

Jesse exhaled a shocked breath. "I can't believe he did that."

"You probably haven't seen it from him yet, but Evan can have a very nasty temper. Not that it was uncalled for that day. I learned later the man was upset by the slow meeting since at that time, Ethan's larynx had already been fully removed and he had to write down all the questions he wanted to ask. The rep asked if Ethan would mind sitting out of the meeting and that was all the provocation Evan needed to throw the man out. Ethan scolded him lightly for it, but even I could tell he wasn't upset. It took sitting in a room with Ethan for about five seconds to realize there wasn't much Evan could do to raise anger in him, if it was even possible for him to get angry. He was the most peaceful, gentle man I had ever met, and he absolutely adored his son."

Jesse absorbed every detail of what Greg told him. Evan spoke of his father quite a bit in the past couple weeks, but it was always sharing good memories. This was all new to him, and to hear someone else's opinion of Evan's father captured his full attention, but with it came a pang that he would never get to meet this man who sounded so kind and who had been so dear to Evan.

"When Evan began recording, Ethan was steadily declining," Greg continued. "Evan actually started out his career in debt to the label. Did he tell you that?"

Jesse shook his head.

"He blew through his advance money to pay off medical bills and take his father to various specialists. And he spent a small fortune when he bought a restored original '67 Mustang Shelby GT500 for Ethan, because Ethan had always dreamed of owning one." Greg turned his head. "But by then, Ethan was too weak to drive it, so Evan would lift him in and out of it, and take him for rides, until the time came when Ethan didn't have the strength for even that anymore."

Jesse glanced away from Greg to give him a moment to regain his composure. From their very first night together when Evan told him the Mustang had been his father's, he knew the car was special. Even though Evan didn't care if he drove his cars and had never told him he couldn't drive the Mustang, something inside him had known it was off limits.

"He still has it," Jesse said quietly. "The Mustang."

Greg looked at him, a smile relaxing his pained expression. "I wondered what had happened to it. I was afraid he got rid of it like he did all his others when he left." He nodded to himself, and cleared his throat to proceed. "There were times when I thought the album would never get finished. Not that I was upset with Evan. I understood that he needed to care for his father. He was the one who took Ethan to all his doctor appointments. He prepared all of his meals for him, helped him bathe, took care of his medications. He did it all."

"He told me his mom didn't handle things well when his father became sick, but I didn't realize he did so much for him."

"Well, Evan pushed her away a lot because of that, but I also think he felt she wasn't capable of caring for Ethan as well as he could, and that was probably true. To this day, I still believe Evan holds some resentment against her.

"At Ethan's the funeral, I expected to see Evan break into hysterics, but he cried so silently you wouldn't even be able to tell unless you looked at his eyes. I didn't see him again for a week, then at twelve o'clock at night there was a knock on my door, and when I opened it, there he was. But there was a strangeness about him, a coldness that hadn't been there before, and he said, 'My album's been out for two months. It's time to get this tour rolling. Make the arrangements tomorrow. I want to be on the road before the month ends,' and he turned to walk away. I called to him to come inside, but he refused, and disappeared into the night. From that moment, he was never quite the same person as when his father had been beside him."

Both Jesse and Greg sat silent. The ghosts of Greg's spoken memories hovered in the air above them. A physical ache tightened Jesse's chest over Evan's emotional pain. After a long pause, Jesse stood up and walked over to Greg.

"I know Ev would've told me eventually about everything, but it's nice to hear someone else talk about his father. He sounds like he was a wonderful person."

"He was. I tried my best to be a father figure to Evan after Ethan passed, but I know I failed. It doesn't change the fact that I love him like a son of my own." Greg looked at Jesse intently. "So, you take good care of him."

Jesse turned for the door. "I will. I already promised that to him."

❋ ❋ ❋

Jesse walked through the house, his thoughts weighing down his mood from everything Greg had told him. To hear how dedicated Evan had been to his father, to picture him so diligently caring for the man he admired and trying to battle an unconquerable foe in the illness, made such sorrow for Evan well up inside him that he could hardly breathe.

Then to think after years of hiding Evan had finally found the courage to make his music public again, and he could be the one to destroy his comeback, made determination mix with the sadness. He wouldn't allow that to happen. No matter what it took, no matter what he had to do, he wouldn't drag Evan down, and he would make sure Evan's comeback was successful, if not just for Evan, then for Evan's father, whose dream had been to see his son share his beautiful gift with the world.

Jesse stopped at the French doors in the music room and looked outside. The sun was beginning to set, turning the sky to burning oranges and reds, misty blues and violets. Evan walked onto the diving board at the far end of the pool. He bounced once, and for an instant, his sleek body became silhouetted against the golden sky. He arched in the air and descended into the water with hardly a splash. He surfaced, shaking his drenched hair from his eyes, the gold and copper highlights bright against the saturated darker tones.

So beautiful, Jesse thought. His gift, his spirit, his physical appearance, all that made Evan who he was, was beauty so supreme to rival the angels. Watching Evan at that moment and knowing what he knew now, if it was possible for the immense love he felt for him to grow, then it doubled its depth into his soul, and he knew whatever future they would have, his love for Evan had melded into his very essence.

Jesse took a breath to pull himself from his thoughts and opened one of the doors. He walked toward the pool, holding one arm behind his back, and watched Evan swim, admiring the ripples in his deltoids and how the water rolled off the muscles in his back.

Evan reached the shallow four-foot section of the pool and touched bottom. His eyes fell on Jesse and a wide smile shone over his features. "I knew you were here," he said, walking through the water and brushing his hair back with one hand.

Jesse went to one knee at the pool's edge. "Did you see me standing inside?"

Evan reached the edge of the pool and shook his head. "I felt you. Does that sound weird?"

Jesse stroked along Evan's cheek with his fingertips. "No. It's happened to me when you're near, too."

Evan gazed up at him, his smile fading slightly. "Are you okay?"

Jesse nodded. "Yeah, I'm fine. I'm just tired. It was a long day and I feel bad for getting home later than I told you."

"Don't feel bad. I know how it goes when you're trying to get stuff done in the studio, especially when you got new people playing for you." Evan smiled up at him. "But pretty soon we'll be going to work together. I talked to JJ today and he's flying in on my birthday. He's planning on taking the next day to recover, but after that, for the rest of the week we'll be in the studio getting things ready to start recording and working with the other guys Greg's bringing in."

"I can't wait to meet him. Are we all going to go out for your birthday?"

"Well, his flight comes in late in the afternoon, and I was planning on picking him up, but I'm not sure he'll be up to partying. He's flying from Australia and he's not the best flyer to begin with, so I'll probably just get a drink with him then come home."

Jesse leaned down, stopping with his lips a fraction from Evan's. "I was thinking about taking your birthday off, so I'll go with you."

Evan put his index finger to Jesse's lips. "No. You're not going to disrupt your work because of me. It's just another day."

"It's not just another day. It's your birthday."

Evan tapped his finger once against Jesse's lips. "No."

Jesse exhaled a frustrated huff. "Fine." He brought his arm forward from behind his back, revealing a gold bag featuring a stylized design of a nude woman with long hair riding a horse. He pulled out a gold box with the same design on the lid, and opened it to neat rows of Godiva dark chocolate truffles. "Even though you're mean to me, I guess I'll still give you these since you were pouting last night about there not being any good chocolate in the house."

"You're scary perfect, you know that?" Evan pulled one of the truffles from the box. He bit it in half and held the other half up to Jesse. Jesse bent down and took the delicacy, along with Evan's fingertips, into his mouth. Evan slowly drew his fingers back and tugged on the bottom of Jesse's khaki shorts. "Are you coming in?"

"Yeah." Jesse set the box to the side and stood up, pulling his T-shirt over his head.

Evan gazed at Jesse's wiry muscles stretching with each movement. "I love watching you strip."

Jesse pushed his boxers down with his shorts, exposing his rapidly rising cock. "I should do a striptease for you one of these days."

Evan chuckled. "You're such a little exhibitionist."

"And you love it."

Jesse sat at the edge of the pool. He slipped his legs in the water and eased the rest of his body in. A shiver shook him from the shock of the cold water, but passed as Evan's warm flesh pressed against him. Evan claimed his mouth, his lips wet and cool from the pool water, his tongue tasting of the chocolate he'd just eaten. Jesse sent a quiet moan from his mouth to Evan's and wrapped his arms around his neck. Evan pushed him back against the pool wall and thrust his hips slowly against him.

Jesse broke the kiss with a soft sigh. As good as Evan's cock felt behind the black nylon fabric of his swimming trunks, he knew it'd feel ten times better without the cloth in the way. He drifted his hands down Evan's back and around to his hips, hooked his thumbs over the top of the trunks and pushed them down.

Evan kicked them off underwater and caught them on one foot, which he lifted to remove the trunks, and tossed them from the pool. He took a handful of Jesse's hair behind his head and pulled his head back, kissing down the full length of his throat.

Jesse groaned and embraced Evan tighter around his neck. "Let's worship each other for the rest of the night. Let's make it last for hours."

Evan briefly sucked on Jesse's bottom lip. "That's what I want, too. I feel like I won't be able to get enough of you tonight."

"I don't think I'll be able to get enough of you for the rest of my life," Jesse said, and met Evan's tongue as their lips closed together.

CHAPTER TWENTY-ONE

Jesse spun away from the mic to glance at the clock behind him. When he saw it was almost three o'clock, he stopped playing his sunburst Fender Stratocaster and pulled the black leather strap over his head, announcing, "I'm outta here."

The music came to a jumbled halt.

"You couldn't wait two minutes until we finished the song?" Kenny asked.

"Nope. Ev didn't want me to take his birthday off, but he didn't say anything about cutting out early. He should've left the house by now to pick up JJ, so that'll give me plenty of time to get home and get things ready for him."

"Awe, isn't that sweet?" Trish scoffed.

Jesse turned to look at her. "At least it isn't some girly excuse like cramps or something."

Trish tapped a steady, annoyed beat with one drumstick. "Do I look like the kind of woman who whines about cramps?"

"No, you're a *manly* strong girl."

Trish's drumstick whizzed by his head and crashed into the window between the live room and the control room.

"Damn, you may drum like a boy, but you still throw like a girl," Jesse laughed.

Kenny set his new black Les Paul down on a stand. "What do you need to do to get ready for him?"

"I'm baking a cake."

"*You're* baking a cake?" Kenny snickered. "Since when do you cook? Maybe we should change our name from Conquest to Suzie and the Homemakers."

Jesse shoved him before turning for the door. "Don't forget I won't be here tomorrow either."

"Then I can leave my Advil at home," Julian teased.

Jesse flipped him off and disappeared into the control room. He said a quick farewell to Jeremy and a silent thank you that Greg had left half an hour before for a teleconference at the Phoenix corporate offices. He headed out of the studios and across the street to the parking garage. His eyes fell on Tim walking toward the exit, causing his elevated mood to become tainted with irritation.

Tim veered directly into Jesse's way. "And where do you think you're going?"

Jesse kept marching forward. "Home."

They both stopped, neither willing to diverge from his path.

"Greg didn't say anything to me about you leaving. He sent me down here to work with you guys for the rest of the afternoon."

"He probably didn't tell you because, unlike me who knows of your incompetence, he assumed you would know today is June 14th and the birthday of the biggest star under the Phoenix label."

Tim's small eyes shrank further as he narrowed them. "Exactly. It's the birthday of Phoenix's most important artist, which isn't you. But I guess you probably have a special little present for him, don't you? You better hurry along home now so you can give it to him. Maybe after you do, you'll be able to hit that high note in 'Euphoria' you seem to think you're capable of."

Jesse burst out with a fake laugh. "It cracks me up that someone as tone deaf as you works in this business. But then I should cut you some slack since multi-tasking between watching Trish's boobs bounce while she drums and actually paying attention to the music is too much for your small mind." He moved another step closer to him, locking his gaze into Tim's in a threatening glare. "Now get your ass out of my way."

Tim stood unmoving, staring back into Jesse's eyes. He took a slow step to the side. "Go. I wouldn't want you crying to him that I was the reason you were late."

Jesse stormed through the space Tim vacated. He jumped in the ebony Enzo and utilized many of the six hundred and sixty horses to get to Evanston in record time, where he ran into a grocery store and bought a dark chocolate cake mix with dark chocolate frosting, then hit a florist shop and cleaned it out of red roses, knowing roses were Evan's favorite flower.

He reached home and set about making the cake, and having never made a cake before, was surprised at how easy it was. While it baked, he ran upstairs to shower, then dressed in a tight V-neck, royal blue T-shirt since Evan loved him in blues. He came downstairs and swung back into the kitchen to set the cake out to cool while he went to the backyard with his supplies for the evening.

He placed tall white candles in silver holders on the glass top of the white wrought iron patio table and set a vase of roses in between. Not far from the patio, he laid a blanket over the thick grass. He put lube within easy reach and set small candles in votives around the blanket. By the time he finished, the sky had darkened to deep blue, the horizon edged with a golden glow in the sun's goodnight wish.

He went back inside, collected two small plates and forks, and brought them out. He lit the candles, put a CD that had the original version as well as different renditions of Pachelbel's Canon in the player, and hit the repeat button. The disc spun under the clear plastic lid, drifting the first soft notes across the yard.

Smiling in approval at his work, he headed into the house a final time to frost the cake. He grabbed the pan and flipped it to shake the cake out, gasping when only half fell onto the serving tray. He stared at it, dumbstruck. He glanced at the frosting and decided the only thing to do was use it as glue to mend it.

As he dotted on the last glob of frosting, the security system beeped, signaling Evan was home. He sprinted toward the door. He heard one of the garage doors open, followed by the deep rumbling of the new Lamborghini Murcielago that had been delivered a few days before, which had Evan bouncing around the house all day until the delivery truck carrying it arrived. The car was an unquestionable work of art, but he still felt it necessary to tease Evan about buying another black car.

The garage door closed, and a moment later, the knob to the access door turned.

Jesse flung his arms around Evan before he was fully in the house. "Happy birthday!"

Evan laughed and hugged him. "I think that's the fiftieth time you've said that today with the way you were calling me every hour."

Jesse stepped back to let him in. "Did I drive you nuts?"

"No, I liked it. But I can imagine how frustrated Greg was getting. How'd things go today?"

"Good," Jesse said, deciding he wasn't about to ruin Evan's birthday with telling him about his confrontation with Tim. He followed Evan down the hall and saw him head toward the kitchen. He pounced on Evan's back and wrapped his arms around his neck. "Where are you going?"

"To get a drink."

"I'll get it. You come this way." Covering Evan's eyes with both hands, Jesse pressed his body against him to get him to walk forward.

Evan stumbled. "What are you doing? I can't see."

"That's the point." Jesse bumped his hips against Evan's butt. "Get moving."

Evan stepped forward, trusting Jesse to steer him through the house.

They reached the French doors in the music room, and Jesse stopped him. "Keep your eyes closed."

"Yes, dear," Evan snickered.

Jesse stepped around him, squinted at him to make sure he wasn't peeking, then opened the doors and took Evan's hands to pull him through. "You can open them."

Evan opened his eyes and stared. The candles flickered with soft yellow light against the dark, the scent of roses drifted with the breeze, the violins sounded through the night. Jesse led him to the table and pulled out a chair. Evan sat, blinking at him in shock.

"I'll be right back," Jesse said, and darted into the house.

Evan gazed around the backyard, emotion filling him that Jesse had gone through such effort. When he heard Jesse's golden tenor singing "Happy Birthday," his eyes widened at the sight of the cake glowing with twenty-seven candles. Jesse placed the cake before him as he finished and dragged a chair closer.

"Well that was the best sounding 'Happy Birthday' song ever sung to me." Evan looked down at the patched cake, which dipped in the middle. "Did you make this?"

"Yeah," Jesse said, wearing a tentative smile. "But it sort of fell apart and I had to put it back together again with frosting, but I think it should still be okay."

"You baked me a cake," Evan said softly. He raised his eyes to Jesse. "I can't believe you did all this."

Jesse's lips curved upward with mischief. "This isn't all I have planned for you, so don't get too overwhelmed." He flicked his head toward the cake. "Make a wish."

Evan closed his eyes, took a breath, held it, opened his eyes, and exhaled a hard gust that extinguished every candle.

Jesse leaned toward him and gave him a light kiss on his lips. "Happy birthday."

"And that would be fifty-one times now," Evan chuckled. He delivered a deeper kiss. "Thank you."

Jesse gave Evan the knife. "I wouldn't thank me until you've tasted it."

Evan gave him one more tender kiss before sitting back to cut the cake.

"How's JJ doing?" Jesse asked.

"Good." Evan slid a piece of cake onto a plate and handed it to him. "He was a little rattled because the plane went through some heavy turbulence, but I got him tipsy and sent him to bed, so he should be fine. He'll need tomorrow to rebound from the flight, but after that, he'll be in the studio."

"I bet he's excited to be playing with you again."

"So excited he started crying when he saw me. When I quit performing, so did he, even though he didn't have to. He could've easily picked up a lead guitar gig with another artist or band, but he made himself believe he could settle down and do the family thing. Of all the people who've ever played for me, he's the only one who's been with me since the start of my career." Evan took a bite of the cake and paused. "Damn," he said with his mouth full. "I was expecting it to suck, but it's actually good."

"Thanks for the faith in my abilities!" Jesse laughed. "I've cooked for us before."

"Yeah, I know. How anyone explodes instant potatoes is beyond me."

Jesse shoved him on the shoulder in a light reprimand.

Evan chuckled and swayed away from the push. "So has Greg set a target release date for the album yet?"

"He's thinking the first week of August for 'Euphoria' to come out as the first single, then release the album the last week of August, which should give us plenty of time to finish recording now that everyone's clicking. Trish is having some issues with 'Vanish' because the beats have to be so hard and fast, she can't keep up with it, but we've decided we'll have Jeremy adjust it during editing, and we'll slow it down a touch when we play live. I'm not thrilled about it, but there's nothing else we can do.

"And Greg told me today that he's got a photo shoot scheduled in July to get some promos and shots done for the liner, and we're going to be making the video for 'Euphoria' then too, so July's going to be a busy month, but I already told him I need the 30th free for Brandon's birthday. Other than some small publicity stuff he's planning on for August, he's already talking up his contacts to have us go to New York in September for interviews and photo shoots. And it looks like we'll be kicking off our tour on my birthday."

Jesse poked at the cake, his voice softened. "You know, I always thought I would be torquered about doing stuff like this, traveling for publicity and interviews, going all over the country on a professional tour, but now I'm dreading the day when I get on the bus. I don't want to leave you behind."

Evan laid his hand over Jesse's. "I know. But with what I'm projecting for recording, my album won't be released until December, so I can catch up to you anywhere you're at until I hit the road, which probably won't be until mid-January or early February."

"But what about after that?"

"Then we'll do the best we can." Evan brushed Jesse's hair back from his forehead. "I trust you. I know you're not going to screw around on me, no matter how long we're apart. And I know you're headlining your own tour, but Greg will probably book you for about a four month run, so if you wanted, when your tour's finished, you could join me on mine as my opening act. If you did, you'd get to play bigger venues and get more exposure since it'll be a world tour, and most importantly, we'd get to be together." He softly touched his lips to Jesse's and grinned. "Just think of all the different countries we'd get to make love in."

Jesse returned the kiss. "I was sold when you offered letting us open for you, now I would beg to tag along on your tour." He saw that Evan had finished his cake. He stood up with Evan's hand in his. "Dance with me."

Evan rose and followed Jesse away from the table. He wrapped his arms around Jesse's waist. Jesse tucked his head into the curve of Evan's neck, his arms embracing Evan's waist as well. As they slowly danced, Evan noticed every time Jesse's right leg moved, something hard pressed against him, but it was too square and small to be what he was used to, and besides, Jesse hung to the left. "What do you have in your pocket?"

Jesse stopped dancing and retrieved a small box wrapped in gold paper from his right front pocket and set it in Evan's hand.

Evan stared at the gift. "You got me a present, too?"

"Of course I did. Open it."

Evan freed the box from the paper and opened the gray velvet lid. Nestled in black velvet was a white gold ring holding a round cut, finely faceted, deep burgundy gemstone. Eight sparkling diamonds embraced the gem, four on each side.

"It's your birthstone," Jesse said. "Well, one of them. June has a couple, the pearl and this one, and I had to get this one because it's called alexandrite. It changes color naturally when different light hits it. In the daylight it'll be bluish-green, but in lighting like this, it's that color."

"It's beautiful." Evan lifted the ring free. His eyes fell on an inscription on the inside of the band, *Forever Yours-Jesse.* He stared at it, then slowly looked up at Jesse. "That's the best present I've ever gotten, and the ring is nice, too."

Jesse's eyes shone as his smile reached them. He took the ring from him and lifted Evan's left hand. "I had the band custom made to get it the right size. The only problem was, the finger I wanted it for you never wear rings on. I still stole one of your rings to get it sized close, and you have so many, you never noticed." He glided the ring smoothly onto Evan's left ring finger. He gazed at the perfect fit. His heart pounded. He raised his gaze to Evan's. "If you don't want to wear it on that finger, I can always get it resized for another."

Evan laid his hand on Jesse's cheek. "There's no other that I could imagine it being on."

Jesse's smile widened, the nervous beat in his chest slowed. He bent at the waist and kissed Evan's knuckle above the ring. When he straightened, Evan embraced him, weaving his fingers through the back of Jesse's hair, and welcomed Jesse's lips with his tongue.

Jesse could feel it in Evan's body, the way he thrust his tongue into his mouth deep and slow, massaging him, filling him. It would be exactly how Evan would take him, easy and gentle. At the last thought, Evan drove his tongue deeper. Jesse groaned and leaned against him, his muscles loose to silently tell Evan he was willing for anything he wanted.

Evan pressed him toward the blanket and broke the kiss long enough to pull both their shirts off. As they passed the table, he took a rose from the vase and brushed the silken petals down Jesse's cheek, along his jaw, over his chest. Jesse closed his eyes at the flower's sensual touch. Evan tickled the petals up to Jesse's cheek again and gazed at him, enraptured by how Jesse's exquisite features shamed the perfect blossom.

They reached the blanket, removing their clothes in the short moments between long kisses. Jesse took both of Evan's hands in his and eased down to his back. Evan laid over him and stroked Jesse's hair as he met his lips once again. Jesse accepted Evan's tongue and sucked it gently, wishing he could keep it forever in his mouth. He rubbed his legs over Evan's and slid them up his sides. Evan eased back from the kiss and grabbed the lube.

Jesse watched him slicking his fingers. "I should probably tell you I'm not going into the studio tomorrow."

Evan looked at him. "Why not?"

"Because I want to spend the day with you and keep celebrating your birthday. You wouldn't let me take today off, but you didn't say anything about tomorrow."

Evan chuckled and shook his head. "Sneaky little brat. You shouldn't have done that."

"Yeah well, I just want to make sure I take advantage of all the time I can get with you since you're an official geezer now."

"Is that so?" Evan drifted his right hand down between Jesse's legs and brushed his fingertips across his opening. "You know what they say? You're only as old as the person you're sleeping with."

Jesse gasped in feigned horror. "That's not fair! That means I'm almost thirty!"

"Twenty-seven!" Evan laughed. "I still have three years!"

Jesse grazed his lips over Evan's. "And I hope I'm there for every one."

"That's the only present I'll ever want," Evan said, and pressed their lips firmly together.

Jesse held him around his neck, his heart drumming a cadence of passion in time to the stroking of Evan's fingertips. Teasing and tormenting, Evan slipped just a tip in and circled around his rim, then pulled out to tickle again. Jesse writhed under him and passed a choked whimper into Evan's mouth. His plea did nothing to increase Evan's pace. Gradually, insistently, he entered and withdrew, entered and withdrew. For need of breath, Jesse broke their long kiss. He pressed his head back on the blanket, panting hushed, desperate moans on each exhale.

Evan watched him. After being together for over a month, it still amazed him how wanton Jesse could be for him. It emphasized what he already knew, Jesse was a man who only knew one form of loyalty, and it was complete and absolute devotion. The thought broke the last of Evan's control, and he grabbed his own cock. Jesse spread wider for him. Seeing Jesse's motions sent a dizzying rush of desire through Evan. The way Jesse always welcomed him was just one more of the countless things he loved about him.

"Jess," Evan groaned, and pushed into him at the same moment.

Jesse sucked in a sharp breath at finally being stretched and filled. His cock reared up against Evan's stomach, the friction sending a sweet shiver through him. Evan nuzzled into his hair, then found Jesse's lips and graced them in a gentle kiss. He moved his hips in long, slow thrusts, and kept his lips on Jesse's, pulling Jesse's breath into his lungs, exhaling his own into him.

Jesse brushed his hand down Evan's left arm to his hand and interlocked their fingers, the white gold of the alexandrite ring, warmed by Evan's body, pressed against his skin. He moved his other hand down to rest on Evan's lower back and lost himself in the feel of the muscles flexing as Evan glided in and out. The first spark of climax heated his stomach and groin, and he moaned and shifted.

Evan breathed a soft sigh over Jesse's lips when he felt his muscles shudder around his sensitive organ. He increased the force of his thrusts, but kept his pace slow. Jesse breathed harder and faster, his orgasm building. He squeezed Evan's hand with painful force, his short nails dug into his lower back.

"Ev…Ev, I love you. I love you so much."

Jesse's words pushed Evan's climax to the surface, but he battled it back to gain a few more moments. "I love you too, Jess. More than anything."

Jesse arched under him, exhaling a loud, shaking gasp as he came. Evan pushed into him hard, and with a soft cry, his climax broke free.

Though their muscles loosened, they still clung to each other. Jesse's chest expanded with deep breaths against Evan's. Slowly, Jesse opened his eyes and looked up at him.

"We'll be like this forever, won't we?"

Evan nodded and kissed him softly. "Forever."

CHAPTER TWENTY-TWO

Jesse sat in the control room watching Evan play the red mahogany grand piano in Studio A. His fingers flicked and floated over the keys, his azure eyes set in concentration. He paused in playing to jot a few notes on a piece of sheet music, then started to sing *a cappella* the notes he had just played, raising and lowering his smooth baritone.

The door to the control room opened. Jesse glanced to see a man in his early thirties walk in. He looked close to six feet tall with a lanky build, his medium blond hair cut short and spiky. A smile took over Jesse's face at recognizing the newcomer as Evan's long time guitarist, Jerry Jeffries. He stood to greet him and noticed JJ's hazel eyes examining him and the smirk tipping up his lips. He extended his hand, but before he could introduce himself, JJ spoke, his Australian accent thick.

"You're Jesse Alexander, aren't you?"

"Yes, I am."

JJ shook his hand. "I knew it the minute I saw you from how the Mad Genius described you. He said you were a real looker, but he didn't say you could give a straight man a second of regret for his preferences."

"Thanks!" Jesse laughed. He caught what JJ had called Evan and gave him a quizzical look. "The Mad Genius?"

"That's what I named him back in the day since he's a bit on the batty side when it comes to his music and can be a damn tyrant in how he wants it played."

"JJ!" Evan bellowed, standing in the doorway between the live room and the control room. Despite his sharp tone, he wore a smile. "Don't tell him things like that! So far, I've been able to hide that I'm not perfect from him."

Jesse winked at Evan. "It's okay. I still think you're perfect."

The door to the control room opened again with Kenny poking his head through and looking at Jesse. "Hey, are you gonna sit in here all day?" His eyes landed JJ. He paused, then the door flew open the rest of the way as he leaped into the room and thrust his hand out to JJ. "Jerry Jeffries! Dude, you freakin' rock! I've watched you play for years."

JJ chuckled and took Kenny's hand. "Thanks, mate, but don't say years. You're gonna make me feel old." He cocked his head in a thoughtful look. "Then you're a guitar player?"

Kenny nodded enthusiastically. "I'm Kenny Cooper, from Conquest."

"Oh, then you're the one who can give me a run for my money, according to him," JJ said, pointing at Evan with his thumb.

Kenny's wide gaze on Evan revealed his surprise at such a compliment.

Evan smiled at him, then slapped his hand on JJ's shoulder. "Since you actually decided you might want to work today, let me play a new ballad I'm working on and see what you think."

JJ rolled his eyes. "A ballad? What the hell am I here for if you're gonna do nothin' but make ballads?"

Evan turned for the live room. "Don't worry. I got others that kick ass, and I've got a guitar solo for this one that's pure genius. I don't even know if you'll be able to play it, it's so genius."

JJ leaned toward Jesse, and whispered, "See why I call him the Mad Genius?"

Jesse chuckled and nodded.

Evan took a seat at the piano, interlocked and stretched out his fingers, then settled them on the keys. He allowed silence to fill everyone's ears. Slowly, softly, he pulled the first notes from the instrument, and let his rich baritone flow,

> *"I used to fear the sunset,*
> *And the cold dark it would bring.*

With it came my memories,
And a past I couldn't leave.
But your soft breath beside me,
Is my shield in the night.
And I finally feel safe again,
As your heart beats with mine.

If you want to bring me down,
Let me hear your sweet voice sing.
If you want to see me fall,
Bring your lips to mine again.
Your kiss broke my nightmare,
Your touch has freed my soul,
I finally found the man I'd once been
When you gave yourself to me.

Touch me softly,
Let me fall for you.
Kiss me sweetly,
Let me be one with you.
Hold me strongly,
Let me belong to you.
Caress me gently,
Let me never be alone."

He kept the tempo gentle through the piano's solo, then raised his sensual voice again,

"Now when the sunset comes,
I welcome it with a smile,

Because you're standing next to me,
Your hand enclosed in mine.
My past has left my dreams.
Your kiss has slain my demons.
With your tender touch guiding me
I'll return once more.

Touch me softly,
Let me fall for you.
Kiss me sweetly,
Let me be one with you.
Hold me strongly,
Let me belong to you.
Caress me gently,
Let me never be alone..."

Jesse felt he could finally breathe as Evan's voice trailed away.

Evan looked up at him. "That's just a rough version, I've got a couple more verses I'm working on, but what do you think?"

Jesse took hold of the P.A. mic. "It's," a slow smile curved his lips, "genius."

Evan laughed quietly and moved his gaze to JJ. "And what about you, you tone deaf bastard?"

"The song's great. You still sound like a cat in heat, though."

Evan laughed louder and flipped him off.

Kenny put his hand on Jesse's shoulder. "I can't believe I'm the one trying to drag you into working, but we gotta start getting the kinks out of 'Vanish.'"

"I know." Jesse stood up, but instead of going to the door that led out, he headed toward the one leading to the live room. He stepped up to the piano and combed his fingers through Evan's hair. "The song is beautiful."

Evan caressed Jesse's upper arm and guided him down. Jesse met his lips in a soft kiss.

JJ nudged Kenny with his elbow. "They always like that?"

Kenny sighed and nodded. "Yeah, it's pretty sick, really. And I don't mean it's sick because they're both guys. It'd be sick if it was a dude and a chick hanging on each other like that, or two chicks. Well, maybe not if it was two chicks. Hot ones."

JJ burst out laughing. "I hear that."

Jesse walked back into the control room. "Alright, I'm ready now."

Kenny stopped at the door and turned to JJ. "Hey, maybe if you get time, you could come down and listen to us."

"Absolutely."

"Awesome!" Kenny said.

Jesse turned up the hall toward the chill-out room. "Did you just meet your kindred spirit?"

"He's so freakin' cool! He's one of the most kickass guitar gods ever! We should all go out tonight to welcome him into town."

"Yeah, that'd be cool." Jesse saw they were nearing the chill-out room and hushed his voice. "Has Trish calmed down yet?"

"She was still slamming things around when I left to go find you," Kenny whispered.

That morning, they had been working on the fast pop/rock track "Vanish," and the rapid, heavy rhythms were causing Trish more trouble than usual. It seemed like her concentration was everywhere but the song. He tried to be patient, but by her fifth screw-up, he had whirled around and yelled, "What the hell is wrong with you today? Is this your first day on the skins or what?" She hadn't taken that well, and started whipping her drumsticks at him, pelting him not only with the ones she was using, but the spares sitting beside her. When her cache was depleted, she stormed out screeching "asshole" so loud it reverberated off the walls and window, and he decided they should all take an extra long break.

Jesse turned into the chill-out room with Kenny to find Julian sitting on a couch trying to hide behind a copy of *Keyboard* magazine, and Trish sitting at the small square table in the kitchen area, her right foot thumping a lightning fast stomp of annoyance.

Jesse marched over to the table. "Damn, if you could drum as fast as your foot is going, we wouldn't be having the little issues we're having now."

Julian snorted in an attempt to not laugh and buried his face deeper in the magazine. Kenny scooted a large distance around Jesse, heading for safety at Julian's side.

Trish slowly turned her head, her green eyes flashing rage.

Jesse stared back at her, his dark blue gaze insistent and unwavering. "Are you going to sit there glaring at me all day, or can we get back to work? We need to get 'Vanish' wrapped up."

Trish looked away from him, defiance dominating her demeanor. "We've got others we can work on. I don't feel like working on that song anymore today."

"Oh shit," Kenny mumbled, tucking back into the couch cushions beside Julian, who peeked over the top of his magazine.

"You don't feel like it?" Jesse said, his tone revealing his disgust. "I don't give a rat's ass if you don't *feel* like it. You made the decision to join this band, and I accepted you. Now if you got a problem being part of this family, then let me know right now. Otherwise, pop a Midol to balance out the bitchiness and let's get back to work!"

Trish leaped out of her chair and into Jesse's face. "Arrogant, narcissistic, cold-hearted, ignorant, smart-ass punk!"

Jesse folded his arms across his chest. "I'll give you arrogant, narcissistic, and smart-ass, and I might be a little bit of a punk, but I sure as hell am not cold-hearted or ignorant."

"You are! You have no idea what I feel, and if you did, you wouldn't even give a shit!"

"Since when don't I care about your feelings? I ask you every day how you're doing and talk to you about things going on in your life."

Trish snapped her gaze away, her cheeks flushed pink. "You just don't get it."

Jesse frowned in complete frustration. "Well obviously. I'm sorry, Trish, but my female needs skills are a bit lacking. I need you to be real blunt here and just tell me what the problem is."

Trish looked at him, her bottom lip quivered, her eyes held a pained shine. "I..." she began, then paused. She glanced behind her to Julian and Kenny. They both quickly bent their heads as if looking at the magazine together. She turned back to Jesse's expectant gaze. She lowered her eyes, blinked a few times, and cleared her throat. "It's just, I don't think it's fair the way you're so much harder on me than anyone else. You never yell at Julian or Kenny."

Jesse shook his head, even more confused. "I bitch at Kenny all the time." He looked around Trish to Kenny. "Don't I?"

"Yeah, but I've learned how to tune you out over the years. Don't worry, Trish, you will, too."

Jesse looked back to Trish. "And I'd bitch at Jules too, if he ever screwed up." He peeked at Julian. "When we go in there, will you do me a favor and mess up so I can bitch at you?"

Julian gave him a two-fingered salute. "No problem."

Jesse focused on Trish and smiled, lifting his voice to be more cheerful. "See? You'll get to watch me rag on Jules now. Won't that be fun?" Before she could answer, he wrapped his arms around her and swayed her back and forth in his embrace. "You should've let me know this was the problem sooner. I would've found more reasons to bitch at them a long time ago, especially Kenny."

Trish forced out a single, strangled chuckle and hugged him in return.

"Awe, look who's pretending to be a man," Tim mocked from the doorway. "Sorry, princess, but holding a woman just doesn't suit you."

Jesse released Trish and whirled toward Tim. "Get your sorry ass out of my face! I'm not in the mood to deal with your bullshit today!"

"Jess," Kenny said cautiously, rising from the couch and moving toward him.

Julian rose also to assist Kenny.

"Settle down, sweetie," Tim sniggered. "I didn't know you're the type that can only dish it out and not take it. Except for when you're on your knees, isn't that right?"

"Fuck you!" Jesse yelled, and lunged for him.

Kenny dove forward and caught Jesse around his waist with Julian leaping to help, but Jesse froze at the sight of Evan appearing in the doorway behind Tim.

Evan slammed Tim on the back with both hands. Tim flew forward, stumbling for balance, and spun to see who had pushed him. As he came fully around, his mouth met Evan's fist. Tim reeled back from the hit. He caught himself enough to leap at Evan and throw a punch. Evan swept back, allowing Tim's fist to blow harmlessly by his face, then stepped forward, his right fist speeding for Tim's left cheek with the momentum of his weight behind it. He connected hard, sending Tim sprawling to the ground.

"Fucking prick bastard," Evan growled, standing over him. "I gave you the courtesy of a warning, and you decided not to listen. Now get your ass up so we can finish this."

Greg and JJ ran into the room. Greg rushed to Tim. JJ caught Evan under his arms and around his chest, and hauled him back.

"Well, that temper certainly hasn't changed," JJ said.

"What the hell is the matter with you, Evan?" Greg demanded.

Jesse stared in shock at Tim sprawled on the floor, blood leaking from his split lip, then lifted his gaze to Evan. Evan's eyes were focused on Tim, his gaze still held a lethal threat, though he didn't struggle against JJ's hold. For his modest size, Jesse couldn't believe the force Evan had struck with, the speed and skill of his maneuvers. He realized that he had witnessed for the first time what Greg referred to as Evan's "very nasty temper."

Evan moved his gaze from Tim to Jesse. Jesse's heart pounded faster at the fierce protectiveness he saw.

The moment broke as Tim slapped Greg's hands away from him. He began to rise, shaky and unsteady, his face filled with vindictive righteousness. "You're done," he hissed, blood spattering from his lips. "Kiss your little comeback goodbye. By the time I'm through with you, there won't be a person in the world who won't know what you are."

The threat struck Jesse harder than it seemed to hit Evan. He pulled away from Kenny and Julian, and stormed past Tim to stand in front of Evan. Acting as a shield between them, he faced Tim. "If you want to come after someone, then come after me, you worthless piece of shit! I'm the one you've wanted to bring down since day one! Leave him out of our fight!"

"Don't worry, princess. I plan on taking you down with your queen."

Jesse felt Evan's explosion a nanosecond before his movement. Evan broke from JJ's hold with such force he almost elbowed JJ in the face. He leaped around Jesse. His arm cocked back and shot forward, the hit carrying not only the momentum of his weight, but also the speed of his lunge. Tim lashed both arms up to cover his face. Evan's fist split the gap between Tim's arms and nailed him in the mouth a second time. Tim flew backward, crashing hard on his back.

In the instant that Evan attacked, Jesse saw JJ step back, clearly not ready to jump in to stop him again. Greg looked frantic and incapable of moving. He already knew Kenny was no fighter, and he doubted Julian was willing to help stop Evan either. That only left him and Trish, and no matter how fit or strong she was, there was no way she could wrestle Evan under control.

Evan grabbed Tim by his shirt and hauled him to his feet. Before he could strike again, Jesse jumped for him. He threw his arms around Evan's waist and pressed his body against his back.

"Ev, stop! You're going to hurt yourself."

Evan stood motionless. Reluctantly, he loosened his hold on Tim and let go, but not without a final shove that made Tim stumble to his knees. Jesse felt Evan's tense back muscles relax a fraction, and tightened his embrace around him.

Evan laid his hands over Jesse's and glared at Tim. "You want to come after me? Go ahead and try. I'd like to see if you can survive my attorneys."

The mention of attorneys snapped Greg out of his panic. He spun toward Tim, his voice and expression harsh. "Going after Evan would be the worst thing you could do, Tim, whether it's talking to tabloids or a lawsuit. You never fully understood what I meant when I would tell you that at all costs, we at Phoenix protect our artists. I hope you understand now. Unfortunately, because of your discrimination against Jesse, I'm going to have to let you go. You know Phoenix has a zero-tolerance policy against discrimination based on age, race, gender, religion, or sexual orientation, and the intolerance you've shown is a direct breach of that policy. I ask that you have your office cleaned out by seven o'clock tonight."

With what strength he had remaining, Tim stomped around Greg and out the door.

Silence pervaded the room, no one knowing what to say or do, except Jesse as he kept Evan in his arms. After a long moment, JJ clapped his hands together, the loud crack making everyone except Evan and Jesse jump.

"Well, it's good times again." He walked up to Evan and slapped his hand down on his shoulder. "I really appreciate you inviting me to join you on this album, mate, but you could've warned me about flying elbows. You almost clocked me a good one."

Jesse felt something warm and wet touch his hand. He peered over Evan's shoulder and gasped at seeing blood trickle from a gash across the index and middle knuckles of Evan's right hand. "You're hurt!"

Evan glanced down at his hand. "It's just a scratch from his teeth."

Not feeling the same indifference toward the injury as Evan, Jesse clenched Evan's wrist and dragged him to the sink in the kitchen area. He got the water running, held Evan's hand under the flow, and gently rinsed the cut.

Evan gazed at Jesse's face, so concentrated on cleaning the wound. "I'm sorry, gorgeous," he said softly.

Jesse jerked his head up, surprised by the sudden apology. "For what?"

"I shouldn't have stepped in like that. You had wanted to deal with Tim yourself, but I jumped in and took over. I should've let you handle it."

Jesse turned his attention back to Evan's cut hand. "Yeah well, that may be true, but I'm not really thinking about that at the moment. What did you mean when you said you had given him the 'courtesy of a warning'?"

A tentative smile touched Evan's lips. "I guess I should've told you how on your first day in the studio, I warned him that if he ever offended you again, I'd punch his teeth down his throat."

"Yeah, that might've been good to know," Jesse grumbled.

"Are you mad?"

"No. Right now the only thing I want is to get you home, strip us both down, and have you throw me to my back on the bed so I can wrap my legs around your neck and you can screw the hell out of me." Jesse looked at him from under his eyelashes, a mischief filled grin on his lips. "Do you have any idea how turned on I am right now?"

"I think I'm starting to figure it out."

Jesse brought his lips to Evan's in a tender kiss that hinted at the many more once they were alone. He drew back slowly and began carefully drying Evan's hand with a paper towel. He inspected the wound closer. "It's not as bad as I thought, but it still needs to be bandaged."

"I'll get the first aid kit," Greg said.

"Don't worry about it," Jesse said, leading Evan toward the door. "We have bandages at home. Let's call it a day, guys. I don't think any of us can concentrate on making music now and we were having a bad day, anyway." He paused as they came upon Greg. "I'm sorry things happened that way with Tim."

Greg laid one hand on Jesse's shoulder. "It's okay, son. I'm still confused about why and how this happened. I knew there was tension between you and Tim, but I guess it went a lot deeper than what I realized. I wish you would've come to me about it in the beginning. We'll have to sit down tomorrow and you'll have to catch me up on all that's happened between you two so I don't get any surprises down the line." He turned his gaze to Evan in a reprimanding look. "You too."

Evan nodded, though by his expression it was obvious he had no intention of doing so. As Jesse led him away, Evan turned to JJ. "I'll call you in a little bit and we'll set up dinner plans."

JJ flipped a thumbs up and watched them disappear out the door. He glanced at Greg. "Looks like he's finally found something that means more to him than music."

Greg exhaled a deep breath. "Frightening, isn't it?"

CHAPTER TWENTY-THREE

Jesse dragged himself out of the black limousine to the sidewalk outside the Phoenix Studios. He looked up at the early evening sky that threw its fiery orange glow over the gray buildings. Finally, the month of July was almost over. When he looked back on things now, everything seemed more of a congealed blur of events than any clear memory.

For the rest of June they worked twice as long and hard to get the album finished and ready for printing and packaging. There were times when he wondered if they were going to be able to get it done, times when he wanted to say screw it and walk away for a few days, but he wasn't about to sacrifice all he had worked for, so he hid his fatigue and pushed Kenny, Julian, and Trish to keep up with him.

Evan was the only person who knew his exhaustion and always seemed to be able to sense when he was ready to crack. It was those moments when he was at his limit that he would look up from the mic and see Evan standing in the control room, watching him. A sense of serenity always came over him, then Evan would whisk him from the studio and take him to get something to eat, or for a drive so they could talk, or one time to a suite at the Ritz-Carlton for a quick stress relief session.

Jesse smiled at the last memory and felt the tension from the final day of the video shoot ease. He had decided after they shot pictures for the CD liner and promos that he would love doing photo shoots. Kenny already loathed them, Trish and Julian found them incredibly boring, but for him, being in front of the camera, trying on different outfits, having people fix his clothes and hair for him, was just too much fun. Of course, part of it could be the extra attention he got since the photographers always wanted him in the front, in the most dramatic or sexy poses, or shots of him solo. Greg told him he better get used to it. He might be part of a band, but with his charisma and looks, the media would be looking to get him one-on-one a lot.

With how much he enjoyed the photo shoots, he assumed he would have a blast making the video for "Euphoria" as well, but it turned out to be more of a pain. It started off bad right away when he got into a fight with the director because the guy wanted to do a mini-movie and actors would have more screen time than the band.

He refused to back down and won the battle by having the video done based off his concept of doing a tribute to Chicago and their local fans. It was going to feature him singing on the steps of the Field Museum solo, then with Kenny playing guitar at Soldier Field. It would move next to him singing on the mound at U.S. Cellular Field where Trish would be drumming behind him, then he would be on the Ferris wheel at Navy Pier with Julian rocking out the keyboards below, and wrap up with all of them playing at Millennium Park. Overall, he felt the finished product should be great, but he didn't know if it had been worth three days of work. Who knew it'd take so long to make a video for a three and a half minute song? Well, besides Evan, who had warned him.

At least it was over, until they had to make the videos for "Vanish" and "Shattered." The thought was almost enough to make him puke. On the plus side, he knew August wouldn't be too bad. Just some light publicity, then the album's release date at the end of the month, which they had decided to self-title *Conquest*, even though he thought it sounded generic.

The only thing that had him nervous was going to New York the first week of September. Greg called in countless favors and arranged for them to be interviewed on MTV, VH1, and by a few music mags, including *Rolling Stone*. Being interviewed for *Rolling Stone* was enough to make him swoon.

Greg told him not to worry. By the time the New York trip came around he would have plenty of experience being interviewed by smaller publications and Internet sites, not to mention the coaching Greg and Evan had done with him so he'd know how to handle himself, but it didn't do much to lessen his nervousness.

Jesse fingered the sixteen-rayed sun pendant dangling from the choker around his neck and shook the thoughts away. There wasn't any point in getting himself worked up over something that was a month away. Greg was probably right. By the time he got through August and the smaller interviews, getting interviewed by bigger media would be nothing. He chuckled inside. Yeah, right.

He turned to cross the street for the parking garage and stumbled forward when a body slammed against his back. As he fought to gain his balance, two thin but strong arms clamped around his neck. He could feel a pair of ample breasts squashed against his back and figured it wasn't Kenny, Julian, or Greg who pounced him.

"Jess, let's go out to dinner," Trish said.

"Not tonight, Trish. I just want to go home and chill."

"Go home and chill? You talk like you're sixty years old."

"Fine. I just want to go home and fuck. Is the truth better?"

Julian laughed. "It's more believable since we were all sitting there when the make-up lady was teasing you about what a kinky sex life you must have when she was trying to find the right shade of body foundation to cover that bite mark on your shoulder. We're all still waiting to hear the story behind that fabu dental impression."

Trish softened her voice to a seductive timbre and raked her fingernails through Jesse's hair. "Yeah, everyone likes a good dirty story. It's fun to imagine yourself in the place of one of the players, especially when one of them is you, pretty boy."

Jesse looked at her. "So you like imagining yourself in Ev's place?"

"Maybe," Trish said coyly.

"Then you might want to imagine a strap-on in the scenario because I've got special needs, you know."

Julian burst out laughing. Trish shoved Jesse on the back of the head to show her lack of appreciation. Kenny rolled his eyes and sidestepped away from the door when it opened.

Evan walked out and stopped so short at the sight of Trish hanging on Jesse that JJ ran into him from behind.

Trish narrowed her eyes the merest of fractions at Evan.

Jesse saw Evan and flashed a radiant smile. "Hey! I thought you would've left for home by now!"

He moved to greet Evan, half dragging Trish on his back before she managed to let go. He almost reached him when Greg slid between them and stopped him with his index finger pointed in Jesse's face.

"What have we talked about, Jess? With 'Euphoria' getting ready to come out, more and more people are going to start recognizing you on the street and you can't jump all over Evan like you're used to doing. You shouldn't have been acting so affectionate toward him in public in the first place, and the only reason you've gotten away with it for as long as you have is because the media hasn't found out he's back yet. But that's going to change with us getting ready to announce he's working on a new album, so you need to learn to control yourself."

Jesse stared at Greg, hurt overriding his anger at having to keep his feelings for Evan hidden.

Evan grabbed Greg's arm. "You don't have to be so harsh about it."

Greg ripped his arm from Evan's hold. "No, Evan, I do, because neither one of you seem to understand the risk behind some snake in the grass paparazzi getting a shot of you two hugging each other or worse."

"*Or worse?*" Evan snapped. "Having people see me give affection to the person I love is one of the worst things that could happen in your mind, isn't it?"

Jesse interrupted the growing tension by spinning away from them both. "Just forget it, Ev. I don't want this to ruin our evening. Let's go home."

Jesse marched across the street with Kenny, Julian, and Trish trailing after him. Evan gave Greg a final dirty look and jogged to catch up with him.

JJ shook his head at Greg and moved to join Evan. "You're pushing too hard, mate."

Evan caught up to Jesse and snagged him by the upper arm to a halt him. "Are you okay?"

Jesse summoned a smile for him. "I'm great since I got to see you earlier than I expected."

Evan could tell Jesse was trying to hide his distress, but decided to let him keep his front up until they were alone. "I wanted to wait for you."

Jesse's smile became more genuine. "Are you hungry? We should get something to eat before we go home."

"Yeah, we can do that." Evan retrieved a set of car keys from his front pocket. "Here. You drive."

Jesse took the keys, confusion causing him to stare at them. "What are these to?"

Evan pulled him around a corner and pointed to a new Ferrari F430 coupe, its custom midnight blue paint lightly touched with a hint of metallic. "They're to that."

"How freakin' sweet!" Jesse darted toward it, slamming to a halt as he came upon it. He stood back, drinking in the masterpiece. He gazed at the engine through the window in back, radiating power though it lay silent. He examined the wheels that bore the yellow Ferrari logo with the black prancing stallion in the center. He peeked in at the black leather seats, and the dashboard and controls accented in brushed aluminum.

"That's a kickass car," Kenny said.

"It's beautiful," Julian added.

"It can really move, too," JJ said. "I went with him to pick it up today."

Evan stepped up to Jesse's side. "It should be able to get out of its own way. It's V8 is pushing out about four hundred and ninety horses." He nudged Jesse playfully with his elbow. "And it's yours."

Jesse snapped his head toward him. "What?"

"It's yours. It's what you've always wanted, right? Well, besides a souped-up Honda S2000. Besides the fact that I couldn't bring myself to purchase one of those, I thought this was a little more to your status now."

Jesse quickly shook his head. "It's perfect, but you shouldn't have spent so much." JJ snorted. "If he hasn't already, you need to have him show you his bank statements, Jess."

Jesse glanced at JJ, then back to Evan. "It doesn't matter. It's too much."

Evan gave him a warm smile. "Gorgeous, JJ is right. And what difference does it make? Do you like it?"

"I love it. But—"

"No buts," Evan said, pushing him toward the driver's side. "Just get in. Consider it a congratulations for finishing the album."

"This is one hell of a present for that," Jesse chuckled. Without Greg to stop him, he wrapped Evan in a tight embrace. "Thank you."

"You're welcome." Evan glanced at Trish over Jesse's shoulder and allowed a shadow of smugness to come into his expression. He drew back from the hug and opened the driver's side door for Jesse.

Jesse looked at the others as he hopped in. "You guys follow us. We have to go out to celebrate finishing our first video."

Trish folded her arms across her chest and glowered at him. "Just a minute ago you said you didn't want to go out."

"Yeah, but that was because I wanted to go home to Ev, and now he's here, so we can all go out." Jesse turned to Evan as he climbed in the passenger seat. "Will you call Brandon and ask him if he wants to join us? He's going to die when he sees this."

Evan nodded and pulled out his cell phone.

Jesse pushed the red "engine start" button. The F430 rumbled to life. He let his body go limp in the seat. "I'm done for the night. That was beautiful."

Evan laughed. "You probably should've held it for when it's actually moving."

With the car backed into the parking space, Jesse put it in first gear and eased it forward. He steered toward the garage exit, popped it into second, and hit the street with the tires squealing.

CHAPTER TWENTY-FOUR

"Evan! It's coming back on!" Brandon yelled from the family room.

Evan rushed out of the kitchen carrying three bottles of Guinness and two bags of potato chips. He headed for the couch, dropped one bag into JJ's lap, and squeezed between Brandon and the coffee table. Brandon went immobile at having Evan's crotch at eye level. Evan swallowed down a laugh, sat beside him, and focused his attention on the TV where Jesse sat next to the VJ for VH1 with Kenny on his right, Julian and Trish behind him.

"I think he's handled himself pretty damn good, if you ask me," JJ said. "Especially considering the mob outside the studio and all the girlies screaming for five minutes straight when he walked on stage."

Evan ripped open the bag of barbeque flavored chips. "For all the coaching Greg and I gave him and the small interviews he's done, this is nothing for him."

An indiscernible grumble rumbled in Brandon's throat.

Evan looked at him. "What's wrong?"

"You can give him all the PR training you want, but it won't change the fact that sooner or later, his old habit of speaking without thinking is going to surface. It's just the way he is."

Evan turned his eyes back to the TV. What Brandon said was true, but so far with the questions he'd been getting drilled with, Jesse answered like a seasoned performer. Most were about his music and the history of Conquest, no one tried digging into his personal life yet, but he knew if they did, Jesse could handle it. They talked about it after the incident with Greg, and even though neither of them was thrilled with the idea of keeping their relationship a secret, they agreed that it was the best thing for now.

In truth, he hated having to stay quiet about it. If he had it his way, he would have gone with him to New York and made out with him in the middle of Times Square for all the world to see, but he had Jesse's career to think about. He held no concerns for his own. If he did come out to the public, he was confident his career was strong enough to rebound, and if he was wrong and it did break his career, then so be it. But Jesse was just getting going, and it was hard enough in the music business to reach the level he wanted without having stigmas surrounding his sexuality holding him back.

For now, keeping their relationship a secret seemed the only way to go. They knew they were together and they loved each other, and that's what really mattered. Though, at this moment when he had to sit and watch thousands of fans crying out their love and devotion to Jesse, it made him want to throw their decision out the window.

He knew it was to be expected. "Euphoria" hit Number One on Billboard and was iTunes most downloaded single within two weeks after it came out. *Conquest* debuted at Number One and dominated retail sales and Internet downloads. Evan gazed at Jesse as the camera zoomed in on him laughing. The love the camera showed him was only surpassed by his army of new fans.

Evan knew thousands of people were looking at Jesse, admiring him. He couldn't fight down the jealously that rose in him and wondered if he really would be able to handle not telling the world that Jesse was his. He took a deep breath and forced himself to focus on the interview.

"So, Jesse," the VJ said, "I think not only did our sound guy have a heart attack trying to balance out all the screaming girls, but half of New York is deaf now. I guess you're a little popular with the ladies, huh?"

Jesse laughed softly. "No, not really. Kenny's a lot more of a ladies' man than me."

"Oh yeah?" The VJ craned around Jesse to look at Kenny. "You got a girlfriend, man?"

"Not right now, but I'm looking for a few," Kenny said.

The studio audience erupted with girls volunteering for the position.

The VJ turned back to Jesse. "Let me ask you this and see if I can make a few thousand girls jump for joy or break all their hearts. Are you seeing anyone right now?"

"I am. I've been in a serious relationship for four months now."

Evan froze with a potato chip halfway to his mouth.

"Four months, wow," the VJ said. "Then I guess that means the buzz starting around you is either crap, or it's true."

"I didn't think I've been around long enough for there to be a buzz about me. What is it?"

"Well, you know everybody's hyped that Evan Arden is working on a new album, and it's said you and him recorded in the same studio, and there's a few folks out there saying you guys are a little closer than friends."

"It's true that he and I are working in the same studio, and it's also true I wouldn't be sitting here now if it wasn't for him. He's my best friend and I love him dearly. And people can say and think what they want about me. I'm confidant enough in who I am to not be bothered by it."

A few people clapped in positive response, but it seemed shock dominated most.

The VJ slapped his hand down on Jesse's shoulder. "Well, I don't have much of a response for that, except stay with us, because after the break we'll be talking about…"

Evan fell back against the couch, staring blankly at the TV, his ears no longer hearing what came from it. "He said he loves me, on national TV."

Brandon looked at him, his mouth still hanging open. He started to say something, stopped, thought, and began again. "Yeah, but, there are a lot of different kinds of love, and he said you were his best friend right before that, so of course he would love his best friend."

JJ snorted. "Not many straight men would admit that to themselves let alone on camera. And poor Kenny. Did you see his face when Jess said you were his best friend? I think that stung a bit."

Brandon laid his hand on Evan's thigh. "Don't worry about it. I'm sure people will blow it off."

A slow smile lit Evan's face. "He said he loves me on national TV! I can't believe he did that!"

"You're not mad at him?" Brandon asked.

"No. How could I get angry with him saying he loves me? I just wonder how the media found out about us already. Since Greg released I was working on a new album, we've been careful when we've gone out. Some paparazzi have been slithering around the studio, but I didn't think they tagged us. Now we have to figure out how widespread the rumors are and how to stop them."

Brandon looked back at the TV as the commercial break ended. "Yeah, but I have a feeling stopping the media is going to be a hell of a lot easier than stopping Jess."

CHAPTER TWENTY-FIVE

Jesse rushed through the airport with his Chicago Bears duffel bag slung over his shoulder. Kenny and Julian on either side of him struggled to keep up, Trish and Greg followed behind. He stood waiting for his other bag, impatiently tapping his index finger against his hip, his only thought being how badly he wanted to get into Evan's arms. It was all he had wanted since his first night away. Missing him so much that he had a constant ache in his chest was just one of the many things to make his first trip to New York not as enjoyable as he'd always envisioned.

From the second they landed, it had been go, go, go. Interviews here, photo shoots there, autograph sessions next, it was one thing after another, and to top it off, he hardly slept the whole trip despite the frantic schedule. At night, he would collapse into bed, physically and mentally exhausted, but unable to sleep without the lullaby of Evan's soft breathing beside him and his firm body to keep him warmer than any blanket. They talked every morning, in the afternoon, and evening, but those phone calls only managed to make him miss Evan more.

Despite his fatigue, the *Rolling Stone* interview went especially well. Originally it was supposed to be a small article with a single band shot about Conquest as a band to look out for, but after the way "Euphoria" and the album were dominating, it was decided they'd be the next month's cover feature. The only thing that hadn't gone so well was the interview on VH1.

At the time, he thought it had gone well. Sure there was a tense moment when the VJ asked about him and Evan, but he thought he smoothed it over pretty good. Of course, he did say he was in a relationship after agreeing with everyone that if questioned about his personal life, he would say he was single, and he *had* really believed he would be able to do that, but when the question was finally asked, he couldn't get the lie out. In that split second, he became filled with an overwhelming sense of betrayal, to Evan and himself, and he realized to be asked to deny the one thing in his life that meant more than anything else was too much. He could keep quiet, he could dance around the questions, but he would never openly say he was available when he had Evan.

He was pretty sure he had given Greg an ulcer after that interview. When the show finished and they went back to the green room, Greg was so pale, his forehead beaded with sweat, and he looked like he had just thrown up. He was surprised Greg never lectured him about what he said, but Greg probably realized there wasn't any changing it. Trish scolded him for his words, but he made it clear it wasn't her place to tell him what to say during interviews. Julian thought it was funny; Kenny had been pissed at him ever since.

What made matters worse was by the time they walked out of the VH1 studios, his legions of fans were joined by crazed paparazzi screaming questions at him about his relationship with Evan. From that moment forward, he only knew peace when locked away in his hotel room. Going out to eat, traveling to interviews and photo shoots, even to the airport to come home, the press tailed him everywhere. Though so far, things were clear now that he was back in Chicago. He knew it wouldn't last. It was just because the local paparazzi hadn't picked up his scent yet. It left him feeling hunted, that if he lingered too long in one spot they'd track him, and once they picked up his trail, a certainty as soon as he went to the studio again, they'd be tricky to evade.

But at the moment, none of it mattered. As soon as he walked out the airport doors, he would be in Evan's arms.

Jesse sighed, grabbed his other bag, and waited for the others to collect theirs. He wondered if Evan really was upset with him. When he asked him, Evan said no, but that had been over the phone. He wouldn't feel fully confident until they talked in person.

Jesse walked out of the airport, his gaze darted about and landed on the Cayenne. He waved to the others and strode quickly toward it, hearing the hatch pop open as Evan unlocked it at his approach. He heaved it open the rest of the way and met Evan's radiant blue eyes.

Evan wore a glowing smile. "Welcome back, gorgeous."

At the sight of him, Jesse felt both calm and excited. "Do you know how badly I've been dying to see your beautiful eyes?"

Evan chuckled. "And here I thought the pictures you have of me on your cell phone would keep you satisfied."

"Not nearly enough."

Jesse tossed his bags in the SUV and closed the tailgate. He rushed toward the passenger side, ripped open the door, and jumped in. The door hardly finished closing before Evan was stretched across from the driver's seat, devouring Jesse's tongue in a deep kiss. Jesse moaned and massaged Evan's tongue with his. He slipped his hand up the back of Evan's shirt, needing to the feel the warmth of his bare skin.

Jesse broke the kiss with a soft laugh. "It's a good thing these windows are tinted jet black."

"Yeah. I might not be able to make it until we get home and wrestle you into the backseat." Evan put his lips to Jesse's neck. "You smell so good."

Jesse nuzzled into Evan's hair, inhaling his scent and Platinum Egoist cologne. "So do you."

Evan slid his tongue over Jesse's bottom lip and sat back in the driver's seat, giving Jesse a playful smile as he veered the Cayenne away from the airport. "As soon as we get home, no clothes for the rest of the day."

Jesse took Evan's hand in his. "Sounds like a perfect way to spend the day."

❋ ❋ ❋

Jesse panted for breath, his arms stretched up on the bed with his hands pressed flat against the headboard, bracing himself against Evan's vigorous thrusts. His legs rested over Evan's shoulders. He opened his eyes and looked at Evan, his torso glistening in sweat. The sight of Evan's body, the feel of his strength in each thrust, drove Jesse closer to climax. He pressed his head against the mattress, moaning high and loud.

The sound of Jesse in pleasure took Evan's passion to a fiercer level. He thrust harder and grabbed Jesse's cock in his right hand. Jesse let out a sharp gasp at Evan's forceful grip, yanking and pulling on it. He couldn't hold back. He arched off the bed, squeezing Evan's neck with his legs.

"Yes, Evan!"

Jesse's words turned to an incoherent shout as he released. Evan continued to pound into him with each pulse of his orgasm, making it feel as though it lasted twice as long. Evan slammed into him a final time with a short yell. Jesse felt Evan's cock throbbing as it filled him with cum.

Evan laid his head against Jesse's right knee, his eyes closed as he caught his breath. It wasn't until his breathing got closer to normal that he stirred. He eased Jesse's legs from his shoulders and pulled out of him, then collapsed on his back beside him.

"Maybe you should go away more often," he said.

A deep chuckle sounded in Jesse's throat. With effort, he rolled onto his side and draped one arm across Evan's chest. "Just imagine how wild it's going to be when we're touring together. Of course, having me be your opening act isn't going to help put the rumors about us to rest."

"I don't think that's going to happen anyway after your interview."

Jesse glanced away from him. "I know you said you weren't upset, but you are a little bit, aren't you?"

Evan flipped toward Jesse. He gently held Jesse's chin and turned his head to look into his eyes, his voice soft and warm. "No, I'm not upset. The media will eventually brush off what you said so long as we don't give them any more ammunition. Sooner or later another big celeb will do something to take the attention off us and make the paparazzi see dollar signs. We just have to be extra careful until things quiet down."

Jesse tried to give him a smile, but only a ghost of one came to his lips. "It's not really *we*, though, is it? I'm the one with the big mouth. The thing is, I know what I was supposed to say, but when I was actually supposed to put it in action, I couldn't. I felt like I was betraying you, and us. And I can't do that."

Evan gazed at him, not having any words to combat Jesse's confession. He held Jesse closer. "I know. I don't want to either."

Jesse held onto him, his mind, his heart a turmoil of confusion and emotion. All his life, the only thing he wanted was to make music and share it with the world. He always felt nothing would ever mean more to him than conquering the masses with his gift. Now that he was on the edge of achieving his dream, when he had already won his first battles, the only thing that felt truly important was the man he had his arms around.

"I have something that'll cheer you up," Evan said. He sat up, pulled open the top drawer of the nightstand, retrieved an envelope, and handed it to Jesse.

Jesse opened it. He bolted upright, clutching tickets for that Sunday's Bears game. "These are for a private suite!"

Evan pulled the tickets out of Jesse's hand and flung them over the edge of the bed. He pushed him to his back and climbed on top of him. "I thought a private suite would be nice if we wanted to invite everyone along, but now I'm thinking maybe it'd be better not to."

Jesse gaped up at him. "There's no fucking when football's going on!"

"Great! At least I know where your priorities are!" Evan ground his hips and quickly rising cock against him. "I guess I'll just have to get it all worked out before Sunday afternoon."

Jesse shook his head. "To even think—"

Evan covered Jesse's mouth with his hand. "Shhh, believe me, if it was the Giants, I wouldn't have even thought of saying something like that. But it's just the Bears."

Jesse pulled Evan's hand away. "*Just* the Bears? Haven't you lived in this city long enough to know you don't insult the Bears?"

Evan rolled his eyes. "How can anyone like a team who did the 'Super Bowl Shuffle'?"

Jesse sighed. "All those years ago, and it still won't go away."

"Even without that dark blemish, I'm sorry, gorgeous, I'll always be a Giants fan. But don't worry, I'll be there to comfort you when they lose."

"I can't believe you said that." Jesse pushed on Evan's shoulders. "You're denied." He flipped onto his stomach and stretched over the edge of the bed to get the tickets.

Grabbing him by the shoulder and one hip, Evan yanked him back under him. "Is that so?"

Jesse smiled. "Yeah."

Evan lowered his head and kissed the back of Jesse's neck. He drifted lower, his lips gliding over his shoulder blades. Jesse closed his eyes as Evan's tongue caressed down his spine to his tailbone and back up. He felt Evan's silken arousal pressing against his ass and moaned deep in his throat as he pushed back toward it.

"That doesn't sound like you're denying me," Evan whispered.

"Don't you dare start teasing."

"Unfortunately, I don't have the willpower for that right now," Evan said, and with a smooth thrust, slipped inside him.

Jesse groaned loud and lifted his body to Evan's thrust, letting him go deeper. Evan took hold of Jesse's hip with one hand, seeking out his hand with the other, and clutched them together.

"I love you so much," he said.

Evan rocked his body slowly, his lips by Jesse's ear. "I love you, too. More than anything in the world."

CHAPTER TWENTY-SIX

The sound of the buzzer echoed through the house, giving Jesse and Evan a brutal awakening that someone was outside the gates. Since it wasn't the day for the housecleaners, gardeners, or pool cleaners to come, and only six other people knew where Evan's house was, and of those, only Brandon had a code to get past the gates, Jesse decided as sad as it was, either Kenny, Julian, Trish, JJ, or Greg were going to have to die for waking them up. He felt Evan tense behind him and knew he was thinking the same thing, especially since they had made it clear to everyone the day before at the Bears game they wouldn't be in on Monday.

Jesse took Evan's hand and put it on his usual morning erection. "Do you think we can drown out the buzzer long enough the idiot will give up and go away?"

Evan tightened his fingers around Jesse's solid shaft, tucked his hips tight against him, and kissed the back of his neck. "I'm positive we can."

Jesse turned his head and found Evan's lips. Evan's cock filled against him and shifted so it nestled between his ass cheeks. Evan deepened the kiss, pushing against him at the same moment.

The buzzer continued its harsh cry.

A deep growl shook Evan's throat. Jesse could tell it was one of annoyance rather than aggressive passion.

Evan drew his lips away and flung the covers off. "You'll have my back in case someone finds the body, right?"

"Of course," Jesse said with a yawn. He yanked the blankets up around his neck. "But Lake Michigan is pretty deep, so I think we'll be okay."

Evan hopped into his black running pants and stormed out of the bedroom, turning away from the stairs and heading down to a closed door at the end of the hall. Opening it, he walked into the security room. He looked at the two monitors for the cameras by the entrance to the private road, swearing under his breath as Greg, in his silver Mercedes-Benz S-Class, repeatedly hit the call button. Evan pounded the keys to manually open the gates.

He opened the gates for the driveway, then stomped down the stairs. When Greg's car stopped, Evan whipped open one of the doors and slammed it behind him as he stepped onto the porch. "What the fuck is the matter with you?"

Greg marched around his car and shoved two magazines against Evan's chest. "This."

Evan took the tabloids and looked down at them. One featured a picture on the cover of him and Jesse eating at a restaurant with a headline reading, "Evan Arden's Special Dinner Date." The second boasted a shot of them walking out of the studio with his arm over Jesse's shoulders and the headline, "Evan Arden's New Love?"

"So what," Evan said.

"That's all you can say? There are more pictures inside of you two!"

Evan handed the tabloids back to Greg. "Unless they show us kissing, groping, sucking, or screwing, I really don't give a shit."

"That's real nice, Evan. I don't think you appreciate how serious this is. Obviously the paparazzi have been slinking around with more stealth than usual looking to finally break a scandal on you since they could never nail you before, and now they've finally done it!"

"You're overreacting. Those pictures are easily explained away as two friends hanging out together. And no one believes those stupid things, anyway."

"Whether they believe them or not isn't the issue. It's enough to put the idea in people's heads, not that it isn't there already with Jesse's little confession on TV. I'm less concerned about the damn media than I am about him."

Evan stared at him for a second, then slowly lowered his gaze.

"You know I'm right, I can see it. He's the hottest thing going right now and if it's left up to him, he's going to shoot his career right down the drain because he's so enamored with you he won't listen to reason about the need to keep your relationship under wraps. Your career could probably rebound if you came out, but this is the most delicate time for him and Conquest. Right now, they're balancing on the line of being the next great super-group or becoming one hit wonders, and the loyalty they build in their fans now is what's going to make or break them."

"Alright! I get it! I'll talk to him—"

"Talking isn't enough anymore!" Greg grabbed Evan's upper arm for emphasis. "He won't listen. He doesn't understand. Jesse's dancing through life in his own little fairytale world where everything's happy and perfect, and anything that disagrees with him, he either blows off or forces to his opinion. So unless you've got some trick up your sleeve to make him see the reality of the world around him, this can't continue. Sooner or later he's going to get a wakeup call, and if it doesn't come from you, then it's going to come in a way where everything he's ever wanted is going to be lost forever."

Evan turned his head, unable to look at Greg. With each beat of his heart coming faster, his blood chilled in fear. He took in a shaking breath, trying to loosen his choked throat. "What...do you want me to do?"

"I think you know what you have to do. If you care at all about him and his dreams." Greg handed the tabloids back to Evan and turned for his car. He looked at him over the roof, then slid in and drove away.

Evan stood staring down at the ground, holding the tabloids loosely at his side. He sank down on the porch steps, his head in his hands.

❋ ❋ ❋

Jesse reached out for Evan, his hand found only cold sheets beside him. He remembered someone ringing the buzzer and Evan leaving to see who it was. He must've dosed off again and Evan must still be stuck with whoever came by.

He rolled over to check the alarm clock and heard paper crinkling beside him. He wiggled his hand out from under the covers and smacked it down until it fell on the source of the sound. He picked up the two tabloids. His heart spiraled toward his stomach that churned with a sick flip. He sat up and opened one of the magazines to the article implying that he and Evan were lovers.

"Pretty good pictures, huh?"

Jesse jerked his head toward the balcony. Evan stood outside with his back to him, staring out over the lake. He wore only a pair of jeans. Jesse gazed at his bare back for a moment before looking at the tabloids again.

"Well, we both are extremely photogenic."

"It's cute you can find humor in this," Evan said, pushing off the railing and turning into the bedroom. "Especially since it looks to me like the fun's over."

Jesse gave a confused shake of his head. "What do you mean?"

Evan veered toward his closet and stepped inside. "I told you we had to be careful. I can't have these rumors flying around me while I'm trying to re-launch my career."

"Your career? What are you talking about? These pictures don't prove anything other than we hang out."

Evan rested his hand on a black T-shirt and closed his eyes, trying to steel himself to continue. He took a deep breath and yanked the shirt off its hanger. "Yeah, the pictures are nothing more than innuendo, but there's not much for people to question when you're going on TV babbling how you love me."

Jesse sat quiet for a moment. "But, you said you weren't upset about that."

Evan stepped back into the bedroom pulling the T-shirt over his head. "I just didn't want you to get worked up thinking I was mad at you, and I thought it would eventually bother me less, but now I'm getting slammed with this. Personally, I think it was pretty goddamn selfish of you to act like that. Did you even think about me, or what I wanted?"

"Of course I did!" Jesse said, his tone turning desperate. "It's because I was thinking of you I said that!"

Evan moved to the foot of the bed, fixing him with a cold glare. "You obviously didn't think hard enough. You really can be naïve, Jess. It's no wonder Brandon's always saying all you got are book smarts and no common sense, because if you had even a drop of common sense, you would've realized the damage you could have inflicted on my career."

"I'm sorry! I'll admit I wasn't thinking of the harm it could do, but the last thing I want is to hurt your career. I thought you would be happy that I didn't offer myself as available to the world. I guess I took it a step too far."

"You're damn right you did," Evan growled.

Jesse slid across the bed to get closer to him. "But I'll do better from now on. I won't ever say anything like that again in public."

"You won't have a reason to."

Jesse stared at him, the ice in Evan's eyes making him almost unrecognizable. Panic's iron fingers began to close around his heart. He felt like he couldn't breathe. "Are...are you...breaking up with me?"

Evan answered him with a silent stare.

"Y-you're not serious," Jesse stuttered. "You can't be."

Evan spun for the bedroom door. "I'm going into the city for the rest of the day. That should give you enough time to get your shit and get out."

"Ev, no! There's no reason for this! Fuck your career! Fuck my career! I don't give a shit about any of it if it means I can't have you!"

Evan paused in the doorway. He kept his back to Jesse and closed his eyes again. He swallowed hard, forcing resolve into his waning willpower. "That's easy for you to say. You've never stood under the burning glow of stage lights with thousands of people screaming for you. It's easy to give up what you've never known.

"If you need to use the Cayenne to move your crap, that's fine. But don't play any stupid games like leaving something behind as an excuse to come back over and get it." On his last word, he walked out of the bedroom.

Jesse leaped out of bed and ran after him. At the bottom of the stairs, he caught him and threw his arms around him from behind. "Please, Ev, don't do this. We can explain those pictures. It'll be easy. Just don't break this off. I love you."

"Let go of me," Evan snapped. He pried Jesse's arms from around his waist and flung them away. "Try to be out by nine o'clock tonight. That should give you plenty of time. You don't have shit of your own, anyway."

Jesse stood frozen, watching Evan walk away. He heard the access door to the garage open, then slam close. A moment later, the 612 squealed out of the garage. His legs trembled under him, his strength beaten from him by Evan. He felt like he was going to either pass out or be sick. His head spun, and he dropped to the ground, his body, his mind, his spirit, drowning in loss.

CHAPTER TWENTY-SEVEN

Jesse sat tucked in a corner of the couch in the chill-out room, his back to everyone. Kenny, Julian, and Trish huddled at the table in the kitchen area making small talk with each other in muted voices in an attempt to keep a neutral atmosphere. Their delicate demeanor made him want to escape from them even more, but since Kenny had shown up at Brandon's that morning and practically carried him out the door to bring him to the studio, he knew even if he did leave someone would come chasing after him. He understood what they were trying to do. They all believed if they could get him playing music again he'd feel better. The problem was, he was waiting to run into Evan at any second.

When Evan left him, he sat on the stairs for half an hour in blank shock. Finally he got to where he could move, but the only thing he found himself able to do was pace from one room to another, not knowing what to do with himself. At one point, he had revitalized by deciding he wasn't going to lose Evan, he would fight for him, he would force Evan to believe they could be together and everything would be as perfect as before. Then in his mind he saw Evan's cold eyes, heard his harsh words, and his battle spirit retreated. As that happened, he came to the hardest realization of his life; as his final act of respect for Evan, he had to leave.

Having nowhere else to go, he called Brandon. He knew he could have called Kenny, or Julian, or even Trish, and any would open their doors to him, but only Brandon would truly understand, and at that moment, he wanted to go to the one person he knew would never walk away from him, the one person who had always protected him.

Brandon had been in the middle of rehearsal, but claimed a family emergency and left to come to him. To his surprise, Brandon didn't push for details. Quietly, they collected his belongings, which true to Evan's words were meager and mostly clothes, and crammed it all into the Cayenne. As for the F430, taking so expensive a gift not only felt wrong, how could he keep it? Every time he'd drive it, he would think of Evan, of the places they'd gone in it, the things they had done.

After they unloaded his belongings at Brandon's new apartment on North Dearborn, he drove the Cayenne back with Brandon following on his Suzuki. When they left the mansion for the final time, he sat behind Brandon on the motorcycle, punching the code into the keypad to close the gates. As they shut, the finality of it made it seem all his and Evan's time together had been nothing more than a surreal dream.

That night, Brandon didn't make pathetic efforts to cheer him up. He sat beside him on the couch in his apartment, not saying a word. Maybe it was the silence that did it, but he broke down. Brandon had wrapped him in his arms as he cried and told him what happened.

The next day, he couldn't bring himself to go into the studio, there wasn't anything important to do besides going over tour stuff and rehearsing, and rehearsing he felt was pointless until they would be able to get into the Auditorium Theatre where their kick-off concert was going to be held, so he ended up calling Kenny, told him everything, and that he wouldn't be coming in.

Wednesday morning came, and once again he refused to go into the studio. In the evening, Kenny showed up at Brandon's apartment with Julian and Trish, but to his relief, Brandon blocked them at the door and spared him from having to deal with the cheer-up brigade.

Thursday, he didn't get out of bed except to go to the bathroom and take a long shower, where he stood under the water more than washed. Brandon brought him a pizza from Uno's, but he only managed to get down half a slice before feeling like he would be sick.

Unfortunately, that morning after Brandon left for the theatre, Kenny came pounding on the door. He had no choice but to answer it and didn't have the will to fight him when Kenny demanded he come to the studio. Evan hadn't been there when they arrived, but he knew without seeing him he was there now.

As he finished the thought, Evan walked into the room.

Jesse kept his eyes focused down. The others silenced their conversation as Evan stopped in front of him.

Evan tossed the Ferrari F430 keys on the couch beside Jesse. "I thought I told you not to leave anything behind."

"I don't want it," Jesse mumbled. "Keep it."

"What do I want with it? It's your little toy, it's not my style. It's parked near the guard booth in the garage." Evan turned to walk away.

All his anger, all his pain, rose faster than Jesse could control. He leaped up and whipped the keys across the room. They crashed into a picture hanging on the wall, shattering the glass. "That's all you care about, isn't it? Your fucking image! What's the best car to drive! The best clothes to wear! The best fuck buddy to have in your bed!"

Evan walked over to the broken picture, picked up the car keys, and walked back to Jesse, stopping inches from him. "Is that what you think? That you were just some fuck buddy?"

"What else would you call me? You kicked me out the door like I was nothing just because of some goddamn pictures!"

Evan grabbed Jesse's upper arm, his grip firm, but careful to not hurt him. "Don't ever…EVER…mock the feelings I have for you!"

He threw the keys down on the couch and spun for the door. Greg, JJ, and Jeremy stood by the door, looking trapped by what they had witnessed. Evan rammed his shoulder hard against Greg's as he passed.

Jesse stared at the floor for a long moment, the phantom of Evan's rough touch lingering on his arm. He picked up the car keys with trembling fingers and walked toward the door. His shoulder brushed lightly against Greg's as he turned down the hall and headed toward Studio B, alone.

❋ ❋ ❋

Jesse glanced up at the clock in the control room. He had been at the studio all day, all night, refusing offers to go to his band members' apartments or out to dinner with them. Now the studio was empty save for the security guard. He turned off his music and sat listening to the silence.

He felt numb. It was as if all his emotions, all his desires, had shut down. He didn't want to eat. He didn't want to drink. Most of all, he didn't want to feel. The thought of smiling or laughing seemed a concept beyond his reach and he didn't want to try and grasp it. The only thing that sounded halfway decent was going back to Brandon's, crawling into bed and lying in the dark bedroom. Thinking about it gave him just enough energy to push away from the control desk and leave the studio.

Walking out to the night shrouded city, he headed across the street to the parking garage. He stepped inside and stumbled to a halt. His eyes locked on the F430, its dark blue paint seeming black in the dim yellow garage lights. He clutched the keys and walked toward it. When he climbed in, he wasn't sure if it was his imagination, but he thought he caught the faint scent of Evan's cologne lingering in the car. Despair closed his throat from air, his eyes began to burn. He pressed his forehead against the steering wheel, his body shaking with tears.

CHAPTER TWENTY-EIGHT

Jesse locked Brandon's apartment door behind him and walked down the hall to the elevator. Almost a week had passed since he'd seen Evan when they had their confrontation at the studio, and during that time, he only went to the studio once to rehearse and found himself mobbed by paparazzi. Studio security held them at bay until he got in, but he found little sanctuary when he ran into JJ, who told him Evan had changed his session times and now didn't come in until seven o'clock at night and recorded well into the early morning hours. JJ gave him the information as if it was something he should care about. He saw it as one more slap in the face from Evan, telling him Evan didn't even want to be in the same building at the same time as him. That information pushed him over the edge.

For the past week, he spent his evenings staring blankly at the TV until the sound of it would get on his nerves and he would turn it off. But without having the images flickering in front of him to keep him still, he would pace around Brandon's apartment. He tried reading *The Iliad* again, but couldn't concentrate on it and put it down. Brandon caused some distraction when home, but rehearsals for *Phantom* were getting more intense, so Brandon wasn't there much.

Tonight, he couldn't take it anymore. He came to the conclusion that he needed to snap himself out of his depression, to force himself to forget about Evan, and there was only one way he knew of to do it.

The elevator stopped at the ground floor garage. He walked toward the F430, the smell of his body spray wafting around him. He disarmed the car alarm, climbed in, and swung it out of the parking garage, aiming it toward the Lakeview area. If Brandon knew where he was going, he'd choke him, but he was long past the point of needing Brandon to watch over him. He didn't need *anyone* to watch over him.

A rainbow-striped flag hanging under a lit streetlight added color to the night and announced he had reached Boystown. He eased off the gas, cruising past clubs and bars, restaurants and stores, many places familiar from times when he and Brandon would come there. With it being a little after nine o'clock and a Thursday night, a fair number of people wandered the streets, making their way to favorite clubs or places to eat. Men eyed him from the sidewalk, some called out for him to stop, but he continued drifting. To him, they all looked the same. Blond hair or black, blue eyes or brown, tall, short, built, scrawny, they were all nameless faces.

He stopped at a traffic light, his eyes fell on a couple walking hand in hand. The two men laughed with each other, playfully shoving and grabbing. Jesse clenched his teeth and faced forward. The light turned green. He smashed the throttle to the floor. The Ferrari roared; tires screeched as it launched through the intersection. Jesse rocketed away from Boystown, not knowing where to go, but not wanting to stay there or go back to Brandon's.

He coasted aimlessly through the city, past multi-million dollar condos to neighborhoods where he all but begged to have the flashy Ferrari jacked. He found himself going past every restaurant he and Evan had eaten at, every store they had shopped. He drove to the studio and stopped in the street, wondering if Evan was inside, but not wanting to look in the parking garage to check for his car. If he wasn't there, his mind would flood with thoughts of all the things Evan could be doing, things he couldn't bring himself to face. It was easier to pretend he stood at the mic working on his next masterpiece, his beautiful voice floating over his perfect lips.

Jesse drove away from the studio and continued his directionless quest. The skyscrapers loomed overhead, the lights glowing through the windows of the structures. A twinge of claustrophobia closed in on him. He felt as though he was being swallowed into a great cave. He looked up at the night sky peeking down between the mammoth buildings. Instead of the infinite space above calming him, the blackness increased his anxiety.

He looked down at his cell phone on the passenger seat. He had turned the volume off, but saw three missed calls; Brandon he figured, since it was a quarter past three in the morning. With a sigh, he headed back to Brandon's.

When he got there, he unlocked the apartment door as quietly as possible and stepped in. The apartment was dark save for the TV, the soft light dancing over Brandon's sleeping face. He had fallen asleep on the couch with his cell phone in hand. Jesse turned off the TV and pulled an afghan off the back of the couch to cover him.

"Where were you?" Brandon asked, his voice rough with sleep.

"I went for a drive, just like the note I left you said."

Jesse turned down the hall to the second bedroom in Brandon's apartment, which had become his bedroom, and stripped down to his boxers.

Brandon shuffled in, looking half asleep, and collapsed face down on Jesse's bed. "You were dressed too nice to have just gone for a drive."

Jesse crawled under the covers and lay on his back. "I went to Boystown."

All semblance of sleepiness vanished from Brandon. He bolted half up on his elbows and snapped his head toward Jesse. "What!"

"Settle down. All I did was drive around. I didn't even get out of my car."

Brandon stared at him for a long moment. Jesse glanced at him and had to restrain himself from pushing Brandon off the bed at the pitying look he gave him.

Brandon turned his head away and lay back down. He was quiet for several minutes before mumbling, "You shouldn't try to force it, Jess."

Jesse flipped over, putting his back to Brandon, and gave the covers an irritated tug toward his side of the bed. "Why don't you go to your own bed and get off the blankets, asshole."

Jesse waited for him to respond and when Brandon didn't so much as twitch, he sat up and craned his neck to look at him. Brandon's back rose and fell in deep, relaxed breaths, his face peaceful with sleep. Jesse sighed and folded the comforter over to cover him. He laid back down, his eyes closing on their own.

Three hours later, he woke practically clinging to the edge of the mattress so he wouldn't fall out as Brandon had taken over almost the entire full-size bed. He contemplated kicking him to get him to move, but decided even if he did gain a few more inches, he was too awake to go back to sleep. He sat up, glowering resentfully at his brother who slept in serene obliviousness.

He eased out of bed and went to his closet where he retrieved a Chicago Bears T-shirt and a pair of gray sweatpants. He headed to the bathroom, brushed his teeth, and got ready for a run. After leaving Brandon a note, he left the apartment, started some preliminary stretches in the elevator, and walked to his car while stretching his arms over his head and bending to the side. He drove down to Grant Park, finished stretching in the parking lot, then hit the trails.

He set a faster pace for himself than usual. With each stride, his head pounded Evan's name. Why did he feel like he betrayed him? He hadn't done anything, and even if he had picked up a guy, so what? Evan was the one who dumped him. It was time he moved on. So why did he feel guilty? Why had he felt during the drive to Boystown that he was making a mistake?

He had wanted to prove to himself he could do things like he used to, that he was the same person he was before Evan. But he wasn't. It was all different now. He could never go back. He wished he could. He wanted more than anything to be able to flirt and hook-up without conscience, without regret.

He let out a hard breath as he ran. That wasn't true. What he really wanted, more than each breath he took into his body, was to be held by the same man every night, to know his body, his voice, his movements, his thoughts, better than his own. He wanted Evan, and only Evan. The one person he couldn't have, would never have again.

The realization hitting fresh made his stomach roil. His vision blackened for an instant, and he stumble hard. He tried to catch himself, knowing he couldn't, and crashed to the sidewalk, skinning the heels of both hands and left elbow. He lay still, fighting back threatening tears. He drew his knees under himself and leaned his weight forward on his shaking arms, sweat dripping from his hair.

"Ev," he whispered.

Something soft brushed against his right arm. He startled back, whipping his head in the direction of the touch. A puppy skittered away from him, looking at him with wary eyes. Jesse stared at it. He shook his head and sat back on his heels to inspect his injuries. He gazed down at his scraped hands, then out the corner of his eye, saw the puppy's shadow inching closer to him. Cautiously, the dog stretched its neck out to sniff him.

Jesse slowly moved his right arm toward it, stopping a half-foot away. He remained motionless and was rewarded by a wet nose bumping over his hand and arm. He couldn't help but smile when its bushy tail wagged. Then as if it had instantly decided it liked him, the puppy marched forward and stood staring at him with an expectant look.

Jesse laughed softly and reached to pet it. As soon as his hand touched it, it leaped onto his lap. Jesse laughed louder. He picked it up and held it out in front of him in both hands, looking at its tawny eyes. The dog was covered in dirt and grim, its coat a nest of mats and tangles. It had a white belly, legs, and chest, tan on its head and sides, black tipped ears, and a black saddle marking on its back. He guessed from the fluffy Collie coat but German Shepherd head it was a mixed breed. He determined it to be male, and it didn't look much more than three months old. From its condition and the fact it wasn't wearing a collar, he assumed it was a stray.

The puppy stared back at him with no fear, its tail wagged with greater rapidity.

"You're pretty bold, aren't you?" Jesse cradled him to his chest and stood up, heading back toward his car. "I'm not sure what to do with you, but if I leave you on your own, you probably won't make it very long, so I guess I'll take you to a shelter."

He reached the F430 and stopped. He looked at the immaculate black leather seats, then down at the little dog that smelled like a garbage can.

"Well, I was planning on getting rid of this stupid thing, anyway."

He climbed in and set the puppy on the passenger seat. He glanced over at it as he pulled out of the parking lot, watching drool drip on the leather seat while it panted, and tried not to cringe, thinking to himself a couple more times, it didn't matter, he was getting rid of the car. He turned his eyes to the road.

"Now I just need to figure out where there's an animal shelter."

The puppy laid down, its eyes on him.

Jesse looked at it as he shifted the car. "Don't look at me like that. I can't have a dog. I'm getting ready to go on tour. You shouldn't have found a singer to save your scrawny ass." He turned his eyes back to the road, softening his voice. "Believe me, I know what it feels like. You probably thought you had someone who loved you too until they tossed you out."

The dog crawled across the center console and laid its head on Jesse's thigh. Jesse took his right hand off the steering wheel and stroked the dog's head.

CHAPTER TWENTY-NINE

Trish glanced up from her magazine, her head cocked to the side. Kenny and Julian paused in their conversation.

"Is that a dog barking?" Kenny asked.

A puppy raced around the corner of the doorway and into the chill-out room.

"Oh my god!" Trish squealed as she picked him up.

Jesse walked in after the dog holding a leash.

Kenny's mouth dropped open. "You got a dog?"

"Not exactly. I found him this morning. I was going to take him to a shelter, but..." Jesse shrugged, leaving that for his answer.

When he'd left Grant Park, he called information to find the closest animal shelter, but as the operator relayed the information, he gazed down at the little dog trying to crawl onto his lap and snapped his phone closed. The next thing he knew, he was walking into a pet shop with the puppy under his arm. Forty-five minutes and a cartload of food, supplies, toys, and treats later, he was on his way back to Brandon's, which had been quite a surprise for Brandon when he came home from grocery shopping and found him kneeling outside the bathtub trying to keep the puppy from shaking water and dog shampoo all over. Fortunately, Brandon recovered from his shock and jumped to help.

Julian fingered the black Lupine collar patterned with silver paw prints over crossbones around the puppy's neck. "Once you buy a collar it's official. Are you taking him on the road with us?"

"I plan to try," Jesse answered. "If it doesn't work out, Brandon said he would keep him until we come back."

"He can be our mascot!" Trish said. "What's his name?"

"Achilles."

Kenny startled at the name. "Achilles? Why'd you name him that? What ever happened to names like Spot or Rover?"

Trish put Achilles on the floor. He galloped to Jesse and hopped on his back legs, pawing up at him.

Jesse bent down and ruffled the thick, soft fur around his neck, speaking to the dog in a babying voice. "Because Achilles was a great warrior, wasn't he? And you're a big, tough boy, aren't you?"

"He's a cotton ball," Julian said.

Jesse sucked in an offended gasp. "Did you not see his paws and crossbones collar? He's a rocker."

"With identity issues then," Julian chuckled.

Achilles started barking and shot out of the room.

"Look!" Kenny laughed, pointing after him. "He's as much of a spaz as Jesse! Don't they say dogs take after their owners? And he's only had him since this morning!"

Ignoring everyone's snickering, Jesse threw Kenny a good-humored dirty look and took off after Achilles. He jogged into the hall and slammed to an instant stop.

Evan stood up the hall with JJ and Greg. Achilles stopped in front of him and stared up at him. Evan gazed down at him with a contemplative look. He picked him up, watching the puppy's tail wag so hard his whole body shook. Evan laughed softly and brought the dog to his chest, stroking his head.

Jesse tried to swallow around the lump closing his throat. It seemed like so much longer than a week since he last saw him. He noticed Evan's face looked thin and pale. His eyes bore circles beneath, his head was covered by a dark blue bandana allowing just the ends of his hair to peek out, and he hadn't shaved that morning, which wasn't like him. But it didn't matter. Even disheveled, he still looked amazing.

Evan lifted his eyes and froze at seeing Jesse. He slowly lowered his gaze, his eyes settling on the leash in Jesse's hand.

Greg put his hand on JJ's arm and led him up the hall away from them.

Jesse shifted his weight from one foot to the other. He wanted to retreat, but he wasn't about to skitter away like a coward. Besides, Evan had Achilles and he couldn't turn his back without a word when it was obvious the dog was with him. He filled his lungs with a deep breath and stepped forward.

"Is he yours?" Evan asked, his eyes focused on the puppy.

Jesse stopped a couple feet away from him. "Yeah. I found him this morning in Grant Park."

"He's really cute. He looks like a baby Rin Tin Tin that got into Lassie's wardrobe."

A chuckled slipped out of Jesse's throat before he realized it. "That's a good way to describe him."

Evan smiled and raised his eyes to Jesse. "Have you named him yet?"

"Achilles."

"That's perfect with how much you love ancient culture. I still think it's funny when we're both reading on the couch, I'll be reading a car magazine, and you're always reading some long lost piece of literature that no one knows about." Evan stopped his sentence short and averted his gaze again.

Jesse also turned his eyes the floor, the memory of such relaxed moments causing a suffocating pain in his chest. He cleared his throat, and said softly, "I didn't think you were recording during the day anymore."

"I haven't left since last night," Evan mumbled.

Quiet surrounded them. Neither looked at the other.

With each silence filled second that ticked by, Jesse felt as if his heart ripped a little bit more. How did it come to this, to where there was such strain between them? Had their months of happiness really been a dream? It seemed so now. Unable to handle the awkwardness, Jesse reached to take Achilles.

Evan caught sight of Jesse's skinned hands and elbow. He snatched Jesse's left arm and turned it to look at the scratches, his voice lifting with concern. "Jess, what happened to you? Are you okay?"

Anger sparked in Jesse at the concern in Evan's face and voice. It seemed a mockery after the coldness he had showed him. He jerked his arm out of Evan's hand. "What do you care?"

Evan's expression turned pained. Carefully, he handed him Achilles. "Please don't be like that."

Jesse held Achilles close to his chest, fixing Evan with as harsh of a glare as he could muster, but he couldn't hold it. He sighed and glanced away. "I fell when I was running this morning."

A somber smile tipped one corner of Evan's lips. "How can anyone who's so graceful on stage be so clumsy off it?"

"Yeah well, we all have things that can bring us down, don't we?" Jesse said, and turned to leave.

"Jess, wait."

Jesse stopped, his back to him.

"Do you...want to grab some lunch, or something?"

Jesse shook his head and continued to walk away. "I can't. I don't want to leave Achilles alone in a strange place so soon. Another time, maybe."

CHAPTER THIRTY

Jesse walked into the studio, Achilles trotting at his side. He sipped on a Mocha Frappuccino from Starbucks, the caffeine already kicking in to help him be more alert despite the headache that seemed ever present. He rubbed one temple with his fingertips, wondering how long Evan's wounded mien would haunt him. It managed to all weekend, popping into his head at moments it shouldn't, like when he remembered how to laugh and smile while playing with Achilles, or when he and Brandon joked around when walking him. More than once he faced the mental image and felt such guilt over not going to lunch with Evan, he almost called him and asked him to dinner.

He held strong through the weekend, but now here he was at the studio at the ungodly hour of six-thirty in the morning under the excuse that since he couldn't sleep, he might as well come in and dink around on the piano. Though under the excuse a painfully honest voice whispered he was there with the hope of running into Evan.

Jesse glanced in the vocal booth as he came upon it. His heart matched his stride in stuttering to a stop at seeing Evan. When it beat again, it was with a pain so deep his soul and body constricted in a strangled sob at Evan's condition. He looked worse than he had the week before. The dark circles were more pronounced on his ashen face. By the pallor of his skin, the thinness in his face, the way his wrinkled shirt hung on his shoulders, it was clear to him Evan had lost weight. He noticed how Evan's hands trembled as he pressed the headphones to his ears, as if that simple act took all his strength, then he saw another thing that sent a jolt through his heart. Evan's fingers were bare of rings save for the alexandrite one he'd given him. Not even the precious eagle ring of his father adorned his finger.

As Evan stood singing, his voice and his body wavered.

> *"Some people think*
> *I live a life of*
> *Fairytales and dreams*
> *But…if…"*

Evan's voice faltered and cracked. His body swayed, he looked ready to collapse. He dragged the headphones off his head, dropping them to the floor, and sank down in a chair behind him, his head lowered, his hands buried in his hair.

Jesse opened the door to the vocal booth and stepped inside. Evan's head remained down. Jesse skimmed the lyric sheet, noted the music and rhythm of the song, took the mic, and started to sing,

> *"Some people think,*
> *I live a life of fairytales and dreams.*
> *But if that's true,*
> *Then where is my happy ending?*
> *They don't know what I'm really like,*
> *When all the lights go down.*
> *And the tears I cry,*
> *In the dark alone,*
> *When no one's around…"*

Jesse stopped singing and glanced over his shoulder. Evan blinked up at him as if he disbelieved he truly saw him. Now that he could get a good look at his eyes, Jesse noticed the edges were red, the whites bloodshot, but what hurt him most was the light behind their radiant blue was gone. Jesse turned back to the sheet music and started making notes on it. He took a deep breath to steady his voice as he spoke.

"I think you'll want to extend the second line by bringing a slight pause after fairytales. Then pause again after happy, and at ending, hold the ing sound for just a second longer so that line plays off the rhythm in the second line, because right now it sounds a little off unless you slow them both down and stretch them out. It sounds okay to pick the tempo up after the fourth line, though."

"Thanks," Evan mumbled. Achilles pawed at his leg, and he reached down to pet him.

Jesse took a tentative step toward him. "I don't suppose you'd want to go get some breakfast with me, would you?"

Evan slowly lifted his eyes to him. "I'd like that."

Jesse picked up Achilles's leash and walked from the booth, pausing in the control room to switch off the recording equipment. He led the way out of the studio, grateful that the early hour meant there were no paparazzi to disturb them, and turned on the sidewalk to check on Evan. Evan leaned against the building, his fingers pressed to his forehead, his eyes squeezed shut.

Jesse went to him and laid his hand on his back. "Are you okay?"

Evan gave a tight nod. "It's just a dizzy spell. I've been getting them lately."

Jesse wrapped his arm around Evan's waist to support him as he steered him toward the parking garage. "You don't look like you should drive. Maybe I should just take you home."

"Maybe," Evan said softly, putting his arm over Jesse's shoulders.

Jesse guided him to the F430 and opened the passenger side door for him. After Evan slid in and got his seatbelt on, Jesse picked Achilles up and put him on his lap. Evan closed his eyes, his fingers buried in the puppy's thick fur.

Jesse climbed in and fired it up, aiming the car toward Lake Shore Drive rather than the interstate. On the way, he glanced over at Evan and saw he had fallen asleep despite the chill wind blowing in through the open windows. He watched the wind toss Evan's hair around his face. He had always thought Evan looked beautiful when asleep, like an angel in repose, his lips parted ever so slightly as if in invitation.

Jesse shook his head quickly and faced forward, clutching the steering wheel.

He pulled onto the road to Evan's house and stopped at the gates. He wondered if Evan had changed the code since he left and decided to give it a try since he didn't have a remote anymore. He couldn't believe it when the gates swung open, and he was able to manually override the driveway gates, also. As he coasted down the long drive, he saw the lawn had turned wild and overgrown, the flowerbeds taken over by weeds, the manicured shrubbery now unruly. He parked outside the garage and gently shook Evan awake, then followed him into the house with Achilles, taking off his leash once inside.

"He's housebroken. He hasn't made any messes in Brandon's apartment."

Evan waved the comment away. "It doesn't matter if he makes a mess."

"I guess not."

Jesse walked into the trashed family room. Empty bottles of Guinness were scattered on the floor around the couch and covered the surface of the coffee table. A nearly empty bottle of vodka was tipped over on the couch, and one completely empty had rolled under the coffee table. The remnants of a third lay shattered against the stone hearth of the fireplace. A bottle of Jack Daniels, barely a splash in the bottom, sat on one of the end tables next to two empty wine bottles. A pizza box with a whole pizza in it lay open on the table and looked a couple days old with crusted, congealed cheese.

Evan stood with his back to him, his shoulders sagging. Jesse grabbed him by the wrist and led him upstairs to the bedroom.

"Why don't you lie down and I'll go get you some breakfast," Jesse said, pulling the curtains closed.

The bed creaked as Evan got in. Jesse turned toward the bedroom door.

"Jess?" Evan said, his voice just above a whisper.

"Yeah?"

"Will you lay with me for a little while? Just until I fall asleep?"

Jesse glanced down at the floor. He looked at Evan from under his eyelashes. Evan's gaze was turned away from him. Jesse sighed. He stepped out of his Nikes and climbed into bed with his back to him. His muscles stayed tense, unable to relax in the bed where he and Evan had shared so many intimate moments. He swore he could hear the spectral sounds of them in pleasure seeping from the walls, the furniture, the bed itself. He felt the tips of Evan's fingers on his back as if he wanted to touch him, but was afraid to.

Evan exhaled a shaky breath. "You're better than I am. Or what I was, I should say. Your voice, your skill, your gift, is so much greater than mine. I realized that a long time ago. But it goes beyond just music. As a person, you're so much better than me."

"That's not true and we both know it."

"It is true."

"I'm not going to argue with you about this. It's stupid," Jesse snapped.

Evan stayed quiet. Slowly, he rolled onto his other side.

Jesse stayed still. He wanted to hold him, to tell him everything would be okay, but the poisonous memory of Evan's harsh words and the coldness in his eyes when he broke up with him invaded his mind, and he wanted to spring out of bed and tell him to go to hell. He was so confused by the dichotomy of his emotions that he felt disconnected with himself. As he lay silent, the part of him that had awoken the day he met Evan, his soul that had fallen silent since they parted, murmured the answer to what he should do. He flipped over and pressed his body against Evan's back, draping one arm over his side. Evan reached down and took Jesse's hand. Jesse nuzzled into his hair and held him closer.

Within seconds, Evan's breathing deepened with sleep. Achilles jumped on the bed and curled up at the foot. Jesse closed his eyes and drifted asleep.

❀ ❀ ❀

Jesse started to wake, still in the same position tucked behind Evan. He came fully awake, feeling more refreshed than in weeks, and wondered how long he slept. He cranked his head around to look at the clock and couldn't believe it was past one in the afternoon. They had slept the whole morning, both so deep in sleep neither so much as twitched. Jesse shifted and felt his erection rub against the inside of his boxers. Well, maybe one part of him had twitched.

He inched out of bed and crept from the bedroom. He let Achilles outside and checked his cell phone, seeing that not even it vibrating in his pocket when Kenny called had roused him. He called him back and let him know he was obviously going to be extremely late for rehearsing at the Auditorium Theatre. Then, since it appeared Evan no longer had the care staff come to the house anymore, he set to cleaning.

He started with the kitchen, throwing away the empty beer and liquor bottles piled on the counters and scrubbed everything down. He tackled the family room next, carrying a garbage bag to chuck the bottles in, and went to pick up the pieces of broken glass by the fireplace. He saw the pictures of him and Evan they had placed on the mantel on the floor, the glass of their frames shattered.

He carefully removed the images from their broken frames, gazing at one of him and Evan wrestling in the pool from when they had thrown Brandon a birthday cook-out party. Another of them sitting at a piano in the studio working together. One more had them snuggled on the couch in the chill-out room taking a nap when they needed to back off from the music.

Jesse sighed and set the photos on the mantel. With everything cleaned, he jumped in his car and ran down to the grocery store, buying a cartload of food he knew Evan liked and some new picture frames. When he got back to the house, he unloaded the groceries and restored the pictures to frames, setting them back on the mantel with a note that read, *Whatever you do, please don't shatter our memories.*

He went into the kitchen to make Evan something to eat and heard him and Achilles coming down the stairs. Jesse glanced at him as he walked in, seeing his hair wet, he had shaved, and he smelled like he just got out of the shower. His eyes went to Evan's left hand, and on his ring finger the alexandrite stone glistened, silently telling him that after showering Evan had put it on again.

Evan sat down at the breakfast counter. "You cleaned and went grocery shopping. Thanks."

Jesse shrugged and turned to the refrigerator. "Are you hungry?"

"Yeah."

Jesse pulled some lunch meat from the refrigerator and started making Evan a sandwich, piling the roast beef, ham, and Genoa salami on thick, one piece of white American cheese, and touching it with mustard, knowing exactly how Evan liked it.

"I called the gardeners, the pool people, and the housecleaners," Jesse said, sliding the plate toward Evan. "They'll be here tomorrow to get this place back in shape. After that they'll come on the old schedule."

"Thanks," Evan mumbled. He took a bite of the sandwich and smiled at Jesse. "You made it perfect, gorgeous." He clamped his mouth shut at saying his pet name for Jesse and dropped his gaze.

Jesse reached across the counter and brushed a tendril of hair away from Evan's eyes. "I have to get going. I'm about seven hours late for rehearsal at the Auditorium, and I've got so much to do before we leave, it's ridiculous. Are you going to be okay?"

Evan nodded. "Yeah."

Jesse picked up his car keys and Achilles's leash. "I bought you some bagels and cream cheese, so make sure you start eating breakfast. You know you can hardly tie your shoes if you haven't eaten."

"I know. I'll start eating better," Evan said quietly.

Jesse clipped Achilles's leash to his collar. "And you really need to get some more rest, so don't go into the studio tonight."

"I won't. I'll get some more rest."

"Good. Well, I'll see you around."

Evan lifted his eyes to him. "Hey, Jess. I really appreciate what you've done."

Jesse stopped in the doorway with his back to him. "If that's true, then pull yourself together. When Conquest beats you on the charts, I want to know you were at your best. Not this lame shadow of a singer that once was." He looked at Evan. "Act like the man I gave that ring to," he said softly, and walked away.

CHAPTER THIRTY-ONE

"Jesse, you can't back out now." Greg stood with his arms folded across his chest in an attempt to look stern.

Jesse looked up at him while stretching his muscles in preparation for hitting the stage. "Watch me."

"You agreed to be his opening act," Greg insisted. "The arrangements have already been made."

"Then unmake them. Every show we're booked for has sold out within minutes. Why the hell would I want to be someone's opening act when we're headlining our own sold-out tour?"

"Oh, I don't know," Greg said, his sarcasm thick. "Maybe because you'll be joining him *after* your sold-out tour wraps up. Maybe because the venues he plays are double, triple, quadruple, the size of the ones Conquest is hitting. Maybe because his tour is a *world* tour."

Jesse stretched one arm above his head and bent to the side. "Then book us in venues that are quintuple the size we play now and we'll outsell him."

Greg snorted. "I have no doubt that someday you'll be able to compete against Evan on a more equal level, but not now."

"I can do it now!" Jesse marched across the dressing room and stood inches from Greg. "'Shattered' is going to hit as a single two weeks after his first single comes out, and I guarantee, it *will* be the Number One song above him."

Greg shifted backward as though forced away by Jesse's intensity. "We'll see." He cleared his throat. "But if that does happen, then you have to see the benefit in the two of you teaming up for his tour."

"Yeah, benefit to him in being able to sell tickets because it'll be the only way people will get to see Conquest live."

Greg turned in frustration to face the rest of the band. "What about you guys? Don't you get a say?"

Kenny shrugged. "It's better if we just do what our fearless leader wants. Things go a lot smoother that way."

Jesse grinned at Kenny and dropped down to a full split.

Trish tipped her head in an admiring gaze. "That's impressive."

"And I'm even more flexible," Brandon chimed in.

Julian gave him a flirtatious smile. "Really?"

Brandon leaned closer to him. "Really."

"Stop it!" Jesse demanded, pointing at them. "It's like watching my biological brother and my adopted brother hit on each other."

"So you're really not going to do it?" Greg interjected.

"Are you still on that?" Jesse said, snapping himself back into a standing position.

Greg rubbed his eyes with the heels of his hands. "Why do I put myself through this?"

"You're a glutton for self-punishment?" Jesse suggested.

Greg glared at him from between his fingers, then dropped his hands from his face. "I took on all the responsibilities of Conquest to see that the job was done right, especially since the illustrious manager of Conquest, *you*, has been too busy to handle things." He exhaled a loud sigh. "Fine. I'm not going to hound you about it anymore tonight since you've got to focus for the stage, but I should let you know, I booked you and Evan to sing a duet on New Year's Eve in Times Square."

"You did what!"

"Sorry, Jess, it's the way it's gotta be. I got the call asking if I could get you both to perform and couldn't say no. It's huge exposure for Conquest and for Evan's comeback. Don't worry, though. You'll each get to perform on your own, then later in the show, you and Evan will take the stage together to do one of his songs, and at the end of the show when the ball drops, you'll be on stage together again, but with all the other acts that will be playing that night and everybody will be doing 'Auld Lang Syne.'"

"No!" Jesse roared. "I'm not doing it! I refuse!"

"The deal's already been made, you can't refuse."

"The hell I can't," Jesse growled through clenched teeth. "Now if you're done, I need some privacy to get changed."

Greg stomped past him toward the door. The others trailed after him.

Jesse paced back and forth in the empty dressing room. Achilles jumped off a chair, pacing with him. Jesse sat on the floor and picked him up, holding him to his chest.

"You're the only one who doesn't drive me totally nuts, 'Chilles. Why Greg is pushing so hard. Can't he understand I have to distance myself from Ev to protect him? Doesn't he get it that if I'm near him, it'll break me?"

He tossed his head back and sighed. Evan. He didn't even bother to show up to Jesse's kick-off concert, and if that wasn't bad enough, it was also October 7th, his birthday. He knew he shouldn't have expected Evan to acknowledge it, but he held on to the hope all day that his phone would ring, or that Evan would surprise him by coming to the concert.

Jesse tried to shake away the growing hurt. He couldn't let Evan affect him. He needed to focus. Everything he ever dreamed of waited for him outside his dressing room door. He lowered his gaze. Almost everything.

He forced himself to stand up. He changed into a pair of black leather pants, and instead of a shirt, he pulled on a short black leather jacket.

He pet Achilles. "You stay here and be a good boy while I go perform."

Jesse walked out of his dressing room to Kenny, Julian, and Trish waiting for him, and the roaring voices of the crowd chanting "Conquest." He held his right hand out, the others fell down on top.

"This is the start of the beginning," Jesse said. "This is where we lay the foundation and let the world know we're a force that won't be stopped. Together, we *will* conquer the world. Let's do this!"

The others yelled with him and headed for the stage.

The arena lights dropped. The crowd screamed louder in anticipation. Julian hit the keyboards, pulling out long, deep notes. Kenny's guitar broke through the darkness with throaty smooth cords. A steady beat from the drums came in, getting louder and louder. Over it all, Jesse's voice began to rise, growing stronger with each note. When he hit the top of his range, he could hardly hear himself over the roaring crowd. The lights flashed on. He ran to the front of the stage, and lit into the fast lines of "Vanish,"

> *"You look in my eyes,*
> *Thinking you can see all the tears I've cried,*
> *You don't know me,*
> *Don't hold me.*
> *I can't believe I bought all the lies that you sold,*
> *Took 'em to my heart to hold,*
> *Then you let me go.*
>
> *You breezed through my life,*
> *Night after night,*
> *Pushing me to the edge,*
> *With your smile so beautiful and cold.*
> *Now you stand before me and cry,*
> *Saying you want me by your side.*
> *But I need to go,*
> *I need to run.*
> *I need to vanish like the sun,*
> *Into the coming night.*

Let me go,
Walk away,
Let me vanish from your life forever.
Let me go,
Turn away,
I need to leave this all behind forever.
Let me go,
Fly away,
I'd be happier alone forever.
Let me go,
Run away,
Let me vanish in the night forever..."

Kenny's guitar solo blasted to life at the end of the chorus.

Jesse looked out over the crowd, seeing nothing but a bouncing, jumping mass of faceless bodies screaming hollow affections to him.

CHAPTER THIRTY-TWO

Brandon looked at his watch, a quarter past two in the morning, then peered over the stainless steel railing beside the booth he sat in, down to the first level of the club where Jesse stood out against the gyrating crowd on the dance floor. Even though he was surrounded by people pushing and shoving, wiggling and squirming, to be the next to dance close to him, Jesse moved to the fast thumping bass driven beat like nothing else in the world existed.

Brandon sighed and faced around. Kenny, Julian, and Trish sat at the table with him, picking at the birthday cake they had gotten for Jesse. A plate with a piece of untouched cake was still where Jesse sat long enough to blow out his twenty-one candles before he hit the dance floor, where he'd been for the past two hours, lost in his own world of music and alcohol.

He had gone down once to tell Jesse to take it easy on the booze, but Jesse laughed at him and spun away, allowing himself to be swallowed in the churning wave of bodies. Kenny and Julian tried talking to him also, but Jesse answered them by tipping his bottle of Guinness back to finish it and signaling for another. Trish attempted to approach him, though she seemed to forget her original intent and ended up trying to dance with him, but Jesse gave her no more attention than he gave all the strange women fighting to grind against him.

Brandon looked back to the dance floor and saw one of the bartenders making his way through the crowd toward Jesse. He glared down at the guy who had been overly attentive to Jesse all night, keeping a constant supply of fresh drinks flowing to him. It was obvious the guy wasn't going through the extra effort to get a bigger tip. He'd have to watch him closely and make sure he didn't try anything.

Jesse raised both arms above his head, dancing with his eyes closed, letting his hips and torso sway with the music. He thought about how good the music felt pumping through his body. So long as it didn't stop, he wouldn't stop. That was the one horrible thing about his concert; the music had stopped. He hadn't wanted it to. He tried to drag the show out for as long as he could, fearing playing the last song of the night, but it couldn't go on forever, and when they played the final song for the last encore, it was one of the worst feelings in the world. As he walked offstage, the reality closed in on him that despite the adoration from the thousands he'd just stood before, he was alone.

But here in this club was music again. Here, he could forget about reality for a few hours more.

He felt someone grip his arm and rolled his head loosely to see who it was. It was the bartender who had been subtly flirting with him all night. Tall with a nice athletic build, dark hair and dark eyes, but he was just another guy. Another nameless face.

"Ready for another?" the bartender asked, holding a fresh beer toward Jesse.

Jesse swiped it out of his hand, gave him his empty bottle, and put the fresh one to his lips in a long drink.

The bartender leaned toward Jesse's ear. "My name's Ryan."

"What?" Jesse yelled over the music.

Ryan pressed closer to him, his lips almost touching his ear. "I said my name's Ryan."

Jesse nodded and moved to spin away. Ryan's grip on his arm tightened. Jesse snapped his head around, giving him a harsh glare, then saw the look in Ryan's eyes, the hunter-like gaze that told him this man wanted to screw the hell out of him. It wasn't anything like how Evan would look at him. Evan could be fierce, rough, aggressive, dominant, but through it all his eyes always held unending affection. Not like this guy, whose eyes unsettled him and gave him warning that Ryan would take what he wanted, how he wanted, and would care little how he felt about it.

Jesse tried to jerk his arm free. Ryan held on and smiled at him, the gesture making him more uncomfortable rather than putting him at ease. He felt Ryan press a small plastic bag into the palm of his hand.

Ryan put his lips to Jesse's ear again. "I have more, if you want. We could have a hell of a party when you're ready to get out of here." He released Jesse's arm and gave him another grin as he maneuvered back toward the bar.

Jesse looked down at the tiny bag in his hand. He had never tried ecstasy, but he had seen it enough in clubs to know that's what the two small white tablets in the bag were. He closed his hand in a fist around the drugs and staggered off the dance floor. He reached the stairs to the second level, managed to only trip on the last one, and went to the table. He crashed down in the booth, almost sitting on top of Brandon.

"Hey! Why aren't ya dancin', super dancer boy?" Jesse asked, his words slurring.

"It's time to go," Brandon said. "You have a tour bus to catch in the morning, remember?"

"Ya think it's gonna leave without me?" Jesse laughed. "And I can't leave now. I haven't found anyone to have sex with yet."

Kenny let out a derisive snort. "Dude, you're so wasted, I doubt you could even get it up."

Jesse snatched Kenny's hand with reflexes that seemed far too quick for his drunkenness. "I'm hard right now. Feel."

Kenny twisted his hand out of Jesse's. "Idiot!"

Jesse burst out laughing and crawled over Brandon's lap on his hands and knees to get to the part of the booth closest to the steel railing.

Brandon pressed back away from him. "Will you sit your ass down!"

Jesse ignored him and knelt on the seat with his back to the table. He hung his torso over the railing, waving down at the dance floor with both hands, and yelled, "Hey! Does anyone wanna have sex with me?"

Brandon grabbed Jesse around his waist and pulled him from the railing. Jesse fell on top of him, laughing so hard he could barely breathe.

"Brandon, look, look," Jesse said between laughs. He brandished the tiny bag of ecstasy before Brandon's face. "That bartender guy gave 'em to me."

Brandon ripped the bag out of his hand. "That son of a bitch! Did you take any?" He grabbed Jesse's face in both hands, looking intently into his eyes. "Did you?"

Jesse shook his head as much as he could in Brandon's hold.

Brandon gazed at him for another moment, then released him. He flung the pills over the rail to the fall on the dance floor and looked to the others. "We need to get him out of here."

"Brandon, Brandon," Jesse said, tugging on Brandon's arm. "I gotta pee. Come with me to the bathroom. I don't want that guy to follow me in there."

Brandon rubbed his hands over his face and through his hair in exasperation. "Alright. But then we're leaving."

Brandon slid out of the booth, waited for Jesse to clamber out, then followed him down to the first level. He walked close behind him to not lose him in the crowd as they worked their way to the restrooms. Glancing over his shoulder, he saw the bartender weaving his way between bodies behind them.

Brandon faced forward, hoping his body remembered enough karate to react if the guy tried something and wishing he hadn't quit practicing it. The guy looked to be around six feet tall and built with solid muscle. If it came to a physical confrontation, he knew he wasn't going to get out of it unscathed.

As they neared the restroom, Brandon glanced back to see the bartender was just a few feet away. He decided he didn't want to start a fight in the restroom. The last thing he needed was to get his head cracked open on a porcelain sink or his face smashed into a mirror. He turned fully around, prepared for a fight.

An elbow shot out of the crowd and nailed the bartender in the nose. The guy's head snapped back, he fell to the floor howling in pain. He covered his nose with both hands, but it didn't staunch the blood from pouring between his fingers. Brandon didn't need to get a closer look to know the guy's nose was broken. He turned his eyes to the crowd to see who had hit him and caught the flash of a white New York Yankees logo on a navy baseball cap before the wearer vanished among the people. Brandon exhaled all his breath in a shocked gasp.

He felt Jesse's hand on his arm and looked at him. Jesse stared in the direction the Yankees cap had disappeared.

"Jess?" Brandon said hesitantly. "Did you see someone?"

"I thought…it felt like…" He shook his head and looked at the bartender.

Kenny and Julian shoved their way through the crowd.

"Jess!" Kenny yelled. "Are you okay?"

Jesse nodded slowly.

Brandon grabbed Kenny's and Julian's wrists. "You guys watch him. I'm going to pay our tab so we can go."

Both looked at him, confused, but nodded in assent.

Brandon watched Jesse stumble into the restroom with Kenny and Julian, then darted in the direction the Yankees cap had gone.

✽ ✽ ✽

Brandon and Kenny half carried, half dragged Jesse into Brandon's apartment with Trish and Julian following behind. They wrestled him to his bedroom, somehow managed not to step on Achilles dancing around them, and dropped Jesse on the bed.

"Whoever thought his skinny ass would be so damn heavy?" Kenny said, flexing his sore shoulder muscles.

"If he hadn't gotten away from us after going to the restroom, he would've been able to walk in himself," Julian said. "But he decided to start doing shots."

Brandon looked down at his brother lying passed out on the bed and shook his head in a mix of pity and disappointment. The call buzzer dinged and he turned to answer it. Kenny and Julian followed him from the bedroom, Kenny asking if he could have a drink of water since he had overexerted himself carrying Jesse, and Julian asking to use his bathroom. Trish stood alone in the bedroom.

She took a tentative step toward the bed, then another. She sat down beside Jesse. Her eyes moved over his face, lingering for a long moment on his lips. She reached toward him and brushed his cheek with the backs of her fingers. Jesse didn't move. She gently touched her fingertips to his lips, amazed at how soft and warm they were. Jesse took a slightly deeper breath, his hips rolled in the smallest of motions.

Trish looked down to his hips. She saw movement behind the black leather, the material beginning to strain against Jesse's organ expanding within its confines. Her heartbeat quickened, heat flushed her skin. She wanted to touch him, to feel the weight of his erection in her hand. He had told her he'd been with women. She knew he could do it again. Now with Evan out of the way, her path to Jesse was clear.

She understood he was still coping with the loss of him, but eventually he'd realize how bad Evan had been for him, that he had poisoned him every day with his obsessive, jealous, and possessive ways. But she could give Jesse the kind of relationship he deserved.

She rubbed her hand down his chest, over his firm abdomen, to the top of his pants.

"Ev," Jesse groaned.

Trish jerked her hand back.

Jesse shifted on the bed. He started to open his eyes, closed them again, then finally opened them almost all the way and looked up at her. "Trish? Where's Ev?"

Struggling to keep the irritation from her voice, Trish said, "He's not here, Jess."

"He's not? I thought I felt him—"

"He's not here," she snapped. "He didn't even bother to come to our show tonight. He didn't even care enough to call you and say good luck, or happy birthday. He doesn't give a shit. He only cares about himself and his career, remember?"

Jesse rolled onto his side away from her. "I thought he was here."

Trish winced at the pain in Jesse's voice. She leaned over him, resting both hands on his shoulder. "It's okay, Jess. I'll stay the night if you want me to so you don't have to be alone."

Jesse lay quiet and unmoving.

From the living room, Trish heard voices, and with the original three of Brandon, Kenny, and Julian, was a fourth she also knew well. Before she could react, Evan walked into the bedroom with the others. She tried to look at him in defiance, to tell him with her eyes that she had more right to be beside Jesse than he did, but at the simmering rage and fierce protectiveness in Evan's gaze, she drew her hands away from Jesse, stood, and stepped back from the bed.

"He moved," Brandon said. "Did he wake up?"

"He was mumbling in his sleep, then he rolled over," Trish said flatly. "I couldn't understand what he was saying."

Kenny yawned and stretched his arms over his head. "Well, I don't know about you guys, but I'm ready to go home since we've got a tour bus to catch in six hours."

"I'm with you," Julian said, and laid his hand on Evan's back. "See you soon?"

Evan gave him a weak smile and small, single nod.

Trish walked toward the bedroom door, her eyes averted from Evan as she followed Kenny and Julian. Brandon left to show them out.

With soft footsteps, Evan walked to the edge of the bed. He gazed at Jesse, then sat beside him. He reached over Jesse's shoulder and gently stroked his hair near his temple.

Jesse stirred. He turned his head toward Evan's touch. He looked up at him, and his eyes opened wider. "Ev, you're here. Trish said you weren't, but I knew you were."

A soft smile graced Evan's lips. "I've been with you all night, you just didn't see me. Happy birthday, gorgeous."

Jesse's face glowed with a smile. He rolled over to lie on his side facing Evan and curled his body around him. He embraced Evan's hips and laid his head on his thigh. Evan put one hand on Jesse's side and continued to stroke his hair with the other. He looked up when Brandon stepped into the doorway.

Brandon folded his arms across his chest, disapproval written on his countenance. After he had left Jesse in Kenny's and Julian's care, he managed to track Evan through the club and cornered him by the doors. Never in his life had he seen anyone look so pained. He knew then how desperately Evan wanted to be close to Jesse, but was afraid of upsetting him. He told Evan he could come over to his apartment to see him, and even though Evan declined then, he knew the second his buzzer rang that he had changed his mind. Now as he stood looking at them together, he wondered if he had done the right thing, or when Jesse came out of his alcoholic stupor, would he suffer greater hurt?

"Everyone's gone," Brandon said, his tone making it clear he felt Evan should do the same.

"I'd like to stay with him a little longer."

"Yeah well, I'd like to win a Tony, but that isn't gonna happen anytime soon."

Evan lowered his gaze and nodded. He shifted to slide out from under him, but the movement roused Jesse. He tightened his hold and buried his face against Evan's abdomen. Evan closed his eyes.

Brandon could see he was searching for the strength to push Jesse away. He looked at his brother clinging to Evan and let out a frustrated sigh. "You can stay a little longer." He turned and closed the door halfway, squinting at Evan. "I'm leaving the door open."

A grin slipped onto Evan's lips at Brandon's parental tone. His attention moved back to Jesse when he felt one of Jesse's hands slide up the back of his shirt to rest on his bare skin. That single soft touch was enough to make his cock fill at a record rate. He tried to adjust how he sat so Jesse wouldn't notice, but he already had. Jesse tipped his head toward Evan's lap and nuzzled his crotch.

Evan exhaled a fast breath, need surged through his body in a heated wave. Since their break-up, he had lived in celibacy. His mind rejected the thought of another man, his heart quivered in fear at letting anyone else get close to him, he felt repulsed at the idea of someone's touch other than Jesse's. He had known before, but now with even greater conviction, Jesse was the only one who would ever be able to fulfill him in body, mind, heart, and spirit. But he knew he couldn't do this, not while Jesse was in such a state, and scooted back on the bed to put some space between them.

Jesse sat up and climbed onto Evan's lap, straddling him.

Evan put both hands on Jesse's shoulders in a half-hearted attempt to keep him back. "Jess, stop. You don't know what you're doing."

Jesse chuckled and pressed firmer against him. "That's something you've never said to me before."

Evan swallowed hard. Somewhere in the back of his mind, he should have anticipated this. He knew how Jesse was when he drank, the stages he went through, first giddy, then wild, then sleepy, then ready to screw like hell, but he thought with everything that had happened between them Jesse wouldn't want it, not to mention he seemed way too tanked to make it to the last stage. He should've known better than to have underestimated him.

Jesse put one hand behind Evan's head and kissed him. A soft whimper sounded in Evan's throat as the last bit of his feeble defense broke. He took Jesse's face in both hands and deepened the kiss. The taste of alcohol told him what he was doing was wrong, that he needed to stop, he couldn't take advantage of him, but under the alcohol was Jesse's taste. He wanted to kiss him just a few seconds longer.

Jesse heaved his weight forward and knocked Evan to his back. Evan took a quick breath to protest, but before he could speak, Jesse claimed his mouth again. A groan rumbled deep in Jesse's throat. He thrust his tongue into Evan's mouth with more force and ground his hips against him. He left Evan's lips and sat back to take his shirt off. He got it wrestled halfway over his head before his alcohol-induced un-coordination took over and he got stuck. Evan sat up and yanked it the rest of the way off for him, thinking that if Jesse was so lit he had trouble getting undressed, they really shouldn't keep going.

"Jess," he started, stopping as he watched Jesse unzip his pants.

Jesse pulled his own cock free and took Evan's hands. He wrapped the fingers of one around his base, the fingers of the other around the middle so it was completely encased in Evan's grip. He held Evan's hands in place with his own over them and thrust into them. His head fell back on his shoulders, a loud moan passed over his lips.

Evan couldn't take his eyes off him. Reveling in his pleasure, Jesse looked so beautiful, so powerful. The moonlight illuminated his nude torso to have a pearlescent shine, his black hair contrasting against his fair skin. Jesse rocked his hips, his leather pants hugging his thighs, the golden sun pendant hanging in the tender hollow at the base of his throat. Evan knew he had been hopelessly defeated.

He flung Jesse's hands away, grabbed him by the waist, and tossed him to the side. Jesse gasped as he hit the mattress so hard he bounced up. Before he finished inhaling his next breath, Evan was on top of him, taking possession of his mouth. He gripped a handful of Evan's hair and pushed his mouth against him, desperate to taste every part of Evan's tongue.

Evan broke the kiss and sat back, tearing his shirt over his head. He kicked off his shoes and yanked Jesse's off while Jesse arched his hips up and wiggled his pants down. Evan ripped them down Jesse's legs the rest of the way, threw them aside, and pushed his jeans and boxer-briefs off together. Jesse slid back to the center of the bed and lay down on his back, his legs falling open wide to the sides.

At the sight of Jesse spread before him, Evan lost all control and climbed onto the bed. Jesse sat partially up to meet him and pulled him down on top of him with his arms wrapped around him. Both sighed at having their bare skin meet after being separated for so long. With his feet planted on the bed, Jesse snapped his hips up to Evan. Evan thrust down hard against him. Their cocks pressed together, unyielding flesh against unyielding flesh, dueling for pleasure from the other.

Grasping, clinging, clawing, their frantic movements made it impossible to keep their lips together, each panted his breath into the other. Jesse raked his fingers down Evan's back to his ass and clamped them around the cheeks, his short nails sinking into Evan's skin. A hard groan forced its way from Evan's throat, and he ground his cock with more force on Jesse's. He felt Jesse's body shudder in ecstasy and knew he was seconds away.

"Ev, Ev," Jesse said between fast breaths. "I love you. I love you, Evan. I love—"

He cried out, his hips jerking up to Evan in massive release. At the same instant, Evan let out a deep shout, adding his climax to Jesse's.

Evan laid his forehead in the curve of Jesse's neck, trying to catch his breath as he listened to Jesse do the same. Jesse's breathing began to steady and deepen. He felt Jesse's hold on him relax and one hand fell limp on the bed. Evan raised his head and looked down at him.

"Jess?"

Jesse lay silent, his lips parted in sleep.

Evan placed a whisper soft kiss on his forehead. "I love you too, Jesse."

Chapter Thirty-three

Evan carefully lifted Jesse's arm from across his chest and slid his leg out from under his. He eased out of the bed and collected his scattered clothing. Once dressed, he stood at the edge of the bed gazing down at him. He pulled the blankets up around Jesse's neck and kissed his cheek one more time.

He walked out of the bedroom, closing the door softly behind, and heard the TV playing. He closed his eyes in a long blink. He had hoped he wouldn't have to face Brandon, not only because he stayed the entire night, but also because after Jesse passed out, he realized he forgot about the bedroom door being open. He put on his jeans so he could get a towel to clean Jesse with, and when he stepped into the hall to go to the bathroom, he saw Brandon's bedroom door closed tight. He didn't hold much hope that Brandon didn't know what had happened.

He took a deep breath and walked into the living room.

Brandon sat on the couch in a pair of sweat-shorts, eating cereal and watching Yu-Gi-Oh!. Achilles was on the couch beside him, begging, but when the puppy saw Evan, he bounded to him.

"Trying to sneak out before he wakes up?" Brandon said without taking his eyes off the TV. "That's real brave."

Evan bent to pet Achilles. "It's not exactly what you think."

Brandon looked at him, his blue eyes dark with anger. "I've woken up alone enough in my life to know exactly what it is, so spare me the bullshit, Evan." He shook his head in disgust and turned his gaze back to the TV. "Just get out. It's my own stupid fault for letting you come over. But for some reason, I thought you were more of a man than to take advantage of him while he was drunk."

Evan slunk toward the door with his head down. He paused, his hand on the knob, and looked back at Brandon. "I know what your answer will be, but I need to ask you a favor."

Brandon slowly raised his eyes, looking at him in complete disbelief that he would dare ask something of him.

"I…" Evan began, "I was hoping you would take care of the house for me while I'm on the road. You can stay there if you want to, I'll handle all the bills, of course, and—"

"Are you fucking kidding me?" Brandon exclaimed. He flung his spoon into his bowl so hard milk splashed up. He set the bowl on the coffee table as he stood and advanced on Evan, stopping inches from him. "After everything you've done, after the way you've treated my brother, you've got the fucking balls to stand in my apartment and ask me to take care of your house? And to say I could stay there, in the house you and him lived in together, do you have any idea what that would do to him? Do you know how that would look? I knew when I met you that you were an arrogant son of bitch, but I never imagined you could be this heartless and I never would have guessed you were this goddamn stupid."

Evan couldn't bring himself to look into Brandon's eyes, or at any part of him, and focused on the floor.

Brandon shoved Evan hard on the chest, making him stumble backward into the door. "Get out."

With his eyes cast downward, Evan turned and opened the door. "I'm sorry, Brandon," he said softly as the door clicked shut behind him.

Brandon spun away from the door and shook his fingers roughly through his hair. He stomped back to the couch and grabbed his cereal bowl, grimacing at the soggy Honey Nut Cheerios, then heard Jesse's bedroom door open.

A second later, Jesse shuffled to the end of the hall and stood staring at the door leading out of the apartment. "He's gone, isn't he?"

"Yeah."

"How long ago?"

"Not long."

Jesse sat in a dark blue recliner catty-cornered from the couch. Achilles trotted over to him, and he reached down to pet him.

After several minutes of silence, Brandon said, "He had the nerve to ask me to take care of his house while he was on tour. Can you believe that?"

"What'd you tell him?"

"I told him no, obviously."

Confusion made Jesse shake his head. "Why?"

Brandon looked at him in greater bafflement. "What do you mean *why*?"

"He doesn't have anyone else he can turn to, Brandon. He's all alone. And he looks at you as family. You can't say no to him."

"Well I did. And if he looks at me as family, then he should've shown more respect in the way he treated you."

"What the hell are you talking about?" Jesse demanded.

Brandon rolled his eyes. "Don't you remember anything from last night? I heard enough to know that asshole should've had more control and left you alone." He softened his voice. "I'm sorry for letting him come over. I thought I was doing the right thing and it'd make you feel better if he told you happy birthday."

Jesse fixed Brandon with a stern glare. "If you ever call him a name like that again, black belt or not, I'll kick your ass."

Brandon choked out a shocked gasp. "You're joking, right? He crept out the freakin' door this morning like a dog and that's an insult to him!" He pointed at Achilles.

"If I'm not angry about it, then why the hell are you? I want you to call him this afternoon and tell him you'll help with the house while he's gone."

Brandon snorted and looked away.

Jesse stood up and marched across the living room to him. "I'm serious, Brandon. If you won't do it because he asked, then do it because I'm asking."

Brandon folded his arms across his chest. "Fine," he said grudgingly.

Jesse exhaled a relieved breath. "Thanks. I'm going to get a shower. The limo should be here in half an hour to take me to the bus." He turned to go to the bathroom and paused at the entrance to the hall. "He did the right thing, Brandon. If he had stayed, I never would've been able to leave. He knows that. He's the strong one, not me. And until I become stronger, I don't deserve to be with him."

Brandon looked at him, taking in his words as Jesse disappeared down the hall.

CHAPTER THIRTY-FOUR

Jesse stood at the window of his hotel suite watching snow float down over Central Park. The others had been so excited about spending Christmas in New York. He could only think that he was in Evan's hometown. At least Trish got to visit with her family, and Julian did as well since Connecticut was only a spit away. Kenny stayed rather than going back to Chicago, and Brandon had arrived the day before on Christmas Eve, but despite having everyone around him, he still felt alone.

He wondered what Evan was doing, where he was. He had a feeling Evan may have come to New York to see his mother, which meant he could be somewhere in this labyrinth of a city and they were the closest they'd been since he had left on tour. At that thought, the city seemed to spread out further, the buildings heightening their already mammoth statures, as if to hide Evan within its great depths.

A knock sounded on his door. Achilles sprang off the couch in the living room of the suite, barking and charging the door. At nearly six months old, the dog looked more gawky and uncoordinated than ever as his German Shepherd body beneath his Collie coat tried to fill out his massive paws. The little bit of worry he held about it not working out having a dog on the road quickly vanquished when he realized Achilles was happy so long as he was with him and that he could take the dog pretty much anywhere, since not too many people wanted to say no to the lead singer of the hottest band in the country.

Jesse put his hand on the dog's head. "Good boy, 'Chilles."

Achilles stopped barking and stood wagging his tail as Jesse opened the door.

Kenny stood on the other side. "Hey. Greg said to come get you because we'll be eating soon."

Jesse sighed and turned back into his room to grab Achilles's leash. "Just because he booked a banquet room and ordered a big dinner, I don't know why I'm expected to be there."

"Because it's Christmas dinner, scrooge boy. I don't know why you've been so pissy the past couple days."

"I haven't been pissy."

He walked out of his room with Kenny and Achilles, and headed to the elevators. He knew his mood hadn't been the best lately. He worked exceptionally hard at being the lighthearted, fun-loving lead singer of Conquest that fans expected him to be, playing it up for the cameras, trying to appear happy and cool, when really, there were days he hardly ate because his appetite was non-existent and all he did was sleep, or try to, at least. It was one of the few escapes he had, and even it wasn't much of an escape since Evan haunted his dreams.

Every day, every night, every hour, he still thought of him. There were times when his mind felt like it no longer belonged to him, thinking what it wanted without his consent.

He needed to move on. He knew that. But it seemed so hard to imagine himself with anyone else, touching them, letting them touch him. He'd start to feel sick thinking about it, and he wondered, had he become a total head case? Was he ever going to be normal again? He had more than a hundred opportunities to have sex since he'd been on the road, and while some of the men had been exquisite in appearance, none, no matter their looks or personalities, were equal to Evan. And yet through all the dreams and fantasies of being with Evan again, he knew it would never happen. Evan had regained his music, shining before the world as he shared it. Evan didn't need him anymore, if he had ever really needed him at all.

The elevator stopped. Jesse followed Kenny out and down the hall to the banquet room. He stepped in to the sound of softly playing Christmas music and a long rectangular table laid out with a red tablecloth trimmed in gold. A tall Christmas tree stood in one corner sparkling with white lights. Everyone sat on the couches close to a fireplace and a piano off to the side.

Along with Brandon, Julian, Trish, and Greg, were Greg's wife, Crystal, and his daughter, Krista, who flirted with him mercilessly.

He caught sight of a server coming in to put some finishing touches on the table, and after requesting a bottle of pinot noir, he moved to join the others.

"Welcome to the party, sunshine," Brandon said as Jesse flopped down on the couch beside him.

"Suck it," Jesse grumbled.

His brother wrestled him around the neck. "That's the way to be, jerk-ass! You keep spreading that Christmas cheer!"

Jesse shoved Brandon away.

Krista sat down on the arm of the couch at Jesse's side and hugged him around his shoulders, her long brunette hair falling on his cheek. "He's right, Jess. I'm not going to have any fun bragging to the girls at school about spending Christmas with you if I have to say you were in a bad mood." She brandished her new digital camera above them. "Just smile for the camera. I need to get a shot of us to make all the girls jealous."

"Then give them this." Jesse took the camera from her and held it out, then put his lips to her cheek and snapped the photo.

"That'll get 'em!" she giggled. She took the camera back and gazed down at the photo of them. "Now I just have to get Evan when he gets here."

Jesse's heart stopped with a hard thump. He looked at Greg. "What?" He whipped his head toward Brandon. "What?"

"I don't know why you're looking at me," Brandon said. "When I talked to him before I left, he said he still wasn't sure if he was coming, so I didn't know until he called me earlier today."

Jesse stared at Brandon, caught between being shocked or angry. With each second, anger began to win. He knew Brandon and Evan had been communicating regularly since he left, even keeping up the tradition the three of them started by having dinner together every Tuesday, and though in his heart he knew it was all innocent, his mind whispered venomous doubts.

"That seems like an awful lot of conversations," he said between clenched teeth. The smile Brandon turned on him grated his frayed nerves further.

"Not really between friends."

The server returned and stepped up to Jesse, bending forward to show him the wine he brought. Jesse took the bottle and glass without moving his piercing glare from Brandon. Greg stood and walked away from everyone. Jesse eased up from the couch and followed him over to the table.

"I was going to tell you, Jess," Greg said. "You know Evan doesn't get along well with his step-relatives and his relationship with his mother is tense, so I thought it would be nice to invite him and them for Christmas dinner. It'd be good for him to be around people he actually enjoys, and whether you like it or not, he's like a son to me and a friend to the members of your band. And seeing him now isn't that big of a deal since you'll have to see him in a couple days to rehearse for the New Year's performance."

"I already told you I wasn't doing that," Jesse hissed in a loud whisper.

"You can't avoid him forever. You need to learn to deal with this, and most of all, talk to him."

Jesse took a breath, ready to let a torrent of protests fly, when the door to the banquet room opened. Evan walked in with his mother, stepfather, and stepsister. Jesse's breath left at the sight of him. He looked more divine than his memories held. There wasn't a hint of darkness under his eyes that somehow seemed an even more dazzling blue. He wore a pair of brown leather pants so dark they were nearly black, and a tan cashmere sweater with a broad neck that revealed a glimpse of his collarbone. Jesse sighed to himself. Evan always did take leather pants from being rock star to supreme elegance.

Achilles barked. Jesse made a grab for his collar, but was too slow. The dog tore across the room toward Evan.

"Achilles!" Evan called. He bent down, clapping his hands a couple times to encourage him. Achilles slammed into Evan's knees, his tail whipping back and forth. Evan went down on one knee, roughing up Achilles's fur and laughing when the dog tried to lick his face. He glanced up at Jesse standing near the table and found himself trapped by Jesse's indigo eyes.

He couldn't believe it was true, but Jesse looked more gorgeous than the last time they had been together. He had on a pair of black dress pants and the midnight blue sweater he wore pulled out the twilight in his eyes. At first, he thought the outfit was making Jesse look more mature, then he saw it in Jesse's eyes, felt it in the air around him; during his time on the road, Jesse had grown even more into the confident leader of his band.

"It's about time you got here!" Krista yelled, running up to Evan.

She threw her arms around his neck, and he lifted her off the ground with his hug. He put her down and took a step back from her, keeping his hands on her arms as he looked her up and down. "Wow. Did Santa bring you a boob job, because I know those things are bigger than the last time I saw you."

"Evan!" Greg bellowed.

Evan glanced at him, a sly smirk spreading over his lips, and turned back to Krista. "Oops, I mean, damn girl, I hope you got some makeup in your stocking because yikes." He held his hand up as if trying to shield his eyes from looking at her.

She giggled and slapped him on the arm.

Julian slid up beside Jesse. "Ah, nothing like being in the presence of the most breathtaking and talented man in the world. Didn't you once say that was your type?"

Jesse gave him an unappreciative look out the corner of his eye.

Julian tugged on Jesse's sleeve. "Come on now, darling. Say hello to everyone like a good boy."

Jesse let Julian lead him over to the group. He walked up as Greg was finishing introductions.

"And this is—"

"Jess doesn't need introductions," Evan cut in, and met Jesse's eyes. "Everyone knows who he is." He took a step closer to him. "You look amazing."

Jesse stared at him, brought off balance by Evan's boldness. Before he could move, Evan closed the distance between them and pulled him into a tight embrace. Jesse stood rigid. He was in Evan's arms. Evan's body, that he knew so well, was pressed against him. His cologne, so familiar, filled his nose. Without warning, everything inside him broke. He pushed against Evan and wrapped his arms around him, melting into his embrace. Evan laid his head against Jesse's and buried the fingers of one hand in Jesse's hair.

Jesse lingered in Evan's arms. It felt so good being held by him, so comfortable, so warm. This was how it should be, how it was meant to be. His throat started to tighten. But it was a lie. Why was Evan even bothering to hold him? Why was he doing this to him? Why did he want to keep hurting him? His eyes started to burn. He pushed back from Evan, blinking rapidly to keep his tears at bay.

He stood silent. He couldn't look at Evan. He couldn't look at anyone. He heard everyone around him making small talk, but their voices sounded muted, and in his mind they were all talking about them. He peeked toward the door from under his eyelashes, judging the distance. How bad would it look if he made a run for it?

He shook the thought away. No. He had to be strong. The last time they were together, Evan had been the strong one. Now it was his turn.

He glanced at Evan and saw he hadn't moved from where he'd been standing during the hug. His eyes were focused on Achilles sitting at his side. Jesse could tell as Evan rubbed the dog behind his ear that even though he tried to hide it, Evan was upset. He cursed himself for it, but he was filled with the need to comfort him.

"He's gotten big, hasn't he?" Jesse said.

Evan kept his eyes on Achilles. "Yeah. I'm surprised he remembers me."

"He likes you. He always has since the first day I found him."

Evan raised his head, a sad smile on his lips.

Jesse felt someone tap his arm and turned to see Evan's mother standing beside him, holding out her hand.

"We didn't get introduced. I'm Sophia, Evan's mother."

"It's a pleasure to meet you," Jesse said, taking her hand gently. He remembered her from the photos Evan had shown him, but now that he saw her in person he realized Evan looked so much like his father. Sophia's hair was a much darker brown and while her eyes were blue, they weren't the same radiant azure as Evan's.

Sophia laid her other hand over his. "I have to admit, I haven't been able to stop listening to your CD. Your voice is just amazing. And 'Shattered,' honey, your singing is so beautiful it gives me goose bumps whenever I hear it."

"That's why I haven't been able to get the top spot back," Evan said, smiling at Jesse. "I took it right out of the gate with 'Addiction,' then the next thing I knew, I was sitting in your shadow."

Jesse couldn't muster even the smallest of smiles. As much as he boasted "Shattered" would take Conquest above Evan, he hadn't really thought it would happen. After all, Evan's first single, the title track to his album *Addiction*, came out the last week of November to massive publicity and success, and knocked "Vanish" out of the top spot, so who would've guessed when "Shattered" hit two weeks later, they'd take it back. When he got the news, he knew he should've been happy about it, and maybe should have even felt that a little poetic justice had been served, but instead he felt miserable. Of all the things he wanted to achieve in his career, surpassing Evan wasn't one of them.

He couldn't stand Evan's praise at being usurped by him and walked to the table. Swiping the bottle of red wine and a glass, he headed over to the couches. He sat down, poured his glass full, downed it in two gulps, and filled it again. He tipped his head back, draining half, and felt someone sit down beside him. He knew who it was without having to look, the warm, strong presence could never be mistaken for anyone else.

"What are you drinking?" Evan asked. Without waiting for Jesse to answer, he took the bottle from Jesse's hand and looked at the label. "This is a nice vintage. Do you care if I have a taste?"

Jesse gave a tense shake of his head. "I'll get you a glass."

He moved to get up, stopping when Evan grabbed his thigh.

"I just want a sip." Evan slid Jesse's glass out from between his fingers. He placed his lips where Jesse had drank, letting them linger longer than the drink he took.

Jesse sat motionless watching him, acutely aware he was growing more aroused by the second and the pants he wore did a poor job of hiding it.

Evan lowered the glass and handed it back to him. "Tastes incredible."

Jesse took the glass. He quickly finished the remainder and poured again.

Evan took in his anxious movements and glanced away.

Harmonious notes from the piano filled the room as Julian's fingers glided over the keys playing "I'll be Home for Christmas." Evan stretched one arm across the top of the couch, his fingertips grazed the back of Jesse's neck.

Jesse could barely breathe. It was an accident. He was sure it was an accident. Everything Evan did was his own wishful thinking that he still held some affection for him. He was acting mental. He needed to cool it. Knowing him, Evan was only laying the groundwork hoping to get a one-night bang. Well it wasn't going to happen. There was no way—

Evan's fingers brushed through the back of his hair.

Jesse's heart drummed faster. That wasn't an accident. Evan had meant to do that. He was tormenting him, testing him, teasing him. Evan's fingers caressed his hair again, but this time stayed, stroking and playing with it like he had always done.

A team of servers marched into the room carrying trays of food.

Jesse sprang off the couch, holding the wine bottle pinned to his front to hide his erection. "Look! Dinner! Awesome, I'm starving!"

His band members and Brandon all gave him strange looks, but he darted for the table. He took a seat at the table laden with a turkey, a ham, garlic mashed potatoes, green beans, corn, fresh rolls, and cranberry sauce. He kept his eyes lowered when Evan sat down directly across from him. Brandon sat on his left, Kenny on his right, and Julian on Brandon's left. Trish sat at the end near Crystal and Krista, and Greg moved to the head by them.

"I guess we should do a toast," Greg said, holding up his glass. "To Evan and Conquest. Thanks for playing your butts off so we can afford this dinner."

Everyone laughed except Jesse. He lifted his glass and clinked it against the others. Evan looked into his eyes as their glasses touched. Jesse closed his eyes, tipping his head back to empty the contents of his glass down his throat.

"Dude, slow down," Kenny whispered to him.

Jesse filled his glass to the top and let out a mocking sigh. "Sometimes it's such a pain in the ass having my mom in the band."

To retaliate for Kenny, Brandon grabbed Jesse's leg close to his knee and clamped down on the pressure point. Jesse smashed his teeth together to keep from yelling out.

"Stop acting like a spoiled brat," Brandon growled, and released his leg with a hard shove.

Jesse threw his brother a dirty look, then turned to piling food on his plate. He ignored all the conversations going on around him, though it was hard to ignore Brandon and Evan talking like old friends, and Kenny and Julian treating Evan like he was the long lost fifth member of Conquest. Trish, however, completely ignored Evan. He didn't even remember if she had said hi to him and wondered if she was being aloof with Evan for his sake.

He glanced up from his plate and watched Evan cut his food. His eyes fell on the alexandrite ring shining on Evan's left ring finger. He stared at it, stunned that Evan still wore it, then raised his eyes and saw Evan looking at him. Jesse quickly dropped his gaze. Achilles laid his head on Jesse's foot, and he picked some turkey off his plate, slipping it to him.

Brandon shook his head. "You know, most people try to teach their dogs *not* to beg."

Jesse passed Achilles another bite of turkey. "But he likes it."

Evan broke in, his voice sharp. "You're drinking more than you're eating anyway, so I guess it's better that the food isn't wasted."

The conversations around the table hushed.

Jesse's body temperature heated with annoyance. Who was he to say anything about his drinking? Hadn't he been the one who cleaned two garbage bags full of empty beer and liquor bottles out of his house? And now here he was passing judgment on him?

In pure defiance, he threw his head back, willed his throat to stay open, and poured the contents of his glass down. As he brought his head forward, he slammed the empty glass on the table and stood.

Brandon snagged him by his wrist. "Where are you going?"

"To the restroom and to take 'Chilles out."

He patted his leg, and Achilles scrambled from under the table. The walk to the restroom did little to cool his irritation. He couldn't believe Evan's stones at criticizing him in front of everyone. Evan of all people should know just how much he was able to drink before getting tipsy. He tied the leash to a table decorated for the holidays, telling the dog to stay and petting him on the head. He walked into the restroom and headed for a urinal.

A moment later, the restroom door opened.

Jesse glanced up and let out a little snort. "Do you miss it so much that you have to follow me and sneak a look while I piss?"

Evan turned half away from him. "Stop it, Jess. This isn't the way you are."

Jesse zipped up and went to the sink to wash his hands. "You don't know how I am anymore, do you?"

He dried his hands and spun for the door, his shoulder brushing lightly against Evan's as he walked by. He untied Achilles's leash from the table leg and headed toward the lobby.

Evan followed him out the front doors of the hotel. "I know you have a thousand things to be angry at me for, but can you tell me the immediate one?"

"You have no right to criticize how much I drink."

"I do when you can't control yourself with it."

"Since when can't I control myself?"

"Do you even remember your birthday?"

"I remember a few choice parts."

Evan looked away from him. "I'm sorry, Jess. That night, I took advantage of you—"

"You've got to be kidding me," Jesse huffed, marching Achilles up the sidewalk. "You didn't take advantage of me, Ev. I'll admit, my memory might not be the clearest, but I'm pretty sure I was the one who crawled all over you. I knew what I was doing and I knew what I wanted. Granted, I passed out before I got all that I wanted, but that's beside the point."

He stopped to let Achilles sniff at a streetlight and faced Evan. "You know, I'm so sick of you and Brandon always treating me like I can't take care of myself. I've got news for you both. I'm a big boy, and guess what? I've been doing pretty damn good on my own these past few months. I don't need someone to follow me around every time I go out, and I sure as hell don't need someone to break the nose of every guy who wants to suck me off."

His voice saturated with jealousy, Evan asked, "So with how *good* you've been doing, just how many assholes *have* sucked you off?"

Jesse narrowed his eyes at him. "Wouldn't Brandon have already told you?"

"What the hell is that supposed to mean?"

"Are you fucking my brother?"

At the hurt that flushed Evan's face, Jesse had his answer.

"I can't believe you would even think I could do that to you," Evan said.

Both stood silent, neither looking at the other.

Jesse watched the gently falling snow collect on his sweater. "I'm sorry," he said softly. "It's just, I know you two have been talking and hanging out a lot, and I know there's nothing between you guys, I honestly do, but," he paused, the next words lingering on the tip of his tongue, but feeling so difficult to get out, "I can't help being jealous, because even though it's just friendship, he has more of you than I do."

"Jess," Evan moved closer to him and took both of Jesse's hands in his, "no one could ever have more of me than you do."

Jesse lifted his eyes to Evan's face. Snow fell on his cheek, melting the instant it met his skin. Without thinking, he pulled his right hand from Evan's and brushed his thumb over the glistening spot.

Evan closed his eyes at Jesse's touch and took another half step toward him. He squeezed Jesse's left hand. "I know I have no right to ask anything of you, but will you go somewhere with me?"

"Now?" Jesse said, surprised by the strange request.

Evan nodded.

"Where?"

"Just say you'll go. Please."

Jesse's heart wrenched at Evan's desperate tone. He glanced at the snow covered sidewalk. "Even now I can't say no to you," he mumbled to himself, then lifted his voice for Evan's ears. "Let me take 'Chilles up to my room."

Evan exhaled the breath he'd been holding. "Thank you."

Jesse tugged on Achilles's leash and led him back to the hotel with Evan walking silent at his side, wondering where Evan could want to take him.

"I'll have my rental brought around," Evan said as they stepped back inside.

Jesse walked toward the elevator. "I'll meet you out front in a minute."

Once in his room, he gave Achilles a handful of dog cookies, checked the water bowl, and grabbed his thick black leather coat. When he walked out of the hotel, a white Cadillac Escalade idled at the entrance. He hopped in the passenger side, chuckling.

Evan looked at him with a grin. "You're remembering the fate of my poor Escalade, aren't you?"

"You tried to play it so cool, but the look on your face was priceless."

"I'm glad my misfortune still makes you smile." Evan put the SUV in gear and pulled away from the hotel. "It was worth it. I'd let someone strip every car I own to relive that night. To relive any of them. They were all incredible."

Jesse's soft chuckling died in his throat. He shifted in the leather seat and focused his gaze out the window. He watched the unfamiliar buildings and streets streak by. The roads and sidewalks were quiet, but as they passed through residential neighborhoods, strings of Christmas lights dotted the darkness and he caught glimpses through windows of people continuing to celebrate the holiday in the warmth of their homes. And here he was with the man he had relinquished his heart to in what seemed another lifetime ago and who he had never been able to take it back from.

He glanced at Evan out the corner of his eye. He drove like he had always driven when they rode together, his left hand on the wheel, his right on the center console. In that other lifetime, they held hands whenever they drove anywhere. He wondered if Evan had placed his hand there in offering. Jesse sat still, then tentatively moved his hand toward Evan's and laid it over his. Evan turned his hand under Jesse's and interlocked their fingers. Though Evan squeezed so tight he caused a dull ache in Jesse's hand and the eagle ring dug into his skin, Jesse refused to let go or ask him to loosen his grip.

He lost track of how long they rode in comfortable silence and was about to ask Evan again where they were going when Evan swung into a driveway, stopped, and honked the horn twice. Jesse looked forward and startled at the sight of closed cemetery gates, then realized where Evan had brought him.

An elderly man trudged through the snow to the gates on the other side and unlocked them. Evan pulled through, taking his left hand off the wheel to wave to him rather than pull right hand from Jesse's.

"Do you know that guy?" Jesse asked.

"Yeah. He's been the groundskeeper here forever and has been really good to me over the years, letting me come here when it's closed so I don't get interrupted in case someone recognizes me. I just call and let him know I'm coming." Evan pulled into a small parking lot. "Sorry. We'll have to walk the rest of the way."

As Jesse got out, he saw Evan reach in the backseat and retrieve a bouquet of two dozen long-stemmed red roses. He fell into stride beside him as Evan maneuvered them through a maze of headstones. He had never been in such a full cemetery. Hardly any space was between the graves. He began to get a sense of how old the place was as he looked at the chipped and weathered headstones, some of the names and dates barely visible. The cold felt deeper there than it had by the hotel, and he shivered. He glanced at Evan and noticed he wasn't wearing a coat.

Evan stopped short, the hand holding the roses dropped to his side. "I can't believe it. I told my mom to get a grave blanket. I even sent her extra money for one."

Jesse followed Evan's eyes to the grave before them marked with a simple half oval stone with the name, Ethan Avery Arden, his dates of birth and death, and the words, 'Beloved Father, Husband, and Son. May you add your golden voice to the angels of Heaven,' chiseled into the surface.

Evan stepped forward and fell to his knees in the snow, brushing the marker clean with his bare hands. "She doesn't care," he mumbled. "She never did."

Jesse stood back, knowing Evan's grief couldn't be comforted with words. All he could do was be there if Evan turned to him in need.

Evan stopped trying to clear the snow and sat slumped on his knees. He put the roses in the cement vase at the base of the gravestone and stared at them. He reached out with his right hand and touched his fingers to the word "father."

"He would've adored you, Jess," he said softly. "I wanted to say that to you so many times before, but I never did. If he could've seen us together, I know he would've been so happy for me to have found someone like you, who accepted me for all my flaws, who saw me for who I really am and gave me unconditional love regardless. But I screwed it all up, and I know he would have been disappointed in me for treating you like I did.

"He would've told me the same thing you did, to forget about our careers because what we have is more important. But I thought I was doing what was best for you. The truth is, I couldn't care less what becomes of my career, but I couldn't stand the thought that I might be the one thing to hold you back from achieving your dreams, so I let you go to not drag you down. But now…" Evan closed his eyes, his left hand balled into a fist, his voice trembled more with each word, "I want to be selfish and force my way back into your life. I need you. I know I can't make it through my life if I don't have your strength to lean on."

He looked up at Jesse, his pain, his desperation, filling his face. Tears welled in his eyes, making them shine in the moonlight. "Tell me, Jess, is there nothing I can do? Do you hate me so much that I can never make amends? I need to know. Even though I know I can never move beyond you, I need to know if you're happy without me."

In less than a single quick heartbeat, Jesse went to his knees in the snow and pulled Evan into his arms. Evan's arms went around him in return, his hands gripped the back of Jesse's coat in two fists, his body shook with a hard sob.

The weeks of pain and loneliness he had fought so hard to keep down overwhelmed Jesse's spirit. Silent tears left his eyes as he held Evan to him. "I don't hate you, Ev. I could never hate you. And no, I'm not happy without you. Every day since we've been apart I've felt like I've been stumbling through a dream, no longer recognizing the things I was doing. I've wanted to call you a hundred times a day and tell you how much I wanted you back, but just like you were afraid of hurting my career, I was afraid of doing the same to yours, and that's the only reason I walked away when you told me to go."

He sat back and cupped Evan's face in both hands, his eyes unwavering as he looked into Evan's. "You're the love of my life. My soul-mate. And even if I act angry or upset, nothing will ever change that. If there's a time beyond eternity, that's how long I will love you."

"Jess." Evan collapsed into Jesse's arms again. "I love you. I love you so much. Please, tell me I'm yours again and that you're mine. I need to hear it."

Jesse held Evan tighter with one arm and gently placed his other hand on the back of Evan's head. "You're mine and I'm yours. We belong to each other. Even when we were apart, that never changed. I'm going to worship you every day, just as you'll worship me, for the rest of our lives." He drew back slightly and smiled as he brushed Evan's hair from his forehead. "Even if you did get snot all over my seven hundred dollar leather coat."

Evan choked out a laugh.

Jesse noticed Evan's fingers were wet and chaffed, and now that he wasn't holding him, Evan shivered. He wrestled out of his coat and flung it around Evan's shoulders.

"No, don't," Evan said, trying to stop him. "You'll freeze."

Jesse gave the coat a tug around Evan's neck and took both of his hands in his. "I just got you back. I'm not going to lose you to pneumonia." He rubbed his hands over Evan's. He held them to his mouth, softly kissed his fingers, and blew warm breath over them.

Evan stretched his fingers and touched the tips to Jesse's jaw. Jesse lifted his gaze. Evan leaned forward, and their lips met in a soft, chaste kiss. They stayed together for a long moment, before each slowly opened his eyes and sat back.

"I have something for you," Evan said, reaching in the front pocket of his pants. He retrieved a small wooden box and held it out.

Jesse took it and said teasingly, "Great. We've just gotten back together, and you're already one up by getting me a Christmas present when I don't have anything for you."

A soft smile graced Evan's lips. "You've saved my life by sharing yours with me. Nothing material could ever surpass that."

Jesse caressed Evan's cheek with his fingers. He lowered his hand and opened the lid of the box.

A ring of white gold edged in yellow gold lay inside on a pillow of royal blue silk. The large square cut diamond in the center rivaled the stars for brilliance. Set into the yellow gold were diamond chips. Traveling around the white gold center of the band was the Greek meander, a pattern that could continue forever without breaking.

Jesse swallowed to free his tight throat and lifted the ring. He saw an inscription on the inside of the band, *All my love forever, Evan.*

Evan carefully took the ring from Jesse's fingers and held his left hand steady as he slipped it onto Jesse's left ring finger. "It's your match to my alexandrite. They're our reminders to ourselves of our love and commitment, but hopefully, someday, we'll have other rings that will tell the world we belong to each other."

Jesse took Evan's left hand in his left hand and entwined their fingers so the two rings were side by side. "I would bind myself to you in every way. I can live my life without fans and fame. I can't live it without you."

Evan laid his other hand on Jesse's cheek. "There's nothing that I wouldn't do to be with you. There's nothing in my life that I need more than you." He met Jesse in another tender kiss.

As they eased back from the kiss, both rose and stood at the edge of the grave, each silently saying his farewell. Hand in hand, they turned and walked back to the Escalade.

When they climbed into the SUV, as if gravity pushed them together, they met over the center console in a firm embrace. Both breathed soft sighs into the other's mouth as their tongues touched. With his lips still on Jesse's, Evan whispered, "Let's go back to your room."

Jesse sat back in his seat, taking Evan's hand again. "Are you staying in a hotel or with your mom?"

"I checked into your hotel and dropped my bags off in my room about five minutes before I met my mom down at the banquet room. And I just happen to be on the same floor as you thanks to Brandon letting me know your room number." Evan grinned at Jesse as he pulled onto the street. "I was going to get my time with you one way or another."

Jesse laughed softly. "Why do I feel like I've been the subject of a conspiracy?"

Evan chuckled and turned his gaze to the road. He sat quiet for a moment, his smiled faded. "Greg told me you've been trying to get out of performing with me on New Year's Eve and you've decided to not join me on the road."

"Yeah, but I was talking more than I was backing it up. Greg knows that, and that's why he hasn't worked to find a replacement band for you." Jesse looked at him and winked. "You know me and my mouth."

Evan's eyes lingered on Jesse's lips. "Yeah, I do."

Jesse's mischievous smirk lit his lips. "So, if you don't mind, I'll be standing beside you on stage New Year's Eve, and we'll be joining you on the road in February."

"I certainly don't mind."

Evan forced his attention back to the road, but Jesse continued to gaze at him.

"What is it?" Evan asked.

Jesse smiled. Evan always knew when he wanted to ask him something. "It's just, with all the thinking I've done in the past couple months, I started to get the idea the only reason you decided to make a new album and tour again was because you thought it was what I wanted you to do."

Jesse waited for Evan to respond and with each second of the long pause, he knew the answer.

"Wasn't it?" Evan replied.

"No. I wanted you to come back because you wanted to. Not for me. You seemed so happy when you began recording, it never even hit me that you didn't want to do it until after I was able to step back and look at everything."

"I *was* happy at first, but it was only because you were there with me. And I'll be happy touring when you join me, but I could be just as happy singing with you as my only audience for the rest of my life."

Jesse laid his head on Evan's shoulder and wrapped his right arm across Evan's chest.

They reached the hotel, and Evan tossed his rental keys to the valet as he followed Jesse in. When they reached their floor, Jesse turned to him. "How obvious would it be if you moved your bags into my room?"

"Not that obvious. Even if housekeeping is suspicious, who cares? They can't prove anything."

Jesse went to Evan's room with him to get his bags. He grabbed one of Evan's suitcases and looked at him with a little grin. "I assume you came prepared."

Evan chuckled as he collected his other two bags and headed out of the room. "I did."

"That's good, because I don't have anything." Jesse's voice became subdued as they walked up the hall to his room. "It's mental, I know, but I felt like if I bought stuff for sex, it'd mean I was getting ready to be with someone else, and I couldn't bring myself to do that."

"Then you really haven't been with anyone else?"

Jesse shook his head as he unlocked the door to his suite. "No, I haven't."

"Neither have I." Evan leaned close to his ear. "I've been surviving off wet dreams about you."

Jesse laughed and gave him a playful shove as he opened the door. Achilles greeted them with a wagging tail and spinning in circles. Evan barely had a chance to touch the dog's head before Jesse grabbed him by the upper arm, hauled him up, and slammed against him in a hungry kiss. Evan's arms went around him as Jesse pushed him through the suite's living room toward the bedroom.

As they passed over the threshold to the bedroom, Jesse broke the kiss and looked down at Achilles. He petted him, then closed the bedroom door to keep him out. He turned to face Evan and saw him walking along the king-sized bed, the fingers of one hand brushing the comforter. Jesse's breath slipped from his lungs. He had never forgotten how gracefully Evan could move, but seeing him gliding by the bed, each movement revealing his desire, reinforced just how beautiful Evan truly was.

Evan retrieved a bottle of lube and sat on the edge of the bed. He leaned back on his arms, slowly lifting his gaze in one of the most sensual looks Jesse had ever seen. Jesse walked toward him, taking his sweater off on the way. As Jesse neared, Evan spread his thighs farther apart to invite him to stand between them. Jesse did, and combed his fingers through Evan's hair.

Evan put his hands on Jesse's hips, taking a long moment to admire his tight, wiry torso. "You look even more gorgeous."

"So do you." Jesse pulled Evan's sweater off. He ran his fingertips over his toned chest, his touch having lost no memory of Evan's body.

Evan rubbed his hands up Jesse's abdomen, each line of muscle exactly how he remembered. He leaned forward, touching his lips to the taut flesh, and drifted one hand down to fondle the hard line straining against Jesse's pants. Jesse sighed softly and pushed harder into Evan's hand. With ritualistic care, Evan unfastened the button and eased the zipper down. He pulled Jesse's pants and boxers off his hips, lingering his lips close to his cock, but not touching, as he brought the clothes down. Jesse slid out of his shoes and bent to pull off his socks along with removing Evan's shoes and socks.

Evan gazed reverently at Jesse's cock. Gently, he brought his fingertips to it in the softest of touches. Jesse groaned and closed his eyes, his hips rolled the slightest bit as he took a handful of Evan's hair at the back of his head. Evan stared at the glistening tip; the memory of Jesse's taste filled his mouth. He ran his fingers down the underside of his length and wrapped them around the base. He took a second to appreciate the heavy hardness in his hand, then dove forward, dragging his tongue over Jesse's tip to get a full taste before pushing him to the back of his throat.

Jesse gasped, his knees buckled at the inferno of Evan's mouth wrapping around his organ. He leaned on Evan's shoulder and looked down at him. The sight of Evan's beautiful lips sliding up and down his length hit him with force, having believed he would never witness, never experience, Evan doing such things to him again. He felt Evan's powerful throat muscle swallow the tip of his cock, the action causing heat to fire through his sac in the first hint of a rising climax. He placed his hand under Evan's jaw and eased his cock from his mouth.

Evan looked up at him with a grin. "I wasn't done."

Jesse stroked Evan's slender jaw with his thumb. "I know, but you were already getting me close, and I want the first one tonight to be when we're fully together."

Evan wrapped his arms around Jesse's waist. He kissed his stomach and laid his head against him. "Jess, will you?"

Jesse softly stroked Evan's hair, knowing when Evan was like this, when his emotions were fragile and delicate, he always preferred to bottom. "You know you don't have to ask."

Evan nodded his head against him.

Jesse placed his fingertips under Evan's chin and tipped his head back as he bowed his head to his lips. He covered his mouth in a gentle kiss, keeping one hand in Evan's hair. With his other hand, he pulled the button free on Evan's pants. He released Evan's hair to bring the zipper down. Evan lay back on the bed and raised his hips for Jesse to pull them off. Jesse flung them and Evan's boxer-briefs aside, and dropped to his knees. Evan slid forward to sit on the very edge of the bed, spreading his legs wide as Jesse moved in to nuzzle between them.

Jesse inhaled deep, the familiar scent of Evan, musky masculinity touched with Platinum Egoist, gave him a heady rush. He licked and laved attention on his delicate sac. Evan groaned deep in his throat and raked the fingers of both hands through Jesse's hair. Jesse moved his mouth to the base of Evan's cock and sucked on the underside where it met his sac, then traced the thick vein up to the head with his tongue. He cleaned the tip with his tongue and teased the slit for more.

"Jess," Evan said, his voice pleading.

Jesse reluctantly withdrew his lips and moved up Evan's body. Evan took greedy possession of his mouth as he slid back on the bed. Jesse moved with him without halting the thrusting of his tongue against Evan's. Evan reached the center of the bed and went flat to his back.

Jesse coated his fingers in lube. He hooked his arm under Evan's leg and bent it back as he pushed two fingers into him.

Evan gasped loud and clung to Jesse's back. Jesse massaged and rubbed him, working to stretch out Evan's tightness. He felt Evan's cock leak fresh drops, just as his own had. Hearing Evan whisper his name, he withdrew his hand, grabbed his own cock, and with a single, forceful thrust, pushed into him. Both let out loud, hard groans at finally having their bodies joined again.

Jesse pushed his length halfway in before pausing. He eased his arm out from under Evan's leg and his head bowed as he fought to calm his overexcited body. Evan clung to Jesse's waist with trembling fingers, needing the respite just as much to collect his control.

With his breathing beginning to calm, Jesse moved his hips forward, slowly sinking into him. He raised his head up, moaning louder with each fraction of his cock that went into Evan until he could go no more. When Jesse stopped, Evan lifted his hips, seeking to take more of him. They stayed still, Jesse savoring the heat and tightness of being sheathed in him, and Evan relishing the strength of Jesse's body and solid rod of flesh that filled him so perfectly.

Jesse gradually eased his hips back and forward again. Evan's breath fled fast, only to have him quickly draw another. Jesse lowered himself down to his elbows, his next thrust coming harder. Evan hugged Jesse's hips with his thighs and clung to him with one arm as he sought Jesse's hand with the other. They locked their fingers together and squeezed with grips that couldn't be broken.

Jesse kissed Evan's lips, his cheeks, his forehead. "I've missed you, Ev. I've missed you so much."

"I've missed you too, Jess. Every day, I dreamed I'd have you again."

Jesse brought his lips to Evan's and sucked his tongue deep into his mouth. He increased his pace, adding more force behind each thrust, rocking Evan under him. He wanted to go slow. He wanted to make it last. But it had been so long, and now he had his Evan under him again. Each thrust was an excruciating torture of ecstasy, and his body trembled for want of release. He felt Evan's muscles constricting and thrust harder. Evan clenched his hand, his body arched up toward him.

"Jess, I love you. Jesse!" Evan cried out, and shuddered hard as his cock pulsed his release between them.

Jesse rammed into him, yelling out his passion as he came. He collapsed fully on top of Evan, still feeling the aftershocks of it. Emotions swirled from his core to his mind, a confusing mix of elation, satisfaction, and heart wrenching love, all edged with hurt that they had allowed themselves to be separated.

Jesse turned his head on Evan's shoulder and snuggled against his neck. "I love you too. And from now on, we'll always put each other before all else. Forever."

Evan held him tighter. "Only you, Jess. Forever and always."

Chapter Thirty-five

Jesse stood backstage gazing at Evan on stage preparing to perform as soon as the show came back from commercial. A soft smile rested on Jesse's lips, a smile that had been present since he and Evan vowed their eternal commitment to each other. Now as he stood watching his beautiful partner get ready to sing before millions of eyes that would gaze upon him in adoration, one thought filled his mind; Evan was his, and only his. It didn't matter how many people screamed their undying love and devotion to Evan, because Evan knew the one who held it truly was just a few feet away.

As if thinking the same thing, Evan glanced at him and threw him a smile and a wink. Jesse blew him a kiss. Evan laughed and looked away as JJ walked up to ask him something.

Julian stepped to Jesse's side. "We haven't gotten to see much of you two these past few days since you've been holed up in your hotel room together, but it appears you both haven't missed a beat in picking up where you left off."

"We haven't, but I suppose that's to be expected. It wasn't like we broke up over something bad. It happened because Ev was trying to protect me, and I left for the same reason toward him. It's hard to hold a grudge against good intentions, even if they were misunderstood."

Brandon tossed his arm around Jesse's shoulder. "You almost sounded like an adult there. It's kinda weirdin' me out."

Jesse chuckled and shook his head.

Kenny quit fiddling with his black and white Fender Stratocaster hanging from a black leather strap over his shoulder. "Then we'll be hitting the road with him for sure?"

"Yeah."

"That's going to be so kickass," Kenny said. "The arenas he plays are crazy huge, and we'll get to run all over the world. I'm really glad now that you gave it up to him to get our contract."

"How many times do I have to tell you I didn't do it for that!" Jesse laughed.

"What's going to happen when you guys come off the road?" Brandon asked. "Are you going to live together again?"

"Yeah. The media's never discovered where the house is. Even if they do find out, they can't prove we're living together. They wouldn't be able to get down the private road unless someone parked and walked around the first gates, and then security cameras would catch them, and they'd never make it past the second gates and wall, so we think we'll be pretty safe."

Julian asked, "Then you're going to continue to keep things secret?"

"For now."

Kenny got an apprehensive look. *"For now?"*

"We decided to appease Greg by not openly admitting anything for a little while longer, but we're not going to deny rumors either. We just won't comment on them."

"But then you're leaving people to believe the rumors are true," Julian said.

"Which is fine. It'll be less of a shock for when we feel the time is right to openly confess our relationship." Jesse realized that out of everyone, Trish had yet to say a word. He hadn't talked to her much since Christmas, or to anyone since he had been so focused on hoarding Evan all to himself, but when they were around her, she was fairly quiet, and he wondered if she still harbored a grudge against Evan for his actions toward Jesse. He made a mental note to get some one-on-one time with her and tell her it was fine to treat Evan normally. He glanced at her standing behind him. "You okay?"

Trish stared at him for a moment, then nodded. "Yeah. I think I'm still in shock that we just played for pretty much the whole country."

"I know," Jesse said with a contented sigh. "And I looked so damn good on camera, too."

"Well, get ready Captain Pretty Boy or else you'll miss your cue," Kenny said.

Jesse turned his attention to the stage.

The stage lights flashed on with blinding brilliance, flames shot up in a quick blast from the pyrotechnics at the front of the stage, all timed perfectly to Evan's band launching into the hard driving rock track, "Addiction." Evan walked toward the front of the stage as if it and the entire world belonged to him, and let his baritone blast out,

"You're in my mind,
You're in my soul,
You're everywhere.
I just can't get away.
There's no help for me.
But how I love this torture so sweet,
The ghost of your memory,
Haunting me.
I feel you there,
When I close my eyes.

This addiction,
It's left me weak and sore,
But I don't want to the cure,
It'd mean not having you anymore.

This addiction,
It's pounding in my brain,
But oh how I love the pain,
Breaking my body down again,
This addiction…"

Just as Jesse prepared to step on stage with Kenny to join JJ in the guitar solo, Evan raised his left hand and dropped it down in a swift motion. The entire band stopped playing, the stage lights blackened. Jesse snapped his head around to look at Kenny, but Julian sprinted past him toward the stage, aiming for a black grand piano.

"Surprise," Julian chuckled as he trotted by.

"Surprise?" Jesse said, his eyes back on Kenny.

Kenny flicked his head toward the stage. "Get ready."

Through the darkness Evan's voice rose pure and celestial with no instruments to interfere,

> *"I yelled for you as you walked away,*
> *My voice a whisper…in the crowd…*
> *And I watched our memories fall with the rain,*
> *Breaking…on the ground…*
> *I want to take it all away,*
> *And believe the truths in the dark.*
> *I want to live the fantasy,*
> *The sweet delusion,*
> *And keep you in my arms…"*

Jesse gasped at Evan singing "Shattered." He stood motionless, listening and watching as the piano added its voice to Evan's after the fourth line and the stage lights turned to a soft golden glow with a single spotlight illuminating Evan. The crowd had exploded at the first line, but now sat silent, mesmerized.

"Alright, go." Kenny poked Jesse on the back with the head of his guitar.

Jesse stumbled forward, clueless as to what to do. This wasn't what they had rehearsed. He and Evan were supposed to duet on "Addiction." There was never any mention of "Shattered." He took a breath and walked on stage, hoping he didn't look completely confused. Another spotlight shone down on him, and for a second time, the crowd erupted with a deafening roar.

Evan turned toward him as he came to the end of the chorus,

> *"Take my hand,*
> *Pull me out,*
> *Please save me.*
> *I'm shattering,*
> *Breaking…"*

Evan wrapped his arm around Jesse's shoulders as the piano interlude took over. He put his lips to his ear. "You've got the next verse, and I'll join you on the chorus."

Jesse nodded and slipped his arm around him. Kenny and JJ joined their guitars with the piano. Jesse took a breath and lifted his tenor,

> *"Now I'm sitting all alone in the darkness.*
> *Listening for your voice in the silence.*
> *All I have left are illusions and dreams.*
> *Your phantom body lying next to me.*
> *Another memory trickles down my cheek,*
> *And I slip a little bit more…"*

Evan tightened his grip around Jesse. They raised their voices together, blending them as one in perfect harmony,

> *"What can I do?*
> *Don't leave me to drown,*
> *In these shattered memories.*

> *I want to scream,*
> *But I can't breathe,*
> *I'm falling away.*
>
> *Can't you see,*
> *That I'm alone,*
> *And I'm slipping away?*
> *I can't stop myself.*
> *Can't catch myself.*
> *Take my hand*
> *Pull me out,*
> *Please save me.*
> *I'm shattering,*
> *Breaking…"*

As the song finished, they bowed in unison to the screaming audience. Together, they walked offstage.

Jesse turned to Evan with a glowing smile. "I can't believe you did that!"

"It was the only right thing to do. After all, 'Shattered' is the more popular song right now, and for your set earlier, Greg made you play 'Euphoria' because it's more upbeat."

"You're so sneaky," Jesse chuckled. His soft laugh slowed as he looked into Evan's eyes. "Thank you."

"Anything for you, gorgeous."

Kenny jogged up and slapped Jesse on the upper arm, forcing him out of his trance. "Come on. We've gotta head over to the other stage and get ready for the finale."

"Alright." Jesse turned to Evan. "Shall we?"

Evan draped his arm around Jesse's shoulders. "Let's go."

❄ ❄ ❄

The crowd chanted the countdown to midnight. The ball crept lower, foot by foot. It touched down to raucous shouts and blasting fireworks. Confetti rained, and on the main stage, a crowd of famed performers lit into "Auld Lang Syne."

Jesse switched off the TV. Silence filled the hotel room. He turned in Evan's arms and found his lips in a long, sensual kiss. Evan pulled him tight against him, took a step back, and fell backward on the bed behind them.

Jesse laughed and braced himself up so Evan could slide higher on the bed. He crawled with him and lowered his body down on top of him. He stroked Evan's hair, his eyes shining with joy. "Happy New Year."

Evan caressed Jesse's cheek with the backs of his fingers. "Happy New Year."

A mischievous smirk played on Jesse's lips. "So, how long do you think it will take the paparazzi to notice we're the only ones who weren't on stage?"

"Considering our performance earlier, I'm sure their little fingers are already flying across their keyboards. Do you care?"

"No." Jesse stretched his left hand out and took Evan's left hand. "It doesn't matter what they say, because we're stronger together than we are apart, and together, side by side, we'll conquer anything that tries to come between us."

Evan squeezed Jesse's hand, pressing their rings together. "I love you, Jess. Everything I am, everything I'll ever be, will always be yours."

"I love you too, Ev. I always will. My future only exists so long as you're with me."

Evan embraced him stronger, and Jesse lowered his head, touching his lips to his once again.

ABOUT THE AUTHOR

S.J. FROST resides on a mini-ranch in Ohio with her husband and son, as well as a kind-hearted German Shepherd, a Collie who is the anti-Lassie, a few kooky cats, and some very special horses. She enjoys experimenting with her writing and dabbling in different genres, though it's guaranteed that no matter what she writes there will be hot erotic action appearing somewhere in the story. She's a romantic at heart, which is reflected in her writing. The majority of her work is m/m, though she's had the occasional m/f piece published too. Her short stories have been featured in several erotic and romance anthologies including, *Best Gay Romance 2007 Edition, Girls on Top,* and *Surfer Boys*, all published by Cleis Press, *Ultimate Gay Erotica 2008* and *Best Gay Love Stories: Summer Flings*, both published by Alyson Books, and *Honey Flava* published by Atria Books.

You can find out more about the authors and upcoming works at: http://www.sjfrost.com/

Turn the page for a Sneak Peek at

NO FEAR

S.J. FROST

Release: ManLoveRomance Press, winter/spring 2010

Unable to contain his excitement, Jesse paced quick strides back and forth across his dressing room. For more than a year, it'd become routine to out on stage night after night, performing for thousands of raucous people. He woke to a new city nearly every morning, and often slept in one different than he's awoken. But tomorrow, he'd be back in Chicago, and tomorrow night, he and his love would sleep in each other's arms in their own bed. A smile rose of its own will to Jesse's lips. He stopped pacing. Home. They were going home. A wave of pure joy surged inside him, making him want to dance, sing, sprint around the room.

Through his thoughts, Jesse caught the voice of his guitarist and lifelong friend, Kenny Cooper speaking. "He's left us again. He's back in Jesse's Happy La La Land."

"It's the Frappuccino he finished a little bit ago. He's always like a gerbil on speed when he drinks those things."

Jesse faced the two. His older brother, Brandon, met his gaze with a smirk on his lips. Of all the people in his life, there were only three he knew he could always depend on, and one was Brandon. Together, they had survived their father, from his fits of rage when they were young to his prejudice against them both for being gay. Brandon stood up to their father to protect him, but in all aspects of his life, Brandon had always taken care of him. The colorful names they used to address each other were more like pet names, their bickering more an act of play than seriousness.

Beside Brandon was the second person he knew he could always depend on, Kenny. Halfway through Conquest's tour, Kenny traded in his longish, shaggy dark blond hair for a cut shorter all around and spiky on top, claiming it wasn't as hot on stage and the fan girls liked the new style better, which he knew was Kenny's main motivation.

"You back with us now?" Kenny asked.

Jesse's smile widened. "No. My mind's already home."

Julian jumped into the conversation. "Just so long as your body and voice are still here. No one's interested in your mind, anyway."

Jesse's gaze turned to his keyboardist and pianist, Julian Forrester. Julian looked at him with a grin reaching his light blue eyes. The Julliard-trained classical pianist completely shocked him a few months ago when he traded in his perfectly groomed ponytail for a cut that made his pale blond hair look wild and messy. But no matter how rock-starred out Julian tried to get, he never could shake his distinguished air.

"There's one person who values my mind just as much as my body," Jesse retorted.

Julian, Kenny, and Brandon all burst out laughing.

"That's highly debatable," Julian said.

Jesse allowed a good-humored glare to pass over the three of them. His ears didn't catch the high laugh he was so familiar with from the other person in the room. He turned toward his drummer, Trish O'Connell. She sat with her back to them all at a small table, the fingers of her left hand expertly twirling a drumstick. Her dark red hair cascaded down her back in a braid. A white tank top patterned with pink roses clung tightly to her curves and revealed her toned arms.

"Hey, Trish," Jesse called. "Don't you want to join in on picking on me?"

Trish glanced over her shoulder at him. "Sorry. I've got my mind on other things at the moment."

Jesse turned when he heard the dressing room door open. His smile returned brighter than earlier as his eyes locked with the brilliant azure gaze of the third, and most important, person he knew he could always depend on, Evan Arden.

To headline his own sold-out tour was a dream achieved for him. To be Evan's opening act on his *Addiction World Tour*, surpassed it. Nothing compared to his joy at being with Evan every day, every night, watching him perform, learning from him, loving him.

For him, Evan's music, his voice, his gift, was a source of unending inspiration.

Jesse coasted his gaze down Evan's body. A light blue shirt of fine, thin silk formed around Evan's lean, fit torso. With half the buttons undone, he admired Evan's smooth chest, the curves of his solid pectorals. Black leather pants hugged his narrow hips and cloaked his legs down to a pair of black snakeskin boots.

No matter the event or situation, when Evan made an appearance, all eyes, all cameras, were drawn to him. His mannerisms spoke of sophistication, his charm enthralled all who spoke to him. For those fortunate enough to have his dazzling blue eyes focus their attention on them, everything else in the world seemed miniscule and unimportant compared to their azure beauty. And for all their days and hours together, Evan still managed to take his breath away.

"Hey," Jesse said, his voice soft.

A smile shone across Evan's lips. "Hey, gorgeous."

Evan closed the dressing room door behind him, muting the sounds of the audience chanting for entertainment. He walked toward Jesse, his eyes moving over him. Jesse wore a pair of stylishly faded Diesel jeans that fell off the tops of his slender hips, and the tight, v-neck, dark purple t-shirt gave his indigo eyes a violet tint. His Jesse, his savior, his shining warrior. The only person who knew all his secrets, who had seen all his flaws, who he trusted completely and fully.

Jesse moved to meet him. The distance between them closed as Evan slipped his arms around Jesse's waist.

Jesse embraced Evan's neck. "You appreciate my mind just as much as my body, don't you?"

A thoughtful expression crossed Evan's face. "That's a difficult question. I guess it depends on the situation."

"Point proven!" Julian called out, Kenny and Brandon laughing.

"That's not what you were supposed to say!" Jesse said over their snickering.

"Well, you have to set the scenario up better." Evan dipped his head down, putting his lips to Jesse's neck, and laid gentle kisses upon it. He drifted one hand lower on Jesse's back, his fingers traced the curves of his ass. "Like how long has it been since we've had sex? Or what are you using your mind for when I'm supposed to appreciate it?" He raised his head to meet Jesse's eyes. "Are you using your brilliance to create beautiful music, or are you babbling about old gods and ancient people? Because if it's the first, we could not have had sex for months and I would still appreciate your mind. But if it's the latter and we haven't had sex within twenty-four hours, then I might be forced to put something thick, long, and hard in your mouth to express my appreciation for your other qualities."

Jesse's attempt to maintain a serious countenance withered under a chuckle slipping from his throat.

❄ ❄ ❄

Jesse gazed out the dark tinted window of the limousine, his hand on Evan's thigh, Evan's hand resting atop his. The streets of Evanston were quiet despite it being late afternoon. With only two weeks until Christmas, snow was piled up along the edges of the road, ice coated the branches of the trees in a crystalline sheen. The grayish-white sky threatened more snow for the evening.

It seemed surreal to him, how different it all looked covered in winter's cloak. He wondered why his heart was beating a nervous cadence, why it felt like he was going home with Evan for the first time. Maybe, because in a way, he was. They hadn't returned home since being reunited. Whenever they had time off on the road, they always stayed in the town they were in or went ahead to the next destination and relaxed in the hotel or explored the area. Coming home together solidified things were truly as they were meant to be.

❄ ❄ ❄

They stepped over the threshold into the mansion. Jesse stopped in the entrance room, feeling a weight he hadn't realized was in his heart lift. He took a tentative step forward, then another. Beneath him, the dark hardwood floor was polished to where his shoes reflected in it. The walls paneled in large wooden rectangles of rich brown traveled up to the vaulted ceiling. Across from him, the broad flight of wooden stairs were the same rich deep brown as the panels and the woodwork that edged the Gothic peaked open doorways, one to the right of the stairs leading into the kitchen, further to the right another opened to the family room, and the dining room to the left.

Jesse walked to the stairs and rested his hand on the banister, the wood smooth and cool under his hand. He heard the door shut and turned to see their bags piled inside and Evan standing at the security system keypad watching the limo make its way down the drive on the monitor so he could close the gates behind it. Achilles, claws clicking on the wood, walked past him with his nose to the floor in an exploration of the house. Jesse looked back to the stairs, his gaze drifting up their height where he knew the master bedroom was.

Evan moved behind him and embraced him around the waist. He touched his lips to the back of Jesse's neck in a whisper soft kiss. "Welcome home, gorgeous."

THE TREVOR PROJECT

The Trevor Project operates the only nationwide, around-the-clock crisis and suicide prevention helpline for lesbian, gay, bisexual, transgender and questioning youth. Every day, The Trevor Project saves lives though its free and confidential helpline, its website and its educational services. If you or a friend are feeling lost or alone call The Trevor Helpline. If you or a friend are feeling lost, alone, confused or in crisis, please call The Trevor Helpline. You'll be able to speak confidentially with a trained counselor 24/7.

The Trevor Helpline: 866-488-7386
On the Web: http://www.thetrevorproject.org/

THE GAY MEN'S DOMESTIC VIOLENCE PROJECT

Founded in 1994, The Gay Men's Domestic Violence Project is a grassroots, non-profit organization founded by a gay male survivor of domestic violence and developed through the strength, contributions and participation of the community. The Gay Men's Domestic Violence Project supports victims and survivors through education, advocacy and direct services. Understanding that the serious public health issue of domestic violence is not gender specific, we serve men in relationships with men, regardless of how they identify, and stand ready to assist them in navigating through abusive relationships.

GMDVP Helpline: 800.832.1901
On the Web: http://gmdvp.org/

THE GAY & LESBIAN ALLIANCE AGAINST DEFAMATION/GLAAD EN ESPAÑOL

The Gay & Lesbian Alliance Against Defamation (GLAAD) is dedicated to promoting and ensuring fair, accurate and inclusive representation of people and events in the media as a means of eliminating homophobia and discrimination based on gender identity and sexual orientation.

On the Web: http://www.glaad.org/
GLAAD en español:
        http://www.glaad.org/espanol/bienvenido.php

If you're a GLBT and questioning student heading off to university, should know that there are resources on campus for you. Here's just a sample:

US Local GLBT college campus organizations
        http://dv-8.com/resources/us/local/campus.html
GLBT Scholarship Resources
        http://tinyurl.com/6fx9v6
Syracuse University
        http://lgbt.syr.edu/
Texas A&M
        http://glbt.tamu.edu/
Tulane University
        http://www.oma.tulane.edu/LGBT/Default.htm
University of Alaska
        http://www.uaf.edu/agla/
University of California, Davis
        http://lgbtrc.ucdavis.edu/
University of California, San Francisco
        http://lgbt.ucsf.edu/
University of Colorado
        http://www.colorado.edu/glbtrc/
University of Florida
        http://www.dso.ufl.edu/multicultural/lgbt/
University of Hawai'i, Mānoa
        http://manoa.hawaii.edu/lgbt/
University of Utah
        http://www.sa.utah.edu/lgbt/
University of Virginia
        http://www.virginia.edu/deanofstudents/lgbt/
Vanderbilt University
        http://www.vanderbilt.edu/lgbtqi/